**Praise for *New York Times* bestselling author
Jill Shalvis**

"Witty, fun and sexy—the perfect romance!"
—*New York Times* bestselling author Lori Foster

"Shalvis thoroughly engages readers."
—*Publishers Weekly*

"Shalvis firmly establishes herself as a writer of fast-paced, edgy but realistic romantic suspense, with believable and likable supporting characters and fiercely evocative descriptive passages."
—*Booklist*

**Praise for *USA TODAY* bestselling author
Natalie Anderson**

"You can always rely on Natalie Anderson to deliver a fun and feel-good read."
—*PHS Reviews*

"Readers won't be disappointed with this passionate, fast-paced and funny romance."
—*RT Book Reviews* on *Dating and Other Dangers*

JILL SHALVIS

New York Times and *USA TODAY* bestselling and award-winning author Jill Shalvis has published more than fifty romance novels. The four-time RITA® Award nominee and three-time National Readers' Choice winner makes her home near Lake Tahoe. Visit her website at www.jillshalvis.com for a complete booklist and her daily blog.

NATALIE ANDERSON

Possibly the only librarian who got told off herself for talking too much, Natalie Anderson decided writing books might be more fun than shelving them—and, boy, is it that! Especially writing romance—it's the realization of a lifetime dream kick-started by many an afternoon spent devouring Grandma's Harlequin romances....

Natalie lives in New Zealand with her husband and four gorgeous-but-exhausting children. Swing by her website anytime—she'd love to hear from you: www.natalie-anderson.com.

New York Times Bestselling Author

JILL SHALVIS

The Heat Is On

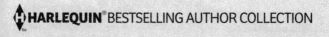

ISBN-13: 978-0-373-18079-0

Harlequin

THE HEAT IS ON
Copyright © 2013 by Harlequin Books S.A.

The publisher acknowledges the copyright holders of the individual works as follows:

THE HEAT IS ON
Copyright © 2010 by Jill Shalvis

BLAME IT ON THE BIKINI
Copyright © 2012 by Natalie Anderson

Printed in U.S.A.

CONTENTS

Dear Reader,

I love putting characters into their own worst-case scenarios. Is that mean? I do give them their happily ever afters—always—but there's something about watching them go through the wringer to get what they want in life that appeals to me. I also love watching them fall in love, hard. In fact, the harder they fall the better.

Take Isabella and Jacob. She's a pastry chef just trying to make it through her day when she stumbles over a dead body at her back door. To further her bad luck, the first detective on scene is the one-night stand she just had.

And Officer Hottie isn't any more thrilled by this than she is. It's hard to investigate a murder when your only witness is someone you've just seen naked.

Oh, how I love writing for Harlequin Blaze, where this book was originally published. *The Heat Is On* is truly one of my own favorites! I hope you enjoy.

Happy reading!

Jill Shalvis

THE HEAT IS ON

New York Times Bestselling Author

Jill Shalvis

To my editor extraordinaire, Brenda.
Thanks for always believing.

Chapter 1

"Oh, yeah, baby, that's good," she whispered. So good that she wanted more. She couldn't help herself, she'd never been known for having much self-control.

Not when it came to chocolate. Isabella Manchelli loved desserts, all of them.

Especially hers.

Which was why she was talking to them. Licking the last of it off her spoon, Bella then tossed the spoon into the sink, nodding in satisfaction and pride at the tray of little chocolate Genoese sponge squares she'd created. She wasn't sure of much, but she felt quite positive that the little cakes were her personal best to date. She went to work making up a second batch, knowing her boss, Willow, owner of Edible Bliss Cakes and Pastries, would be clamoring for more for her customers as the day progressed.

And the day had a lot of progressing to do. By the very nature of her job, she was routinely up before dawn, baking, and today had been no exception. At just the thought, she yawned.

That's what you get for staying up way too late last night...

Having her absolute last one-night stand.

Her last, because as much as she enjoyed the occasional social orgasm, she never got much pleasure out of the morning after. The slipping out of bed, hunting down her clothes from off the floor, carrying her sandals so as not to wake him up...

No, none of that ever felt good as good as the night before.

Even if this time, her first in a damn long time, now that she thought about it, the night before had been so admittedly terrific that she suspected she was still wearing a grin advertising just how terrific...

She angled her stainless-steel mixer so that she could use the appliance as a mirror and turned her head right and then left, inspecting herself.

Yep.

Ridiculous grin still in place.

She couldn't help it. Mr. Tall, Dark and Drop-dead Sexy had really had it going on. She'd met him through the local rec center's singles club, when Willow had somehow talked her into signing up for their Eight Dates in Eight Days. Tall, Dark and Drop-dead Sexy had been her eighth date, and the only one she'd let so much as kiss her.

The kiss had been shockingly…wow. Which had led to one thing or another, and some more wow, along with a good dash of yowza, and then…the whole morning-after thing.

He'd caught her in mid-tiptoe and off-kilter; she'd decided to go with her standard protocol for such situations.

She'd told him she was moving to Siberia, and then she'd left.

No feelings hurt, no strings. Just the way she liked it.

So why she felt a little hollow, a little discontented, she had no idea.

Probably it was all the chocolate on an empty stomach. Or possibly not. Possibly, the impossible had happened, and her mother's mantra—it's time to settle down, Bella—was right.

And how disconcerting a thought was *that*.

Bella didn't settle well. After growing up one of many in a huge family, she'd taken off soon as she'd been able, loving being alone. Loving the adventure of silence, the lack of planning ahead. It'd been bliss. She still felt that way, still preferred to roam the planet, touching down here and there as it suited her, never staying in one spot too long.

Except this time.

This time she'd landed in Santa Rey, California, the latest stop on the Bella's Train of Travels, and she loved the small beach town. Loved the job she'd taken on as a pastry chef at Edible Bliss, in the heart of a most adorable little downtown, only one block from the beach.

She'd been working here for a month now, and things were good. She had a roof over her head, she had pastries to make, and best yet—she'd gotten that orgasm last night.

Make that multiple orgasms…

She took a moment for a dreamy sigh. It really was a shame that she'd forced herself out of Tall, Dark and Drop-dead Sexy's bed after such a fantastic night, because he'd been both sharp *and* fun, her two top requirements in a man.

He'd also been focused and quietly controlled in a way that suggested cop or military, making her want to break the rules of the Eight Dates in Eight Days contract and ask him what he did for a living. But they'd been forbidden from discussing details like their vocation or age of residence until a second date, if a second date came to be.

He'd been the only one to spark her interest. He'd certainly been the one and only to get her to a bed, and in fact, if things had been different, he might even have had a shot at being that elusive keeper everyone talked about.

With a sigh, she moved through the front room of Edible Bliss, straightening tables and chairs, making sure everything was perfect before she opened them up for business.

She was raising the shades on the windows when she thought she heard a scraping sound from the kitchen's back door. She headed that way, thinking maybe it was Willow a little early. But today was Tuesday, and on Tuesdays Willow took a drawing class at the city college. It was male-model day. *Nude*-male-model day.

Willow's favorite.

It wouldn't be Willow then, no way.

Maybe it was Trevor, the rangy, sun-kissed cutie who worked part-time bussing tables and serving customers.

Walking through the kitchen, Bella peeked out the window in the back door—no one.

So now she was hearing things. Seemed that's what sleep deprivation did to a person. Good to know. Maybe next time she was faced with the prospect of some seriously fantastic sex, she'd say, "No, sorry, I can't, it appears wild monkey sex causes auditory hallucinations in me."

Shaking her head at herself, she checked the Cannoli batch she had in the oven, waving the heat blast from her face. Needing air, she went to crack open the back door, but it caught on something. She pushed, then squeezed through the space onto the back stoop to take a look, and tripped over—

Oh, God.

A body.

It was a guy, in jeans and a T-shirt, a small bouquet of wildflowers clutched in his fist.

Heart stuck in her throat, she dropped to a crouch and put a hand on his shoulder. "Hello?" There was an odd stillness to him she didn't want to face. "Are you okay?" Beneath her fingers, he felt warm, but she couldn't find a pulse. Panic caught her by the throat, choking off her air supply, as did the sight of the blood pooling beneath the man. "Not okay," she murmured, horror gathering in a greasy ball in her gut—which did not mix well with all the chocolate already there.

She closed her eyes on a wave of dizziness, doing her best not to throw up her sponge squares. "Hang on, I'll call 911."

But even as she hit the buttons on her cell phone, even as she stumbled back and stuttered her name and address for the dispatcher, she knew.

The man on her back stoop was beyond needing help.

After being assured by the dispatcher that an ambulance was on its way, Bella practiced the breathing techniques she'd been learning in yoga.

Not helping.

She went to visualization next, trying to imagine herself on the beach, with the calm waves hitting the shore, the light breeze brushing her skin… She had a lot of beaches to choose from, but she went with the beach right across the street because there was just something about Santa Rey's long stretch of white sand, where the salt water *whooshed* sea foam in on the gently sloping shores, and then *whished* it back out again. She swallowed hard, telling herself how much she loved the contemplative coves, the bluff-top trails, the dynamic tide pools, all off the beaten path. Here she was both hidden from the world, and yet doing as she loved. Here, unlike anywhere else in her travels, she felt as if she'd come home.

Better.

But then she opened her eyes and yep, there was still the dead guy on the concrete at her feet.

At least he hadn't gone belly up in the kitchen, she told herself, taking big gulps of air. The Occupational Safety and Health Administration probably frowned on dead guys in an industrial kitchen.

Oh, God.

Legs weak, she sank to the ground, feeling weird about being so close, but also like she didn't want to leave him alone. No one should die alone. She set her back to the wall and brought her knees up to her chest to drop her head on them. She was a practical, pragmatic woman, she assured herself. She could survive this, she'd survived worse.

She could hear the sirens now, coming closer. Good. That was good. Then footsteps sounded from the front of the shop, heavy and steady.

The cavalry.

Paramedics first, two of them, tall and sure, dropping to a crouch near the body. One of them reached out and checked the man beside her for a pulse, then shook his head at the other.

Behind the paramedics came a steady parade of other uniforms, filling the small pastry kitchen, making Bella dizzy with it all.

Or dizzier.

She answered questions numbly and eventually someone pushed a cup of water into her hands. One of Willow's pretty teacups.

She answered more questions. No, she hadn't heard any gunshots. No, she hadn't recognized the victim, but then again, she had yet to see his face. No, she hadn't noticed anything out of the ordinary, other than a noise that she'd barely even registered much less investigated....

God.

How could she have not have actually opened the door when she'd heard that odd scraping sound?

After the endless questions, she was finally left alone in the kitchen, by herself in the sea of controlled chaos. She backed to the far wall, attempting to be as unobtrusive as possible. Her legs were still wobbling, so she sank down the wall to sit on the floor, mind wandering.

She wished she'd never gotten out of her bed.

Correction: Tall, Dark and Drop-dead Sexy's bed.

If she'd only broken her own protocol and stayed with him, then she wouldn't be here now. And she might have, if she hadn't been so surprised at how badly she *hadn't* wanted to leave his bed.

That didn't happen often—hell, who was she kidding—sex didn't happen for her often, and certainly not during Eight Dates in Eight Days. She cursed Willow for talking her into doing it, but what was done was done. Besides, it wasn't as if she'd been finding her own dates since she'd put down anchor in Santa Rey.

Date one had been nice but a snooze.

Dates two through seven had been pleasant but nothing to write home about.

But date eight? Holy smokes. Date eight had blown all the other dates not only out of the water, but out of her head, as well.

Jacob.

She knew him only as Jacob, since last names hadn't been given. They'd agreed to meet at a new adventure facility on the outskirts of the county. He'd been there waiting for her, leaning against the building, tall and leanly muscled, with dark wavy hair that curled at his nape and assessing brown eyes that reminded her of warm, melted chocolate when he smiled, which he'd done at first sight of her.

Flattering, since though she was five foot seven and curvy, she knew she was merely average in looks. Average brown hair that was utterly uncontrollable. Average eyes. Average face…

In comparison, Jacob had been anything but average, oozing testosterone and sex appeal in a T-shirt and board shorts that emphasized his fit, hard body. Sin on a stick, that's how he'd looked.

For the next two hours they'd bungee jumped, jungle canopied and rode on a Jet Ski, none of which were conducive to talking and opening up, but she hadn't cared.

They'd flirted, they'd laughed, and she'd been in desperate need of both, even knowing he would be nothing but trouble to her heart. She'd had a blast, and afterward, her car had sputtered funny in the lot.

Jacob had said she had a bad spark plug and that he was a car junkie and had extras at his place. If she wanted, he could either follow her home to make sure she got there okay, and then return with the plug to fix her car, or she could follow *him* home and he'd fix it now.

She'd looked at him for a long moment, ultimately deciding that no guy who looked as good in that ridiculous bungee protective gear as he had—and he *had* looked *good*—could be a bad guy.

Naive? Not really. Just damn lonely. Besides, she

assured herself, she knew just enough self-defense moves to feel comfortable. She could always knock his nuts into next week if she had to.

And then there was something else. He had that air of undeniable control, that raw male power radiating from him that made her feel safe in his presence. Safe from harm, but not necessarily safe from losing her mind over him. She might not know his last name or what he did for a living, but she knew she wanted him.

So she'd followed him home.

She'd called her own number and left a message. "If anything has happened to me, check with Jacob, sexy hunk, and mystery date number eight."

But nothing had happened to her that she hadn't initiated.

He'd changed her spark plug. And there on his porch, she'd given him what she'd intended as a simple good-night peck.

He'd returned it.

Then they'd both gone still for one beat, their eyes locked in surprise. And the next thing she'd known, she'd been trying to climb up his perfect body.

And she meant *perfect,* from the very tips of his dark, silky hair all the way down to his toes and every single spot in between. Just thinking about it gave her a hot flash.

He'd actually resisted.

The thought made her want to smile now. He'd

really tried hard to hold back, murmuring sexily against her mouth that there was no need to rush things, they could go out again sometime.

Sometime.

She'd lived her life doing "sometime," being laidback and easygoing, not keeping track of anything, much less something that mattered.

For once she hadn't wanted *sometime,* she'd wanted right then. She'd *needed* right then. It'd been so long, she'd been taking care of her own needs for so damn long...

Startling her out of her own thoughts, there was new movement outside the pastry shop as the ME was finally ready to have the body removed. Once again, Bella set her head down on her knees, feeling a wave of emotion for whoever the guy had been, for his family, for whoever would grieve for him.

A pair of men's shoes appeared in front of her, topped by faded Levi's, and she closed her eyes, not up for more unanswerable questions. She heard a rustle and knew the owner of said shoes and jeans had just crouched in front of her.

When she peeked, she saw long legs flexing as he set his elbows on his thighs and waited on her.

He finally spoke. "You okay?"

Wait a minute. She knew that voice. It had coaxed shocking responses from her only last night, and she lifted her head, wondering if her mind was playing tricks on her.

Nope, it was Tall, Dark and Drop-dead Sexy, no longer wearing board shorts and a relaxed, easy grin.

Instead, he wore a light blue button-down that emphasized his lean, hard body, the one that had taken hers to heaven and back.

The man she'd told that she was moving to Siberia.

Oh, God.

He had a detective's badge on his hip, and he was either carrying a gun on his other hip or was very happy to see her, which she sincerely doubted, given the expression on his face.

Gulp.

"Hey," she whispered with a little smile.

He returned the little smile, his eyes warming, but he didn't "hey" back.

Yeah.

She'd had it right last night. She was in trouble with this one.

Deep trouble.

Chapter 2

Detective Jacob Madden looked into those jade-green eyes and thought *Ah, hell*. What had already been a really rough morning shifted into something else entirely, except he wasn't sure exactly what.

Not only was he running on less than two hours of sleep, he was he looking into the face of the reason for that lack of sleep.

The sexiest reason he'd ever had...

And there hadn't been a wink of sleep involved. Nope, it'd been a physically active sleepover, and just thinking about it had certain parts of his anatomy twitching to life, though those certain parts should be dead after the night they'd had.

Christ.

He knew he shouldn't have answered his damn cell this morning. He hadn't been scheduled to work today. In fact, he'd planned on hanging out with his brother Cord, recently injured on one of Uncle Sam's missions. Today's physical therapy was to have involved the beach, with a net and a volleyball and some good-old-fashioned ass kicking.

But dead bodies always trumped days off, so here he was. It was what he did.

Work.

His job took over much of his life, and it wasn't as if he was petting puppies for a living. Murder and mayhem was his thing, and he was good at it.

But sometimes it got to him.

And in this case, *she* got to him. Bella, with those slay-me eyes, heart-stopping smile and tough-girl attitude, got to him.

"Jacob?" she whispered.

"Yeah." They knew each other's first names, that they both liked adventure and seafood and that they had physical chemistry in shocking spades. He'd held her, he'd touched her. Hell, he'd had his mouth on every inch of her.

He knew he liked her.

A lot.

That had been the biggest surprise, he thought, considering the fact that the guys at the P.D. had signed him up for the date in the first place. As soon as he'd realized he'd been set up, he'd canceled out his singles club profile, but there'd already been one date planned and it'd been too late to cancel on her.

Bella.

He wasn't sorry. Or he hadn't been until she'd walked away sometime before dawn. He'd told himself that had been for the best and, considering her line about moving to Siberia, had figured he'd never see her again.

And yet here she sat, in the middle of his crime scene, looking anxious and stressed. He'd never been able to walk away from a perfect stranger, much less a woman he'd had panting and coming beneath him, so with a sigh, he reached for her hand. "Bella."

Her fingers, icy cold, gripped his. In complete contrast, she kept her voice even. Guts. She had guts.

"I have a little problem, don't I?" she asked.

He found his lips curving slightly. "Little bit, yeah."

Letting out a long breath, she pulled her hair out of its messy ponytail. Wild waves immediately fell in her face. "I tend to do that, you know," she said, trying to corral the hair back into the ponytail holder. "Walk into problems."

Shit, he did not want to know this. "Define 'problems.'"

She blew out another breath.

"Bella." He waited until she leveled him with those eyes. "Dead-people problems?"

"Oh, my God. *No.*" She rubbed her temples. "I really should have stayed in Cabo. That's where I was before this. The kayaking was good, and I was learning how to make the most amazing strawberry-and-honey friand—"

"Bella, about the dead-people problems."

"Right. Sorry. I tend to talk when I find gunshot victims."

"Again," he said carefully. "Does this happen often?"

Her gaze met his. "You're a cop."

"Detective."

She nodded. "I guessed cop or military last night."

She'd made him? "How?"

She sent him a wry smile. "Have you met you? You give off this *I'm relaxed* vibe but really you're totally alert, taking in everything around you."

He took another deep breath and let it out slowly, considering his response. Last night she'd been wearing strawberry lip gloss, her sweet, seductive lips full and curved in an open, easy smile. Her eyes had been warm and welcoming. This morning her lips were bare, and no less kissable for it, but she was breathing a little erratically, and the pulse at the base of her throat was racing.

Dammit.

He'd been a cop since college, a detective the past five years, and he never, ever got used to the punch of empathy when dealing with a victim.

Question was, was she really the victim? "You work here at Edible Bliss."

She nodded, her light brown wavy hair bouncing into her eyes again. Yesterday he'd loved that hair flying free around her when they'd been cuddled up on a Jet Ski, her arms wrapped tight around his middle.

Even later, that gorgeous hair had trailed down his body...

Don't go there, man. "You're the pastry chef," he said.

Another nod. "My lone talent."

He didn't believe that. Last night might have been nothing more than a really great one-night stand, but he'd seen a lot of sides to her. She was adventurous as hell, tough as hell and sexy as hell.

She had layers, lots of them. No way was she just her job the way he was. "You found the victim on the stoop when you got to work," he said, wanting to clarify.

"No. He wasn't there when I first came in." She paused. "Someone shot him."

Yes. Right in the forehead. At close range.

"Shot him dead." Her voice was a little hoarse. "There was blood..." Her eyes went a bit unfocused, and her tan faded to gray. "Huh. I see spots. Black spots. Do you?"

Shit. He pressed her head down between her knees, his hand curled around the nape of her neck.

Last night her skin had been warm and silky. Today it was cold and clammy. "Breathe," he commanded softly.

"I'm sorry." She grabbed a shallow breath. "I don't like blood much. You'd think I'd be used to it, given that once I was an assistant to a butcher in Rome, but I'm not. Used to it. God." Reaching out blindly, she grabbed on to the leg of his jeans and held on. "God, Jacob."

"Keep breathing," he murmured, stroking the tender skin of her neck with his thumb. "Slow and deep."

She did her best to comply, sucking in air in a shuddering gulp. "That's it, Bella. Good." Again his thumb swept over her.

"I'm really sorry about the whole Siberia thing," she whispered, eyes squeezed shut, her hands tightly fisted.

"Just keep breathing."

"I shouldn't have said Siberia. I don't even like Siberia. I didn't— I just don't do the long-term thing, I'm not good at it, and you seemed— You're a long-term guy, you know? I didn't want to mislead you—"

"Shh. It's okay." Was he a long-term guy? He'd always thought so, but his last two relationships had fallen apart and both his ex-girlfriends had put the blame square in his lap, citing his job, the hours and the danger. So he'd begun to wonder about his long-term potential.

Then he'd gone out with Bella.

He'd been pissed off about the setup, but prepared to make the best of the situation. He'd figured he'd have an okay time, then go home and watch a late game.

Instead, he'd been instantly entranced by Bella's easy smile, sweet eyes and take-no-prisoners attitude.

He could use more of that, all the way around.

And yet here they were, at a murder scene. He knew she was tough, and he hoped she was tough enough for this.

"There's a freaking dead guy on the back stoop," she said out of the blue. "And I nearly tripped over him. Can you imagine? I actually asked him if he needed anything."

His thumb made another gentle pass over her creamy skin. He couldn't help himself.

Which was why he couldn't be on this case. "Bella, don't. Don't tell me anything more."

"I was here for an hour and a half before I saw him," she whispered, not listening. "Do you think I could have—"

"No." His voice was low but firm. She couldn't have saved him. He believed that much. He looked around them. There were two uniforms and two plainclothes; himself and Ethan Rykes, Jacob's sometime partner. Also Ramon Castillo had just arrived, their detective sergeant.

Shit.

Castillo was a tough son of a bitch who went by the book. Jacob swore to himself and gently pulled Bella to her feet.

"What?" she murmured, still a little gray as she shivered.

Goddammit, she was shocky. He had no idea why no one had noticed it before, but she needed out of this room and she needed to be checked out. She'd already been questioned, but protocol would entail her going to the station, where she'd be checked for gunpowder residue, and further questioned.

Normally, this would be *his* job. Not today. Not with her. Having been naked with a possible suspect was considered bad form.

There was a walk-in pantry off to the side of the kitchen, and Jacob pulled Bella into it. He shut the door and leaned her back against it, his hands on her arms.

She set her head against the wood and gave him a ghost of a smile. "The last time we were this close to each other," she murmured, "you dropped to your knees and put your mouth on my—"

"Bella." Christ. She drove him crazy. So did the memory.

Because she was right. He had dropped to his knees in front of her, tugged her pretty pink lace thong to her ankles and had his merry way with her.

She'd returned the favor.

"You have to listen to me," he said, looking into her eyes.

"Are you in charge of the case?"

"Yes. *No.*" He shook his head. "I am, but in about two minutes when I talk to my sergeant, I won't be. I can't be."

"Because of last night? Because we—"

He put a finger on her lips. A direct contrast to only a few hours ago, when he'd wanted to hear every pant, every whimper, every cry she made for more. "Yeah. Because of that. I'm not exactly impartial now."

She stared at him a moment, then pushed his finger away. "Am I a suspect, Jacob?"

"As a formality, everyone on the premises will be."

"A formality." She shook her head. "I'm the only one on the premises. Willow lives in the apartment upstairs next to mine but she's in class. The store isn't open." She met his gaze and he was gratified to see hers had cleared.

Yeah. She was tough enough for this.

"I didn't kill him," she said. "I don't even know who he is."

His life had been saved on more than one occasion by nothing more than his wits and instincts. Those instincts were screaming now, telling him that this woman, this smart, funny, walk-on-the-wild-side woman could never pull a trigger to kill someone, much less at close range, in cold blood.

But then again, he'd seen worse.

"Who is he?" she whispered.

"Don't know yet. He had no ID on him, no wallet, no keys, no money, nothing. He didn't appear to drive himself here."

She blinked. "Then how did he get here?"

"I guess we were hoping you could shed some light on that subject."

She said nothing, just stared at him.

At a hard, single knock on the door right behind Bella's head, she jumped, then turned and stared at the door as if it'd grown wings. "They're coming for me."

"No one's coming for you." He pulled open the door and faced Ethan.

"Can anyone join this party?" Ethan asked lightly.

Jacob wasn't fooled. Ethan might look like a big, rough-and-tumble linebacker, with more brawn than brains, but underestimating him was a mistake. Ethan was sharp as a tack, and *always* solved his case. Jacob nudged Bella out of the pantry. "Why don't you get yourself some more water."

When she nodded and moved away, he looked at Ethan.

"What the hell, man?" Ethan asked quietly, his smile still in place for anyone who happened to look over at them. "You screwing with protocol for a pretty face? And don't get me wrong, that is one pretty face..." Ethan turned his head, his gaze slowly sliding down the back of Bella as she walked away, from her wild hair to the sweetest ass Jacob had ever had ever sunk his teeth into. "Pretty *everything*," Ethan corrected.

Jacob let out a careful breath. "I can't be on this case."

"You afraid to get tough with Cutie-Pie?" Ethan grinned. "That's okay. Big, bad Ethan will do it for you. I can take one for the team."

"I have a conflict of interest," Jacob said tightly. "And it's your fault."

"Huh?"

"That date you signed me up for last night? It was with her."

"And?"

"And the date didn't end until a few hours ago."

"Nice." Ethan's grin faded as the implications sank in. *"Oh."*

"Yeah."

Before Ethan could say another word, Sergeant Castillo moved in close, leaning over both their shoulders like a bloodhound on the scent. "Ladies, we have a problem?"

"Yes," Jacob said.

Ethan smirked. "Casanova here not only slept with the key witness, but he also slept with our only suspect so far. But at least it's the same person, so..."

Jacob let out a controlled breath and resisted punching Ethan. *Barely.*

Ramon, dark skinned, dark-eyed and tougher than any of them on a good day, quietly stared at Jacob. "Ethan, coffee."

Ethan didn't budge. "I want to hear you chew him a new one."

"Coffee. Now."

"You aren't serious."

"As a heart attack." Ramon never took his eyes off Jacob, waiting until Ethan stalked off. "Talk."

"You remember the guys telling you yesterday that they'd signed me up for a date with the singles club."

Ramon's eyes lit with a quick flash of humor—the equivalent of a belly laugh on anyone else. "Yes."

"It was last night."

Ramon's gaze slid across the kitchen to where Bella was standing in front of a baker's rack, inspecting whatever she had on it. It looked like cream puffs.

They smelled like heaven.

His mouth watered and he wondered if under different circumstances—say, her not running out on him, and him not answering his cell phone—he'd still be at home right this minute, once again sampling her considerable wares—

"Let me take a wild stab at this," Ramon said. "The date those assholes set you up on was with one Isabella Manchelli."

"I guess that's why they pay you the big bucks."

Ramon didn't cut a smile. "You slept with her. Hell, Madden."

Across the room, Ethan approached Bella, fun, laid-back guy gone, cop face on, his pad out.

Ramon let the silence hang between them a minute, then blew out a breath. "Bad timing."

Yeah.

Ramon was quiet another moment, then shoved his fingers through his dark hair. "Okay, well, we'll deal with it."

They didn't have much of a choice. Jacob glanced over at Bella again. She was still talking to Ethan, but looking past him, right into Jacob's eyes, her own soft and compelling.

She'd planned on never seeing him again, and he'd reconciled himself to that as being for the best.

But fate had intervened now. He wondered just where it would take them, and if they were going to enjoy—or regret—the ride.

Chapter 3

By the time Bella finished talking to Ethan at the police station, it was nearly two, which was when her shift ended. She checked in with Willow, who told her that there was still yellow crime scene tape blocking off the shop, so she'd never opened for the day, disappointing their customers.

All those delicious pastries and cakes, going stale…

Ethan drove Bella home from the station. Home was, temporarily at least, one of the two small apartments above Edible Bliss.

"You're new to town," Ethan said lightly, idling at the curb while Bella unhooked her seat belt.

They'd been over this, but she nodded. "Yes."

"You planning on sticking?"

"I don't tend to stick, I never intended to stick."

"Are you...unsticking anytime soon?"

"Not this week."

"Good enough," he said. "Thanks for cooperating this morning."

She'd been raised right enough that she automatically thanked him in return, even though she had no idea what she was thanking him for. Asking intrusive questions? Plying her with bad cop coffee until she was so jittery she was in danger of leaping out of her own skin? He seemed like a good cop and a decent man, but she was on overload now, facing an adrenaline crash. "How long until we can go back inside?"

"Another couple of hours, tops. Just long enough to let CSI finish. You'll call me if you think of anything else you can tell me?"

"Yes," she said, then asked him the question she'd been wondering all day. "Are you Jacob's partner?"

"We work together sometimes, but not on this case."

Something in his voice had her taking a second look at him.

"Conflict of interest," he clarified.

She hesitated, knowing that they both knew *she* was the conflict of interest. "Is he in trouble?"

He started to say something and then stopped.

"Is he?"

"For being with you? No. For not being able to keep his nose out once he's feeling protective about someone he cares about? Not yet, but give him a day or two."

"We're not together. It was…just a one-night thing. You need to make sure your commander, or whatever he's called, knows that. I don't want Jacob to be in trouble over me."

"I'll be in touch."

She nodded, ignoring the unease in the center of her gut, and got out of the car. She looked at the front door to the shop. Edible Bliss, the cute little paisley sign read. The interior was just as unique. Done up like a sixties coffeehouse, the colors bold and happy.

And just a little psychedelic.

She loved it here.

But at the moment, she also hated it.

There was still yellow crime tape blocking the front door. Willow was sitting on the steps. She was forty, tiny, with a dark cap of spiky hair tipped in purple this week. Her eyebrow piercing glinted in the sun as she watched Bella approach with a worried tilt to her mouth.

It'd been a while since Bella had stayed anyplace long enough to make friends, been a long time since she'd wanted to, but Santa Rey had snagged her by the heartstrings.

So had Willow. They'd spent only a month together, but it felt like more. She sank to the step at Willow's side. "I'm so sorry."

"Not your fault." Willow had sweet, warm eyes and a smile to match, and she hugged Bella tight. "We don't see a lot of murder in Santa Rey," she murmured. "They asked me a bunch of questions and I didn't get to ask any of my own. Do you suppose they have any leads?"

"At the moment, I might be their only one."

Willow pulled back, clearly shocked. "They suspect *you?*"

"I think it's standard procedure to suspect everyone."

Willow was quiet a moment. "It's probably not appropriate to ask, given what's happened, but I never got to ask you. How did last night go? Date number eight?"

In spite of everything, Bella felt herself soften. "Nice."

Willow blinked, then let out a slow grin. "Honey, a smile that like means a whole helluva lot more than *nice*."

"Yes, well, it got complicated."

"Uh-huh. Most good stuff is. Is he good looking?"

"Yes."

"Good kisser?"

"Willow—"

"Oh, come on. I haven't had a date in three months. Let me live vicariously through you."

"Yes," Bella breathed on a whisper of a laugh. "He's a good kisser. But—"

"Oh, crap. There's a but?"

"A big one, actually. He's the detective assigned to this case. Or he was, until it was established that he'd slept with the person who found the dead guy."

Willow stared at her. "Oh, shit, Bella."

"Yeah. That about covers it."

They stood together and walked past the yellow tape to the alley between the building and the one next door. It was narrow and lined with two trash cans. Passing through, they came to the rear of the shop, where there was more yellow tape across the back door.

Bella took in the sight of the stoop and shivered. Willow hugged her, then they took the stairs to the second-story landing. Her boss moved to her door. "You going to be okay?"

"Absolutely."

Willow blew her a kiss and vanished inside her place.

Bella entered her own apartment, where she stripped, pulled on her bathing suit and headed back out, walking the block to the beach. The boardwalk stretched out in front of her, but she didn't walk it as she normally did. Today she wanted to swim.

Hard.

This particular beach drew sunbathers looking to soak up the California sun, and fishermen seeking fish and crab. It was a popular spot, and not much of a secret, but this afternoon, there wasn't a crowd. Standing at the water's edge, Bella stared out into the waves, inhaling the warm, salty air. The scent was intoxicating. With a purposeful breath, she let loose some of the tension knotting her shoulders and neck, and kicked off her flip-flops. She dropped her towel to the sand, and then her sunglasses on the towel, and without pause, dived out past the waves. There, she swam parallel to the shore for half a mile, and then back.

By the time she walked out of the water at the same spot she'd started, the sun was slanting lower in the sky, perched like a glorious burning ball hanging over the horizon.

The beach had completely cleared. Instead of the pockets of families dotting the sand, there was only the occasional straggler. She bent for her sunglasses, slid them on, then straightened, coming face-to-face with Detective Jacob Madden.

He looked her over slowly, taking in her dripping wet suit without a word. He wore the same loose jeans and the shirt she'd seen him in earlier, and still had his gun at his hip. The shirt was snug across his shoulders and loose across the abs she had every reason to know were flat and ridged, as she'd spent some time running her tongue across them.

All day her thoughts had drifted to him.

He was easy to think about. He looked great

when he was smiling. He looked great when he was just standing there. Hell, he looked great naked and sweaty, and that was hard to do—no pun intended.

He was wearing dark sunglasses and looked like a movie star. She squeezed the water from her hair, quiet as she eyed him. "Definitely Tall, Dark and Drop-dead Sexy."

"Excuse me?"

"Well, maybe *drop-dead* aren't exactly the right words today."

He grimaced, and she had to let out a low laugh. "Are you embarrassed?"

"No. I don't do embarrassed."

But he was. She could tell, and she shook her head. "You do own a mirror, right?"

He ignored that, probably out of self-defense. "I wanted to know if you were okay."

"I was thinking of asking you the same."

"I'm not the one who had a pretty rough morning."

"Are you sure? Because I hear you lost a case just by sleeping with the chick who found the dead guy. I'm really sorry if it was because of me, Jacob."

"I'm a big boy. I'll be fine."

She nodded, but the tension she'd just worked so hard to swim off had come back. Worse, her stomach chose that moment to rumble, *loudly,* reminding her she hadn't eaten all day.

He arched a brow, and she shrugged. "Listen, I've got to go."

"You're hungry."

Usually when she shooed a man away, he went. And stayed gone.

Not Jacob. He stood there, hands on hips, unconcerned that she'd just dismissed him. "I'm thinking they can hear your stomach in China. Let's get something to eat."

Here was the problem. She wanted to gobble *him* up. But she wasn't going to get him in any more of a bind. "I'm fine." Again her manners got the better of her. "But thank you."

He was quiet a moment, then blew out a breath when she shivered. He bent for the towel she'd left on the sand and handed it out to her. "Bella, I—"

"Look, I hate that you got in trouble for me, okay? And I know you did." She dried herself off.

"I'm not in trouble."

"You got taken off the case!"

"I *took* myself off the case. Officially." He paused. "Unofficially, I'm still involved."

"What does that mean?"

"Let's just say I feel invested."

"In the dead guy?"

He just looked at her.

In her. "Oh, no. *No.*" She added a head shake. "You aren't going to risk your job for me."

"I'm not risking anything. I'm off duty at the moment, and my time is now my own, however I wish to spend it. Turns out I wish to spend it helping you."

"You think I need help?"

"I think, if nothing else," he said with terrifying gentleness, reaching for her hand, "that you could probably use a friend."

Dammit. Her throat burned. Too much swimming in the sun. Too much caffeine at cop central. Too much adrenaline still flowing. But it had nothing, nothing at all, to do with having him at her side. "I really didn't kill him," she whispered.

"Well, that makes this a lot easier." Not letting go of her, he tugged her close, looking into her eyes. "How about we figure out who did."

She bowed her head a moment and watched the water drip from her, vanishing into the sand at her feet.

Jacob pulled off her sunglasses and then his, studying her face with his cop's eyes. "You look done in."

"I—" Yeah. Yeah, she was.

Without another word, he tugged her hand again, leading her across the beach to the boardwalk. Willow's shop was off to the right, but he went left.

"Hey," she said.

He didn't answer. He didn't say a word, in fact, until they'd crossed the beach, stepping onto the back deck of Shenanigans, a lovely outdoor café, one of Bella's favorites. Her favorite, because they bought their desserts from Edible Bliss, Bella's own creations, serving them for their nightly dinner run.

Jacob pulled out a chair for her and she shifted on her feet. "I'm all wet."

Jacob had slid his dark sunglasses back on, but she felt his gaze go from mild to scorching in zero point four.

Her body answered the call.

"I meant from the ocean," she clarified wryly. "I'm wearing a bikini here, Jacob."

"Trust me, I noticed."

Her belly executed a little flutter. She told herself it was nerves and an empty stomach, but that was one big fat lie.

It was all Jacob.

He excited her. Even just sitting across from her the way he was, slouched in his chair, long legs spread carelessly out in front of him, just breathing and watching her, he excited her.

"It's a no shirt, no shoes, no service sort of place," she said.

"Fine." He started to shrug out of his button-down.

"Wait— What are you doing?" she asked in a horrified whisper.

"Helping you out with the shirt part." Beneath, he wore a pale blue T-shirt advertising some surf shop in Mazatlán.

And a lot of lean muscles.

A *lot*.

Not that she was noticing.

The light in his eyes said that he noticed her noticing, so she made a conscious effort to shut her mouth and surreptitiously check for drool.

Jacob stood up and walked around to the back of her chair, draping the shirt over her shoulders.

It was warm from his body heat, and it smelled like him, and she had to work at not moaning out loud. Her eyes drifted shut.

Bending so that his mouth brushed her ear, he murmured, "Stand up, Bella."

As if her brain had disconnected from her body, her body obeyed. She stood up.

Still behind her, he guided her hands through the sleeves and rolled the cuffs up, the insides of his arms grazing the sides of her breasts. "Better?"

"Uh-huh," she managed brilliantly. *God, please let me find the bones in my knees so I don't collapse to the floor in a puddle of longing...*

His fingers were sure and firm as he buttoned her up, but somehow gentle, too, evoking memories of last night.

Of course, he'd been *removing* her clothes then, with lots of hot, openmouthed kisses and hands stroking down her body in a way that had brought pleasure and heightened her need and hunger.

As if she'd needed help with the heightening.

Hell, by the time he'd slid his clever, knowing fingers between her thighs, she'd been primed to go off.

And go off she had, like a bottle rocket.

At the memory, her nipples hardened even more. She clasped his shirt to her, her fingers brushing his. "Thanks."

He nodded.

And yet neither of them moved for a long beat. They just stood there, locked in an embrace, her back to his front, his arms around her.

A few customers walked by and broke the moment. Bella slid back into her chair.

Jacob's gaze ran the length of her, a light in his eyes that said arousal, and just a hint of possessiveness.

Clearly, he liked the look of his shirt on her.

Her nipples throbbed. She felt them shrink to two tight points. And thanks to her very wet bathing suit, the shirt immediately suctioned to her breasts so that he could see her happy nipples. "Not good," she muttered, hugging herself.

His mouth curved in a slow smile that heated her up almost as much as the shirt had. "Depends on your point of view."

Chapter 4

Jacob looked away from Bella when the waitress came to their table. "Hey, handsome," she said. "On duty?"

He'd known Deb since high school. "Not today." He glanced back at Bella, who gave a little wince, making him wonder if she still felt responsible for the fact that he wasn't working.

He didn't want her to feel guilty. In his life, there was *always* work. Hell, there'd be work tomorrow.

Today, he wanted to make sure she was okay. And he could tell by her pallor, by the dull look in her eyes, that she wasn't.

"So what can I get for you kids?" Deb asked.

Bella didn't answer. She was staring down at her menu, already lost in thought, a million miles away. "Bella?"

No answer.

Jacob turned to Deb and ordered for them both.

"Something to drink?" Deb asked.

Again he glanced at Bella. Still looking a little shell-shocked. He'd seen this a hundred times. It'd finally all caught up with her. She was worrying her napkin between her fingers in a motion of anxiety, and he covered her cold hand with his.

She jerked and met his gaze. "I'm sorry, what?"

"A drink? You want some hot tea to warm you up?"

She mustered a smile. "That'd be nice."

Not moving his eyes off hers, he spoke to Deb. "We'll take whatever comes up first, Deb, thanks." And when she'd smiled and moved off, he kept his hand on Bella's.

"You ordered for me?"

"Only because you didn't." His thumb brushed over the backs of her fingers.

"Sorry. What are we having?"

"Pizza, fully loaded. Also a sushi platter and a turkey club."

"For you and what army?" she teased.

Deb came back with the hot tea and some crackers. Jacob opened the crackers while Bella doctored her tea. He handed her a cracker and waited while she ate it. Sure enough, less than a minute later, her color came back, which relieved him. "How long since you've eaten, Bella?"

"Do my sponge cakes and cannoli count?"

"Yeah. Against you."

"Hey, I'll have you know they're the best cannoli on the planet."

He was watching her carefully, noting her fingers shook when she reached for her tea. "Is there someone I can call to stay with you tonight? Family?"

"God, no." She looked at him, seemed to realize that hadn't eased his worry and sent him a little smile. "I have family, Jacob. Don't look so concerned. Six sisters, five brothers-in-law, four grandparents, and at last count, twelve nieces and nephews. They all live in Maine within a three-block radius. If you contacted any of them, they'd roll their eyes and ask what I've done to warrant trouble now, and then converge on Santa Rey like the Second Coming. They'd huddle and hover and nag and smother, all in the name of love. But fair warning, if you call them, I'll have to hurt you."

He found himself smiling. He did that a lot around her. "They're that much fun, huh?"

She shrugged. "We're like a pack of pit bull puppies. Can't stand to be together, but we'd fight to the death for each other."

He supposed that wasn't all that different from

him and his brothers. "That's a lot of family—were you all raised together?"

"Yep. Growing up, my sisters and me shared one bedroom with five tiny beds. I was the youngest, so I did without my own bed."

"That must have been tough."

"Nah. They loved me." A brief shadow crossed her face, as if knowing that hadn't quite made it okay that they hadn't been able to accommodate her.

"I slept with a different sister each night." She shrugged. "You'd think that it might have given me a twisted sense of belonging, but actually, it made me feel like I belonged anywhere."

Or nowhere...

"Which is where the traveling bug came from," he guessed, fascinated by this peek into her life.

"Yeah. I'm definitely uniquely suited to moving around, it's in my blood. I wander, stick for a little while, and if I don't find what I want, that's reason enough to go on."

"What are you looking for?"

She blinked. Clearly, she'd never been asked that question. "You know," she mused, "I have no idea, really. But as I moved from place to place, I learned about baking and pastry making from all different cultures."

"Quite the experience. You must have some great recipes."

"Actually, I don't use recipes all that much. I've

memorized the rules and ratios, so I can get away with winging it."

"Rules?"

"Yeah, like egg whites and eggs yolks cook at different temps, and that adding sugar to eggs causes the protein in the eggs to start setting." She lifted a shoulder. "I know a ton of boring stuff like that."

He smiled. "You couldn't be boring if you tried."

The sushi plate arrived, and Bella's stomach growled loud enough for him to smile.

"Shut up," she said good-naturedly, and stuffed a California roll in her mouth, and then a spicy tuna roll. And then another, chewing with a loud moan. "God, this is good." She ate for another minute before she seemed to realize he was just watching.

He couldn't help himself.

"You get off on watching women eat?" she asked, looking amused.

"Not usually," he said, having to laugh at himself. "Apparently, it's just you."

A flash of amusement, and then regret, crossed her face, and she put down her next roll. "Listen. I said I was sorry about the Siberia comment, but—"

He nudged her fingers back to her food. "It's okay. It was to be a one-night thing, I get it. But you could have just said so, you know."

"I should have. I'm sorry. But I really have been to Siberia, you know. I used it because it seems like the farthest possible place from here…" She gestured to the beach over her shoulder.

"Why use it at all?"

"Because sometimes guys don't take rejection well."

"I didn't exactly get rejected," he reminded her.

"Because you stalked me on the beach."

He laughed, and she smiled. "Okay," she said. "Not exactly stalked, and obviously I want to be here or you'd be walking funny."

He arched a brow.

"My signature self-defense move is a knee to the family jewels."

He winced. "I'll keep that in mind."

"No need. Like I said, I want to be here." She paused. "With you." She took a sip of her tea and hummed in pleasure.

"Bella," he said, staring at her mouth. "I love that you love food, and that you seem to experience everything to its fullest. I *really* love that, but you're killing me here with the moaning."

She stared at his mouth in return. "I'd say I'm sorry…"

"But you're not."

Slowly, she shook her head, and when he let out a low groan and had to shift in his chair—she got to him, dammit, like no other—she smiled and broke the spell. "The tea is peach mango," she said. "My sister makes tea like this."

"You ever get homesick?"

"Only for the tea." She paused. "Okay, maybe sometimes for the people. They miss me. A lot."

"They love you."

"Yes, well, I'm very lovable." She smiled again, her gaze holding his. "So, Detective…"

"So."

"You know all about me, and yet all I know about you is that you feel protective over girls you sleep with, and have a food fetish."

He ignored the protective thing. Fact was fact. "No, I have a watching-*you*-eat fetish. There's a difference."

"Don't distract me," she said, scolding him. "It's your turn."

"To what?"

"To tell me about you."

Bella smiled when Jacob just stared at her. The detective was far more comfortable dissecting her than himself.

"What about me?" he finally asked, his eyes shuttering a little bit.

"Well, you could start with why you were one of my blind dates. You don't seem like the blind-date type."

"Is there an easier question?"

"That *is* easy," she said.

He was quiet a moment, studying her. "You might not like my answer."

"Try me."

"Okay, the guys at the P.D. thought it would be funny to sign me up for the singles club."

"You mean, without your knowledge?"

"Yes."

He was right. She found she didn't like the thought of that at all. She picked up another California roll. "So you didn't want to go out with me."

Letting out a long breath, he reached across the small table for her hand, entwining their fingers, his thumb running slowly over her knuckles in a little circle that was unbelievably soothing.

And arousing.

"Bella?"

"Hmm?" She lifted her gaze from their fingers.

"Did I seem all that unwilling to you?"

His gaze was clear, open and honest…and heated.

She remembered the night before, how he'd looked at her as he'd slid in and out of her body in long, slow strokes while murmuring hot, erotic words in her ears, holding her gaze prisoner as he'd taken her over… "No," she whispered, squeezing her thighs together beneath the cover of the table. "You didn't seem unwilling."

"One thing you should know about me. I never do anything I don't want to."

She looked away and cleared her throat. "So, are you the youngest in your family also?"

"The oldest of four boys. I was born and raised here." He lifted a shoulder. "I'd guess you'd say I'm your polar opposite. I like roots."

She didn't correct him, tell him that she was beginning to see the light on that subject. That she'd never disliked the idea of roots, she'd just not felt the slightest urge to cultivate them. Until now anyway.

"My brothers are here in Santa Rey—or least two of them are. Wyatt's air force, and in Afghanistan, but we think of this as home."

"You're close to them then?"

"Whether we like it or not," he said with a dry smile that spoke of easy affection and an easier love.

It made her feel a little wistful. It also tweaked that odd sense of loneliness that had been plaguing her of late. Sure, she could go home and live near her family, but that wasn't the answer for her.

She hadn't found the answer yet. And wasn't that just the problem. "What about your parents?"

"Retired and living in Palm Springs. I try to see them several times a year."

"That's sweet."

"Sweet?"

He said this as if it was a dirty word, and she smiled. "What's wrong with being called sweet?"

"Not something I'm accused of all that often."

She bet. Hot? Yes. Big and bad? Yes and yes.

But the sweetness he had buried pretty deep. Still, it was undeniable. "I have to tell you, I'm sitting here, trying to figure out why your friends thought you needed help enough to set you up with the singles club."

"It was a joke."

"Rooted from what?"

"Christ, you're persistent."

"Uh-huh, it's my middle name. Spill, Detective."

He let out a low, slow breath. "I live the job."

"Lots of people live the job. Hell, I live *and* eat the job."

"Cops are...different. We go to work and tend to see the worst in people every day, and sometimes we face things that make it hard on whoever's waiting for us at home."

"Things like a bullet?"

"Yeah," he said. "Or the business end of a knife, or a hyped-up druggie determined not to go in peacefully, whatever."

"That makes you very brave," she said softly. "Not a bad relationship risk."

"But there are the long, unforgiving hours. People really don't like the hours."

"By people you mean women," she said.

"I've had two serious, long-term relationships, both of whom walked away from me because of the job."

"Were you a cop before you dated them?" she asked.

"Yeah."

"Then that was *their* fault." She squeezed his hand. "Not yours. You shouldn't have to change who you are for a relationship, Jacob." She cocked her head and studied him for a minute, seeing more of the story in his eyes and taking a guess. "So, actually, when it comes down to it, a blind date is right up your alley. Little to no danger of getting too attached, the anonymity of being strangers, et cetera."

"Yeah."

Ironic. Here was the first guy who'd tempted her to stick around in a damn long time, and he wasn't looking for more.

The pizza arrived, steaming hot and smelling as delicious as Jacob.

Almost.

She dug in with a huge bite, and moaned again. "God, this is good." She licked cheese off her fingers. "So why were you waiting for me on the beach? I doubt it was to find out how many siblings I have, or that I have a healthy appetite."

He was watching her suck the cheese off her fingers, but he answered her question without trying to bullshit her, or misdirect. "There's news on the case."

She swallowed and looked at him. "Tell me."

"Have you had any odd phone calls or letters or anything out of the ordinary going on?"

"No. Why?"

"Did you know a Seth Owen?"

The name took her a minute, and she stared at him as shock hit her. "The dead guy. It was Seth?"

"Yes."

"I didn't know his last name," she whispered, covering her mouth. "Seth was date two of eight." Oh, God. He'd been a nice guy, friendly and sweet. He loved puppies and his mom.

And he was dead.

Dead on her back stoop, holding flowers. Her stomach rolled, and she pushed away her plate.

Jacob waited, eyes warm and patient while she struggled with control.

"I keep thinking I could have prevented this," she finally said quietly. "If I'd only looked earlier, maybe called 911 sooner—"

"No. Bella—"

She looked away, toward the ocean, her happy place. The sun was a huge ball of orange fire on the horizon. The late breeze was soft and gentle, but still she shivered.

Because suddenly she was cold, very cold.

"I didn't recognize him this morning," she murmured. "But I never really saw his face, just his back."

And his blood.

"He was so nice. I just didn't— We didn't click." She met his gaze. "I was looking for the click."

She hadn't found that until date number eight, as they both knew.

Jacob's eyes held hers, dark and filled with things, things she didn't intend to spend a lot of time thinking about if she could help it. "I'm sorry. Thanks for dinner, but I have to go." She surged to her feet, needing to bake, needing to be anywhere but here.

He stood up with her, but she shook her head. "I'm okay, really. I just have to…go."

Now.

Yesterday.

He was standing close, looking a little protective and a whole lot intense, but when he reached for her, she took a step back.

He dropped his hand. "Bella."

"I'm okay," she whispered.

Not arguing with her, he nodded slowly, his see-all eyes taking her in carefully.

"Look, I'm sure you're used to this…murder thing," she said. "But I'm going to need some processing time."

"Understandable."

She ran her hands down herself, realizing she didn't have any pockets. Or money. Hell, she was barely dressed. "I don't have any cash, but I'll—"

"I've got it, Bella."

"See? Sweet." She hugged herself, her fingers brushing over the material of his shirt. "And your shirt. I promise I'll get it back to you—"

"It's okay."

She nodded, grabbing her towel and backing away from him and the table. "Thanks for..." *Everything.* "You know. Coming by, feeding me, et cetera."

"Bella—"

She didn't stick around to hear what he had to say.

Couldn't. She needed to blot out the images of that innocent man bleeding on the shop stoop. She needed some time to untangle the newly complicated knot that now represented Jacob. She needed to breathe, to find some sort of center.

She needed to bake.

Chapter 5

Bella walked back to Edible Bliss to find Ethan sitting on the steps that led up to the two apartments above the shop. Unable to summon the most basic of manners, she stared at him and sighed. "Didn't I already give you the better part of my day?"

"You had two calls."

"What?"

"Yeah, you left the window open in the shop's kitchen—" He gestured above his head. "So when the phone rang, I could hear the machine pick up. Mrs. Windham wants a three-tiered lemon birthday cake for her pug for next Wednesday, and Trevor wanted to see if you want to go for a sail."

"Is that why you're here, to play assistant?"

"Victim has been identified," he said. "Seth Owen."

Grateful to Jacob for breaking the news first, she nodded and hugged herself. "Date number two."

Ethan pulled a small pad from his pocket and wrote something down. "From Eight Dates in Eight Days."

"Yes."

Ethan made another note. "And you hadn't seen nor heard from him since you went out?"

"I didn't say that." She sighed when Ethan lifted his hand and looked at her. "He called me, asking for another date. I reminded him of the rules, that we weren't supposed to go out with anyone again until all eight dates were over."

"And?"

"And he said he'd call after all eight dates, if I was interested."

Ethan was watching her carefully. "To which you replied...?"

She sighed. "That I'd be moving out of the area."

Ethan arched a brow. "You blew him off."

"I—" She hesitated. Yeah. She had. "He was a perfectly nice guy, I just didn't feel any sparks."

And now he was dead.

"So why was he at Edible Bliss?"

"I don't know."

"Good enough, thanks." Ethan pocketed his pad.

"I'll be in touch." He moved past her, and when Bella turned to watch him leave, found Jacob behind her.

The two men exchanged long looks. There was some sort of silent communication, then Ethan nodded and walked away.

"What was that?" Bella asked. "That whole conversation you just had without words? And you followed me."

"Yep." Ignoring her first question, he brushed past her, grabbing her hand as he did, pulling her up the stairs. At her door, he held out his hand.

"What?"

"Your key."

She stared at him.

"I want to look inside," he said. "And make sure you're safe."

The thought that she might not be hadn't occurred to her. She stared at her door and shivered.

"I'm not trying to scare you," he said quietly. "But you need to be aware of your surroundings. Have an escape route, always. When you walk up these stairs alone at night, you don't have a lot of choices on this small landing."

"I can defend myself."

"How?"

"I'd kick him in the nuts."

He nodded. "Good. But you might need a backup plan. I can show you some moves, if you'd like."

Yes. She'd like to see some of his moves.

Especially if they were anything like the moves he'd shown her last night.

"Key?" he repeated.

She hesitated, knowing he wasn't going to like this.

He took in her expression. "Tell me the door's locked, Bella."

"It's locked." She let out a low breath, then stooped and pulled the key out from beneath the doormat.

He stared at her as she dropped it into his hands. "Are you kidding me?"

She lifted her chin. "I've always felt safe here."

Until now...

"Jesus." Shaking his head, he unlocked her door and handed her back her key. Hands on hips, he silently dared her to put the key back beneath the mat.

She didn't. She almost wanted to, just to see what he'd say.

Or do.

She was pretty sure he could see that particular wheel turning in her head, so she resisted.

He looked at her for another beat, then shook his head again. "Stay here."

She pictured him walking through her tiny seven-hundred-square-foot apartment like something out of a 007 movie, and wasn't surprised that when he came back to the opened doorway, he was tucking his gun into the back of his jeans.

"Any boogeymen?"

"All clear." He stepped aside to let her in, nodding to the two huge duffel bags lined up against the wall in the living room. "Going somewhere?"

"Not quite yet." She nudged one of the bags with her toe. "I don't usually unpack."

He lifted a brow.

She was used to that look. It was the genuine bafflement of someone who'd centered his life around one place, someone who'd made a home for himself. And she'd seen his house. It was big and open and… guy. There was a large, comfy couch and a huge TV. He'd had sports equipment lining his foyer and dishes in his sink. It'd been warm and lived in, and had reflected his personality.

It'd definitely been a home.

She'd not really had a home in years, and never one she'd made for herself since she tended to leave before she wore out her welcome. She realized that she was a contradiction—wanting to belong, yet doubting it would ever happen. But it was who she was. "It's easier," she said. "This place came fully furnished. I'm just borrowing the space."

He absorbed that, looking as if he might say more, but he didn't. And she was glad. She thought maybe they could have a good thing, and she was afraid to hope that this one time, she'd be able to stick around for a while.

He walked past the tiny kitchen table, upon which sat her ratty old notebook.

Last night, she'd written in her journal. It wasn't a typical journal filled with thoughts and expressions, but held notes of her cooking adventures. Desserts were truly her happy place, and she could think about them, or write about them, all day. She'd meant it when she'd told Jacob that she didn't follow recipes, instead using ratio, temps and conversion rates permanently in her brain. Mostly she went with her gut, and with the formulas she knew worked, things like her 1-2-3 method for sweet-crust pastries, which meant one part sugar, two parts butter and three parts flour.

But at the end of the day, if she'd done something new, she liked to scribble it down, and she did mean scribble.

Since she was always in a hurry, her handwriting was pretty much chicken scrawl, and illegible to anyone but her.

"Practicing your Greek?" he asked, raising a brow, proving her point by being unable to read her writing.

"Make fun of my writing all you want," she said, lifting her chin. "Maybe those are *secret* recipes. Maybe I use a special decoder ring. You can never be too careful."

He flipped the notebook closed. Beneath it was a shopping list.

Also nearly illegible.

He grinned. "So you do have a fault. You can't write worth shit. Ever think of taking up medicine?"

"Hey."

He just smiled at her, and it pretty much diffused any righteous indignation she might have mustered.

He came up close and swept a stray strand of hair back from her face. "You're going to lock up behind me."

She saluted him. Her little attempt at levity. When he didn't smile, she rolled her eyes and nudged him in the chest. His very hard, very warm chest. "I'm a big girl," she said softly, leaving her hand on him. Maybe she even gently ran her hand from one pec to the other. She couldn't help it, he was built. And the way he was standing over her, big and bad and protective, doing his cop thing…

"Bella."

And God, his voice, all low and warning, and completely sexy.

He wanted her again.

And he didn't want to want her again.

Well, welcome to her club. "Thanks for making sure I got home okay," she said. "Did you check my closet for monsters?"

"Your closet's monster free. So's your shower. Nice underwear, by the way."

She'd hand washed a bunch of it and had left it hanging in the shower to dry. She grinned. "Did you like the black lace?"

"Yeah, I liked the lace. And the yellow satin thong and matching bra."

Her nipples got perky. This was becoming a habit. She wondered if there was documentation of Pavlovian response involving sexily voiced innuendo and nipples. There should be.

Then he leaned in and put his mouth to her ear. "And while I bet they look hot on you, they're not my favorite. At least not on you."

She'd left her hand on his chest, and her fingers involuntarily fisted in his T-shirt.

"W-what is?"

Backing her to the door, he put a hand on either side of her head against the wood and let his knee touch hers. "Nothing at all."

Oh, God.

His thigh slid in between hers, and desire skittered across her belly, heating her from the inside out. "Yeah?"

His mouth skimmed her jaw. "Oh, yeah. But back to keeping yourself safe." He had her pinned to the door, their bodies flush. She couldn't have fit one of her wafer-thin phyllo pastry sheets between them. She squirmed, trying to get even closer, and discovered to her delight that either his gun had moved to his crotch, or he was hard.

"Do you remember what I told you, Bella?" He ran his lips over her jaw and she let out a helpless moan.

"Um—"

He nuzzled just beneath her ear, and she lost her concentration. "Don't keep the key beneath the mat?" she managed to say.

"Before that."

"You told me—" His mouth was on her neck. He drew on a patch of skin and sucked. "Oh, God, Jacob."

"Told you what, Bella?" He dipped his tongue into the hollow at the base of her throat.

"T-to have an escape route." God. God, she needed another taste of him. Just one. "You're it tonight, Jacob. You're my escape." She lifted her mouth and he met her halfway. His hands slid from the wood to her, one cupping the back of her head, the other sliding down her body with a new familiarity that thrilled, and as he devoured her mouth, she couldn't hold back her moan.

He reached for her shirt—*his* shirt—pulling it open, making his hands comfortable on her bare skin, gliding them up her bare thighs, over her back, making her moan again. She felt those fingers catch on the back tie of her bathing-suit top, a light tug, and then it loosened over her breasts. "Jacob?"

"Yeah?"

"My bed's about ten steps away."

His fingers went still. Then he kissed her lips softly and dropped his forehead to hers, breathing heavy. "This can't happen," he said.

She rocked against his raging hard-on. "Hate to break it to you, but your body is in disagreement."

He looked down at his hands. One cupped her breast, his thumb slowly rasping back and forth over her nipple, making it stand up to attention for him, his other was spread wide over her hip, his fingers beneath the material of her bikini bottoms. He still had a hard thigh thrust between hers, and with a muscle ticking in his jaw, he closed his eyes.

Bella's hands had been busy, too. Her fingers were curled in the waistband of his jeans, heading for the hidden treasure. When she wriggled them, he groaned. Grabbing her wrist, he dropped his head to the door, hard.

"What are you doing?"

"Knocking some sense into myself." He opened his eyes and stepped back, face tight, body tense, erection threatening to burst the buttons on his Levi's. "I'm leaving now."

"But—"

His hot gaze swept down her body one more time. He pressed in close, kissed her hard and just a little bit rough, and loving it, she kissed him back in the same way, but then he was pulling free, shaking his head as he moved away. He shoved his hands into his pockets as if he didn't quite trust himself. "We can't— I can't sleep with you while this case is open."

"It's not your case."

He let out a long, slow breath, as if struggling for control. "You need to be careful with what you're saying to me. Only last night, you wanted me to think you were moving to Siberia."

This was unfortunately true. "Yes, but there's something I didn't anticipate."

He just looked at her.

How to explain that last night, when he'd been pulling off her clothes, his hands everywhere on her, both demanding and somehow gentle at the same time, she'd been aware even then that being with him was going to be different.

Better than anything she'd known.

It'd scared her in the heat of the moment. But now, she wanted to experience it again.

Just one more time…

The fact was, in the dark of the night, he'd made her body sing the Hallelujah Chorus, and in the light of day her body wanted a repeat. "We seem to have a little chemistry problem."

He didn't move, but she could see the agreement in his eyes. Plus, he was still hard. Gloriously hard. Her fingers itched to touch, and she reached for him to do just that, until his words stopped her.

"How long are you staying in Santa Rey?"

"I don't know. Why? Trying to figure out if this still qualifies as a one-night stand?" She smiled. "Because I have no problem with a two-night stand. Maybe even a three-night stand if you play your cards right. And by the way, I don't have an aversion to daytime sex, either."

He ran his gaze over her features. Finally, he turned to the door.

"Let me guess," she said to his back, fascinated by the play of muscles as he reached for the handle. "This time it's you who's moving to Siberia?"

When he looked back at her, the heat was still in his gaze. His mouth barely curved in a hint of a smile, testosterone leaking from his every pore. "No. I stick, remember?"

"Then?"

"Maybe I'm just giving you time to absorb what's happened."

"The murder?"

"The fact that we're drawn to each other like a moth to the flame. The fact that it's only a matter of time before I get you in bed again—if you're still around. And this time, there'll be no pretty lies at the end. It is what it is."

Every single erogenous zone in her body quivered. "And what is it?"

He flashed her a wicked, naughty grin, and opened the door. "Lock the door," he said, and then he was gone.

Jacob drove home to his ranch-style house in the sprawling, rolling hills that backdropped Santa Rey. He'd bought the house back when it was a piece of shit and no one had wanted to live all the way out here, and as a result, he'd gotten it and the land damn cheap. Good thing, as he could never afford it now that the area was in fashion.

He'd slowly fixed the place up one room at a time, using his own hands and cheap labor—his brothers. He'd found that for the price of beer and pizza, he could coax them out on the weekends, and as a result, his place had become Madden central.

So he wasn't all that surprised when he pulled up and found Cord and Austin in his backyard, drinking his beer and idly watching his two horses roam the pen they'd all worked on putting up.

Austin handed him a beer.

Cord offered an opened tin of cookies, half-empty.

No one spoke until Jacob had taken a long pull from the beer and put away two chocolate-chip cookies, obviously homemade. Since Cord could burn water, he said, "Tell Lexi these were amazing."

Cord grinned stupidly. He'd finally gotten smart and for the last month had been dating his sweet, sexy next-door neighbor, a woman who would most definitely give Cord a run for his money.

"Long day, I hear," Austin said. He was a private investigator working insurance fraud, but his office monitored the police scanners. "You caught a murder."

"And lost it." Jacob took another pull of his beer and told them the story, making sure to face Cord as he spoke, since his brother still suffered fifty percent hearing loss from the explosion he'd lived through overseas.

"So you boinked the prime suspect." Cord shook his head and grinned. "And I thought I was the screwup."

"Bella didn't commit murder," Jacob said.

"So I guess that means you've taken interrogation to a whole new level," Austin said, cracking Cord up. Jacob sent him a don't-make-me-kick-your-ass look, which only made Cord laugh harder.

Whatever. Jacob took the last cookie and Cord stopped laughing.

"That was mine."

Jacob shrugged. "Two types of people in this house. The fast and the hungry."

Cord watched the cookie vanish into Jacob's mouth. "I can go home and talk her into making me more." He added a love-struck little smile, and both Austin and Jacob stared at him. Each of them had had women in their lives before, plenty of them.

None had stuck.

But there was a different element to his brother's expression lately, an inexplicable light in his eyes that signalled something that they hadn't seen in a long time.

Happiness.

After the hell Cord had been through with his

long, painful recovery, he deserved that. So very much, he deserved it, and Jacob was happy for him.

And also just a little envious.

The next morning, Jacob found Ethan waiting for him in his office. He'd made himself at home, sitting back in the guest chair, feet up on Jacob's desk, legs crossed as he sipped coffee and thumbed through his iPhone.

"Something new on the case?" Jacob asked him.

"Crime lab lifted a tread print from the top step to Edible Bliss's back door," Ethan said. "They're working on tracing it." He looked up from his phone. "And I thought you were staying out of this one."

"I am."

"Yeah?" Ethan cocked his head. "Is that why you saw Bella last night?"

"We went out for a bite. I walked her home to make sure she got there safely."

"Dude, I came back to ask her a question and heard someone pressing someone up against her front door."

When Jacob narrowed his eyes, Ethan smiled. "I was going to ask her if Seth Owen had brought her flowers on their first date. But I heard that rustling up against the door and figured you two…had your hands full."

Jacob had no response to make because it was true. He'd had his hands full.

"Maybe you were frisking her," Ethan suggested with a smile.

In return, Jacob suggested something with his middle finger.

"Huh. Again with the no comment," Ethan noted. "Maybe she wore out your tongue?"

Jesus. Jacob drew in a breath, and purposely let it out, refusing to let Ethan push his buttons.

"So. You get laid again?"

Jacob shoved Ethan's feet off his desk and sat behind it. "None of the above."

"No frisking, no tongue exhaustion, no getting laid. Got it." Ethan looked at him for a long moment. "Makes sense since you're so grumpy." He paused. "You're into her."

Jacob booted up his laptop.

Getting no response from Jacob, Ethan pressed, "So into her."

"Not that it's any of your business, but we're just—" He broke off, because he had no idea what they were just.

Seeing right through him, Ethan laughed softly. "Look, I get it. You wanted it to be casual because women end up dumping us for the job. It's a damn fact, man. But if it's more, it's more."

Again, Jacob didn't answer. Didn't know how to answer.

"Fine. Be the big, strong, silent type." Ethan rose

lithely to his feet. "But if she's nothing to you, maybe when this is all over, she'll go out with me."

Jacob slid him a long look.

"You know, since you're not into her or anything."

And though Ethan was an ass, he wasn't stupid. He was quickly out the door, a wide, obnoxious grin in place.

Probably if Jacob had consumed any caffeine yet, he'd have caught up with him and pounded him into dust. Probably he could have done it even without the caffeine, except for one thing.

Ethan was right.

Jacob was into Bella.

Luckily, his workload was off the charts, and he managed to keep busy the entire day. First he was called out as backup on a domestic violence case. They had to pull the wife off her husband, and were listening to the man's side of the story when the wife hit the guy over the head with a flowerpot, right in front of Jacob and his partner. A few minutes later, Jacob was reading the woman her rights, the husband standing there dripping blood, potting soil and daisies.

Boggled the mind.

In the afternoon, he sat in a hot car for two hours staking out a corner near Fourth Street with binoculars, hoping to catch sight of a known identity thief he'd been trying to pull in. By six o'clock, he'd seen a handful of public sex acts, one or two of which had surprised even him, but not a single sign of his man. By the time he got back to his desk, it was far past dinnertime.

But his paperwork had piled up, threatening to topple over. It took him two more hours to make even a dent, and by then, he was starving. He shut down his computer and was nearly to his motorcycle, when a call came in.

Another shooting.

Instead of going home, he met Ethan on scene. "Male, shot once with a through-and-through hit to the thigh," Ethan told him.

"Connected to the first shooting at Bella's place?"

"Don't know. Going to guess yes, since bullet type matches. The guy was just coming home from being out all day. He had ducked to tie his shoe or he'd have taken the hit to the torso and we'd be calling the coroner about now."

"His lucky day," Jacob said. "ID?"

"Banning Jefferson. Ring a bell?"

"No."

"He lives in the building. His neighbor reported seeing an unidentified male running from the scene."

"Anything else?"

"Perp's around six feet and Caucasian."

Much preferable to five foot seven and female.

"Now, get out of here," Ethan said. "I'm going to nail his ass and I don't want any technicalities holding me up."

"And I'm a technicality?"

"If these shootings are connected, you could be."

Jacob got back on his bike. He needed to go home, eat and sleep.

But first he wanted to make sure Bella was okay. He'd just follow up, he assured himself, and it had nothing to do with their obvious sexual chemistry.

Nothing at all…

Ten minutes later, he was in front of her building. There were no parking spots. With no qualms whatsoever, he parked illegally, telling himself that the salary raise the city hadn't been able to afford to give him for three years running could be paid back in special parking privileges.

He got off his bike, removed his helmet and was at the bottom of her steps, just outside the pastry shop's back door when he heard a scream.

Chapter 6

*T*he man standing in front of her was faceless. He had a huge bullet hole where his forehead should have been, and he was reaching for her with a hand that held a bouquet of wildflowers. "Bella," he said in a zombie voice. "Bella!"

She screamed and took a step backward, stumbling in shock when she realized that she held a smoking gun.

She'd shot him.

She'd shot his face off.

"Bella!"

She jerked away and fell out of bed. "*Ow.*"

Two big, warm hands scooped her up and pulled her into what felt like a wall of muscle.

Even with her eyes closed, she recognized Jacob by his scent and the feel of his arms, and she melted into him, pressing her face to his throat. He brushed the hair away from her damp face, his warm lips settling against her temple. "Bad dream?"

"Zombies." She stayed there in his arms, the sound of her accelerated, panicked breathing and heart pounding in her ears all she could hear as the rest of the world stopped existing.

Moonlight came in through her shutters, slanting the room in glowing stripes. Jacob was on the floor with her, holding her, and there was nowhere else she wanted to be.

He pulled back enough to see into her eyes. "Better?"

Was she? She tried to figure that out. She was damp with terror sweat, wearing only a tiny tank and boy-cut panties. But there was no dead guy without a face, and she wasn't holding a smoking gun. *And* she was in Jacob's lap. "Really bad dream."

"Zombies?"

She let out a shaky breath. "A dead guy. With no face and a hole in his forehead, carrying wildflowers. Chasing me." She shuddered. "And I had the gun."

With a low, wordless murmur, he hugged her closer. Chilled to the bone, she burrowed in. His hands grazed her arms, her back, her bare thighs—

He froze for a single beat as if just realizing only now how undressed she was. Then she shivered again, and a big hand cupped the nape of her neck. "When I heard you scream, I lost about two years of my life during the time it took me to get in here to you."

She tightened her grip. "I didn't put the key under the mat."

"I know. You had it under the flowerpot. We'll talk about *that* later."

She pressed her face into his shoulder. "You smell good."

"Yeah? So do you." He buried his nose in her hair. "Like vanilla and sugar. Good enough to eat."

She squirmed at that image. "I made cookies."

"For the shop?"

"For me." She sighed. "It's a destress thing." She knew she was wrapped around him like Saran Wrap but couldn't make herself let go. He was strong and solid, and she could feel the even, steady beat of his heart. Hers was still racing. "I'm not dressed."

"I noticed that." If her voice was shaking from adrenaline, his was low and husky. His *aroused* voice, which added an entirely new element to her adrenaline rush.

"Not that I'm complaining," she said. "But what brought you here?"

He didn't answer, and it was her turn to pull back a little bit and look into his face. "Uh-oh." She couldn't see him clearly, but she could certainly feel the tension in him, tension she'd missed before because she'd been too busy recouping from the nightmare. "Jacob?"

"I was just leaving work."

"This late?" It was ten-thirty. A long day by any standards, and she was quite certain his hadn't been spent hanging out baking in a kitchen, or sitting and staring at the waves. He'd been out there, catching bad guys, and probably risking life and limb while he was at it.

"It was one of those days," he allowed, in what was undoubtedly an understatement.

"Lots of bad guys?"

"Always." He paused. "And a late call came in."

More tension, she felt it in his thighs beneath her, in the chest she'd set her head on and in the arms he'd banded around her. She climbed out of his lap, stood and flipped on the light by her bed, because she had a feeling she needed to see his face.

From the floor, he blinked, adjusting to the light as his gaze ran over her from head to toe, slowing at all the places in between. "God, Bella."

"I was hot."

His eyes flared, letting her know exactly how hot he thought she was.

"I have to go downstairs in a few minutes and beat up some dough for the morning." The fib popped out of her mouth automatically. But that's how she operated, always giving herself a way out with a man. She called it her safety net.

Except at the moment, for the first time in memory, she didn't want a safety net, and regretted the lie the minute it left her lips.

Jacob remained on the floor. He leaned against her bed, dropping his head back on the mattress and closing his eyes as if afraid to look at her too long. His dark silky hair was tousled, as if he'd shoved his fingers through it repeatedly. There was a grim set to his mouth, and fine lines of tension fanning out from his eyes.

"You look exhausted," she said softly, and came back to him, curling up at his side, mirroring his pose but setting her head on his chest instead of against the bed.

He wrapped an arm around her and pulled her in. "There was another shooting, Bella. The guy took a hit to the thigh, and should live."

She looked at him, but his head was still back, eyes closed. "Who?"

"Banning Jefferson. You know him?"

She let out a breath. She didn't, not that it made it any less horrifying. "No. The name doesn't ring a bell." She relaxed slightly, grateful this one at least didn't involve her.

His fingers brushed low on her spine, against the bare skin between the hem of her tank and her low-cut panties. "Bullet type matches." Lifting his head, he met her gaze. "In a big city, this wouldn't be enough to connect the shootings, but here in Santa Rey, we don't get shootings every day. Not even every month. So just having two in a matter of days is enough to possibly connect them."

They were close enough to share air, and one thing she already knew about Jacob, he was good up close. Very good. He had a way of looking at her, of touching her, like now, that made her feel both safe and sexy, and that was a lethal combination.

Suddenly she wanted him to use those traits to help her escape, to forget the horror of finding Seth's body even for a few minutes, and it was all she could do to resist setting her hands on his flat stomach, sliding her fingers over those hard muscles as she leaned in and took a bite of him—

"Look at me, Bella."

She was. She was looking at his chest and wondering how long it would take to get him out of that shirt...

"At my face," he said with what might have been amusement.

As if his face was any less dangerous....

Adding an assist, he cupped her jaw and tilted it up to his, looking her over carefully with that intense, all-seeing gaze that made her want to confess to state secrets, and also take off what little clothing she still wore. She squirmed a little, working her way even closer to him.

"Are you okay?" he asked quietly.

"Working on it. Jacob?"

"Yeah?"

"I'm glad I didn't move to Siberia," she whispered. "And I'm glad *you* didn't move to Siberia." She brushed her lips lightly over his. "I was really scared tonight. I'm glad you're here."

He almost smiled. "You just want me to check for the boogeyman again."

She dipped her head and brushed another kiss on him, this time on his chest. "That would be great."

"Christ, Bella." He ran a hand up her back, wrapped his fingers around her loose, unruly ponytail and gently tugged until she was looking up at him again. "What am I going to do with you?"

Do me was the first thought that came to mind, but he rose and did his cop thing, thoroughly checking out the small apartment, even looking beneath her bed and in her bathtub.

"There's no one here but us," she said when he came back.

"I know."

"Then why did you search the place?"

"So you could go back to sleep."

Which meant he was leaving. Disappointment settled in her belly, which was ridiculous. She'd been the one to formulate the escape plan. "Jacob?"

He lowered himself to a crouch in front of her,

running a finger over her temple, tucking a strand of hair behind her ear. "Yeah?"

Reaching up, she cupped her hand around his wrist. "What are we doing?"

"Other than checking for the boogeyman?"

"Yeah. Other than that."

He looked into her eyes. "No idea."

"Casually seeing each other?"

He thought about that a moment, then nodded.

"How casually?"

"Asks the woman with one foot already out of Santa Rey."

Fair enough, she supposed. She'd made a big deal out of leaving, and he knew it.

"And I've done the long-term thing," he said. "It doesn't mix well with being a cop."

Right. She knew this, knew all of it, which in no way explained the ball of discontent deep in her belly. She managed a smile. "I know who you are, Jacob. Being a cop is part of you. No woman should ask you to change that."

"Yeah." He grimaced. "It might be more than the cop thing."

"Such as…?"

"I've been told I can be obstinate, single-minded and doggedly aggressive." He said this with a tone of slight admission that it might all be true, and she laughed.

"Well, hell, if you're all that, forget about it," she teased.

"Bella—"

"No, listen to me." She grabbed his arms when he would have straightened. "Those are the very things that make you such a great cop." And, she thought, a great lover. "You're okay, Jacob, just the way you are."

He let out a slow, appreciative breath, then took her hand in his as he rose and walked to the front door. There he stopped and looked down at her, not smiling, but his eyes were warm as he leaned down to kiss her.

"Bye," she whispered.

"Bye," he said against her lips, but instead of opening the door, he threaded his hands into her hair and kissed her again, leisurely this time, allowing his tongue a very thorough farewell.

Her nipples had been hard since he'd first appeared in her bedroom, but the rest of her body joined the fray now, and she rubbed up against him. She'd have crawled into him if she could. "Keep that up," she managed to say, breathless as hell. "And I'm going to fake another nightmare to keep you here."

He stared at her from heavy-lidded eyes, then backed her to the door and kissed her again, kissed her until she was gripping his shirt in two tight fists. His erection pressed into her, nestling against the crux of her sex, and he made a guttural sound deep in his throat. "No faking anything," he said against her mouth.

"Ah, but how would you know?"

"I'd know," he said firmly, and when she let out a low laugh, he paused meaningfully. "I'm sensing a challenge."

"I'm just saying."

"Saying what exactly?" he wanted to know, all male pride and ego, his expression suggesting she'd somehow questioned his manhood or testosterone level.

She tried not to laugh and failed. "Look, faking is nothing but a polite lie designed to avoid hurting anyone's feelings."

He blinked, looking genuinely confused. "But why lie at all? I mean, if you're going to fake, then why not fake *not* having an orgasm, so that the guy keeps at it?"

"Huh." She laughed again. "Never thought of it that way."

He shook his head, his eyes still heated, his body still taut and tense…everywhere.

Hers tightened in response. She was going to have to accept that whenever she saw him, this crazy heat would be there. But also there was more. What exactly that more was, she couldn't say, but it was a little disturbing given that she'd known him all of a few days.

And even more disturbing, he made her laugh.

God, she was a sucker for that.

She realized he made her both laugh and want, a double whammy, one she wasn't sure she could resist, or why she even wanted to try.

He was just watching her watch him, another thing she liked about him. He was tough and edgy, a cop through and through, and yet he had seemingly endless patience.

But just behind that patience was hot, simmering passion that took her breath away.

He said her name once, softly, then let go of her hair to slide his hands up her back, and down, cupping her bottom, a cheek in each of his big palms, cheeks that were more than half bared by her scrap of panties. A sound of distinct male satisfaction rumbled from his chest, and he squeezed before lifting her to nestle her best part against his best part.

A movement that had them both stopping to gasp in pleasure.

She didn't know about him, but she was instantly back to quivering with need, burning up with it. Her breathing was unsteady, ragged, making her breasts brush his chest with every breath of air she gulped.

He ran his mouth over her jaw to her ear while his fingers explored her body. "If I stand here any longer, Bella, you are not going to make it downstairs to deal with your dough."

"Yeah." She winced. "Remember when you said

I always need an escape route? Well, I usually do, when it pertains to men."

"And what, the dough thing was it?"

"Yes. Sorry."

His eyes were two dark pools. "Tell me to go, Bella."

She opened her mouth to do just that and said "stay" instead.

He groaned and once again pressed her into the door, lifting one of her legs to wrap around his hip, opening her up so that when he rocked again, he slid his erection directly against the core of her. The only thing that separated them were his jeans and her very thin, very wet panties.

"Do you want this, Bella?"

In answer, she took the hand he had on her ass and brought it around until he cupped her. Again he groaned low in his throat, and then his mouth found hers, crushing her lips, his tongue delving deep.

Yeah, she wanted this. And even as she thought it, he lifted her up and turned to her bedroom. Suddenly she found herself airborne and then she hit the mattress with a bounce. With a laugh, she started to sit up but found herself pinned by two hundred pounds of solid muscle, and she shivered in anticipation.

"Cold?" he murmured in her ear, his hands sliding beneath her tank, settling on her ribs.

She shook her head and clutched at him. "No."

He held her gaze as his hands slid farther north,

covering her breasts, his thumbs slowly rubbing over her nipples.

A shuddery breath escaped her.

He tugged her tank up and off, baring her to his eyes, and then his mouth.

Already half gone, she shivered again, and panted his name.

He groaned in approval, then stood to strip out of his clothes, stopping to pull a condom from his pocket.

She'd thought she had the image of his perfect body etched in her brain, but the reality was even better than the memory. Clueless to how gorgeous he was, he kneeled on the bed at her feet. His hands hooked in the material at her hip, slowly sliding her panties down her legs and off before he parted her legs.

And then his gaze skimmed down at what he'd unwrapped for himself. "God, Bella. Look at you." He kissed a rib, dipped his tongue into her belly button. "I need to taste you, all of you." Urging her open even farther, his thumb made a slow, barely there graze right over her center, and she nearly came off the bed.

"My toes are curling!" she gasped.

"I have the cure for that." And he replaced his thumb with his mouth and proceeded to drive her right out of her ever-loving mind. She came with such force that her entire body was trembling, and still he didn't stop. *"Jacob."*

"Making sure you aren't faking anything," he murmured against her wet flesh.

She laughed, then moaned as his tongue got busy again, ravaging and plundering as he brought her to orgasm once more before finally releasing her.

When she opened her eyes, he had a forearm on either side of her shoulders and was gazing into her face. She had just enough left in the tank to laugh breathlessly. "Show-off."

He smiled, a mixture of wicked intent and fierce affection that didn't just take the last of her breath but also turned her heart over and exposed its tender underside.

What he did next cracked it wide-open.

He entwined their hands beside her head, murmured her name softly, and then, condom somehow miraculously in place, drove into her with one fierce thrust.

"Oh God, Jacob, *God*..."

He filled her so deeply, so completely, she felt as if he was touching her soul, and her hips rocked mindlessly up to meet his. He nudged her face with his jaw, then looked into her eyes as he moved within her, his thrusts deep and steady.

So good, it was so damn good. That was all she could think, and lost in the waves of pleasure crashing over her, her eyes began to drift shut.

"No, don't close them. Look at me."

Somehow she managed to drag them open for him, open and on his, which were letting her in, letting her see what she was doing to him.

Unbelievably, she was on the precipice again, hovering on the very edge. "Please. Jacob, *please.*"

"Mmm." He nipped her jaw, then her lower lip. "I like the begging. More of that."

She laughed breathlessly.

Eyes nearly black with desire, he rubbed his jaw to hers and her laughter faded away. Arching her back, she wound her legs higher around his waist, gripping him as tight as she could.

Now they were hand to hand, chest to chest, breathing as one as their movements sped up, becoming almost frantic, and then, at the very end, she cried out first as she came, hearing and feeling him immediately follow her.

It was the single most sensual, erotic experience of her entire life, and she wondered for the first time how she would ever be able to walk away from this.

Chapter 7

Jacob woke up, the sun shining on his face. He was alone in Bella's bed, which was not only a new experience, but also a little humiliating.

He was a cop, for crissakes. As a rule, he slept light, able to wake at the slightest sound or movement.

And yet he'd slept through her leaving, like the living dead.

Of course, he thought, bleary-eyed, as he looked at the clock—7:30 a.m.—he hadn't gotten all that much sleep. Last night, after having his merry way with Bella in bed, they'd moved to the shower where she'd returned the favor.

And then, starving, they'd ended up downstairs in the shop's kitchen, where they'd pulled miniature raspberry turnovers out of the fridge at two in the morning, feeding them to each other.

Licking the raspberry filling off each other...

Jacob rolled out of bed and recovered his clothes from where they were strewn across the floor. He had a raspberry stain across his chest in a shape that looked suspiciously like a handprint, and he had a flashback to Bella sitting on the counter, him between her legs teasing her, and her fisting her fingers in his shirt so he couldn't get away.

As if he'd wanted to.

Probably no one would be able to tell what the stain was from, he decided, and grabbed his gun and cell phone from the nightstand. He took a stab at his hair with his fingers and helped himself to Bella's toothbrush.

That was all the easy part.

After he'd laced his boots, he made his way down the stairs. He intended to get on his bike and head straight to work, but the back door to the shop was open and the most delicious scents wafted out, making his stomach rumble.

He needed more than raspberry filling.

Bella, her back to him and the door, wearing hip-hugging jeans and a snug red tee, was talking to Willow.

"I can't commit to the Walker anniversary cake, I

don't know if I'll be here next month," she said, and for a minute Jacob forgot to breathe.

"Honey," Willow said, sounding as if she was having the same problem. "You're the best pastry chef Santa Rey has ever seen. Please consider staying longer, maybe the whole summer."

"I don't know." She spoke with real regret and steely determination. "I was up front with you from the beginning."

"I know, but just think about it, okay? You have the place, you have the beach right here, it's gorgeous weather, and you have a hot guy in your bed. What more could you want?"

"How do you know about the hot guy in my bed?"

"Well, because you've been wearing a just-got-some smile all morning. And because he's standing right behind you." Willow winked at Jacob, and grabbing a tray of fresh pastries, made her way out of the kitchen toward the front of the shop.

Bella whirled around to face him, surprise on her face.

"Didn't mean to eavesdrop," he said. "All the amazing smells coming out of here drew me in."

She tugged him out of the doorway. "I'll feed you."

"I have to go to work."

"Food first." She stared up at him for a moment, her mouth slightly curved.

"What?" he asked, having no idea what she could be thinking when she looked at him like that.

"You look...uncivilized," she said.

"Uncivilized?"

"Yeah." She was still staring at him, eyes warm. "You look sleepy and a little bit rumpled, and a whole lot hungry." She eyed the bulge of the gun on his hip. "And armed. It's a good look on you, Jacob."

He pulled her in and put his mouth to her ear. "Keep looking at me like that and I'll show you what I'm hungry for."

She bit her lower lip and slid a gaze to the closed pantry, making him both groan and laugh. "Bella."

"Hey, you put the suggestion in my head." She gave herself a visible shake. "Food. I have fresh croissants that are, if I may say so myself, out of this world." She grabbed one from a tray on the counter and took a bite, moaning softly as sheer bliss crossed her face.

Last night, he'd seen that look directed at him.

Smiling softly, she held out the croissant. Deciding one hunger at a time, he leaned in for a bite, purposely nipping the tip of her finger.

She sucked in her breath, then let it out slowly while the croissant melted in his mouth, making him moan. She'd been right. Best croissant ever.

Willow came back into the kitchen. Her dark hair was spiked around her head today, and she'd put in more piercings than he could count this early. "Bella, honey," she said, taking in Jacob. "He's wearing raspberry."

Bella looked at Jacob's shirt. Dragging her teeth over her lower lip, she appeared to be fighting a smile. "Uh-oh," she said. Grabbing Jacob by the shoulder, she nudged him into the tiny hallway between the kitchen and the dining area, and pushed him against the wall.

"What—" he started, but she cut him off.

With her lips.

He wasn't often surprised or caught off guard, but she kept doing both without effort. Staggered by the kiss, he slid one hand to the small of her back, the other to the back of her head, holding her to him while she kissed them both stupid, stealing conscious thought and detonating brain cells with equal aplomb.

Breaking for air, she murmured, "Morning. And can I just say, casual has never felt so good."

He laughed softly. "No, it sure hasn't."

"Come on." She led him out to the dining area and with a pat on his ass, pointed him toward a bar stool.

A few catcalls rent the air, and shocked, Jacob looked around.

Most of the tables were full with the usual morning crowd seeking their sugar and caffeine rush.

"Ignore them," Bella said loud enough for everyone to hear. "Sit tight and I'll serve you. I had some trouble with the second batch of croissants, but the third batch is just about ready."

The closest table had four women of varying ages starting at around eighty, and they were cackling like a gaggle of hens.

"Saw you come down the stairs," the one with the candy-red lipstick said slyly, gesturing to the café's side window, where there was indeed a view of the building stairs. "From Bella's apartment."

Great. He'd made the walk of shame with an audience.

The woman across from Red Lips arched a penciled-in brow. She had blue hair and her glasses were perched on the very tip of her nose as she looked Jacob over, giving him bad flashbacks to his Catholic-school days when he'd been regularly disciplined. He still twitched whenever he saw a nun.

But this was worse, especially since he would have sworn the two of them were licking their lips over him.

He shuddered inwardly and looked around for Bella. She'd deserted him.

"You have a little something there on your shirt," Blue Hair said, getting up and adjusting her reading glasses, pressing her face so close to his chest her nose brushed him. "Looks like fruit sauce."

Christ. He backed up, bumped hard into the counter behind him and rubbed at the stain, assuring himself they couldn't possibly have any idea what he and

Bella had done with that raspberry sauce, which he was pretty sure was illegal in several states.

"Raspberry turnovers were yesterday's special," Blue Hair announced shrewdly, lifting a hand to touch.

He ducked, dodged her, and then whirled around with a yelp when he felt a hand slide down his backside and pinch.

"Nice and firm," Red Lips said wistfully. "They don't make 'em like that in my age group."

He refused to run. But he walked very fast into the kitchen, realizing what he was. "I'm a piece of ass."

"Yes," Bella said, then came up behind him to whisper in his ear, "But you're one fine piece of ass." She offered him a taste of something warm and chocolate and mouthwatering from a wooden spoon. When his mouth was full, she leaned in close and pressed hers to his rough jaw.

He sighed, having to shake his head. What the hell else could he do? "I really have to go."

She lifted a brown bag. "I know. Breakfast to go."

"Thanks." He caught her before she could move away. "You'll call if anything feels off or weird."

Her eyes laughed at him. "I'm pretty sure I've got the croissants under control now."

"Not that, smart-ass." He tugged on her hair. "If you see anything odd, or someone so much as looks at you cross-eyed, you'll call." Unable to resist, he kissed her. He'd meant for it to be a light, easy kiss, but as usual, he'd underestimated her innate ability to drive him crazy.

He wasn't sure how long he'd been kissing her when he came up for air.

Her eyes were closed and she was wearing a dreamy smile. "Um," she said, and opened those gorgeous eyes, staring at his mouth as if she wanted another.

"You'll call," he repeated.

"Mmm, hmm."

He ran his thumb over her lush lower lip. "I'm going to assume that was 'Yes, Jacob, I'll call if anything seems off, or anyone so much as crosses their eyes at me.'"

With a smile, she pulled him down and kissed him again.

It was a diversion, but he couldn't summon irritation when it was such an effective one. She'd been right about one thing—casual had never felt so good. It took a shocking degree of control to remind himself that he'd only meant to make sure she was okay, that it was time to go, and even then he took a minute to press his face against her hair before walking out the door.

While he still could.

"You ever going to tell me about that kiss?" Willow asked Bella later that afternoon as they were cleaning up the shop after a day of brisk business.

"What kiss?"

"The one you laid on Tall, Dark and Drop-dead Sexy earlier, the one that looked like something right out of a movie." She fanned air in front of her face. "Goodness, it was hot. That man is hot. The way he cupped your jaw and looked at you for a beat before molding you to every single inch of him…" She slid Bella a long look. "And I have a feeling there are a lot of inches to him—"

"Willow!"

She grinned, unrepentant. "Sorry. I'll stop. It's giving me a hot flash anyway. But just tell me this much—you going to keep him?"

If I can, Bella almost said, but squelched it. Casual. They were going for casual. She'd agreed. And casual didn't worry about things like keeping someone. "Undetermined at this time," she finally said.

"Seriously? Because if someone was kissing me like that, I'd keep him. I'd keep him naked and handcuffed to my bed."

Bella shook her head just as Trevor came in from the front room, carrying a heavy tray of dirty dishes. He looked like the typical California surfer boy with his deep tan and easy good looks. "Getting kinky again, Willow?" he asked with a wink.

"Not me. Bella."

Bella rolled her eyes and headed to the door. "I'm out. I'm going for a swim."

"Hold up." Trevor flashed a smile her way. "You

shouldn't swim out there alone," he said. "I'm off, too, I'll come with."

It wasn't a hardship to have his company. He was a strong swimmer, plus he was just damn fine scenery, all tanned and buff and gorgeous. His quick grin didn't hurt, either. But though she'd given some thought to him when she'd first come to Santa Rey, he was younger than her, and they worked together... and she'd decided against it. But no one could blame her for enjoying the view.

Still, she found herself yearning for the view of another man, a big, bad, sexy detective named Jacob...

After the swim, she and Trevor sat on the sand. "Dinner?" he asked, tilting his head back to the warm sun.

She hesitated. Swimming as friends was one thing. But having dinner, too, might put it into another category. "Trev—"

"Just dinner, Bella." He smiled. "Unless you plan on breaking my heart over sushi."

"I'm taking a break from breaking hearts."

"Didn't look that way this morning."

She grimaced. "Don't ask me what I think I'm doing."

He shrugged. "Hey, sometimes the heart wants what it wants."

She sighed. "Yeah." And sometimes the heart wanted what it couldn't have...

After they dried off, Trevor left to meet up with friends for that sushi he wanted, and Bella went back to her apartment to change out of her wet suit before going back down to the shop. She pulled on a halter sundress in deference to the heat and headed into the downstairs kitchen to make the dough for tomorrow's shortbread, wanting to give it time to rise. She'd just finished when she heard a knock on the front door. Moving through the tables, she saw a face pressed up against the window.

Tyler Scott, date number three. She knew his last name because he was a bookseller here in town. She'd been fascinated by his brains and sheer volume of knowledge, and just a little bit intimidated.

But he was a good guy, a very nice guy, and so she opened the door with a smile. "Tyler, hi. I'm so sorry, but we're closed."

"I know. I was just hoping…" He paused. "I know this is so rude of me to ask, but I'm heading to my mother's in San Luis Obispo and I'm expected to bring the dessert. I guess I was wondering if you wouldn't mind setting me up with something, but now I realize what an imposition it would be, and—"

"No. No imposition," she said. "Let's go see what we have left over in the back."

Five minutes later, she'd sold him a small chocolate sandwich cake, and she walked him back through the shop to the front door.

"My mom's going to take one bite of this and start harassing me to bring you home," he teased.

Bella smiled. There was no doubt she enjoyed his company, but there was something pretty vital missing—the zing.

She'd never really pondered the mystery of the elusive zing until Jacob. Because, holy shit, she and Jacob had zing. They had real, gut-tightening, goose-bump-inducing, brain-cell-destroying zing, and they had it in spades. She hated to compare men, but she could honestly say that not a single one of the other seven guys she'd dated during the Eight Dates in Eight Days had come even close.

And while she was being so honest, she might as well admit that no man in recent history had come close.

Maybe no man ever.

And wasn't that a terrifying thought all on its own?

"Thanks again, Bella," Tyler said, and stepped outside the door. She followed, wanting to see if the early evening had cooled down any.

A loud shot sounded, echoing in the still air, and the glass window just behind them shattered. Before Bella could even begin to process any of it, Tyler grabbed her and knocked her to the ground.

It seemed like forever, but it was probably only seconds before the glass finished raining down over them. Finally, Tyler lifted his head. "Bella?" When he sat up, his glasses were crooked on his nose. "You okay?"

Her knees and palms were skinned, but that was nothing compared to being dead. "Yes. What the hell was that?"

"Something exploded your window."

"Something?"

"I think someone shot at us." Tyler stood, then pulled her to her feet, as well, running his gaze down her, then down himself. "No injuries. No injuries is good. It means we can freak out now."

Bella stared up at the blown-out window of the shop. "A gunshot?" Oh, God. Not again. "Are you sure?"

There were a few people gathering on the sidewalk, murmuring amongst themselves. "I phoned 911," one of them called out. It was Cindy, who worked at the art gallery across the street and bought a croissant from Bella every morning without fail. She was still holding her cell phone. "I don't think I've ever heard a real gunshot before."

Bella was still staring at the hollow window, a matching hollowness sinking in her gut.

Looking shell-shocked, Tyler sank to the curb. Just as shell-shocked, she sat next to him. "Can I borrow your phone?" she asked, and when he handed it over, she punched in Jacob's cell number. It went straight to voice mail. "Hi," she said. "Nobody looked at me cross-eyed, but I did get shot at. That probably counts as something you'd like to know, right?" She drew in air. "I'm okay," she said, and disconnected.

He would come. And that brought a now-familiar tingling that yesterday had started and ended in all her erogenous zones, but today...today nicked at a certain vital organ that clenched hard at the mere thought of him.

She remembered how he'd looked this morning sprawled on his back across her bed, the sheets and blankets on the floor, revealing him in full glory.

And then there'd been how he'd looked coming into the shop all rumpled and sleep deprived, a two-day-old shadow darkening his strong jaw, his eyes narrowed and probably already filled with thoughts of his cases, his shirt wrinkled, that raspberry stain over one pec.

Armed and dangerous.

And badass gorgeous.

She might have dwelled on that, but there was the whole just-been-shot-at thing, and the police arrived.

Then she heard the motorcycle. Jacob came off it at a dead run, slowing only when he saw her standing in the midst of the organized mayhem, clearly fine.

Or as fine as she could be.

Normally in a stressful situation—and she considered this pretty damn stressful—she'd already be out the door. Gone. Moved on. After all, she'd grown up in chaos, and it'd never suited.

But she didn't have the urge to run right now. It was the place, she thought. Santa Rey seemed to be making a home for itself in her heart. And so were its people.

One in particular.

Jacob came toe to toe with her. He removed his sunglasses and ran his gaze over her carefully, thoroughly, noting the scrapes on her hands and knees.

"We're okay," she said. "Tyler pushed me down. Thank you for that, by the way," she told him.

Jacob flicked a glance in Tyler's direction and nodded, then surveyed the damage around them with one sweep of his focused, sharp eyes before returning his attention to her. He pulled her to her feet, picked a piece of glass from her hair and shook his head, then slipped an arm around her, tugging her close enough to press his mouth to her jaw. "Calls like the one I just got suck."

"I'm sorry."

He murmured something too soft to catch and wrapped both arms around her, holding tightly now, as if he needed it as much as she. Snuggling in, she absorbed his warmth and strength. After a long moment, she said, "I'm really okay. You can let me go now."

"I'll let you go when I'm good and ready." But he sighed and pulled back, cupping the nape of her neck to look into her eyes. Whatever he saw must have reassured him because he nodded. "You good to talk to Ethan?"

"Yes."

"Good. Because he's right behind you, giving me the evil eye, waiting for me to let go of you so he can ask you some questions. Also, just so you can brace yourself, we're going to put a man on the shop."

"A man?"

"A squad car. We're talking murder, and now attempted murder."

"This is getting old."

Jacob looked deep into her eyes, his own dark and troubled. "There's always Siberia."

"You want me to leave?"

"I want you safe."

So did she. But she'd never felt as safe anywhere as she did right there, in his arms.

Chapter 8

Two hours later it was finally just Bella again.

Well, just Bella and the policeman assigned to watch over the building. She couldn't see him, but she knew he was around somewhere, and that was just fine with her.

Feeling as calm as she possibly could, she stood in the shop kitchen and let out a deep breath, nearly screaming when she turned in a circle and came face-to-face with Jacob.

Yeah, apparently her nerves were shot.

He'd watched as the EMTs had bandaged up her knees, then helped board up the front window before leaving for a task-force meeting with Ethan, but apparently he was back, looking his usual big and bad and edgy.

She did the first thing that came to mind. She walked right into his arms.

They closed around her, warm and taut with muscle, tightening on her, surrounding her with his virility, the scent of him. The police had questioned her, Tyler and then Willow, who'd shown up when she'd heard. Trevor, too. The shooting might have been random and unconnected to the other shootings, but until the ballistics came through, no one would know for sure.

Tyler had left, completely unnerved. Probably he wouldn't be a returning customer, Bella thought with a sigh.

"You okay?" Jacob asked.

She'd had to ask herself that several times now, and she wasn't used to not being sure. She was always okay, it was her M.O. And if she wasn't, well, then, there was always someplace new. "Aren't you getting tired of having to ask me that?"

Silent, he stroked a big hand up and down her back.

"For two people who aren't involved," she murmured, "we sure are seeing a lot of each other."

She felt him smile against her hair, and pulled back to look into his eyes. "I've always felt so safe here," she said. "It's why I stayed. I never thought of it before, but I *like* feeling safe. But now someone's shooting at me. I know we joke about Siberia, but holy shit, am I really going to have to go?"

"Would you?"

When she thought about leaving, she felt a clutch in her gut. "No."

He nodded, clearly already guessing as much. "We're going to figure it out."

"We? You mean, the police?"

He made a vague response deep in his throat and pulled her out of the kitchen's back door, carefully locking up.

Then he led her upstairs toward her apartment.

"I appreciate the sentiment," she said to his broad back. "But fair warning, it's going to take an act of Congress and possibly hypnosis to get me in the right frame of mind for sex."

He glanced back at her, his mouth slightly curved. "I'll keep that in mind, but that's not what we're doing. I want you to pack an overnight bag."

"Excuse me?"

His hand tightened on hers when she tried to pull free. "You're not staying here tonight, Bella. Maybe not tomorrow night, either. Not until we know what the hell is going on and why you nearly took a hit today."

"Jacob—"

"This is nonnegotiable, Bella. We have a man here but for tonight at least, you're gone."

She looked into his eyes, fierce and protective and utterly stubborn.

"I'm not saying you have to stay with me," he said, bringing their joined hands to his mouth so that when he spoke, his lips brushed against her fingers. "I'm not trying to exert power or authority over you, just common sense. You can stay in a hotel, you can stay with a friend or you can stay with me. I don't care, but you're not staying here alone. Please," he said very softly when she opened her mouth.

She had a feeling he wasn't a man to say please very often. Touched, she nodded her head, and turned to go into her place.

He stopped her and moved inside first, once again thoroughly checking it out, giving her the go-ahead when he deemed it safe.

Normally she liked watching him do his cop thing. It was macho and alpha and on any other day it would have made her knees weak and other parts quiver.

But not now. Now she wanted the nightmare to go far, far away.

He was helping with that just by being here for her instead of running off soon as he was done being questioned, like Tyler. Willow and Trevor had both left rather quickly, too, soon as they were able.

Not Jacob.

He wanted her safe. He was willing to do whatever it took to keep her that way.

She racked her brain to try to remember the last time someone outside of her family had truly cared and worried about her, and she couldn't come up with anything. This was easy enough to explain. Until recently, she hadn't stuck around long enough for such ties.

She would have to decide if she liked it.

She filled a small backpack, and then realizing Jacob probably had his motorcycle, she slid on a pair of denim shorts beneath her halter sundress.

They left her apartment, locked up, and in the lot, Jacob nodded to a guy walking the alley between the shop and the building next door.

He nodded back.

"My bodyguard?" she asked.

Jacob actually smiled. "Tonight, I'm your bodyguard." And he handed her a helmet.

"What about Willow?"

"Didn't she tell you? She went to her mom's."

No, she hadn't mentioned that...

"Where are we going?" she asked, getting on his bike behind him, hiking her dress up until it looked like a loose summer top over her shorts. She slipped her arms around him, her hands sliding across his washboard abs.

"For food. You smell like sugar and vanilla and you're making me hungry."

"I have—"

"Your desserts are heaven, Bella, but I need real sustenance. And so do you. You're pale."

And that was new, too. He was a guy who said what he meant, no sneaky charm to try to get her into bed, no pretty lies just to make her feel better. He told her what was on his mind and expected her to be mature enough to deal with it.

Her first grown-up relationship, she realized, "casual" as it was—

She broke off the thought with a startled squeak when he revved the bike and hit the throttle. The engine roared between her legs and suddenly, blessedly, just like that, her mind was off murder and bullets and she couldn't decide which was better, hugging up to Jacob's hard body, or the way he maneuvered them through the streets as if he were a part of the bike.

She was still trying to decide when he pulled up to a small diner, where they were greeted by yet another smiley-faced waitress ready to serve his every need.

After they'd ordered, Bella looked at him. "Must be tough, being so hated everywhere you go. Have you dated them all?" *Slept with them all...?*

He looked at her for a long moment. "Who?"

She rolled her eyes. "The women who fall all over themselves to make you smile."

"People in Santa Rey like cops."

And he was all cop. He was also all man.

He pulled out a pad and pencil from his pocket and looked at her. "I want to hear about your eight dates," he said, clearly done discussing women, his or otherwise.

"Nice subject change."

He looked at her, torn between amusement and irritation. "Do you want to discuss the waitress—who, by the way, used to babysit me—or whoever's screwing with your life?"

Well, damn, when he put it that way… "I've already gone over all of this with Ethan. Twenty-five million times."

"So let's do it twenty-five million and one. Maybe we've all missed something. Names and impressions."

"You think one of my dates is a crazy stalker." She shivered at the thought. "Which doesn't explain the second guy who got shot, the one across town."

"True, but there are a lot of possibilities here. Let's work at narrowing them down."

He was all focused and fiercely intense, and when he was really concentrating—like now—he got that deep furrow in his brow.

She wanted to forget the hell that was her current life and kiss that furrow away. What could she say. Yes, her sexual thoughts were inappropriate considering the moment, but it was a defense mechanism. And an easy one to cling to. For God's sake, just look at him. Still watching him, she reached for her soda and sucked her straw.

Immediately his eyes homed in on her mouth.

Huh. Maybe she'd been wrong about needing an act of Congress to want sex. She smiled.

And he raised a brow.

She sucked some more soda down. "About that hypnosis I mentioned, to get in the right mind for sex…"

His eyes dilated. "Distracting me isn't going to end this conversation," he said, voice husky.

"You sure?"

His gaze never left her mouth. "Positive. I can't be distracted. It's one of my gifts."

She was in a position to know that he had other gifts… Lightly, she ran her fingers down the straw, then sucked some more.

Jacob let out a shaky breath. "Okay, new plan."

"Which is?"

"You talk fast, and then we're going back to my place."

"To…watch a movie?"

"Guess again."

A little frisson of heat raced up her spine, something she'd have thought impossible tonight. "Play a game?"

He smiled, and it was filled with so much fire, she nearly had an orgasm on the spot. "Sure, we can play a game. How about Seven Minutes in Heaven."

"I might need more than seven minutes."

"You can have as many minutes as you want." He pulled the soda away from her, and the straw popped out of her mouth with an audible sound that made his eyes darken even more. "But this first."

"Damn. You're so strict."

"You know," he said, "I was hoping I could get you out of that quiet, protective shell you had going, but I didn't think it would happen at my expense."

She sipped more of her soda.

Now he out and out grinned, looking so freaking sexy she could hardly stand it. She had no idea what was wrong with her. She didn't go back for seconds, much less thirds, and yet she had a feeling she could have this man every night until she left for her next destination, and it still wouldn't be enough.

Jacob gently tapped her forehead with the end of his pencil. "Anyone home?"

"Sorry."

"The dates," he said.

Right. "Number one was Bo. Cute, nice, sweet. And too young for me."

"How young?"

"Like five years."

"Huh."

"Huh what?" she asked.

He lifted a broad shoulder. "I doubt he feels too young for you. Next?"

"Seth was number two." She let out a low, pained breath and fell quiet for a minute, remembering him with an ache in her chest. "Date three was Tyler, the bookseller. You saw him today."

"Yeah. What did you think of him?"

"Sweet. Nice. And so smart as to be a little intimidating."

He was making notes. "A dweeb."

"That's not nice."

"Good. Remember that when you're describing date eight, cuz I don't want to hear I'm sweet or nice. Date four."

She shook her head. "A guy named Brady. He seemed…" She nearly said nice but bit it back. "Harmless."

Jacob lifted his head. "Brady, the guy who owns the coffee shop on Third?"

"I think so, yes."

"You think Brady is harmless."

"I do."

He shook his head and kept writing.

Cocking her head to the side, she tried to read what he was writing. "What's wrong with him?"

"What's wrong with him? He dates a different woman every night of the week. He drives a scooter, which for some reason, women think is…*nice*. And he looks like a poet."

"He *is* a poet."

Jacob did a palms up, like *see?*

She held back a grin. "I liked him."

"Did you sleep with him?"

"Is that for your notes?"

Frowning, he wrote something on his pad, pressing hard enough on the paper that his knuckles turned positively white. "Date five."

Okay, so they were moving on. Worked for her. Their food arrived and she dug in. "Juan Martine," she said around her BLT. "I know his last name because I recognized him."

Again he lifted his head and looked at her, that furrow firmly in place. "The model."

"Do you know everyone in town?" She shook her head. "Never mind. Why don't you tell me what's wrong with him, too."

"He wears hair product."

She burst out laughing.

Jacob's furrow deepened. "He does."

"Are you going to find something wrong with each of them? Because it's cute. And yeah, that's going in your description."

This did not help his mood. "I am *not* cute."

She grinned. "You think the word insults your manhood."

"Jesus." He tossed down his pencil and scrubbed his hands over his face. "Forget it."

"Fine. Forget that I think you're cute. I'll never say cute again. Let's go with…" She paused, considering him carefully. "Edgy, grumpy and…"

"We're supposed to be talking about *you*. About your dates. Not me."

"Sexy."

He stared at her. "You drive me crazy."

"Ditto. Can we get back to the rest of the dates, or are you too jealous?"

"I'm not jealous."

"Whatever."

"I am not jealous, Bella."

"Date six. B.J. Sorry, I don't have a full name, but he works in sales, and is a really nice guy."

"What is it with you and nice?"

She ignored that. "Date seven was Lorenzo Ramos, and though I shouldn't know his last name, I do because he's a chef, and works at the Hilltop Lodge."

Jacob wrote the name down and remained silent.

"What, no comment on Lorenzo?"

"No."

"Oh, come on," she said with a laugh. "You know you want to."

"Hey, it's none of my business if you want to date a guy who drives a twenty-year-old Rabbit."

"It saves gas, a lot of gas. And what is it with you and a guy's ride?"

He didn't answer.

"I think this brings us up to date number eight," she said.

"Yeah. Him I've met." By this time they were done eating. He stood and dropped some cash on the table.

"What, you don't want my impression?"

He flashed her an unreadable look, then grabbing

her hand, pulled her up and toward the door in one smooth movement.

"What are we doing now?"

"Going home to discuss your impressions of date number eight. In detail…"

Chapter 9

Jacob's cell buzzed as he led Bella into his house. It was Ethan. "Make yourself at home," he said to Bella. "I have to take this." He moved to the laundry room off the kitchen and flipped open his phone. "Madden."

"She with you?"

"Yes."

"I'm glad she's safe."

There was something in Ethan's voice that tipped him off. "What do you have?"

"The print from the first shooting. The crime lab found marina sand in the tread."

"We need to have the marina checked out."

"Already there. Checking the hotels, motels and all the boats. There's something else. The second gunshot vic. Banning Jefferson. Apparently he goes solely by a nickname. B.J."

Oh, Christ. "Bella's sixth date."

"Yeah. We didn't catch it earlier because B.J. wasn't on any of his IDs."

Jacob stared sightlessly out the laundry room window. "Bella wasn't the target today."

"No," Ethan agreed. "That would be Tyler Scott, date number three. And if he'd been hit, it'd have made three from her list of eight."

"Which puts me on the short list."

"Yeah," Ethan said grimly. "It does."

"I'll watch my back."

"See that you do. We're sending a squad car to your house, as well as to the other guys on the list. It leaves us strapped, but we have to stop this perp."

Jacob shut his phone and went into the kitchen. He grabbed a bottle of wine, two glasses and his laptop.

Bella had wandered into the living room, and was standing with her back to him in front of the huge picture window, looking out to the gentle rolling hills that lined his property. "It's so pretty out here." She turned and looked at him. "The land is beautiful. Are those your horses?"

"One's mine, one's my brother Wyatt's."

"The one in Afghanistan, flying for the air force."

"Yeah." Jacob set the laptop on the coffee table

and poured the wine. "As for the land, I bought it a long time ago, before Santa Rey spread out this far. Back then, this place was a POS." He held out a glass of the wine.

She looked at it, then into his face. "Am I going to need that?"

His gaze didn't waver from hers. "Yes."

She sighed, then took it and sipped. "So. POS. Piece of shit?"

"Got it in one. I redid a room at a time, assisted by a brother or two. Took almost four years, but it's getting there."

She sipped some more wine, looking around her at the oversize, comfortably worn furniture. The only other adornments were a huge plasma TV on the wall and a variety of sports equipment.

"I keep meaning to put all that away," he said.

"Your house is big and warm and feels lived in, like a real home." She said this almost wistfully as she met his gaze. "Tell me what you've got, Jacob. I'm strong enough."

"I know."

"Then just put it out there, like ripping off a Band-Aid."

"All right." He took the wineglass from her fingers and set it aside, then pulled her closer, nudging her down to the couch. "Two things. The guy hit on the other side of town. His name is Banning Jefferson. But he goes by B.J."

She looked at him for a beat before it struck her. "Oh my God."

He took her hand. "He survived, Bella. Remember that. He's going to be okay."

"I need to see him."

"Tomorrow."

She stared at him, and he braced for a fight, but in the end, she simply nodded. "Thing two."

"Thing two." He looked into her eyes. "Today's shooting. You were with Tyler Scott. One of the eight."

"Yes, he came for dessert. He—" She gasped and covered her mouth. "The bullet was meant for him."

"It's likely."

She surged to her feet. "The others. We have to warn the others—"

He straightened and grabbed her before she could run for the door. "They're all being protected."

"And you?" She pulled back, gripping his arms in her hands, her fingers digging into his biceps. "You're in danger, too, just by being with me. You have to go. *Now.*"

"Bella—"

"Oh, God. You can't go, we're at your house. Okay, *I'll* go. I'll call a cab and—"

He pulled her back against his chest, wrapping his arms around her from behind. "I'm not sending you away."

"But—"

"We've got men on the shop, on all the dates, and now here, as well."

"Really?"

"Yes. And don't forget, the perp doesn't know where I live, my home address wasn't on my profile. The guys were punking me, not trying to get me stalked and shot at."

"That's right," she murmured. "I keep forgetting you weren't on that date by your own choice."

"Maybe not at first." Turning her in his arms, he stroked a finger down her temple, tucking a strand of hair behind her ear. "But that changed pretty quickly."

She stared up at him. "When?"

"When a pretty, wild-haired brunette showed up, willing to have a first date that involved adventure seeking and getting her hair wet and her hands dirty."

She smiled at him, some of the panic leaving her eyes. "So what now, Jacob?"

"I want you to show me the profile you filled out, the one that the singles club used to line up your eight dates."

She moved back to the couch and opened his laptop. She waited until he leaned over her and typed in his password, then using his browser program, she accessed her e-mail and then opened a Word document.

"Bella?"

"It's pretty detailed."

He knew because he'd seen the one the guys had filled out for him. There'd been some innocuous questions, like favorite foods and colors. And some not-so-innocuous questions, like sexual likes and dislikes. And fantasies. The profile wasn't to be shared between any of the daters, only used to line up potential matches and, the club promised, would be destroyed afterward.

The guys at the P.D. had bullshitted their way through Jacob's. Since Bella hadn't had her so-called friends "help," most likely she'd answered truthfully, which meant that by allowing him to read her profile, he'd be reading her innermost thoughts and desires. It would be like peeling back the layers of the real Bella.

She made a sound that said "screw it" and thrust the laptop at him.

He looked at her, but had no idea what to say, so he began to read. Her favorite color was the color of the sun because it made her happy. Her favorite food was, surprise surprise, dessert of any kind. Her favorite clothes were anything that felt good and moved with her, she didn't care about labels or designers. Her favorite amusement ride was anything with speed. Her favorite thing she'd *not* yet done— fall in love.

He looked at her.

She lifted a shoulder. "I think I should try everything at least once, including love. You know, someday."

She was embarrassed, but for him he was struck by her honesty and bravado. Since she'd hate for him to point that out, he nodded, and ignoring his suddenly tight throat, quietly read on. The next section was a list of sexual preferences. She preferred one lover at a time, didn't mind toys when they were appropriate and didn't need a bed in order to get in the mood.

She'd left sexual fantasies blank.

"They should be individual to whoever you're with," she said.

He lifted his gaze to hers.

"Yes," she said.

"What?"

"You were going to ask if I have one for us. I do."

His body processed this faster than his brain. "Are you going to share?" he finally asked.

"You first," she said.

He felt a little thrown. A feeling he was starting to get used to around her. He knew now wasn't the time to be playful, but it felt like exactly the right time. They needed this. "Is this a show-and-tell sort of thing?"

"I think it just might be," she said, and for the first time since they'd gotten to his house, he smiled. "How bad do you want to know, Bella?"

She took the computer from his lap and set it aside. "Bad. Besides, you owe me."

"How do you figure?"

"I trusted you with my profile."

True. And, he realized, he trusted her. He, who because of his job and all he'd seen and done on that job, rarely trusted at all, trusted her to the bone after only a few days. He wasn't sure how he felt about that, but he wasn't quite jaded enough to let it go unappreciated. Pulling her onto his lap, he shifted her so that she was straddling him.

"Wait," she said, standing up and removing the jean shorts from beneath her dress. "More comfortable."

He was all for comfort.

She settled back on his lap, once again straddling him. "I like this sundress," he said. "It's the same one you wore after we went on a Jet Ski." He ran his hands slowly up her smooth thighs, pushing up the hem as he went. "In my fantasy, you're not wearing anything beneath."

"That's it? That's your fantasy? That's…surprisingly tame."

"You didn't let me finish." His fingers glided higher on her thighs, and anticipation drummed between them. She was still covered by the hem of the sundress, but barely. "In my fantasy," he went on, his voice thick and hoarse to his own ears, "we go out on my bike, and the whole time we're riding, I can feel the heat of you, bare against me when you hug up close. You're covered from view to everyone else by the wide skirt of your sundress, only I know you don't have on panties."

Her breathing had definitely changed. Actually, he wasn't quite sure she was breathing at all, but the pulse at the base of her throat leaped wildly. "Then what?" she whispered.

"I take you out to dinner. While we're waiting for our food, I slip a hand beneath the table, under your dress. You're hot for me. You press yourself against my fingers, wanting more."

She opened her mouth a little, but nothing came out. Her eyes went glossy with arousal. He knew if he slid a hand beneath her dress right now, he'd find her hot and wet like in his fantasy. "We dance afterward. And every time I touch you, I'm reminded that you're bare-ass naked beneath the dress. Then you lean in and whisper in my ear that I'm making you wet, and I can't get you off the dance floor fast enough."

She drew in a shuddery gulp of air. "And then we make a run for the closest coat closet?"

"Mmm, good plan. We'll add that in. You'll scream my name, but no one but me will hear over the music."

"I want to make you lose control, too," she told him breathlessly. "You scream out my name, too."

He shook his head. "Guys don't scream. It's not manly."

She paused with a small smile. "Manly?"

"*My* fantasy."

"You're right," she said, pacifying him with a pat on the shoulder. "You can groan my name loudly. But hate to break it to you, it's still pretty tame."

"*Still* not finished." He ran a finger over her shoulder. "Someone keeps interrupting me."

"Sorry. Do go on."

"We get back on the bike and ride along the bluffs overlooking the ocean. There's no one around, so when your skirt blows up, you leave it."

He could tell by the way she nibbled on her lower lip that she liked that idea.

A lot.

"I reach back and feel you," he murmured, sliding both hands up to her hips, bringing the hem of her dress up, as well.

She was wearing a light blue silk thong. "You're completely exposed," he murmured. "And completely turned on by it. We pull over to the side of the road and—"

"Have some fairly acrobatic beneath-the-moon sex?" she asked hopefully, eyes dilated, voice husky.

"You have no patience." Giving in to temptation, he nudged her forward, lightly sinking his teeth into the spot where her neck met her shoulder, loving the shiver that racked her. "First I get off the bike and just look at you."

"Is my dress still hiked up to my waist?"

"Yeah. And you've unbuttoned the top part, too."

"No bra?"

"No bra, and when I pull the dress all the way off, you look up at me with a sexy little smile and slowly spread your legs."

"Like this?" And eyes on his, she did just that, opening her legs even farther over his.

Christ. "Yeah," he said hoarsely, watching the silk stretch tight over her mound. "And then you touch yourself. We both know anyone could walk by and see us at any time, but it doesn't stop you from opening my jeans and—"

"Wait a minute." She cocked her head. "I'm nearly buck-ass naked in the great outdoors, and you get to pull out just the essentials?"

"Yes, but the essentials are the important part." He wanted to laugh at the indignation on her face. "My fantasy," he reminded her.

"Men suck."

"Actually, you suck. It's what comes next in this scenario. Male Fantasy 101," he admitted. "But don't worry. Afterward, I lean you up against the bike, spread your legs, drop to my knees and return the favor until you're screaming my name again."

"You like that, the screaming thing."

"I do."

"Then what?" she asked.

"I turn you around, bend you over the bike and—"

"Let me guess. Make me scream." She shook her head. "You are such a guy." The mock annoyance wasn't fooling him. Her eyes were bright, she was having trouble breathing and her hands kept sweeping restlessly over his body, his shoulders, his abs… "How about the water?" she asked. "Do we get in the water and go skinny-dipping?"

"Most definitely. And there's no male shrinkage at all."

She burst out laughing, and he grinned, loving the sound. "In fact, you're so impressed with me, we do it again."

She snorted.

"And again," he said, gliding his hands along her smooth thighs.

"I wouldn't be able to walk." When his fingers got high enough to brush her panties, she closed her eyes and swallowed. "Or ride home."

"Fantasy," he reminded her, groaning when he stroked a finger over the taut silk and found it wet—

As if galvanized into action, she once again leveraged herself off him, evading his hands when he tried to stop her. "You're going to like this," she said. Lifting her hands, she untied the back of her halter dress, cupping the material to her breasts as it began to slide down.

She was right. He was liking this.

With a little smile, she slowly let it slip to her waist, exposing her bare breasts.

Her nipples had hardened into two tight peaks and his mouth went dry.

She slid her hands under the hem, giving him a quick peekaboo hint of that silk. Then she wriggled, and her hand reappeared with that blue silk, which she tossed over her shoulder.

Ah, yeah. He was liking this a lot.

"We're not on your bike," she murmured, slipping back onto his lap, straddling him. "But maybe we can improvise."

Chapter 10

"I'm good at improvising," Jacob murmured in Bella's ear. The rough timbre of his voice made her shiver. It was true, she thought. He was really good.

Always.

He kissed her lips and she curled her fingers around his neck. She slid them into the soft, silky hair at the nape, making him let out a low sound that was half growl, half purr, as if her touch had suffused him with pleasure.

He wasted no time in once again pushing the dress up to her waist, but of course this time she was commando.

"Christ, look at you," he breathed reverently. "So

pretty here." Lightly, he dragged his thumb over her wet flesh. "And here."

Her head fell back, mouth open as she tried to suck in some air, but someone had used it all. She tightened her fingers on his hair as he continued stroking her with that rough, callused thumb. His other hand gripped her hip, slowly rocking her against the hard bulge behind his button fly. Then his mouth joined the fray, hungry and demanding as it devoured hers.

It was all too much—and not enough. *"Jacob."*

"You feel so good, Bella." Sliding his hand around to cup her ass now, he pulled her harder against him, letting her experience just how good she made him feel.

She felt the same. Having him look at her like this had feminine power surging through her, and caused her pulse to throb in every erogenous zone in her body, of which there was suddenly so many. "Jacob—"

"Right here." His grip on her hips was tight, controlling as he ground against her rhythmically, causing the heat to spread. Her every muscle tightened, leaving her about an inch from orgasm.

"I can't get enough of you," he murmured, opening his mouth on her throat, still rocking, always rocking.

"Yes, but—" But she was going to go off far too quickly, she could feel it building within her even before he kissed and sucked and nibbled his way to her breasts.

"Oh God." She couldn't suppress the whimper, or slow the train down. Her mind was spinning with it, with the shocked realization of what he did to her, how he could make her so completely lose herself so that nothing, *nothing* else mattered but this.

Him.

His mouth fastened on her nipple, and with another helpless whimper, she arched her back as he continued to grind his erection hard between her legs, assaulting her senses, finding a spot deep inside her that no one else had touched. "You have to stop," she gasped, trying to pull free. "I'm going to—"

He merely tightened his grip, and then lightly clamped his teeth down on her nipple.

With a soft cry, she exploded—and lost her ability to see or hear anything over the roaring of the blood in her ears. When she could stop trembling and blink her vision clear, she pressed her face to his throat and moaned in embarrassment. "That was all your fault."

He slid his hands into her hair and lifted her face, his eyes scorching, his voice low and fierce. "I love the sounds you make when you come." He looked at her for a moment, then rose to his feet, effortlessly holding her. "Bed," he said, apparently done talking, preferring to move onto the doing portion of the evening. *"Now."* And he kissed her deep and wet while, without missing a beat or taking his tongue out of her mouth, he strode down the hall to his bedroom. At the side of his bed, he slowly let her slide down his body.

She opened his Levi's, pulled out just the "essentials" and stroked the thick, hard length of him. "Condom?"

He pulled one from his nightstand.

"In the name of fulfilling fantasies," she murmured, and with a last look in his eyes, turned from him and bent over the bed, knowing by the rough groan torn from his throat that he was enjoying the view. She felt his hands glide over her, gently murmuring in her ear when she jumped a little, soothing her with his touch as he pulled her back against him.

Then he slowly pressed into her, wrenching a sigh of pleasure from her and a deep groan from him. He went still a minute, letting her adjust to his size, then began stroking her in long, slow thrusts that had her trembling, once again on the very edge. His mouth was on her shoulder, one hand on her hip, the other gliding back and forth between her breasts, teasing her nipples into two hard aching points. Then his fingers trailed down her quivering belly, slipping between her thighs.

Gripping the blankets beneath her in two fists, Bella pressed her forehead into them as she gasped for air, making dark needy sounds that might have horrified her if she could have put a thought together. But Jacob's mouth was on her neck, his fingers strumming between her legs as he moved within her, and suddenly there was no thinking at all.

Behind her, Jacob groaned, struggling for control, a battle he lost as he followed her over, her name on his lips.

Afterward, Jacob took her into the kitchen to raid his fridge. He wore his jeans, unbuttoned. Bella wore his shirt.

Also unbuttoned.

He handed her a bottle of water and she drank as if she hadn't had anything to drink for a week. "Your turn," he said, watching her throat convulse as she swallowed. Fascinated, he ran a finger down her throat to the center of her chest, changing directions to glide the pad of his calloused thumb over her nipple. It hardened into a tight bead, and his body had a matching reaction. Jesus. He was never going to get enough of her. "Your fantasy next."

She looped her arms around his neck, sinking her fingers into his hair, making him practically purr. "You really want to know?"

He looked down into her face and felt something catch deep within him, and he knew in that moment that Ethan had been right.

He had it bad for her.

"I really do."

Tilting her head up, she met his gaze. "You show up at my place unannounced."

"Yeah?" His hands slid up the backs of her thighs, beneath the shirt.

"I open the door to you and tell you…" She affected a look of mock shame. "That I've been bad. Very, very bad."

"Mmm." His mouth was busy on the spot where her neck met her shoulder, his fingers cupping and squeezing her sweet, bare ass. "How bad?"

She kissed one corner of his lips, then his jaw. His throat… "You have to cuff me."

His eyes drifted shut. "Do I?"

"Uh-huh… And then—" She licked his nipple.

"And then?" he managed to say.

"And then you exercise your authority," she whispered against his chest. "Because I've been so bad and all. I mean, *really* naughty."

He picked her up in tune to her surprised gasp, and carried her down the hall toward the bedroom, grabbing his cuffs on the way.

"Where are we going?" she asked breathlessly.

"To see just how bad you've been."

Bella woke up and took assessment. She was toasty warm, and someone had stolen all the bones in her body. She cracked open an eye.

She was face-first in Jacob's chest.

Not a bad place to be, as it was a world-class chest. She was snuggled up to his side with one leg and an arm thrown over him, hugging him to her like her own personal body pillow. The blankets were long gone. Only a sheet covered them, and it was pooled low at their waists. It was still dark outside but there was enough light slanting through his window from the predawn to see that Jacob was asleep.

As they'd not passed out until very late, and it was debatable as to whether it was officially still very late or very early, she couldn't blame him.

He was on his back, far arm stretched above his head, the other wrapped around her. His face was turned toward hers, eyes closed, jaw whiskered in dark shadow. He looked younger, and extremely relaxed, as if maybe someone had stolen his bones, too, and the thought brought a knowing smile to her mouth. *She'd* put him in that state.

She could stare at him all night. Except she couldn't. She had to go.

He shifted, and drew in a deep breath. Eyes still closed, his arm tightened on her, and he pressed his face to the top of her head. "Mmm. Good way to wake up." His voice was sleep roughened and sexy as hell vibrating in her ear.

"Don't get stirred up," she said. "I have to get to the shop."

"Too late."

She crooked her neck and look down the length of him. Yep, it was too late. He was stirring.

Everywhere.

She watched as the sheet became an impromptu

tent, and because she couldn't help herself, slid a
hand beneath the fabric to wrap her fingers around
him.

He groaned and covered her hand with his. "I like
where this is going."

"It's not going anywhere. I have to start baking
or we won't have anything to sell today. I'm not sure
we'll have customers after all that's happened, but
I know Willow is going to be hoping for the best."
But because she couldn't help herself, she shoved
the sheet free and bent over him, kissing him on the
very tip of his most impressive erection.

It bobbed happily.

She gave one last sigh of regret and slipped out
of his arms and off the bed.

"That's just mean," he said as she padded off to
his bathroom. "Cruel and unusual punishment."

She was smiling when she turned on his shower,
smiling when she used his soap and pressed her nose
into her own arm to get as close to his scent as possible, smiling when she felt the door open behind her.

And then she was pulled back against a solid,
hard chest. "No funny business," she warned him.
"If you behave, I'll meet you for lunch, but for right
now, I've got to go. Just cleaning up here, that's it,
then I'll call a cab."

"Hmm," he said noncommittally as his hands slid
up her soaped-up, slicked-up body and cupped her
breasts, his fingers grazing her nipples.

Her entire body quivered. "I mean it, Jacob."

"Fine. We'll do lunch."

"You mean, we'll do each other."

He grinned against her skin. "That, too, if you'd like. I'll come to the shop, pick you up and feed you first. Okay?"

"Mmm." It was all she could manage with one of his hands on her breast, his other heading south—

She dropped the soap.

"Uh-oh," he murmured silkily. "Better get that."

When she bent over to get the soap, he sucked in a breath and gripped her hips. She felt him hard against her ass. "Jacob—"

"Just pretend I'm not even here," he said, both laughter and arousal in his voice.

"I'm only cleaning up," she repeated weakly, her body on high orgasm alert. Good Lord, it was crazy. They'd had each other so many times last night she'd lost count. How could she *still* want him like this? "I've really got to get going…"

"Oh, Bella." His voice was low and full of sexy promise. "You're going to get going. And coming…"

The words themselves almost edged her over. "The shop—"

"You're going to be late." He took the soap from her and directed her hands to the tile in front of her, gently kicking her feet farther apart as though he was about to frisk her. Then he slid a hand down her ass and groaned again. "*Very* late."

* * *

Later that morning, Jacob was at his desk handling paperwork while reliving the morning's shower—look at him, multitasking—when Ethan stopped by.

"Just visited your girlfriend," Ethan said, annoying smirk in place. "She has the same just-been-thoroughly-laid look on her face that you do."

Jacob leaned back, lacing his hands over his abs. He was feeling far too mellow to put his fist in Ethan's mug, probably due to the just-been-thoroughly-laid feeling that was indeed running through his veins today.

Ethan dropped into a chair and stretched his legs. "We've put every spare man we've got on this case."

"I know. We're going to get him now."

Ethan nodded. "I've interviewed Willow, Trevor, all the neighboring shop owners and their employees, and all of the men Bella dated through the singles club."

"Except me."

"Except you. You haven't been contacted by the club since the date, right? Or by any of the other participants, other than Bella?"

"Nope."

"And no sense of being watched in any way?"

"No."

Ethan nodded. They both knew that once a cop,

always a cop. If someone had been watching him, chances were Jacob would have noticed.

"Your club date with her was different than the others in two ways," Ethan said. "With everyone else, they had a meal or a drink, that was it. But with you, you changed venues and did quite a bit."

"Yeah. What's the second way it was different?"

Ethan waggled a brow. "You're the only one who slept with her. Did you know that was forbidden?"

"No, it wasn't."

"Okay, it wasn't," Ethan agreed. "But it was discouraged. So the question is, why you? Why did she sleep with you?"

"Thanks, man."

Ethan grinned. "I'm actually serious. It was out of character for her."

Truth was, Jacob didn't know why Bella had slept with him. All he knew was that from the moment they'd met, there'd been a spark—a physical, visceral spark—and it was still there, every time he saw her.

Every.

Single.

Time.

"You've kept seeing her," Ethan said. "Not that anyone could blame you. But she hasn't made a move to see any of the others again."

"So?"

"So are you exclusive already?"

"And that's pertinent to the case how?"

"Oh, it's not. Just wondering what that sweet little thing sees in you. I mean, look at her. She's warm and funny and sexy as hell. You on the other hand are grumpy, usually scowling, and I'm having a hard time imagining you bringing the funny or the sexy." He rose lithely to his feet when Jacob's eyes narrowed, and wisely moved to the door.

"Ethan?"

"Yeah?"

"I can't see a rhyme or reason to the order in which the eight of us are being targeted."

Ethan shook his head. "Me, neither. Just be careful out there," he warned. "And though I don't believe she's the target, I've advised Bella to do the same."

At lunchtime, Jacob shoved the reports he'd been working on aside and left the building. He was halfway to Edible Bliss when he was called to check on a material witness for a case he was building involving the identity-theft ring.

Thanks to an uncooperative witness and an unhappy victim, by the time Jacob was back on the road again, it was nearly two.

Bella had probably eaten lunch without him long ago.

Still, he headed over there, needing to see her. It had nothing to do with his own emotions and feelings, he assured himself, and everything to do with what Ethan had said.

She needed to be careful.

Something bad had happened each day for three days running, and he just wanted to lay his eyes on her—and maybe his hands—and know she was okay.

Over the years he'd had hundreds of cases, and had met countless people he'd worried about in the scope of the job. But this wasn't just the job. This was personal.

Almost too much so.

He parked his bike in the back lot next to the squad car assigned to the shop, nodding to the cop inside. It was Tom Kennedy, a rookie of less than a year. They spoke for a minute, and when Tom said he hadn't had lunch yet, Jacob told him to take off and grab something, that he'd watch the place until he got back.

Jacob stepped up to the kitchen door, wanting to take a quick peek inside before he made a complete check around the perimeter of the building.

Bella was alone, bustling around in tune to the sound system, which she had blaring Radiohead. She wore a pair of tiny denim shorts, an oversize white men's T-shirt knotted in the small of her back, a siren-red apron, and matching red high-tops on her feet. That made him smile.

Hell, *she* made him smile.

Her wild hair was piled up on top of her head, a few wispy tendrils escaping, sticking to her damp temples. He knew just how that damp skin would

taste, and he felt himself stir with arousal just looking at her.

Then he pictured her in that apron, and nothing
else.

Christ, he needed help. If he had ever doubted the
necessity of removing himself from the case, this
moment made it irrefutable.

She hadn't seen him yet. She was singing to herself as she cleaned the countertop, the motion making her hips rock back and forth.

And making him ache.

Christ, he was gone. Completely gone over her.
He hoped she'd decide to come out and get some
air, but clearly she was getting ready to close up.
Leaning against the doorjamb, he stood there with
a ridiculous grin on his face, just soaking her in. He
figured he could probably stand there and watch her
all damn day long and not get tired of it, but then she
vanished into the front room of the shop, where he
could no longer see or hear her.

And he had a job to do first before he went inside. He straightened up to get on with it just as the
hair on the back of his neck suddenly stood up. He
jerked around at the exact moment the shot rang out.

He jerked again at the impact, and fire burned
through him.

He really hated getting shot.

He opened his mouth to yell a warning to Bella,
since he knew she couldn't hear a thing over her

music, but nothing came out. His last thought at he hit the ground was that at least he wasn't holding a bouquet of flowers.

Chapter 11

Bella moved to the front door of the shop, locked it, then looked over the freshly installed window. Remembering the reason for that had a shiver racking her as she flipped the Closed sign. She moved to the iPod dock in the closet and hit the power button, and in the sudden silence, another shiver, this one of dread, raced up her spine. She stepped out of the closet and looked around for the cause.

Everything looked normal.

Then Willow's face appeared in the front door's window, and Bella near fell back on her butt in surprise.

"Sorry," Willow said when Bella had opened the

door for her. "Forgot my key and my purse." She frowned. "I don't know where my head is."

"I do. It's on the shootings, and the fact that we had half our usual customers today."

Willow sighed. "Yeah. That's it."

Her hair was spiked straight up and out today, like Cher in her seventies Oscar run. She was wearing retro derby gear complete with polyester shorts and a green-and-white rugby top. The only thing missing was a pair of skates and the pads. "You're wearing your mom's clothes again."

"Yeah, I love her closet. I'm going to stay there again tonight. There's an extra couch…"

"Thanks. I'll let you know."

Hands on hips, Willow's eyes narrowed as she studied Bella. "You're eating your short-crust pastry."

Bella looked down at the pastry in her hands and sighed. "Had so much left over today. And it's good."

"It's great," Willow corrected. "It's soft and flaky and *perfect*. But according to you, it also goes right to your hips."

"You forgot your purse and keys due to stress. I'm eating due to stress. We're quite the pair." Bella sighed again and tossed the pastry into the trash.

"Well, Jesus, if you were going to throw it away…" Willow looked wistfully at the trash can.

"Don't you dare." They moved into the kitchen,

where Bella gave her a new one from the leftovers bin, and Willow happily bit into it.

Bella shook her head. "I hate that you can eat like this and stay as skinny as a rail."

Willow grinned and took another pastry. "Good genes." She cocked her head and her smile faded. "There's something else wrong. Aw, honey. Is it Sexy Cop?"

"No. Yes. I don't know." She shook it off. "It's nothing. He was supposed to meet me for lunch and didn't. No biggie."

"He's got an important job. He probably just got held up."

"Yes. Maybe." But maybe not. Maybe he'd decided their casual fun was over.

"He doesn't seem like the sort of man to play with a woman's feelings," Willow said quietly. "And anyway, I've seen him look at you. He'd never play with you like that. Something came up. He'll call."

"Yeah."

"You keep going down that path," Willow said, grabbing her purse, "and you're going to be insane by the end of the day. I'm going to the movies. Trevor's driving. Come with us?"

"Not today, thanks."

Willow gave her a fast hug. "You're just afraid because you're feeling more than you meant to, because you're falling for him."

Bella squeezed her eyes shut. "Maybe."

"Don't worry, Bell, I think he means to catch you."

And then she was gone, out through the dining area and the front door, and with a sigh, Bella locked up. For the tenth time, she pulled out her cell phone.

No missed call.

Fine. He hadn't called. That was fine.

You're falling for him. Willow's words echoed in her head. They were a scary truth. *Her* scary truth, because she *was* falling.

But was she the only one? Hard to tell. But if so, that was okay. He'd said casual. It wasn't his fault that she hadn't managed to keep it that way. She'd get herself together.

She would.

She sagged a little, feeling the ache behind her ribs that showed her up as a big, fancy liar. With a shake of her head, she turned off the lights, grabbed her key and went to push open the back door, but it got stuck on something. She pushed a little harder, and when it moved enough for her to squeeze out, she nearly tripped over—

A body.

He was on his side facing away from her. Dark hair, buff arms, broad shoulders, blood pooling beneath him on the ground—

Oh, God.

This wasn't just any body, this one was as familiar to her as her own.

With a groan, Jacob shifted, and she stepped over him and dropped to her knees with a shocked sob. *"Jacob!"* His shirt was light blue, so she could clearly see the hole in his shoulder, and the blood pumping from it. Panic clenched her hard in the gut, and she ripped off her T-shirt, wadding it up to press it to his wound as she whipped out her cell phone and pounded 911.

He rolled to his back, face tight in a grimace as she gave the information to emergency dispatch.

"Goddamn," he said through his teeth when she was done and pressed harder on the wound. "That hurts."

She slid a hand beneath his head to move it to her lap, and her fingers came away bloody. "You must have hit your head."

"Well, that's a relief." He was staring up at her and blinking rapidly. "Explains why there's four of you." He closed his eyes. "Get inside and stay away from the windows."

"What? I'm not leaving you!"

"Goddammit, Bella. The shooter could still be out here somewhere."

She lifted her head and looked around, heart pumping so hard she could scarcely breathe. "No one's out here."

"Did it go through?"

"What?"

"The bullet. Did it go through?"

She let out a breath and looked him over. Hole in the front. Gently she leaned over him so she could see the back.

God.

God, there was so much blood. "Yes," she said shakily. "It went straight through."

"That's good." His eyes were a little glazed and fixed on what was right in front of his face—her chest. "Nice bra."

She made a sound that was a half laugh, half sob, and applied more pressure.

"Oh, shit," Jacob rasped through his teeth.

"I'm sorry. You're bleeding so much."

"Call Ethan. Have him tell Tom his lunch break's over."

Again she used her cell. Onlookers were starting to trickle into the parking lot, one of whom brought her a shawl to wrap around herself. Two of the adjacent shop owners were there, too, and several people that Bella didn't know, all standing a respectful distance back.

She heard sirens. "They're coming."

He didn't move or open his eyes and she gripped him tight. "Jacob!"

"Shh," Jacob whispered. "He's sleeping."

"No. Stay with me," she said fiercely, leaning down to put her face right in his. "Don't you dare leave me."

"Bella," he said softly, sounding pained. He squeezed her hand. "I'm not going anywhere."

"Okay, then."

He didn't say anything more, but she could see his chest rising and falling. Breathing. Breathing was good.

The ambulance pulled into the lot and everything happened in super speed then. She was pulled free of Jacob, who was quickly assessed, his vitals taken and an IV started. She heard the EMT report to the hospital that they had a thirty-two-year-old male with a through-and-through GSW to the shoulder, vitals stable, possible slight concussion.

She never took her eyes off Jacob. He was clearly woozy, but he'd been able to give his name, age, the time and place. That had to be good, she told herself.

Then he was loaded up.

She tried to go with him, but another EMT detained her, gaze running over her gently as he assessed her to make sure the blood all over her wasn't hers. By the time it was determined she was fine, the ambulance with Jacob had left.

Fine. She knew just where the hospital was, since on her first week in Santa Rey she'd cut her finger with her paring knife and had required three stitches. She needed a shirt anyway, and she had to lock up, and she had to—

"Bella."

She turned and found a grim-looking Ethan, and nearly lost it at the familiar face.

Right. She had to talk to the police.

Yet again.

"Oh, Christ," he said when he got a good look at her. "Were you hit?"

"No, it's Jacob's blood."

He backed her into the kitchen, keeping a tight grip on her until she sat in a chair. Without a word, he went to the refrigerator and got her a bottle of water. "Drink," he said, and went to the sink to wet a towel.

"Someone shot him," she said softly.

"I know." Gently he pulled the shawl off her, then ran the towel over her arms. He rinsed it out, then handed it back to her, presumably so that she could do her own torso. "What did you see?" he asked.

"Nothing. I saw nothing. I got a sort of hinky feeling, and I shrugged it off." She shook her head. "Willow came back for her purse—"

"Willow was here?"

"Yes, briefly. After she left, I came to the back door here to leave, and nearly tripped over him. He was just lying there." Her hand was shaking so badly she couldn't drink. "And I'm shaking. I never shake."

He shrugged out of his shirt and wrapped it around her. "Are you going to take me to the station again?" she asked him.

"I'm not a complete asshole. I'm going to wait for

you to collect yourself, then I'm going to drive you to the hospital to see him."

She lifted her head and met his gaze. "You're worried about him, too."

A muscle ticked in his jaw. "Yeah."

She stood up. "Consider me collected."

He looked her over as if to make his own assessment, then he reached for her hand and took her to his car.

Chapter 12

Getting shot sucked. Being X-rayed and MRI'd sucked. Lying in a hospital bed sucked.

Jacob kept his eyes closed because somehow he hurt less that way. What else sucked? he wondered. Oh, yeah, wearing a stupid hospital gown with his ass hanging out—

At the slight rustle at his side, he gave up the pity party and opened his eyes.

The room immediately started spinning wildly. Thank you, morphine.

The lights were low. He could hear the soft muted sounds of monitors and sensed activity just outside his door, but inside his room, all was fairly quiet.

Turning just his head, he came face-to-face with Bella. She was sitting in a chair by his bed, hunched over the raised mattress, head down on her folded arms.

Given her slow, even breathing, he concluded she was sleeping. Her hair was a wild, riotous wreck. He was fairly certain there was blood in it, and his heart picked up speed until he realized it was probably his. She wore a man's shirt, not his, shoved up to the elbows, and with her face turned to the side, he could make out the very faint tracks of whisker burns on the underside of her jaw.

Those were his.

She was a quiet, tousled, clearly exhausted mess, and maybe it was the fact that he was as high as a kite, but no one had ever looked better to him.

The door opened behind her, but thanks to what he knew from experience was a combination of a severe adrenaline letdown and an emotional exhaustion, she didn't so much as stir as his brother Austin walked in.

He and Jacob were only a year and a half apart, and on a normal day, when one of them wasn't lying in a hospital bed trussed up with bandages and on some good mind-altering drugs, they could have passed for twins. Dark hair, matching dark eyes and a tendency for walking headfirst into trouble.

"Just talked to your doctor—" Austin glanced at

Bella, raised a brow, then silently sat on the other side of Jacob's bed. "That her?"

"Who?"

"The woman you went out with, the one you dropped off the face of the planet for over the past few days."

Jacob felt the stupid smile cross his lips and couldn't do a damn thing about it. "Her name is Isabella Manchelli—Bella. She works at Edible Bliss. She's a pastry chef and a friend."

"Great," Austin said. "But none of that answered my question."

"Keep it down, she's asleep."

Austin raised a brow. He looked Bella over, taking in the wild hair, the way her mouth was slightly open, and he smiled. "She's cute."

Bella shifted, turned her head over to the other side, and in the process, lifted up briefly enough to reveal more blood in her hair.

Austin's smile faded. "Tell me she's not hurt."

"It's my blood. Tell me what the doctor said."

"X-ray and MRI were negative, no bullet fragments. Mild concussion. You're going to hurt like a son of a bitch, but while you're in here you get morphine. You're probably going to be woken every two to three hours, but the good news is that the nurse on duty is pretty damn hot. Still, the next time you're going to be stupid enough to stand on the back stoop of a woman who tends to get her men shot at, the least you could do is wear a vest." He paused and looked over Bella again. "So you're dating her?"

"Why?"

"Why? Because you met her through a singles club. Seems kind of cheesy, man."

"Should I have met her on a bar stool like you meet your one-night stands?"

"So she's a one-night stand?"

Their gazes met and Jacob sighed. "I don't know. I can't think straight. Are you on the merry-go-round or am I?"

Cord entered the hospital room at a dead run, or more accurately, a limping run on a leg that hadn't quite healed yet. Eyes a little wild, he stopped short and gripped the doorjamb. "You were shot."

"Yeah," Jacob said.

"You're breathing."

"Yeah."

"And wasted," Austin added.

Cord let out a slow, careful breath, then sank to a chair. "I didn't get details, just a text from Mr. Talkative here, and I—" He broke off with a shake of his head and put a hand to his heart. "Christ, man."

"I'm okay," Jacob said. "Though you've split into two. You need some help."

Cord just stared at him. "Christ," he finally said again. He hadn't been back from his last overseas mission all that long and was still a little jumpy.

"What I need is whatever you're on." He turned to Austin. "Prognosis?"

"Hard head still intact, and expected to make a full recovery," Austin told him. "He's going to be okay, Cord."

Cord nodded but still looking shaken, leaned his head back to the wall.

Austin turned to Jacob with a raised brow. "Why don't you tell baby brother here how you're on, what, date number three? With the same woman. That woman, in fact." He gestured to a still-sleeping Bella.

That seemed to knock Cord out of his own thoughts. "She must be a walking fantasy or something." He cocked his head. "Kinda hard to tell with the crazy hair."

"Fantasy," Jacob repeated, brain fuzzy. "We knocked out fantasy number one. Need to move on to fantasy number two."

That had both Austin and Cord giving each other a speculative look. "What's fantasy number two?" Austin wanted to know.

"Her in her apron and nothing else."

Cord grinned, the hauntedness and hollowness gone from his gaze. "Those must be some good drugs."

Austin took in Jacob's expression and shook his head. "Oh, Christ."

"What?" Jacob asked, his eyes at half mast now. They were closing on him without his permission.

"You've got that look, the same stupid, love-struck look that Cord had right before he admitted he'd fallen for Lexi."

"Hey," Cord said. "True, but—hey."

"I'm pretty sure I'm just high," Jacob said in his own defense.

"I actually hope that's true," Austin said. "Because if you fall, too, that leaves me hanging out here all alone, and even I can't handle all the single women in town by myself."

Cord grinned. "You can try."

"You still have Wyatt," Jacob said, reminding Austin that their other brother was still single. "He'll be home soon enough."

A shocked silence echoed between them as Jacob's words said sank in. "Wait a minute," he said. "I didn't mean that I *am* falling."

They all turned their heads to stare at a still deeply sleeping Bella, and Jacob's gut tightened. His heart tightened, too. Typically when he looked at her, his dick tightened, as well, but nothing there. Damn meds.

A little snuffling whimper escaped from Bella, and Jacob stroked her arm with his hand. "Shh," he said. "It's okay now."

Her frown smoothed out and she let out a shuddery breath.

And just like that, his dick twitched. Good to know he was in fine working order after all.

Austin was staring at him. "You're soft around her."

"Soft?" He begged to differ.

"You know what I mean." He looked at Bella and then shook his head. "What does she see in you?"

Jacob sighed. "Thanks for coming by."

"But go away?"

"That'd be great."

When Jacob was released from the hospital late the next evening, Bella was waiting to take him home. She'd spent the night with Willow at her mom's, then gone back to her place to shower and change, and now had a purse full of happy pills and two pages of doctor's instructions as she slid her arm around Jacob for the walk out.

"I'm not an invalid," he said, smiling down at her.

He'd been smiling a lot since he'd started the happy pills. He'd smiled at the nurse, and she'd dropped her supplies. He smiled at his brother, who was currently on his other side helping Bella get him to the car, and Austin just shook his head and said, "You're a sap."

"Love you, too, man," Jacob said, making Austin laugh.

Austin turned to Bella. "Take care of the idiot, will you?"

"Plan on it."

And now the "idiot" was smiling at her as she

drove him home, making her heart catch in her throat.

Her life had turned into a *Law & Order* episode, and he was smiling at her.

God. She could hardly bear to think about what had happened to him, or how much worse it could have been.

Ethan and most of the P.D. were on this case, she told herself. They would find the shooter, Ethan had promised. They would take care of it.

She knew it, she believed it.

She just hoped they'd do so before anyone else got hurt.

At Jacob's house, she guided him to the couch, removed his shoes and sank back on her heels to look up at him.

"You stopping at the shoes?" he asked, and wriggled his toes.

"Yes. Why?"

"I'm not comfortable. I want to be in sweats."

She dutifully pulled off his socks.

"And?" he asked with a sweet grin that was so amiable and easygoing—unlike his usual stoic, tough, badass self—she laughed. "You are feeling no pain today, Detective." But she obliged him by unbuttoning his shirt and carefully easing it off his shoulders, working around the splint and sling his left shoulder was immobilized with. At the sight of all the thick bandages, her mirth faded.

He hadn't required surgery—a miracle. Nothing vital had been hit.

Another miracle.

He was a walking miracle…

"And?" he murmured again, arching a brow.

She looked at his jeans. Levi's, button fly. She ran her finger over his corrugated abs, which contracted beneath her touch. She popped the top button and felt him harden beneath the denim, and then it was her turn to arch a brow.

"He's excited to see you," Jacob explained.

"You say that like it's been so long," she murmured, crawling between his long legs and leaning in so that she could rest her head on his stomach. "It's only been a day and a half."

"He's greedy when it comes to you."

With a soft laugh, she turned her face and nuzzled his belly button. His skin was silky smooth, with the ripple of hard sinew just beneath. "I think this is my favorite spot on you."

He was lying back against the couch, his eyes at half mast, his long, thick lashes shielding his thoughts. He brought his good hand up to her hair. "I was hoping your favorite spot was down a little."

She stroked the spot he was talking about, and he let out a sigh, which turned into a ragged groan when she dragged her tongue south to the Levi's waistband, snaking it just beneath.

"Christ, Bella." His hand tightened in her hair.

He kept his head back, his eyes now closed, throat exposed. She watched his Adam's apple as he swallowed.

"You have no idea what you do to me," he murmured.

She eyed the growing bulge behind the button fly. "Oh, I think I do... You know, you might be right about my favorite body part. Let me take a look." She popped open the rest of his buttons, and he sprang free. In the same way she'd nuzzled his belly, she leaned in and pressed her face against him, then gave him a kiss.

His breathing had accelerated, but other than that, the rest of his long body was stone still, clearly waiting for her next move.

"You do realize," she whispered, her lips brushing him with each word, "this isn't doctor recommended."

"He said I should go with what feels good. Trust me, Bella. You feel good."

"Well, stop me if anything causes you any pain." She let her tongue dart out and run the hard length of him.

"You're not hurting me." His voice was raw. "You're *killing* me. But, Christ, please don't stop."

In less than three minutes, she had him quivering, alternating between swearing and begging. In two more, he was panting, boneless and completely sated.

"You okay?" she whispered, sitting back on her heels.

"If I was any more okay, I'd float out of here and into bed."

She smiled. "I'll help you." She got him down the hall and onto the mattress, and he lay there, eyes closed, color a bit ashen. She'd never rebuttoned his jeans, and she already knew he was commando beneath them, but she still couldn't help but stare as he one-armed them down his legs and kicked them away.

She'd had her mouth on every single inch of that glorious, gorgeous body and still, she wanted him. She was afraid she always would. "You hungry? Thirsty? Need anything?"

He made an almost inaudible negative sound.

She covered him with a blanket and moved to leave the room, but, eyes still closed, he reached out and unerringly snagged her wrist.

Seemed he was down for the count but still in complete control of his instincts. "You okay?" she asked.

"It's late."

"Yes. So?"

"So…" He tugged, and with a gasp, she sank down beside him on his good side.

"Jacob, careful—"

"Don't drive home this late, don't go be by yourself."

"I won't be alone. There's still a man on the shop."

"Just stay."

"But you need to rest. You're not up for—"

"I won't be able to rest if I'm worried about you, and if you go back there, I'll worry."

She went still for a long moment, her eyes closed, chest aching, wishing he'd say, "Stay with me because I want you to."

She'd told herself she didn't need to hear that from him but she did.

God, she did. She needed to hear it from someone in her life, someone who wasn't family, who didn't have to say it.

"You should know," she finally whispered to him in the dark, her hand caught in his. "I'm…afraid. Of you. Of me. I don't do things like this, Jacob. I don't let guys in. I like to keep my options open, I like to be free to up and leave whenever. And I'm due to leave." She paused, then decided what the hell. She'd already anted up, might as well play out the round. "But even with an entire lifetime of experience of keeping my emotions in check, with you I let go. I let go and let myself feel, all in a matter of days, which is where the terror comes in." She let out a low laugh, and dropping to her knees beside the bed, she hugged his hand to her chest, pressing her face into his good shoulder. "Fact is," she murmured, "I think I'm beginning to maybe, a little bit, fall for you."

He said nothing.

Lifting her head, she looked into his face.

His eyes were closed, his face relaxed. "Jacob?"

Nothing. The happy pills had done their job and knocked him out.

Chapter 13

Jacob woke up slowly, groggy and disoriented. He blinked at the ceiling. It was *his* ceiling. He was in his own bed.

That was good.

He closed his eyes, trying to figure out what he remembered last.

He'd been shot.

Yeah, he remembered that really well. He remembered Bella holding his head on her lap and crying softly over him.

He remembered her begging him not to go to sleep, and remembered staring into her eyes and wanting to promise her anything, his motorcycle, his bank account, his life, if only she wouldn't cry.

He didn't remember the ambulance ride or the E.R., but he remembered Bella sleeping at his side, and Austin and Cord coming to see him, the two of them looking at him with dark, worried eyes, and Austin saying that if Jacob was going to be stupid enough to stand on the back stoop of a woman who tended to get her men shot, then the least he could do was wear a vest.

Point taken.

He needed protection when it came to Bella. Unfortunately the kind of protection he needed was a heart guard, and that hadn't been invented yet.

But he was home now…

How had he gotten here?

His bedroom door opened and Bella slid in, carrying a pitcher and a glass. She set them down very quietly then turned to smooth his covers, and nearly jerked right out of her skin when she saw that his eyes were open.

"Oh! You're awake! Are you in pain? Do you need—"

"You. I need you." With his good hand, he tugged her down to the bed. The shift nearly killed him, but he sucked in a breath and managed a smile. "You're a sight for sore eyes."

She visibly softened and cupped one side of his

jaw, pressing her mouth to the other side. "Right back at you. Do you need another pain pill?"

"Yes, but don't give me one. I can't even remember getting here."

Her eyes widened. "You don't remember the... um, couch?"

He went still as it came back, her kneeling between his spread legs, her mouth on him, and the memory had pleasure suffusing his body. "I thought that was just a really great dream." He met her gaze. "Thank you, by the way. But I still don't remember getting into bed."

She nodded and looked away, and he'd swear that was relief crossing her features. He stroked a thumb over the backs of her fingers. "What did I do, Bella?"

"Nothing."

"Did I say anything to upset you?"

"No, nothing like that." She sagged a little. "It was me, okay? *I* said something I shouldn't have." She bit her lower lip and stared at him.

He blinked. "What was it?"

She groaned and pressed her forehead to his good shoulder. "Never mind. Are you thirsty? I brought you water, the doctor said not to let you get dehydrated."

"Bella—"

"Here." She sat up at his hip and poured him a glass.

He lifted a hand to her wrist and she shook her head. "Please?"

He looked at her for a long moment, then nodded his reluctant agreement to let the subject go. She held the glass to his lips and, looking over the edge at her, amused, he sipped.

"Hungry?" she asked. "I can cook you up some breakfast before I have to go."

He smiled. "In your apron?"

She arched a brow.

"Sorry. That was fantasy number two. We never got to it."

"You have a fantasy about me in an apron?"

He shook his head, feeling a little fuzzy. "I'm sorry. It's a guy thing."

"Huh." She got off the bed. "Breakfast. I'll get it." And then she was gone.

He went back to studying the ceiling. *Way to go, Madden. You had her in here, warm and smiling, then you scare her off with some stupid, sexist, subservient-male fantasy—*

She came back into the room, and holy shit. If he hadn't been lying down, he'd have fallen. She was wearing a black bra and matching panties, low on her hips and sexy enough to put him into heart-attack danger. She'd created an apron out of one of his kitchen towels and used another to create a little cap on her head.

"At your service, sir," she murmured throatily, giving him a little curtsy. "What can I get you?"

"What are you doing?"

"Well, I was going for a French-maid thing, but I can't pull off the accent."

He could only stare at her as she sashayed across the room and sat perched at his hip with a small, warm smile. Leaning over him, she lightly brushed her lips to his.

He was afraid he was drooling. "God, Bella," he said on a low, baffled, bewildered laugh. "I—"

Austin walked into the bedroom and stopped short with a choked breath at the sight of Bella sitting on Jacob's bed, leaning over him in nothing but her underwear. "Um," he said brilliantly.

"Jesus, Austin," Jacob snapped as Bella squealed and dived under the covers with him, hiding her face in his armpit. "Get out."

"Sorry," Austin said, then just stood there with a broad grin on his face. "I came to see if you needed anything, but I can see that you are being extremely well taken care of."

From beneath the covers, Bella squeaked again.

Austin just continued to grin like a jackass. "Fantasy number two. *Nice.*"

Still out of sight, Bella punched Jacob in his good arm. *"You told him?"*

Jacob shook his head. "No. I—"

"Yeah," Austin said. "You told us at the hospital.

Don't be mad, Bella," he said to the lump under the sheet. "We totally took advantage of him being high."

While Jacob was appreciating—and loving—the feeling of Bella wearing only her panties and bra all pressed up against him and squirming, he figured he had about three seconds to get his brother out of here before she killed him. "Austin?"

"Let me guess. Get the hell out?" With a grin, he said, "Going. But next time you play dress up, you really should lock the door."

"Maybe next time you should knock."

"And miss out on all the fun?" With a laugh, Austin turned toward the door. "I'll be in the kitchen making myself something to eat. Loudly, so I can't hear you two do your thing."

Jacob decided it was worth the pain and reached for the phone on the nightstand to chuck it at his brother's head, but Austin laughed again and hastily shut the door behind him.

Leaving a stunned and awkward silence.

For a beat, the only thing visible of Bella was a few strands of wild hair, then suddenly she was in motion, leaping out of the bed, her makeshift cap all askew, the apron half on, half off, one of her bra straps slipped to her elbow.

She looked hot as hell.

"So," he said. "Where were we?"

She whirled, eyes reflecting her disbelief. "You have got to be kidding me."

"He said he'd make lots of noise so he couldn't hear you—"

"Oh, my God." She hauled open his closet door. Her underwear was riding up in back, giving him a heart-attack-inducing view. "He said he'd make lots of noise so he couldn't hear the *two* of us. He didn't specify *me*."

"Honey," Jacob said with a smile.

She went still, then turned on him in her half-naked glory, eyes narrowed. "Honey, what? And be careful here, because it seems like you might be suggesting that only one of us makes a lot of noise in bed."

Jacob wisely wiped the smile off his face. By the look on hers, he wasn't entirely successful.

She yanked off both the cap and the apron and helped herself to a pale blue button-down from his closet. It came to her thighs and she looked just as hot as she had in only her underwear. "Sweats," she demanded.

"Third drawer down." He pointed to his dresser.

"I can't help it if I'm…noisy," she said, helping herself to a pair of dark blue air force sweats that dragged on the floor. She pulled them up with a hip shimmy that made his eyes cross.

"Bella?"

"What?"

"I love the noises you make," he said. "Especially when I'm—"

"Shh!" She rolled the sweats at her waist a handful of times, shot him another indecipherable look and stalked barefoot to the door.

"Where are you going?"

"I promised Willow I'd pick up some supplies and fill a couple of restaurant orders."

"Bella, I don't want you to go into the building—"

"I know. But they have a unit watching the place, and they said it was okay. I'll be very careful. I just have some things to take care of."

"I thought I was one of the things you were going to take care of."

She slid him a bemused look. "Are you saying you need me to stay, or you want me to stay?"

Okay, he knew a trick question when he heard one. Problem was, he didn't know which was the right answer, the one that would have her stepping out of his clothes and sliding into his bed.

And this wasn't about fulfilling a fantasy. He really needed to keep her here so that he would know she was safe. But his mind was fuzzy with meds, and the emotion he'd almost let slip right before Austin had walked in. If his brother hadn't shown up and Jacob had said, "I love you," Bella already would have gone running for the door. And running from him. "Um…"

At his lack of response, something came and went in her eyes, and he got the very bad feeling that he'd somehow hurt her.

"I think Austin can handle anything you need," she said.

"Yeah, but he won't look nearly as good in that apron." Even to his own ears, his words rang hollow. Why couldn't he just say what he was thinking? Jesus, he was pathetic.

She stared at him, then stared at her feet a long moment. "Nice try." Leaning in, she kissed his jaw. "Bye, Jacob."

She was going to walk away, and his heart skipped a beat. "Hey," he said, snagging her hand. "Forget the apron thing. I shouldn't have—"

"It's okay. It's not that."

"Then—"

"Forget it. It's all good." She smiled, but it didn't quite make it to her eyes, and he knew for sure that he'd hurt her.

Dammit. "Wait—"

But she was already gone from the room. He lunged out of the bed after her, and gray spots danced in his vision from getting up too fast, dropping him to all fours, where he struggled to stay conscious. It took a long thirty seconds for the spots to fade before he could stagger to his feet. He stumbled down the hall in time to hear a car rev, and whipped his front door open. It wasn't until he felt the chilly morning air that he realized he was naked.

"Hey," Austin said, coming around the corner

from the kitchen. "Do you want eggs— Holy shit, man. Put some clothes on."

"Why did you let her go?"

"Um, because they frown on unlawful detainment in this country?"

"She left upset."

Austin gestured to Jacob's nudity. "Yes, well, have you seen you?"

"Austin?"

"Yeah?"

"Shut up." Jacob took his sorry, naked ass back to bed, where he called Ethan and asked him to double the watch on Edible Bliss. He called Bella, who surprise surprise, didn't pick up. "Please come back out here when you're done," he said to her voice mail. "And call me when you're leaving the shop, okay?" Then he laid back down, pensive and unsettled, knowing he'd in all likelihood just ruined the best thing that had ever happened to him.

Bella was dropping off the supplies in the shop's kitchen when Willow came in. "Honey, you should be playing doctor with Sexy Cop."

"I wanted to get us set up for when we reopen."

"Or you wanted to outrun your guilt."

"How do you know I feel guilty?"

"Honey."

Bella shook her head. "It's not that. I mean, I

feel…" She closed her eyes. "I am devastated over the shootings, but I know it's not my fault. I'm—"

Willow raised a brow.

And Bella let out a long breath. "I'm in this fight with myself. My head and gut are telling me to go, to leave town and move on, but—"

"But your heart is telling you to stick."

"I don't know." Bella had to purposely draw in another breath and let it out again. "Maybe. A little. Santa Rey was supposed to be nothing more than a pin on my map. A quick stop. But—"

"But you want to grow roots."

Bella had to smile. "I like the finishing-my-sentences thing."

"Yeah? See if you can finish this one for me. You're in the shop, worried about my business, maybe risking your life to be here instead of nursing your man because…?"

"Because he's *not* my man. Because he doesn't know what he wants. I mean, he wants me, but he doesn't *want* me."

"Huh?"

Bella rolled her eyes. "Forget it. Even I don't understand me."

"Hey, I saw him kiss you. Lord, I need a cold shower every time I think about it. Yeah, he wants you bad, but it's more than lust. You're not alone in this."

Bella wanted Willow to be right, but the fear of

not being loved and accepted was an old one. Logic didn't seem to be able to make a dent against it. Hell, even stone-hard facts didn't have a chance against an irrational decades-old fear like hers.

Willow helped her put things away. Afterward, the cop on duty escorted Willow to her car where she planned on heading to her mom's, with Bella agreeing to follow as soon as she put a bag together.

The cop then escorted Bella upstairs, where she took a quick moment to grab her mail, going still when she came to a plain piece of paper, folded in thirds.

"What?" the cop said.

Silent, she handed him the note.

I am the man for you. The others will be eliminated one by one.
Your cop is up next.

"Shit," the officer said, and pulled out his cell phone.

Bella allowed herself a moment of panic, a full sixty seconds, before she grabbed her purse and keys.

"No, no one's come or gone that shouldn't be here," the cop was saying into his phone. When he'd disconnected, he walked Bella to her car, his gaze vigilant and alert. "Where are you going?" he asked her.

She sighed. The only place she'd probably ever

intended to end up tonight, in spite of the fact that she had no idea why he wanted her there. And at the moment, none of that mattered. The note had been a clear warning—he was in danger.

Because of her. "Jacob's."

He nodded, and as he watched her drive off, pulled out his cell phone again.

On the road, she pulled out her own cell phone and called Jacob.

"Jesus," he said in clear relief. "I just heard from Ethan, and I've been going nuts."

"I had protection."

"Yes, but I still want you out of the apartment," he said in an unmistakable demand.

"Already ahead of you."

In the following beat of silence she could hear his anger that she'd left her protection behind. "Where are you? I'll call an escort—"

"I'm halfway there. I'm on Highway 1 already."

"Jesus, you must be flying."

"Do you have a squad car there? Are you protected?"

"Yes." His voice softened. "It's going to be okay, Bella."

"The eliminating part," she managed to say. "That's a little troublesome."

"We'll protect them."

"You," she said, throat tight. "I'm worried about

you, Jacob. And here I am, on my way to your house, maybe leading someone right to you." Oh, God.

She looked in her rearview mirror. Light traffic.

No way to tell if anyone was following her. "I can't do this. I'm not coming to you."

"Yes, you are," he said in that same calm, even voice, and only because she knew him did she hear the undertone of anger and worry.

For her. "Jacob—"

"Listen to me. If you don't come here, I'm going to get on my motorcycle to come get you, and I'm on narcotics, Bella. It won't be pretty." He softened his voice. "Please. Please come here. *Now.*"

Okay, so the domineering "now" ruined the "please" but she nodded. She would do as he asked, and once again she'd be with him, spend time with him—not because he *wanted* her to come and stay, but because his sense of protectiveness insisted on it.

Fifteen minutes later, she pulled up his driveway and parked next to the squad car already parked there. She saw Jacob move away from where he'd been talking to his protection. She got a quick glimpse of faded Levi's low on his hips, the splint and nothing else as she opened her car door.

And then he was right there, pulling her in close against that bare, warm chest. His good arm tightened around her, his warm lips brushing her temple. "You're safe now, Bella. I've got you."

She slid her arms around his waist and felt the

reassuring bulk of his gun in the back of his waist-band. "It's you I'm worried about."

"I'm safe, too."

Yes. Yes, he was, and she sucked in air for the first time since she'd found the note, rubbing her cheek over a hard pec. Melting into him, she let the rest of the world slip away, leaning forward until her head was tucked under his chin.

She was safe in his arms.

Or at least her body was.

She just wasn't nearly so sure about her heart.

Chapter 14

Ethan met them at Jacob's house, and took the note for evidence. Bella called Willow, to tell her about the latest development, and discovered her boss had gone to Trevor's instead because her mother had been hosting bingo for thirty-five seniors. Trevor got on the phone and told Bella to come, as well, but she said she was fine where she was for the night.

And then hoped that was true.

Jacob had left her alone in the living room to give her privacy for her calls, and done with them now, she went to the kitchen. There she grabbed Jacob's pain pills and a glass of water, because she hadn't missed how pale and shaky he'd seemed during the meeting with Ethan, but when she moved down the hall to his bedroom, it was empty.

The bathroom door was open, and the shower was running. She stepped into the steamy room, and thanks to the glass tub enclosure, had a perfect view.

Jacob stood facing the water, his good arm straight out in front of him, braced on the tile, head bent so that the water beat down on his shoulders and back.

"What are you doing?"

He lifted his head. "Cleaning up."

"You'll get your bandage wet."

"It has to be changed anyway."

He reached for the shampoo, and she didn't miss his wince. "Wait." Peeling off her clothes, she stepped into the tub and met his hot, hot gaze.

"That should have been on my fantasy list," he said.

"What?"

"Watching you strip."

"Do you ever think of anything besides me naked?"

He smiled. "I think of me naked, with you."

"Turn and face the water, perv, I'll help you soap up."

When he turned, she wrapped her arms around him from behind, and then, because she couldn't resist, kissed first his good shoulder, and then moved to the other, kissing all around the edge of his bandaging. When she got to the center of his back and pressed her lips to his spine, he sucked in a breath and dropped his head forward with a moan for more.

Pouring some shower gel into her hands, she pressed her body against his so that there wasn't a breath of space between them, and ran her soapy hands over his chest, his abs, and then guiding her fingers downward, wrapped them around his erection.

Another rough groan escaped him and he leaned back into her. "God, Bella."

Her mouth continued to skim over his spine as she stroked the length of him in her slicked-up fingers, apparently applying just the right amount of pressure, because he actually whimpered.

"Okay?" she whispered, sliding her other hand down the front of a rock-hard thigh, then up again to cup him, gently squeezing.

"Christ." His voice was thick and husky. "If I was any more okay, I'd be a puddle on the tile at your feet." He covered her hand with his and stroked himself along with her, showing her how hard he liked it. After a minute, he groaned and pulled away. "Stop," he gasped. "I'm going to come if you keep that up."

She peered around his arm to take in the sight of him fully aroused, wet and glistening, and her mouth actually watered. "Sit."

"What?"

She pushed him down to the tub ledge along the back, then straddled his legs and kissed him.

Gripping her hip with his good hand, he dived

into the kiss, taking her mouth roughly, stroking her tongue with his while his one hand ran feverishly over her, gliding over her breasts, cupping and squeezing her ass. "You feel so good," he murmured against her wet skin. Dipping his head, he pulled a nipple into his mouth at the same time his thumb stroked between her thighs, directly over ground zero, and that was it for her.

In that moment, she didn't care what this was, or why she was trying to hold back.

She needed him.

"Inside me," she gasped.

"But you're not ready—"

"I was ready before I even got here." Lifting up, she slid herself down onto his hard, throbbing length all in one motion, fully seating him deep within her.

"Oh, Christ, Bella."

Her body clenched hard, making him groan again.

"Condom," he groaned.

"It's the wrong time of the month." Then she gave him the line he'd so often given her. "It should be okay." She listened to the sound of his quickened breathing, loving how his arm tightened on her as he kissed her throat, a breast, licking his tongue over her nipple as he thrust up within her.

Her arms tightened on him, too, and she shifted restlessly, feeling filled, feeling desperate, feeling so hungry and achy, *needing* him—

Needing.

God, she was half out of her mind with the need, and also halfway to heaven, and only partially aware that she was spreading hot, desperate kisses over his neck in tune to the hot, desperate words she was whispering, "Don't stop, Jacob. Please, don't stop loving me..."

"I won't," he swore, wrapping his good arm solidly around her back as he began to move, flexing his hips, doing his best to meet her thrust for thrust as he kissed, bit and sucked the skin of her neck and throat, all of it turning her on all the more, as if she needed to be any more turned on.

"God, Bella." He paused to devour her mouth again, his tongue tangling with hers. "You're so wet, so tight." He was looking into her eyes, holding her gaze prisoner, and she couldn't look away, didn't want to.

"Mine," she thought he whispered, but then she burst and could hear nothing but the blood rushing through her head and the faint guttural sound of Jacob's rough groan as he came, his entire body contracting with hers, taking her over the edge yet again in a longer, protracted orgasm she wasn't sure she'd survive. Then his mouth touched hers, sharing air, sharing everything he had, and there were no more thoughts.

For a week nothing more happened on the case. No shootings, no notes, nothing out of the ordinary.

The men on Bella's date list were still watched and protected to the best of the P.D.'s ability, but every day that passed seemed to drain some of the urgency away.

Not Jacob. He remained frustrated and worried about Bella's safety, especially given that his shooting arm was, well, shot.

But he was glad for the reprieve from more death and mayhem. It gave him time to obsess over whatever he'd done to make Bella pull back.

Not physically.

Physically, they were still setting records for condom usage and the number of times they could drive each other insane in bed.

And out of it.

But emotionally...emotionally Bella had changed, albeit so slightly it was hard to be sure. Still, ever since that day after his shooting, when Austin had walked in on them, she hadn't been quite as open, quite as...his.

And nothing he did seemed to bring her back. The only time she allowed any kind of connection with him was when they were making love. And that should have been enough.

But it wasn't.

Another adjustment was the whole being off work. For the first time in years, he wasn't working 24/7, and he...liked it.

He liked it a lot.

He liked having free time, which he did his best to spend with Bella. She and Willow were determined to reclaim Edible Bliss and get over the shootings, and their customer base was slowly returning, but when she wasn't toiling away in the kitchen, she came out to be with him.

He'd played the injured-patient card for the first few days, and had indeed coaxed a Nurse Bella out of the deal. And then, though he was up and about, he managed to still need her help with as many tasks that involved dressing and undressing as possible.

She'd been game.

So maybe he'd imagined the other, the slight pulling back. Maybe it was just her way of keeping it "casual" like they'd agreed.

If so, he had to respect that.

And so it was that one week after getting shot, he'd conned Austin into bringing Shenanigans takeout for him and Bella. She was due off work any time, and had said she'd drive over.

He'd have preferred to take her out in person. Maybe for paddle boarding, or kayaking. Or a ride on his bike.

Something wild and fun and adventurous.

But he was still so limited. The shoulder was healing, but slowly, *painfully* slowly. He'd started physical therapy, except it would be a month yet before he had full movement.

At least his doctor had promised to clear him back to desk duty next week.

Woo-hoo. Desk duty. He could hardly wait.

Austin let himself in and set down the bag in the kitchen. "Where's the wife?"

"Funny."

"No, what's funny is that you think I'm kidding."

Jacob pulled out the containers of food and…a couple of X-rated magazines. He slid a look at Austin.

"What? You're married, not dead."

"Will you stop with the married thing? We're just…seeing each other."

Austin snorted.

"What?"

"Jacob, she has a drawer of her stuff in your bathroom."

"So?"

"So when a woman has a drawer in a guy's house, it's *not* casual."

"It's just while I'm recuperating."

"Really? So when you're back to work, you're going to tell her the license for the drawer is revoked?"

Jacob opened his mouth, and then shut it.

Shit.

He hadn't thought of it like that. Hell, he'd not thought of it at all.

"Look," Austin said, taking pity on him. "As a

cop, you're careful, methodical. It's what makes you so great at the work. But you suck at the real-life shit."

"I do not."

"Real-life shit can't be run off a careful, methodical plan of attack, man. Or by the book. Sometimes you have to wing it. Sometimes you have to go with the flow."

"I can go with the flow as good as the next guy."

Austin wasn't buying it. "Going with the flow would mean accepting that Bella isn't just a casual fling. That things have changed, and you want more with her."

"More doesn't work out for me, remember?"

"Yeah, but that was when you were with the wrong women, and when you were just a badass detective and nothing else."

"What are you talking about? I'm still a detective."

Austin eyed Jacob's board shorts, which was all he was wearing. "No, now you're also part beach bum apparently. Maybe *that* guy could go for more and keep it."

"Would you quit it already. We're just messing around." There wasn't more, there couldn't be, even if he sometimes lately found himself wishing for it. No woman in her right mind would want more from a cop, and he knew this from personal experience.

"Hey, guys."

They both whipped around to find Bella in the doorway.

"Didn't mean to startle you," she said. "I knocked, but no one answered."

As usual, she was a sight for sore eyes. She wore a knit top that crisscrossed her breasts and was the color of her eyes, with a short denim skirt that made the best of her mouthwatering legs. Jacob headed for her, pulling her in, pressing his mouth to her jaw, then her lips, and though she met his kiss, it seemed devoid of its usual wattage. "You okay?" he asked, running his good hand down her arm.

"Always."

"You kids enjoy," Austin said, and pulled Jacob away from Bella in the guise of giving him a brotherly noogie. "You might want to explain that 'just messing around' comment to her," he whispered.

But Jacob knew that no explanation was necessary, not for Bella, who'd set the rules herself. He shoved Austin out the door and smiled at Bella. "Hungry?"

Her gaze met his, a little too shuttered for his liking, but she was smiling warmly and was clearly happy to see him. "Starving," she murmured.

When Bella opened her eyes a few hours later, it was ten o'clock at night and the sun was long gone. Jacob was asleep beside her, both of them naked.

They were sideways in his bed, blankets and sheets long ago tossed to the floor.

Jacob was on his back, his good arm being used as her pillow. She'd thrown a leg over him and had drooled on his chest. Carefully she untangled herself, rolled off the bed and began to search out the various articles of clothing that had been strewn around the room.

Jacob had been right. He was recovering nicely, and had proven it.

Three times.

She slipped into her clothes, grabbed her sandals, and tiptoed to the bedroom door.

"Hey."

With a grimace, she plastered on a smile and only when she was sure it was light and casual—God, how she'd grown to hate that word—did she turn. "Hey."

Sprawled out, lit only by the moonlight slanting in his window, Jacob sent her a lazy smile, a wicked smile, the kind that suggested maybe a late-night snack to regain some strength, and then another heart-stopping round of naked fun. "Where're you going?"

She hesitated. "I thought I'd stay at Willow's mom's tonight."

"Bella, it's late. I don't want you driving back into town now."

Then ask me to stay...

"Stay," he said.

Oh, God. Her heart actually skipped a beat as hope and affection and something far trickier all tangled for space in her heart, which had just lodged itself in her throat. She held her breath and moved closer to the bed. "Why?" she whispered.

"I just said why, it's late."

Disappointment nearly choked her. No worries. She'd go home and drown it out with chocolate. "I have to get up early anyway, and you don't. You need your rest."

He sat up, the muscles in his abs crunching.

God, he was beautiful. It wasn't fair just how beautiful, and with a sigh, she leaned in to kiss him.

She couldn't help herself.

He cupped the back of her head and deepened the kiss, fisting his hand in her hair, pressing her in toward him until she began to melt.

She knew what would come next.

Her clothes would fall away again and then he'd put that mouth on her, that talented, greedy, knowing mouth, and she'd never leave.

She'd never want to.

Which was why she was going, dammit. Sleeping with him was doing something to her, making her want things she had no business wanting, not from him. Knowing it, she forced herself to pull away, forced her hands into her pockets and her eyes off his. "If you keep that up," she quipped, "I'll never go."

"Maybe you've discovered my evil plan," he murmured, his naked body calling to hers.

Maybe, he'd said.

Did that mean he wasn't certain? She wasn't sure, but it sounded to her like he wasn't ready to admit that he wanted her to stay. Not because he needed help, not because she was in danger, but because he wanted *her*.

That settled her mind as nothing else could have.

Dammit.

It was her hang-up, not his, but she couldn't ignore it. Not when her flight reflex was suddenly screaming. At the door, she turned back to look at him, and found his dark eyes on hers, silent and assessing. Her throat tightened, her eyes burned. "I'll see you later," she said, and left before he could touch her again with his magic body and change her mind.

Chapter 15

They did a wash and repeat for three days, with Bella coming over to Jacob's after work, and then leaving late at night.

There'd been no more shootings and though Edible Bliss hadn't reopened to the public, they were still operating the kitchen for their direct-to-restaurant customers. Willow was back in her apartment, being watched over by the cops, but she'd asked Bella to be around whenever possible.

Which is how Jacob once again found himself lying on his bed, watching Bella gather her things to leave. Two minutes ago he'd come so hard he'd been rendered blind, deaf and dumb.

Hell, he still couldn't feel his legs. Somebody had taken out all his bones.

Not Bella. She'd put herself back together with alarming ease.

Jacob didn't move or change his breathing because if he did, he'd sit up and ask—beg—to know why she had to go.

Why she seemed to want his body plenty, but didn't want to sleep with him.

At first, he'd shrugged it off. They'd said casual, and she'd certainly kept it that. Besides, how could he complain? He was getting fantastic, mind-blowing sex without the worry or awkwardness of the morning after.

And given their typical humiliating morning after—what he referred to as the Raspberry Incident came to mind—he should be fine with that.

Which in no way explained why it was bugging the hell out of him. Maybe because it meant he was far more vested in this than she, and he hated that. She was happy enough to see him, hang out with him, he knew this. In fact, she seemed more than happy.

She glowed.

But just how content could she really be if she couldn't wait to leave him at the end of the evening in spite of the looming, omnipresent danger?

There had to be a reason. He just didn't know what. He was missing something, something big. But for two nights in a row, he'd let her go without a word because it was embarrassing that he wanted more than she did, and also because he didn't want the inevitable confrontation that might facilitate their end.

The end of the happiest he'd been in too damn long.

But he couldn't do it any longer, couldn't keep quiet. "Why do you always go?"

She went still for a beat, then turned back from the door. "What?"

"You heard me."

"It's late, Jacob."

"But that's the very reason you should stay."

She was quiet a moment, just looking at him, and he knew right then—he'd most definitely missed something, but hell if he could figure out what. "I'll come with you."

"Not necessary," she said. "I have to get up really early."

It was his turn to be quiet a minute. "Are you afraid to let me go to your place because we haven't caught the shooter?"

"Partly."

"Then stay here."

"Another reason I leave is because I don't live here," she said. "Actually, I don't really live anywhere."

"What does that mean?"

She turned back to the door, which frustrated the

hell out of him because now he couldn't see her face. "It means maybe I've been thinking it's time to move on again."

"You've been thinking about moving on?" Listen to that, listen to him sounding all cool and calm, when he suddenly felt anything but. "Since when?"

"I always think about it."

He pushed off the bed and moved toward her, taking her purse out of her hands, backing her to the wall. "Where will you go this time?"

"Don't know yet."

"Why now?"

"Why not? There's really no reason to stay.…"

He cupped her face with one hand and made her look at him. "No reason?"

"It's not like I have my own shop, or a real relationship. I mean, we're just messing around…"

Jesus. He stared at her, his thoughtless words to Austin coming back to haunt him. *Hello, missing piece to the puzzle.* "You know what I meant by that, right?"

"Yes," she said. "I believe it's fully self-explanatory."

He shook his head as unaccustomed desperation welled up from within him. Not knowing what to do with it, he pressed her against the wall and kissed her. He kissed her until she softened and slid her hands up his chest, around his neck and clung.

He'd never been one to crave physical closeness, but having Bella in his arms suited him.

It suited him a lot.

Only, Bella had changed the rules, the game, *everything,* turning it all upside and sideways on him.

And she was leaving.

Right now, unless he said something to fix it, to bridge the big, gaping hole between them. He opened his mouth and let out the first thing that came to him. "Santa Rey has a lot to offer you. Your pastries are already gaining fame, and Willow told me she suggested you create a Web site. You could go huge, Bella. Right here."

"I don't think this is about my job," she said.

"Is this about *my* job?"

She just looked at him.

Quick, Madden, think quick. "I've never been with a woman who could handle my work."

"A woman who chooses to be in your life should accept you, Jacob, just as you are."

"Should. But they don't. Look at you, running for the door."

"My leaving has nothing to do with your job. Or changing anything about you." She cocked her head and studied him. "Would you ask me to change?"

Would he? Would he get down on bended knee and beg her not to leave here when the time came, simply because he needed her?

"Because I'd never ask you to change who and

what you are, Jacob. Never." With that, she went up on her tiptoes and pressed her mouth to his temple. "'Night."

"Bella—"

"It's late," she murmured, pressing her lips to his other temple, his jaw, and then far too briefly, his lips. "Gotta get some sleep. You're starting work tomorrow, you should get some sleep, too."

And then she was gone.

Two days later, Bella and Willow were just closing up the kitchen when Jacob came in the back door with two cops, one on either side of him. He thanked them and they went back to their perch outside.

One look at Jacob had Bella's heart taking a good, hard leap. She could tell herself that she was good and fine and well with everything that had happened until she was blue in the face.

But she was one big, fancy liar.

She wasn't good and fine, not when every muscle in her body tensed with the urge to run across the kitchen and throw herself at him.

He'd gone back to work, and for two days had been buried under by the backlog, hardly coming up for air. Or so he claimed when he called her at night.

As for her, she'd been…well, she'd been thinking entirely too much.

But no matter how much she'd been remembering and reliving, the reality of Jacob in the flesh was so much more potent than the memories.

He wore a dark suit and tie and his splint, and he looked disturbingly...hot.

"Wow," Willow murmured, leaning back against the sink, looking him over with heated eyes. "You clean up nice, Detective."

"Thanks." He didn't take his gaze off Bella. And those eyes were filled with frustration, temper, hunger and so much bafflement that Bella didn't know whether to laugh or get rid of Willow so she could have him right here in the kitchen.

"You hungry?" she asked.

"Yes."

Not for food.

Those words went unspoken, but they shimmered in the air between them.

Willow had a bag of popcorn, her favorite lunch, and was dividing a curious stare between them as if they were the latest number-one movie at the box office.

Finally, Bella looked at her, brow raised.

"Oh!" Willow let out a little laugh and grabbed her purse. "I'm out." She looked back at them. "Don't do anything I wouldn't do and just so you know, that doesn't cover a lot of ground."

Jacob smiled at her, then turned his attention back to Bella, not saying a word, just giving her that look that never failed to make her nipples hard and her panties wet. "So," she murmured. "A suit?"

"I was due in court this morning, had to testify on a case."

"Did it go well?"

"Yes." His eyes never left her face as he reached out and slowly pulled her in. "Missed you, Bella."

Her heart took another hard leap against her ribs. At this rate, she'd be in heart-attack territory in under five minutes. "You did?"

He pressed his forehead to hers. "Yeah. I'm hot and starving. Come with me, let's get a pizza and go to my house. It's going to be a full moon. We can take the horses out on a moonlight ride."

"The moon doesn't come up until late."

He slid her a long look that said *this again?* "So stay, instead of driving back."

Her throat tightened. No. No, dammit. She wasn't going to go through this again. She couldn't. Not when she knew she was hopelessly, pathetically falling for him. "I can't." It took her another extremely long minute—where she pressed her nose into his throat and just inhaled him as if maybe it was going to be the very last time—before she forced herself to pull free. "I can't tonight."

"But—"

"I can't," she repeated. "Listen, I have to go. Let yourself out." And grabbing a wet cloth, left him to go wipe down the tables in the front room, even though they were perfectly clean since they still didn't have walk-in customers.

She ended up just standing there, staring sightlessly at nothing.

When, finally, she heard the back door close, she sagged into a chair and covered her face.

The front door opened and Trevor popped his head in. He was wearing surf shorts and a weatherguard tee, and his usual contagious smile. "Hey, what are you doing? I'm going sailing. Come with, it's gorgeous outside—" He broke off, looking her over. "You okay?"

"Yes."

"Liar." He took the towel out of her hands, crouched at her side and cupped her face. "You know what you need?"

"A one-way ticket to the South Pacific?"

"A sail," he said gently. "With no worries, no plans, nothing but a few waves. Come on, baby, let me show you a good time."

It was such a cheesy line that she managed to laugh, as he'd intended, and he smiled into her face. "Attagirl."

Jacob went home and stared at his empty house. He looked at his living room and pictured Bella standing before the huge windows, eyeing the view. He saw her sitting on the couch with that light of wicked intent in her eyes. He saw her sitting on his kitchen counter.

He couldn't even look at his bed.

Or his shower…

Her presence was here in every room of his house, and in every part of his heart.

He was such an idiot. He wasn't just messing around with her. Why hadn't he told her that?

He could say this was casual until he was blue in the face, he could pretend with the best of them that he was okay with her walking away from Santa Rey, away from him, but he wasn't okay with it and he never would be.

And he owed it to her to at least have the balls to say so.

Undoubtedly, he'd get his stupid heart broken for the effort, but hell if he'd let her go without at least putting it all out there on the line. That decided, he whipped out his cell phone and called her. It went right to voice mail, and he absently rubbed his aching shoulder as he left her a message. "Call me, Bella. I'm coming back to the shop, I need to see you, we need to talk." He paused, wondering if he'd sounded too scary and would maybe cause her to bolt before he could get there. "I told you that I miss you," he said, drawing a deep breath. "But what I should have also said was that I love you." Hoping that would cover everything, he started to close his phone, then added, "I'm on my way. Please—" He closed his eyes. "Please be there."

* * *

Bella's phone was on speaker, so both she and Trevor heard the message.

"Sweet," Trevor said. "A little too little too late, but very sweet."

She was driving, but she took a quick look over at him. How had she never seen the menace just beneath his surface before? And now that she had, how the hell was she going to get out of this without getting hurt? Or worse. "If I don't call him back, he's going to come over."

"Yes. And find you already gone." He affected a regretful expression. "So sad."

"He'll look for me."

"No, he won't. He'll see that your duffel bag is gone—thanks for staying packed, by the way, I've got your bag in my trunk. Face it, Jacob is going to assume you've done what you've been talking about, that you've left town. Which you are doing. He won't try to come after you. He has far too much pride and testosterone for that."

She'd have thought so, too, until that phone call. In his voice had been bare, heart-wrenching emotion.

For her.

"Turn right at the marina, Bella."

She didn't want to.

She wanted to turn left and get back on the freeway and head north to Jacob's house. She wanted to reverse time, to the time before she'd told Jacob to let himself out, the implication being that he should let himself out of her life while he was at it.

She wanted to plant both her feet in the ground and make roots. She wanted to tell him she loved him, too, so very much.

Why hadn't she told him?

"Turn right," Trevor repeated softly, and gestured with the gun he had pointed at her.

She turned right.

Chapter 16

When Jacob got back to the shop, it was empty. He went upstairs and knocked on Bella's door.

Across the narrow hallway, Willow's door opened and she poked her head out. With tears in her eyes, she shook her head. "She's gone."

"What?"

Willow handed him a note. "This was taped to my door."

Thanks, Willow, for the lovely memories. I'll never forget you, but it's time to move on.

Willow sniffed. "Lord, I'm going to miss that girl."

Jacob's heart had pretty much stopped at the "she's gone" but he read the note again, looking at the handwriting. Neat, and legible.

His heart started again, with a dull thudding that echoed in his ears.

"What is it?" Willow asked.

"It isn't Bella's writing." Or if it was, she was trying to tell them something. He ran down the stairs and found Tom in the lot. "Did you see Bella leave?"

"No," Tom said. "I just got here. Hang on, I'll check with Scott, who I relieved." He pulled out his cell.

So did Jacob, and immediately called Ethan. "We have a problem."

"That's okay, being as I'm the solution king today," Ethan said. "Did you know that the marina started fingerprinting people to store their boats? The chief told me just today. He found out when he went to store his new boat. It's a new security system, letting people in the gate by their prints."

"Fascinating, but—"

"So the chief puts his fingerprint in, and starts to think. The first shooting, we found that tread, with the marina sand. We canvassed the docks, all the hotels and motels on the marina, ran the boat owners, and found no one connected to Bella. But the fingerprint list doesn't just include the owners, but anyone they allow to use their boat. I'm only half-way through the log and I've already found two of the Edible Bliss's regular customers, the coffee shop guy who was Bella's fourth date, and her coworker, Trevor Mann."

"Trevor," Jacob repeated slowly, just as Tom hung up his phone.

"Yeah, his stepfather owns a thirty-two-foot Morgan," Ethan said.

"Trevor and Bella left twenty-five minutes ago out the front," Tom reported. "We were watching for unauthorized people going out only—"

"Tom says Bella left with Trevor," Jacob told Ethan. "And there's a note here from her saying she's leaving town."

"On Trevor's sailboat?"

"Doesn't say, but I can tell you if the note was written by Bella, it was written under duress."

There was a beat of silence. "You sure?"

"I'd bet my life on it," Jacob said.

"Okay, so she's a missing person."

"Yeah. I'll meet you at the marina."

Bella watched as the marina came into view, and her stomach cramped. This wasn't going to be good. "I still don't get why you're doing this."

"Don't you?" Trevor asked.

"No!"

"You were meant for me, Bella."

She stared at him. He looked so normal. How could someone who looked so normal be so insane?

"Breathe, Bella," he reminded her gently.

"Look, if we go back now, I'll talk to the police for you. I'll help explain that you need help, and that—"

"I don't need help. I got what I wanted, and that's you." He stroked a finger down her jaw and she shuddered.

"Don't worry," he said very softly. "It's going to be okay."

She sincerely doubted that. She really wished she'd finished those self-defense classes. If she had, she'd probably have been able to come up with a better escape plan then having an overdue panic attack.

"Turn here into the parking lot," Trevor told her.

She wondered if she could slow down enough to jump right out of the car. Maybe. But an older man was walking along the sidewalk. What if she jumped out of the car and it ran him over?

"Ten points for the old guy," Trevor said lightly, a small smile in place.

"You're sick."

"Aw. I'm just a guy in love."

"I'm sorry." She shook her head. "This just doesn't make sense. If you wanted me so badly, why didn't you ask me out?"

"I did."

"No, you joked about it, I never thought you were serious."

"Your mistake."

No kidding! "Why did you stop the shooting spree? You only hit three out of eight."

"I shot Seth because you liked him. A lot."

Oh, God, Bella thought, sorrow nearly choking her.

"I shot B.J. because he kept calling you and asking you out. I tried to shoot Tyler just because he was bugging the shit out of me with all that snooty talk. How could you stand him?"

When she didn't answer, he went on, unperturbed. "None of the others posed a threat until Jacob. Goddamn perfect Jacob."

Bella took her eyes off the road to stare at him with a mirthless laugh. "He only started coming around because you started shooting people! How did you get the information on my eight dates?"

He shrugged. "I know one of the coordinators, and he let me get on his computer to let me do some research. I neglected to tell him the research was you. And later, Jacob."

"Oh, my God. If you would have stayed *sane,* I'd never have seen him again."

"Yeah." Trevor let out a long-suffering sigh. "Maybe I made a mistake there. But it wasn't necessarily *his* feelings for *you* that got him shot." He paused. "It was your feelings for him. With Jacob around, screwing you senseless, you didn't give me the time of day." He looked at her solemnly. "You'll have to forget him now, Bella. He might be the big, strong, silent type, but there's a limit to a guy like that. He'll never be romantic and sweet and loving. I'll be that guy for you, I swear it."

"No, you won't," she told him. "I love him. I love him for exactly who he is. You can kidnap me and force me to be with you—" Only until she got a chance to run like hell. "But I will not stop loving him."

"Yes, you will."

Resisting the urge to thunk her head into the steering wheel and put herself out of her misery, she pulled into the parking lot, brain racing for a plan. Maybe she could keep him talking until…until what? No one was going to save her. She'd been seen leaving with Trevor, who no one had ever considered a threat.

But maybe…maybe if Jacob went back for her like he said and saw the note that Trevor had made her write, maybe he'd realize that she was trying to leave him a clue…

"We're going to go sailing on a nice, long vacation," Trevor said. "And live the way you've always lived, taking each day at a time. It's how you love to do things, right? No ties, no hold to anyone or any place."

That was true, that's how she'd always lived. But that no longer made her happy—not that she planned on sharing that life-altering epiphany with Trevor. "You can't make me stay with you."

"We'll be out on the open sea, you won't have a choice. If we stay out long enough, you'll fall in love with me the way I love you."

The way he loved her was cuckoo crazy, but she kept her mouth shut.

"Park here," he said, pointing to a spot. "Out of the car."

She got out of the car, and extremely aware of the gun, she kept silent.

For now.

Trevor stepped out, as well, his eyes on her. His hand was in his pocket.

On the gun. "Slowly, Bella," he said. "We're going to walk to the building. No funny stuff, we don't want anyone to get hurt."

She bit back a sharp laugh that probably would have sounded hysterical anyway and tried to appeal to reason, assuming he had any left in his addled brain. "Trevor, this is ridiculous. Jacob isn't going to believe I just up and left without a goodbye."

"He'll move on to another woman easily enough. He wasn't looking for anything permanent, remember? You were just a quickie, a one-night stand that extended a few extra nights, that's all."

Only yesterday she might have been willing to believe that, but she'd seen the look in Jacob's eyes this morning. She'd heard it in his voice, and when it counted, he'd given her the words.

He loved her.

"I'm never going to love you, Trevor. I'm going to escape at the first opportunity and you're going to go to jail for murder and attempted murder two times over, not to mention kidnapping."

His jaw tightened. "You need to be quiet now."

"*Murder,* Trevor," she repeated. "You're going to sit in jail and—"

"Christ, I said shut up!" He accompanied this by putting the gun right in her face.

She gulped and closed her mouth, hoping that *someone* would notice the insane guy with the gun, but naturally there wasn't another soul anywhere to be seen.

Trevor shoved his gun back in his pocket and took Bella's hand. "Better. Now we're going to walk into the marina, smile, then get on my boat and sail away. You're going to behave."

"I don't tend to 'behave.'" Well, actually, there'd been that one night, when Jacob had handcuffed her to the bed and they'd spent some fun role-playing bad cop/bad girl, but she was pretty sure that wasn't what Trevor meant.

Surely there would be someone inside that she could recruit to help her…

They walked into the marina building, hand in hand like lovers. The large reception area on the right was filled with open seating facing huge wall-to-wall windows that revealed the docks and the ocean beyond. Another wall was lined with vending machines, and a third was wallpapered with a map of the planet.

The place was empty except for a teenage girl sitting behind the reception desk. She was reading Cosmo and texting at the same time, her thumbs a whirl of motion.

Bella looked at her and felt the first wave of despair. She couldn't involve this girl and risk Trevor getting trigger happy with her, not when he'd proven how easily he could kill.

So Bella said nothing as Trevor pulled her over to the far double glass doors. There, he pressed his thumb to a small screen, and the doors clicked open. "New security," he said proudly, and pulled her through. "You have to be a boat owner or on file as a guest to get to the docks."

Bella dragged her feet along the dock. All she knew was that she didn't want to get on the sailboat. If she did, and Trevor was able to get them out to sea, she was in big trouble. Maybe she could fall into the water, or just start screaming. Or—

"Don't," Trevor said in her ear, his hand gripping hers hard.

"I didn't do anything."

"You're thinking it."

She was. She was also thinking if she shoved him hard enough, he might fall in, and—

"I'll shoot you on my way down."

Yeah. Yeah, he probably would. Note to self: next

time try to wade the psychos out of your friendship pool. "How do you possibly imagine you're going to be able to keep me on the boat?"

His eyes gleamed. "I have my ways."

Oh, good. He had his ways. Lucky her.

"Don't forget, Bella. You *will* behave."

Uh-huh. She'd get right on that.

His Morgan sailboat was in the sixth of eight slots, with the last two being empty. No help there. It was blue and white with teakwood trim, and looked well loved and cared for.

"Home sweet home," Trevor said.

She eyed the door that led to belowdecks, where there was undoubtedly a place he planned on restraining her. Her stomach cramped at the thought.

Now or never, Bella...

"Get on," Trevor said.

Stall. Run. Make a scene! "I'm hungry," she said, albeit a little wildly. "We should go back and get some food—"

"Get on *now.*"

"But we need—"

"I have everything you'll ever need, Bella. Trust me."

Like hell. "I need sunscreen—50 SPF. I bet you didn't get 50 SPF—"

"Get. On."

He added a little shove to this command and it was either fall into the water or board.

She took a big gulp of air, hoped a bullet couldn't travel through water—probably if she'd paid better attention in high school physics class she might know this—and jumped off the dock.

Jacob made it to the marina in five minutes by running just about every red light and hitting Highway 1 at seventy-five miles per hour.

When he pulled into the parking lot, Ethan was just getting out of his car, and they met up with a handful of others led by Ramon Castillo.

"Trevor Mann's boat is in slip D06," Ethan told them, consulting his pad.

The marina was large, and had five rows of docking that stretched into the bay like fingers. There were hundreds of boats, but not nearly as many people—the place looked completely deserted.

As they stormed their way into the building toward the docks, a shot rang out in the air, echoing over the water.

Chapter 17

The moment Bella plunged into the water, she heard the shot ring out, and involuntarily screamed.

Not a good idea underwater.

She inhaled a cold lungful and promptly choked, forcing her back to the surface. She gasped quickly and plunged beneath again, bumping hard into the hull of the boat and knocking the air right out of herself. *Good going, Bella. You get away from the crazy stalker and then try to help him kill you.*

Still beneath the water, she struggled with the strong urge to kick to the surface again, and just before she had to have air, someone splashed into the water next to her. Propelled by the momentum, again she hit the hull, hard. She didn't scream this time, she didn't have the air left. And she had even less when two hands grabbed her.

Trevor.

Oh, no. Hell, no. In that moment, her fear was replaced by fury. Because of Trevor, Jacob would think she'd run away, think she was yet another woman who didn't believe he was worth fighting for. Because of Trevor, Willow would accept her skipping out as just part of her pattern. Because of Trevor, her chance to change had been taken away from her.

So she fought back. Reaching up, she closed her hands around his throat, squeezing as hard as she could, which wasn't hard enough.

She was too weak, and this wasn't going to work. Frustrated, she shoved him, trying to swim away down the narrow space between the slip and the boat.

She heard a dull thud. Trevor's hands fell from her neck, but before she could assimilate that, two more hands grabbed her and hauled her up to the surface.

She came up swinging, and managed to get in a good punch to the gut.

"Shit!" said someone who definitely wasn't Trevor.

Yet another set of arms slipped around her. "I've got her."

This voice she knew, and immediately she relaxed into the hard wall of muscle. *"Jacob."*

He hauled her in close, holding her above water. "I've got you, Bella. You're safe."

She always was safe with him, she thought, blinking water out of her eyes as he lifted her up to someone on the dock already reaching for her.

Ethan.

He set her down but her knees were weak and she dropped to them. Directly in front of them was Trevor, facedown and being cuffed by a handful of uniformed men. He had blood flowing from a gash on the back of his head.

"You knocked him off me." She coughed as Jacob was pulling up out of the water.

"No." He dropped to his knees in front of her, running his hands over her as if he needed to make sure for himself that she was okay. "That was all you. You smashed his head against the concrete pillar under the dock. Nice going, by the way."

She stared at the boat that Trevor had planned to force her onto, the water she'd been pulled out of and then into Jacob's eyes.

"You did amazing," he said softly, taking a blanket from a uniformed officer and tugging it around her shoulders. "You were in a bad situation and you kept your head. I'm so proud of you, Bella."

The words bathed her in desperately needed warmth. Weak and shaking from the adrenaline letdown, she dropped her head to his shoulder. She'd barely dragged in a breath before he wrapped his arms around her hard and shuddered. "I thought I'd lost you. I don't want to ever lose you."

"I wasn't leaving. Not willingly anyway." She lifted her head, needing to see his face. "I didn't want to leave you, Jacob. I know I was sending mixed signals, but that's because I didn't want to push you into this. I thought you weren't ready, that you needed more time."

He shook his head. "I don't need more time. I love you, Bella."

"I love you, too," she whispered. She hadn't gotten the words out before he lowered his head and kissed her.

An EMT dropped beside them with his med kit. "She needs to be checked out, looks like she hit her head, too."

Yeah. Now that he mentioned it, she was feeling a little dizzy...

Jacob looked deep into her eyes, his clouded with worry. "Stay with me," he said, repeating her words from when he'd been shot back to her.

"I'm okay," she promised. "I'm not going to faint."

His laugh was nothing more than a breath against her temple. "I meant here. With me. Stay here with me. Because I want you with me more than anything else."

"You mean, here in Santa Rey?"

"In Australia. In goddamn Timbuktu. I don't care where, as long as we're in the same place."

The warmth from the blanket and his own body continued to seep into her, but the warmth from his words penetrated even deeper, heating her from the inside out. "Yes, I'll stay," she breathed. "For as long as you want me."

His smile spread across his face. "That's going to be a while. Forever a while."

"I can't think of anything I could want more."

* * * * *

Dear Reader,

Have you ever sent an email or text to the wrong person by accident? I have, and let me assure you, it is alarmingly easy to do. One of my errors was inadvertently emailing a joke to someone in senior management who truly didn't appreciate it and who had no compunction in letting me, my boss and the rest of my department know. Ouch!

In *Blame It on the Bikini*, Mya's mistake was to text a joke picture of herself wearing a "never-in-a-million-years" bikini to her best friend's brother, Brad. Unfortunately he's the guy she's harbored a crush on for years, but he's never so much as glanced at her. Until now.

Yet somehow Brad giving her that look only *after* she accidentally flashes him so much skin doesn't endear him to her. Yeah, Brad is going to have to work for it now....

I loved writing Brad and Mya's story, and feeling the sparks from their sometimes fierce, sometimes funny interaction. Having a heroine try so very hard to hold her own against a superwicked playboy shark was great fun! But both of them, like all of us, make mistakes. And sometimes a wrongly sent text is just the beginning....

I do hope you enjoy *Blame It on the Bikini,* and if you ever want to share your own email/internet/text snafu, do get in touch with me: natalie@natalie-anderson.com—I love to hear from readers!

Natalie Anderson

BLAME IT ON THE BIKINI

USA TODAY Bestselling Author

Natalie Anderson

For Dave, Dave and Gungy:

Thank you so much for giving up your time to help construct "The Plotting Shed"—

I can't tell you how fabulous that room of my own is. Thank you!

Chapter 1

Can I get away with it?

It was harder than you'd think to take a picture of yourself in a small, enclosed space wearing nothing but a bikini. Biting back the giggle, Mya Campbell peered at her latest effort. The flash had created a big white space over at least half the screen, obscuring most of her reflection, and what you could see was more dork than glam.

With a muffled snort—a combination of frustration and laughter—she deleted it and twisted in front of the mirror, trying for another. Her teeth pinched her lower lip as she glanced at the result—maybe the skinny-straps scarlet number was a step too far?

"Is everything okay?" the clearly suspicious sales assistant called through the curtain, her iced tone snootier than her brittle perfect appearance.

"Fine, thanks." Mya fumbled, quickly taking another snap before the woman yanked back the curtain. She needed to get it away before being— ah—busted.

Both she and the assistant knew she couldn't afford any of these astronomically priced designer swimsuits. But that long-suppressed imp inside her liked a dress-up and it had been so long and if she were to have such a thing as a summer holiday, then she'd really love one of these little, very little things…

Giggles erupted as she tried to send the text. Her fingertips slipped she shook so hard. She was such an idiot. Typos abounded and she tapped faster as she heard the assistant return.

"Are you sure you don't need any help?"

She needed help all right. Professional help from those people in white coats. Too late now, the soft whooshing sound confirmed her message had gone. And she couldn't afford this scrap of spandex anyway.

"Thanks, but no, I don't think this style is really me." Of course it wasn't. She tossed the phone into her open bag on the floor and began the contortions required to get out of the tiny bikini. She caught a glimpse of herself bent double and at that point she blushed. The bikini was basically indecent. Would she never learn that bodies like hers were not built for tiny two pieces? She'd bend to pull off her shoes at the beach and instantly fall out of a top like this. Not remotely useful for swimming. She'd have to lie still and pose, and that just wasn't her. Mind you, a summer holiday wasn't for her this year either.

And never in a million years would she send such a picture to anyone other than her best friend and all-around pain in the butt, Lauren Davenport. But Lauren would understand—and Mya didn't need her answer now. It was a "no" already.

Brad Davenport looked at his watch and stifled the growl of frustration. He'd had back-to-back cases in court all day, followed by this meeting that had gone on over an hour too long. He watched the bitterness between the parents, watched eleven-year-old Gage Simmons seated next to him shrivel into a smaller and smaller ball as accusations were hurled from either side of the room. The boy's parents were more interested in taking pieces out of each other and blocking each other instead of thinking about what might be best for their son. And finally Brad's legendary patience snapped.

"I think we can leave this for now," he interrupted abruptly. "My client needs a break. We'll reschedule for later in the week."

He glanced around the room and the other lawyers nodded. Then he glanced at the kid, who was looking at the floor with a blank-slate expression. He'd seen it many times, had worn it himself many times—withdrawing, not showing anyone how much you hurt inside.

Yeah, it wasn't only his client who needed a break. But Brad's burden was his own fault. He'd taken on too many cases. Brad Davenport definitely had a problem saying no.

Twenty minutes later he carried the bag full of files out to his car and considered the evening ahead. He needed a blowout—some all-physical pleasure to help him relax, because right now the arguments still circled in his head. Questions he needed to ask and answer lit up like blindingly bright signs; every item on his to-do list shouted at him megaphone-style. Yeah, his head hurt. He reached for his phone and took it off mute, ready to find an energetic date for the night—someone willing, wild and happy to walk away when the fun was done.

There were a couple of voice messages, more emails, a collection of texts—including one with an attachment from a number he didn't recognise. He tapped it.

Can I get away with it?

He absorbed that accompanying message by a weird kind of osmosis, because the picture itself consumed all his attention. He could see only the side of her face, only half her smile, but that didn't matter—

he was a man and there were curves in the centre of the screen. Creamy, plump breasts pushed up out of the do-me-now-or-die scarlet bra she'd squeezed into. Brad swore in amazement, his skin burning all over in immediate response. The picture cut off beneath her belly button—damn it—but he really couldn't complain. Her breasts were outstanding—lush curves that made him think…think… Actually no, he'd lost all ability to *think*.

Can I get away with it?

This doll could get away with anything she wanted.

Startled, but happily so, he slid his fingers across the screen to zoom the picture, adjusting it so it was her partially exposed face he focused on now. She was smiling as if she was only just holding back the sexiest of laughs.

Brad stilled, his heart hiccupping as disbelief stole a beat. There was only one person in the world with a smile like that. Slowly he traced her lips. Her upper lip was sensual—widening, just as the bone structure of her face widened to those sharp, high cheekbones and wide-set green eyes while her lower lip was as full, but shorter; it had to be to fit with that narrow little chin. And between those slightly mismatched lips was that telltale gap between her two front teeth. It had never been fixed. Her whole body was untainted by cosmetic procedures, indeed any kind of cosmetics.

Mya Campbell. Best friend of his wayward sister, Lauren, and persona non grata at the Davenport residence.

In that minute that Brad thought about her—the longest stretch of time he'd *ever* thought about her—a few images from the past decade haphazardly flashed through his head. Glimpses of a girl who'd been around the house often enough, but who'd hidden away whenever he or his parents were home. Who could blame her? His parents had been unwelcoming and patronising. Which of course had made Lauren push the friendship all the more. And Mya had come across as less than impressed with those in authority and less than interested in abiding by any of the normal social rules. The two of them had looked like absolute terrors. And the irony was that Mya was the most academically brilliant student in the school. An uber-geek beneath the attitude and the outrageous outfits. That was why she was *at* the school; she was the scholarship kid.

He'd only ever seen her dressed up "properly" the once. She'd still looked sullen, exuding a kind of "cooler-than-you" arrogance, and frankly at the time he'd been otherwise distracted by a far friendlier girl. But now he saw the all-grown-up sensuality. Now he saw the humour that he'd heard often enough but never been privy to—never been interested enough to want to be privy to. Now he saw what she'd been hiding all this time. Now the heat shot to his groin in a stab so severe he flinched. And she'd sent him…?

No. He laughed aloud at the ridiculous thought. Mya Campbell had *not* just sent him a sexy summons. She didn't even know he existed—other than as her best friend's big, distant brother. Hell, he hadn't seen her in, what, at least three years? He tapped the screen to bring it back to normal—correction, completely amazing—view. No, this playful pose wasn't for him. Which meant that certified genius Mya Campbell had actually made a mistake for once in her life. What was he going to do about it? Crucially, where was Mya now?

Questions pounded his head again, but this time they caused anticipation rather than a headache. He tossed the phone onto the passenger seat of his convertible, ignoring every other message. He put his sunglasses on, stress gone, and fired the engine. Now the night beckoned with a very amusing intrigue to unravel.

Can I get away with it?

Not this time.

The music was so loud Mya could feel the vibrations through her feet—which was saying something given her shoes had two and a half inches of sole. But she was used to the volume and she had enough experience to lip-read the orders well enough now. Shifts six days a week in one of the hottest bars in town had her able to work fast and efficient. The way she always worked. No matter what she was doing, Mya Campbell was driven to be the best.

Her phone sat snug against her thigh in the side pocket of her skinny jeans, switched to mute so it didn't interrupt her shift. The duty manager, Drew, frowned on them texting or taking calls behind the bar. Fair enough. They were too busy anyway. So she had no idea whether Lauren had got the pic or what she'd thought of it. Though, given Lauren was welded to her mobile, Mya figured there'd be an answer when she got a spare second to check. She grinned as she lined twelve shiny new shot glasses on the polished bar, thinking of Lauren's face when she saw it. She'd be appalled—she'd always shrieked over Mya's more outrageous "statement" outfits.

"Come on, gorgeous, show us your stuff!"

Mya glanced up at the bunch of guys crowded round her end of the bar. A stag party, they'd insisted she pour the trick shots for them, not her sidekick, Jonny, down the other end of the bar. She didn't get big-headed about it—truth was Jonny had taught her the tricks and she was still working towards acing him on them. It was just these guys wanted the female factor.

She'd mixed three for them already and now was onto the finale. She enjoyed it—nothing like lighting up a dozen flaming sambucas for a bunch of wild boys who were megaphone loud in their appreciation.

She flicked her wrist and poured the liquid—a running stream into each glass. Then she met the eyes of the groom and flashed him a smile.

"Are you ready?" she teased lightly.

The guys nodded and cheered in unison.

She held the lighter to the first shot glass and gently blew, igniting the rest of the line of glasses down the bar. The cheers erupted. She glanced at Jonny and winked. She'd only recently mastered that one, and she knew he was standing right where one of the fire extinguishers was kept.

Grinning, she watched them knock the shots back and slam the glasses onto the bar. Some barracked for more but she already knew the best man had other ideas. Her part in their debauched night was over; they were onto their next destination—she didn't really want to know where or how much further downhill they were going to slide.

"A thank-you kiss!" one of the guys called. "Kiss! Kiss!"

They all chanted.

Mya just held up the lighter and flicked it so the flame shot up. She waved it slowly back and forth in front of her face. "I wouldn't want you to get hurt," she said with a teasing tilt of her head.

They howled and hissed like water hitting a burning element. Laughing—mostly in relief now—she watched them mobilise and work their way to the door. And that was when she saw him.

Brad *High-School-Crush* Davenport.

For a second, shock slackened every muscle and she dropped the lighter. Grasping at the last moment to stop it slipping, she accidentally caught the hot end. *Damn.* She tossed it onto the shelf below the bar and rubbed the palm of her hand on the half-apron tied round her waist. The sharp sting of that small patch of skin didn't stop her from staring spellbound schoolgirl-fashion at her former *HSC*. But that was because he was staring right at her as if she were the one and only reason he'd walked into the bar.

Good grief. She tried to stop the burn spreading to her belly because it wasn't right that one look could ignite such a reaction in her.

Back in the days when she'd believed in fairy tales, she'd also believed Brad would have been her perfect prince. Now she knew so much better: a) there were no princes, b) even if there were, she had no need for a prince and c) Brad Davenport was nowhere near perfect.

Although to be fair, he certainly looked it. Now—impossible though it might be—he looked more perfect than ever. All six feet three and a half inches of him. She knew about the half because it was written in pencil on the door-jamb in the kitchen leading to the butler's sink, along with Lauren's height and those of their mum and dad—one of the displays of Happy Familydom his mother had cultivated.

Topping the modelicious height, his dark brown

hair was neatly trimmed, giving him a clean-cut, good-boy look. He was anything but good. Then there were the eyes—light brown maple-syrup eyes, with that irresistible golden tinge to them. With a single look that he'd perfected at an eyebrow-raising young age, he could get any woman to beg him to pour it all over her.

And Brad obliged. The guy had had more girlfriends than Mya had worked overtime hours. And Mya had done nothing but work since she'd badgered the local shop owner into letting her do deliveries when she was nine years old.

She tried to move but some trickster had concreted her feet to the floor. She kept staring as he walked through the bar, and with every step he came closer, her temperature lifted another degree. This despite the air-conditioning unit blasting just above the bar.

He was one of those people for whom the crowds parted, as if an invisible bulldozer were clearing the space just ahead of him. It wasn't just his height, not just his conventionally handsome face with its perfect symmetry and toothpaste-advertisement teeth, but his demeanour. He had the *presence* thing down pat. No wonder he won every case he took on. People paid attention to him whether they wanted to or not. Right now Mya wasn't the only person staring. Peripheral vision told her every woman in the bar was; so were most of the men.

She needed to pull it together. She wasn't going to be yet another woman who rolled over and begged for Brad Davenport—even if he was giving her that *look*. But why was he giving *her* that look? He'd never looked at her like that before; in fact he'd never really looked at her at all.

Her heart raced the way it did before an exam when she was in mid *"OMG I've forgotten everything"* panic. Had she entered a parallel universe and somehow turned sixteen all over again?

"Hi, Brad." She forced a normal greeting as he stepped up to the space the stag boys had left at the bar.

"Hi, Mya." He mirrored her casual tone—only his was genuine whereas hers was breathless fakery.

It was so unfair that the guy had been blessed with such gorgeousness. In the attractiveness exam of life, Brad scored in the top point five per cent. But it— and other blessings from birth—had utterly spoilt him. Despite her knowing this, the maple-syrup glow in those eyes continued to cook her brain to mush. She ran both hands down the front of her apron, trying to get her muscles to snap out of the spellbound lethargy. But her body had gone treacly soft inside while on the outside her skin was sizzling hot. What was she waiting for? "What can I get you?"

He smiled, the full-bore Brad Davenport charming smile. "A beer, please."

"Just the one?" She flicked her hair out of her

eyes with a businesslike flip of her fingers. That was better—the sooner she got moving, the more control she'd regain. And she could put herself half in the fridge while she got his beer; that would be a very good thing.

"And whatever you're having. Are you due a break soon?" He stood straight up at the bar, not leaning on it as most of the other customers did. In his dark jacket and white open-neck shirt, he looked the epitome of the "hotshot lawyer who'd worked late".

Mya blinked rapidly. She *was* due for her break, but she wasn't sure she wanted to have it with him around. She felt as if she was missing something about this. It was almost as if he thought she'd been expecting him. "It's pretty busy."

"But that stag party has left so now's a good time, right? Let me get you a drink."

"I don't dri—"

"Water, soda, juice," he listed effortlessly. "There are other options." He countered her no-drinking-on-the-job argument before she'd even got it out.

Good grief. Surely he wasn't hitting on her? No way—the guy had never noticed her before.

These days Mya was used to being hit on—she worked in a bar after all. The guys there were usually drinking alcohol, so inevitably their minds turned to sex after a time. Any woman would do; it wasn't that she was anything that special. Naturally they tried it on, and naturally she knew how to put them off. She deliberately dressed in a way that wouldn't invite attention; her plain vee-neck black tee minimised her boobs and the apron tucked round her hips covered most of her thighs in her black jeans. She did wear the platforms, but the extra couple of inches helped her ability to look customers in the eye.

She still had to look up to Brad. And right now he was looking into her eyes as if there were nothing and no one else in the room to bother with. Yeah, he was good at making a woman feel as if she were everything in his world. Very good.

"I'll have some water," she muttered. There was zero alcohol in her system but she really needed to sober up. Not to mention cool down. She swallowed, determined to employ some easy bartender-to-customer-type conversation. "Been a while since I've seen you. What have you been up to?"

"I've been busy with work."

Of course, he was reputedly amazing in the courtroom, but she bet his work wasn't all he'd been busy with. The guy was legendary even at school. She and Lauren had been there a full five years after him and there'd been talk of his slayer skills. Lauren had been mega popular with all the older girls because they wanted to get to him through her.

"You need to get away from the bar to have a break," he said once she'd set his drink in front of him.

Actually she quite liked that giant block of wood

between them. She'd thought herself well over that teen crush, but all it had taken was that one look from him and she was all saucy inside. But there was a compelling glint in his eyes, and somehow she didn't manage to refuse.

As he shepherded her through the crowd, she steeled herself against the light brush of his hand on her back. She was *not* feeling remotely feminine next to his tall, muscled frame. She was *not* enjoying the bulldozer effect and seeing everyone clear out of his path and him guiding her through as if she were some princess to be protected. Surely she couldn't be that pathetic?

The balcony was darker and quieter. Of course he'd know where to find the most intimate place in an overcrowded venue. She pressed her back against the cold wall. She preferred to be able to keep an eye on the punters, and it gave her unreliable muscles some support. But in a second she realised it was a bad idea because Brad now towered in front of her. Yeah, he was all she could see and there was no way of getting around him easily.

The loud rhythm of the music was nothing on the frantic beat of her pulse in her ears. But he must be used to it—women blushing and going breathless in his company. She hoped he didn't think it was anything out of the ordinary.

"Will you excuse me a sec?" she said briskly. "I just need to check a couple of messages."

"Sure."

She slipped her hand into her pocket, needing to fill in a few of her fifteen minutes and catch her breath. Besides, the imp in her wanted to know Lauren's reaction to the photo she'd sent. But there were no messages at all—which was odd given Lauren's tech-addiction. She frowned at the phone.

"Did you need to make a call?" he asked quietly.

"Do you mind? It won't take a second." And it would fill in a few more of the fifteen minutes.

"Go for it." Brad lifted his glass and sipped.

Mya turned slightly towards the wall and made the call.

"What did you think?" she quietly asked as soon as Lauren answered.

"Think of what?"

"The pic," Mya mumbled into the phone, turning further away so Lauren's big, bad brother couldn't hear. "I sent it a couple of hours ago."

"What picture?"

"*The* pic." Mya's heart drummed faster. She glanced at Brad. Standing straight in front of her—a little too close. His eyes flicked up from her body to her face. She didn't want him listening, but now she'd looked at him, she couldn't look away. Not when she'd seen that look in his eyes. It wasn't just maple syrup now. It was alight with something else.

"I haven't received any pic. What was it of?" Lauren laughed.

"But I sent it," Mya said in confusion. She'd heard that whooshing sound when the message had gone. "You must have got it."

"Nup, nada."

Mya's blood pounded round her body. Sweltering, she tried to think. Because if that message hadn't gone to Lauren, then to whom had it gone?

She stared up at the guy standing closer than he ought and gradually became aware of a change in him. His eyes weren't just alive with the maple-syrup effect; no, now they were lit with unholy amusement. Why—?

Impossible.

The heat of anticipation within Mya transformed to horror in less than a heartbeat. And to make it worse, Brad suddenly smiled, hell, his shoulders actually shook—was the guy *laughing at her*?

"I definitely haven't got it," Lauren warbled on. "But I'm glad you rang because I haven't seen you in…"

Mya zoned out from Lauren, remembering the rush in the change room, the way she'd been giggling and not concentrating, the way her fingers had slipped over the screen…

No. Please no.

Lauren's voice and the noise from the bar all but disappeared, as if she'd dived into a swimming pool and could hear only muted, warped sound. Her stunned brain slowly cranked through the facts while the rest of her remained locked in the heat of his gaze.

Her contacts list automatically defaulted to alphabetical order. She'd never deleted all the contacts already on it either—and it was an old phone of Lauren's. No doubt her brother's number had been programmed in a long, long time ago. And *B* came before *L*. So first in the phone list?

Davenport. Brad Davenport.

Chapter 2

Mya ignored the fact that Lauren was still babbling in her ear and jabbed the phone, shutting it down. She shoved it back in her pocket and tossed her head to get her fringe out of her eyes. "It seems my phone's died," she said with exaggerated effervescence. "Can I borrow yours?"

Brad's silent chuckle became a quick, audible burst before he summoned the control to answer. "Really?"

She nodded vehemently, pretending she couldn't feel the rhythmic vibrating against her thigh.

"But your phone is ringing."

Yeah, there was no pretending she couldn't hear the shrill squawks over the beat of the bar music.

"What is that?"

"It's a recording of dolphins talking to each other," she answered brightly before hitting him with a bald-faced lie. "But while my ringer is working, the person on the other end can't hear me."

"Maybe you hit mute."

"Look, can I use it?" She dropped all pretence at perky and spoke flatly. Oh, she wanted to curl into a ball and roll behind a rock. Now. This was why he was here tonight. What had he thought? Surely he hadn't thought the picture was meant for him and he'd come to her? As if she'd called him?

Mya bit back hysterical laughter. Teen Mya would have loved Brad Davenport to hunt her down for a hook-up. Adult Mya had learned to avoid sharks. And of all the people she had to mistakenly send a picture to, it had to be her best friend's brother? Her best friend's completely *gorgeous*, speed-through-a-million-sexual-partners brother?

Brad held her gaze captive with his warm, amused one. "But my phone cost a lot of money and I don't like the way you're holding that glass of water. I don't think my phone can survive the depths."

Was the guy a mind-reader? Of course she wanted to drown the thing—she'd drown Brad himself if she could. Or better still, herself.

How could she have made such a mistake? This ranked as the most mortifying moment of her life.

Why had she gone with the scarlet bikini with the see-through sides?

"How come you have my number anyway?" he asked lazily, confirming the worst.

"This was an old phone of Lauren's." Mya groaned. "She passed it on to me."

"One of the ones she lost and made Dad replace?"

Hell, that would be right. For a while there Lauren had made her father pay—literally. "She told me he'd given her a new one and she didn't need this one any more." She didn't like the frown in Brad's eyes.

Yeah, she was the bad influence, wasn't she? The one who came from the wrong side of the tracks to lead Lauren astray. Did he think she abused her relationship with Lauren to get things? Lauren's parents had thought that. Indeed, Lauren *had* tried to give Mya things. Mya had refused to take most of them. The little she had, she'd hidden from her own parents. She didn't want them feeling bad that they couldn't afford those kinds of gifts—indeed any. Even then Lauren had tricked her into taking this phone and she'd taken nothing since.

And now? Now there was no dignity left in this situation. "Would you please delete it?" she asked. Yeah, begging already.

"Never."

Incredibly, his instant laughing response melted her but she couldn't be flattered by this. She just *couldn't.* "It wasn't meant for you."

"More's the pity," he said softly. "Do you often text pictures of yourself in underwear to your friends?"

"It wasn't *underwear*," she said indignantly.

His chin lifted and the sound of his laughter rang out, crashing and curling over her like a wave of warmth. "It's a bra."

But Mya couldn't float in that tempting sea. "It's a bikini."

He shook his head, his brown eyes teasing. "Sorry, Mya. It's a bra."

She was still too mortified to be teased. "I was in a swimwear store. I wanted Lauren's opinion on it. It was a bikini."

"There were see-though bits." He gestured widely and half shrugged. "There was underwire. Looked like a bra to me."

"You'd know because you've seen so many?" She tried to bite, but felt her blush rise higher.

"Sure," he chuckled. "And for the record, yes, you can definitely get away with it."

Brad watched Mya closely and couldn't bring himself to take the polite step back despite knowing the doll was embarrassed beyond belief. But no way in hell was he ever deleting that image. She was gorgeous—far more gorgeous than he'd realised. The picture had been the teaser, but seeing her like this now? All flushed and snappy, pocket-sized but bright-eyed—he was beyond intrigued.

Her hair was swept into a ponytail. Now he re-

membered the colour had frequently changed. She
and Lauren had spent for ever in Lauren's room,
giggles emanating as they did outrageous things to
their hair. Though right now, instead of hot pink and
purple, Mya's hair colour looked almost natural—a
light brown with slightly blonde streaks round the
front. Her wickedly high cheekbones created sharp
planes sloping down to that narrow little chin. Those
teeth and that impish smile broke the perfection, yet
were perfect themselves. The all-black ensemble was
unusual for her but it didn't hide her body. Despite
her slender limbs and pixie face, she wasn't boy-
ishly slim. Her jeans were painted on, and the apron
around her hips didn't wholly hide her curvy butt.
As for those breasts… Plumped up by the bikini/
bra in the picture, they'd been so bountiful they'd
spilled over the edges. Now, disguised under that
plain black tee, their silhouette was minimised. But
no simple cotton covering could fully hide the softness that seemed sinfully generous in proportion to
her small stature.

His heart drummed a triumphant beat. Blood
pulsed, priming muscles. Because he'd seen the way
she'd looked at him—the flash she hadn't been able
to hide when he'd first walked into the bar. There'd
been that pull, that instinctive reaction. He knew the
signs—the second glances, small smiles, the heightened colour. The sparkle in the eyes, the parting of
the lips. Brad Davenport also knew his worth. He

knew he had a body that attracted a second glance—
oh, and the cynic in him knew most women would
never forget his trust fund. So he was used to being
wanted and he knew when a woman wanted him.

Now the tip of her tongue briefly touched that too-
wide top lip and then she bit back her smile. Yeah,
she still had that gap between her two front teeth.

With just a look she'd had those stag-party guys
competing to catch her close and hold her. Only she'd
held them off with a few words and a hint of fire. And
he wasn't thinking of the lighter flame.

Brad's entire body was on fire, and for the second time that night he gave in to impulse. He took
her glass from her and put it on the table next to his.

"What are you doing?" A breathless squeak.

"We're old friends," he said softly. "We should
greet each other properly."

"I wouldn't have said we were *friends*." Her voice
wobbled.

He smiled at the sound. He'd stirred a small response from her, but he wanted more. And he was
used to winning what he wanted. Before she could
say anything more, he stepped close and caught her
mouth with his.

She instantly tensed, but he kept it light. When
the stiff surprise ebbed from her body—pleasingly
quickly—he lifted his head a fraction and stepped
closer at the same time. He flicked his tongue to feel
her soft lips, tracing their uneven length, and then

sealing his to hers again and tasting the delight inside her mouth. And then she kissed him back and that fire exploded. Man, Mya Campbell was a hell of a lot hotter than he'd ever thought possible.

For a split second Mya wondered if she were dreaming. Then the heat blasted into her and she knew not even *her* imagination could come up with this. She held her head up without even realising—no thought of pushing him away. Because the guy did wicked things with his tongue—sweeping it between her lips. Deeper and deeper again. Caressing her mouth as if it were the most delicious pleasure. She softened, opening more. And he stepped closer, taking more, *giving* so much more.

His chest pressed into hers. She could feel how broad and strong he was. It was a damn good thing she had the wall behind her—she was sandwiched between two solid forces and it was utterly exquisite. His mouth was rapacious now. His body insistent. Like yin and yang—hard versus the soft. And yet there was tension in her body too, that fierce need for physical fulfilment unfurling inside.

She slid her hand over his abs, the heat of him blazing through the white cotton shirt. She could feel those taut muscles and shivered at the thought of them working hard above her, beneath her—every way towards pleasure.

Her rational mind spun off into the distance while her senses took centre stage, demanding all her attention. She all but oozed into him, utterly malleable, his to twist and tease. And he did—grinding against her, kissing her mouth, her jaw, her neck and back to her mouth. She threaded her fingers through his hair, opening yet more for him.

His hand slid to the curve of her hip, lower still to her butt. He spread his fingers, pulling her hips closer to the heat of his—so she could feel his response even more. A moan escaped as she felt his thick erection pressing against her belly. So hot, so soon, this was just so crazy.

But all thought vanished as his other hand slid up from her waist, cupping her breast. She momentarily tensed, anticipating the pain—she was too sensitive for touch there. But his fingers stilled, not following through on their upward sweep; a half-second later he moved again to cup her soft flesh, avoiding her nipple. Good thing, as both were overloading already just with the pressure of his chest against hers. She relaxed against him again as she realised he somehow understood. Instead he pressed deeper—his tongue laying claim to her mouth, his body almost imprinting on hers.

And despite this oh-so-thorough kiss, she wanted so much more than this.

She moved restlessly—tiny rocking motions of her hips. It was all she could manage given how hard he was pinning her to the wall. But with every small movement she drew closer and closer to the hit of ecstasy that she suddenly needed more than anything else in the world.

It wasn't a kiss; it was a siege—he'd encircled her and demanded her surrender. It hadn't taken her long to cave at all. Her fingers curled instinctively into his cotton shirt as wicked tension gripped her. Almost at breaking point—the convulsions of ecstasy were a mere breath away.

"Excuse me!"

Mya froze and she felt Brad's arms go equally rigid. She pulled back and met his eyes—he looked as startled as she felt.

"Mya, you're way over your break time." Drew, her boss, snapped right beside her. "What do you think you're doing?"

All but stupefied, Mya turned and stared at her boss. She literally didn't know. Couldn't think. Couldn't answer. She was still trying to process the chemical reaction that had ignited every cell while in Brad's embrace. But as she looked at the extreme irritation on Drew's face, reality rushed back. Her boss was furious. Panic slammed the door shut on the remaining good vibes—she couldn't afford to lose this job. What on earth *had* she been thinking?

"Drew, I'm so sorry," she said in a breathless rush, stepping further away from Brad. "I wasn't aware of the time. I didn't—"

"No kidding," Drew interrupted rudely, her

scrambled apology having no effect on his temper. "This is—"

"My fault." To Mya's horror, Brad coolly interrupted Drew. "I distracted her."

Drew turned his glower on Brad. But within a second his expression eased a fraction as he got a good look at the man now stepping up in front of him.

Mya watched the two men square off. All of a sudden Brad seemed both taller and broader as he moved to put himself partly between her and Drew. Oh, this wasn't good—she really didn't need Brad interfering; she was on the line as it was. She could handle Drew herself without any macho-male stuff.

Brad sent her a quick glance but seemed oblivious to her wordless plea to shut the heck up and back off. Instead he turned back to Drew.

Mya held her breath but then Brad smiled—that big, easy smile, with just a hint of the "born to it all" arrogance. "My name's Brad Davenport." He extended his hand as if it were not in the least embarrassing that he'd just been caught kissing the brains out of Drew's employee when she should have been working. "I want to hire out your bar."

"Drew." Mya's manager paused a moment and then shook Brad's hand. "This is a popular place. I'm not sure you'll need the whole bar for one small party."

"It's not going to be a small party. I want the

whole bar," Brad answered calmly. "Obviously we'll pay to secure absolute privacy for the night."

Mya watched the change come over Drew as he assessed Brad's worth. It didn't take much to know the clothes were designer, the watch gold, the self-assurance in-built…

"I'm sure we can come to some arrangement." Drew's demeanour changed to sycophantic in a heartbeat.

"I'm sure we can." Brad smiled his killer smile once again. "It should be good. This place has an atmosphere I like."

Mya watched the Davenport charm in action as he arranged a meeting time with Drew. He got everything his own way *so* easily. Utterly used to doors swinging open—and women's legs parting on sight of that smile too. And while she was totally relieved he'd just saved her neck from the block, she was also irritated with the ease with which he'd done it. The man had everything. Money, looks, brains, charm. Had he ever known what it was to have to fight for something? To really have to work for something? Mya knew what it was to work, *hard*.

"You have two minutes," Drew said to Mya, as if he were an emperor granting a favour to a lowly serf. "Then back behind that bar."

"Of course." Mya nodded as he disappeared into the crowd. Then she turned back to Brad. "I'm afraid you're going to have to follow through on that meeting."

"I'm looking forward to it." Brad didn't look at all bothered. "I think a night here could be fun."

Mya chose to ignore the hint of entendre in his expression. "Have you got a reason to party?"

"Who needs a reason?" Brad shrugged.

"Because life's just one big party?"

He merely chuckled and then stepped closer. "I'm sorry we were interrupted. Things were getting interesting there."

But that close call had firmly grounded Mya. "Things were getting out of hand," she corrected, opting not to look any higher than his collar. "I'm sorry about that. You took me by surprise."

"Wow," Brad said after a pause. "I'm intrigued to think what it'll be like when I give you fair warning."

Mya shook her head and stepped away. "You're not getting another chance."

She felt his hand on her elbow turning her back towards him. His hand slipped down her arm to take her fingers in his.

The touch made her look up before she thought better of it. His surprisingly intense expression incinerated her but she hauled herself from the ashes of easiness. Mya liked sex, but she preferred it within the context of some kind of relationship, not the one-night-stand scene Brad was champion of. And she was steering well clear of *any* kind of entanglement for the foreseeable future. Long-term future. She had too much else to do—like work, study and occasionally eat and sleep.

Also, this man had always had everything too easy. She'd just seen him in action—twice already tonight. He wasn't having her that way again. She truly had just been caught by surprise, and her response to him was simply a reflection of his expertise and her lack of any physical release in the last while, right?

The swirling frustration and embarrassment inside her coalesced and came out as temper. "You thought that picture was a booty call, didn't you?" She called him out with sarcasm-coated words. "From a woman that you haven't spoken to in at least five years?"

"Have we ever spoken?" He laughed off her accusation. "I thought you and Lauren just paraded around fake-Goth-style and giggled behind closed doors. Interesting to think what was really going on behind those doors given the pictures you send each other. Thinking about it, you two went to prom together, didn't you?"

"With her boyfriend," Mya answered.

"Oh, a threesome." Brad laughed harder.

"If you remember, she tried to get you to take me."

"Oh, yeah." His eyes widened as he thought about it. "That's right."

Unlike him, Mya had *never* forgotten what for her had been the most mortifying moment of that night.

He'd been home from university. He'd had some silvery-blonde girlfriend with him. Tall and sleek, she'd had the obligatory blue eyes and the label clothes and the "born to it all" attitude. Mya had hated her on sight. The girlfriend had spent most of the time spread on a sofa being kissed to glory by Brad.

"You were wearing one of Lauren's dresses," he said slowly.

"Yes." She was amazed he'd now remembered that detail. Mya had butchered one of Lauren's many formal dresses. A soft, pretty pink dress—never a colour she'd normally wear. She'd taken to it with a pair of scissors and completely cut away the back and secured it with long, trailing ribbons. She'd been aiming for a soft romantic look.

It was the dress that she'd hoped might garner her the attention she'd thought she'd wanted. All she'd wanted to do was fit in—to be popular and accepted. To be just like the rest of them and *not* different for once. She'd wanted it to all be easy. But it was never as easy as a change of clothes. Make-overs didn't change the person underneath. She hadn't just been sixteen and never been kissed. She'd made it all the way to eighteen and first-year uni before that honour had fallen to a fellow student who'd seemed sweet enough until he'd had what he wanted.

But back at that night of the dance, she'd had the whole prom fantasy. What wallflower schoolgirl didn't? The one where the hottest guy in school asked her to dance and it was all perfect and ended with a kiss. Or the super-hot brother of the best friend asked her? Yeah, she'd been such a cliché. And she'd felt like a princess for all of five minutes, until Brad had ignored her. She'd been pretty and dressed up and hadn't even been able to turn the head of the most sexually hungry male she knew back then.

"You were too busy wearing that blonde to answer at the time," Mya said dryly.

The dimple in his cheek deepened. "Yeah, that's right."

He hadn't appreciated his younger sister's interruption. Mya had seen the raw lust in him, the tease, the firmness with which he pulled the girl onto his lap—his strong arm wrapped around her waist, his confident hand close to her breast. And for a few minutes, she'd wanted to be that girl. Now for five minutes she had been. And it was better than any fantasy.

Mya sucked up her stupidity and turned her self-scorn towards him instead. "That's all irrelevant anyway. What's really the issue here is how pathetically horn dog you are. You get a look at a woman in her *bikini* and you're suddenly hot for her? When you've never so much as looked at her in the last decade?"

Amusement still burned in his eyes. "You were a child a decade ago."

"It's still pathetic." And frankly, insulting.

"Maybe that prom night isn't so irrelevant at

all." His smile widened. "Did you have a crush on me back in high school? Your best friend's older brother?"

She gaped.

"Because," he leaned closer and drawled outrageously, "you wouldn't have been the only one."

Hell, the guy had an ego. Unfortunately what he'd said was true. There were several girls who'd done the faux-friendship thing to Lauren just to get close to her brother. Mya shook her head and denied him anyway. "Girls that age are at the mercy of hormones just as boys are and they fixate on the nearest object. Their fixating on you was probably more a matter of locality than your attractiveness."

He grinned wolfishly. "So if it wasn't me your hormones fixed on, then who?"

"I didn't have the time."

"Everybody has the time." He moved closer as his voice dropped to an intimate whisper. "Who did you used to dream of?"

"No one."

"So rebellious on the outside, such a square inside." He shook his head.

Mya gritted her teeth.

"No wonder you erupted with one touch—you've been repressed too long."

Mya couldn't answer because that was actually true. She'd been without too long; that was the reason she'd inhaled his touch like an attention-starved animal.

"Did you wish I'd said yes to Lauren and taken you to the ball? Is that why you're trying to cut me down now? Did I burst your love-struck teen bubble?"

He was so close to the mark it was mortifying. But she'd never, ever admit it. "I'm sure you've burst many poor girls' bubbles, but you never burst mine." Mya willed a languid tone. "Fact is I've always seen through your charm to what you really are."

"And what am I?"

"Selfish, spoilt, arrogant. Insufferable."

"Is that all?" He paused a moment. "You don't want to add some more about how unattractive you find me?"

Very funny. "You're so up yourself it's unbelievable."

"But you still want me." He breathed out and then laughed. "You're never going to be able to deny it. Not when you kissed me like that."

"You were the one who kissed me." Cross, she licked her extremely dry lips.

"It started that way but within two seconds you were clawing my shirt off."

"I was trying to push you away."

The rogue laughed harder. Mya pulled her hand free of his grip and strode back through to the bar. She got behind it and found he was right there in front of her, waiting to be served—and still annoyingly amused.

"You have to go now," she told him firmly, determined not to let that smile affect her. "I have work to do." She pulled out a chopping board, some lemons and a knife to prove it.

"No." He shook his head. "I need you more than ever now."

Yeah, right. He'd never needed her before. And while she didn't want to think he'd kissed her on a whim, the fact was he had. He'd never wanted to kiss her before, remember? The guy who had his pick of every woman in every room in the world hadn't noticed her until she was hardly dressed. It really didn't do much for her ego. And even less for his character. It showed he was simply attracted to the lowest common denominator—bared flesh.

He shook his head in mock despair. "You suspect my motivation."

"Your reputation does precede you." She maintained her cool. "And all you've said and done so far tonight merely confirms the worst."

"Actually, Mya, I really do need you." His expression went serious. "I'm not just going to hire out the bar. I'm going to hire you."

Chapter 3

"I'm not interested." Mya was telling herself that over and over but her body wasn't listening. Her pulse still pounded, her ears still attuned to every nuance in his words. But her ego was piqued. He'd kissed her only after seeing her breasts in a skimpy bikini—and now he wanted to *hire* her? For what exactly?

"Sure you are." He winked. "I have to have a party now and you're the perfect person to organise it for poor helpless me."

She shook her head. "Poor and helpless are the antithesis of what you are. You don't need anyone, let alone me."

He grinned, obviously appreciating the unvarnished truth, but behind the smiling eyes she sensed his brain was whizzing. Yeah, the guy was wickedly calculating. And far too together already after the kiss that had shattered her. She needed to keep her guard well up.

"Lauren's finished her degree," he said.

Momentarily thrown by the change in topic, Mya blinked. Then she nodded, but said nothing. If she hadn't been such an idiot, she'd have been a lot nearer to finishing her degree too.

"For a while there it didn't seem likely she'd even finish high school let alone a university degree," he added.

He was right. When Mya had started at that school, Lauren's wild streak had been on the verge of going septic and that hadn't been in the perfect Davenport family plan at all. They were all graduates with successful careers—and expected Lauren to achieve the same. Whereas Mya was the *only* one in her family to have finished school. She was supposed to be the first in the family to finish a degree too. Honours no less, having won a prestigious scholarship. Except she'd screwed it up, and now she doubted that she'd ever deserved it. But she'd finish her degree all on her own account—independence was now everything to her. This time she was taking the lead from Lauren. So she nodded. "She defied everyone's expectations and did it. Brilliantly too."

There was a pause and she couldn't help glancing at him. And then they both laughed at that one unbelievable aspect of Lauren's success.

"It's more than a little ironic, don't you think?" he said, his face lightening completely. "That she almost dropped out and now she's going to be a teacher?"

"She'll be a dragon too, I bet." Mya bit her lip but couldn't quite hold back the chuckle. "Super-strict. She won't put up with any illegal nail polish." Back in the day, Mya and Lauren had broken more than the nail-polish rules. Their favourite look had been purple splatter.

"So we'll have the party for her. It's as good an excuse as any," Brad said confidently. "Exam results are out. It's not long until Christmas. Many of her friends are going overseas and won't be back for her graduation ceremony next year. She's worked hard for a long while." He faced her square on again. "So we'll surprise her."

"You're going to have it as a surprise?" Mya asked. "You want me to distract her?" She'd be happy to sneak Lauren out and be there for the big surprise moment.

But he was shaking his head. "I want you to organise it."

Mya's enthusiasm burst like a kid's balloon encountering the prick of a needle. Of course he did. He had to have this party but she'd be the one copping all the extra work to get it ready? Her ego suffered another blow—and more importantly she just didn't have the time to do it. "Isn't partying *your* area of expertise?"

"Darling, I've never *planned* a party. I *am* the party." He mimicked her emphasis.

"Oh, please."

"Who better to arrange it than my sister's best friend? I said I'll hire you. You'll be paid."

She bridled. "I'm not taking money from you. I'm her *friend*." The thought of him paying for her services irked her. She'd always put in an honest day's work but the thought of *Brad* owning her time spiked her hackles.

"I'll get in a planner instead." He shrugged.

Now she was even more ticked. He was too used to getting everything his own way. "You think you can just throw some money on the table and have some flash event happen? Lauren wouldn't want some impersonal, chic party put together by cutesy PR girls she doesn't even know." Mya shook her head. "Wouldn't it mean more to her if *you* put in some personal effort? She doesn't like cookie-cutter perfection." Lauren had had so many things bought for her—by impersonal secretaries. She liked the individual—that was part of what had drawn her and Mya so close.

He looked sceptical. "You think I should choose the colour scheme and the canapés?"

"Why not?" she asked blandly.

"You're not tempted by an unlimited budget and

licence to do anything? Most women would love that, right?"

"I'm not like most women. Nor is Lauren. You should organise it—it's your idea." She sent him a cutting glance. "Or are you too selfish to spend time on her?"

He laughed. "Sweetheart, every human on this planet is selfish," he said. "We all do what's ultimately best for ourselves. I am doing this for very selfish reasons and not many of them to do with Lauren herself. It's mainly so *I* don't have to deal with my mother's hand-wringing and a frozen dinner out with my parents to celebrate Lauren's graduation. And so *you* don't get in trouble with your boss and take it out on me. Does that make me a bad person?"

Heat ricocheted round her body like a jet of boiling oil as she saw the intense look in his eye. He didn't want her to think badly of him? And he *was* doing this to prevent her from getting in trouble. "No," she conceded.

"You have to help me," he said softly.

That was one step too far. "We wouldn't be in this position if you hadn't kissed me." She tried to argue back but felt herself slipping. "You created this problem. You don't need me."

"Do I have the names and numbers of half her friends? No. I don't know all her university mates the way you do. Of course I need your help."

Silent, she looked at him.

"*I'm* thinking of Lauren. Are *you*?" he jeered.

She sighed. "For Lauren's sake, I'll help. But you're not paying me."

"What a good friend you are," he teased.

"I am, actually," she declared.

"We all do what is best for *ourselves*," he murmured with a shake of his head. "Wasn't insisting I be actively involved in the planning really because *you* wanted to spend more time with *me*?"

She gaped—how did he turn that one around? "No. I'm only thinking of Lauren." She vehemently denied that tendril of excitement curling through her innards at the thought of spending time with him. He had an outsize ego that needed stripping. "You think you're irresistible, don't you?"

"Experience has led me to believe that's often the case."

His eyes were glinting. He might be laughing, but she suspected part of him meant it. *Outrageous* wasn't the word. The guy needed taking down a peg or forty. "Not in *this* case."

"No?" He chuckled, radiating good humour. "So that blush is pure annoyance? Then you've nothing to worry about, right? We can organise Lauren's party together because you can resist me no problem."

Could she resist him? For a second Mya wondered and then her fighting spirit came to the fore. Of *course* she could. "No problem at all."

He leaned closer. "I'm sorry I haven't seen much of you in recent years."

"Maybe you should have turned up to a couple of Lauren's birthday parties."

He winced, hand to his chest. "I was overseas."

She knew he'd studied further overseas before coming back and setting up his own practice. "So convenient. For work, was it? You learned well from your father."

"Meaning?"

"Doesn't *he* use work for emotional avoidance too? Earns millions to buy the things to make up for it." Lauren had been given so many *things* and none of them what she'd truly yearned for.

The laughing glint vanished from Brad's eyes. "Formed a few judgments over the years, haven't you?"

Mya realised she might have gone more than a little far. "I'm sorry, that was out of line. I'll always be grateful for the kindness your parents showed me," she said stiltedly, embarrassed at her rudeness.

But he laughed again, the devil dancing back in his eyes. "Their *kindness*?"

Okay, maybe he did remember the ultra-frosty welcome she'd got for the first year or three that she and Lauren hung out. "They didn't ban me from their home." Even though she knew they'd wanted to. Now they realised they owed Mya something.

"Don't worry about it. I know even better than you what a mess it was."

He'd certainly left home the second he could. Mya had been the one who'd spent every afternoon after school with Lauren in that house. She and Lauren hid up in Lauren's suite, laughing and ignoring the frozen misery downstairs. The false image of the perfect family. "But Lauren's the one who's made the conscious effort to be different from how she was raised."

"You're saying I've not?"

Mya shrugged. "You're the mini-me lawyer."

"You do know my father and I practise vastly different types of law. I'm not in his firm."

Blandly she picked up a glass and polished it. That didn't mean anything.

"What, all lawyers are the same?" He snorted. "I don't do anything he does. I work with kids."

She knew this, and at this precise moment she point-blank refused to be impressed by it. "You think your save-the-children heroic-lawyer act somehow ameliorates your womanising ways?" Because Brad *was* a womaniser. Just like his father.

"Doesn't it?"

See, he didn't even deny the charge. "You think? Yeah, that's probably why you do child advocacy," she mused. "To score the chicks by showing your sensitive side."

He laughed, a loud burst of genuine humour that had her smiling back in automatic response.

"That's an interesting take. I've never really thought about it that way." He shrugged. "But even if it does give me some chick-points, at least I've done something with my life that's useful. Is igniting alcohol for party boys useful?"

She shifted uncomfortably. Serving drinks was a means to an end. But she managed a smooth reply. "Helping people relax is a skill."

His brows shot up. "I'm not sure you're that good at helping guys *relax*."

She met his gaze and felt the intensity pull between them again.

"Are you still at university or are you finished now?" He broke the silence, looking down and toying with the pile of postcards on the edge of the bar.

"I'm there part-time this year."

"Studying what?"

"A double degree. Law and commerce."

"Law and commerce?" he repeated. "So you're going to become a greedy capitalist like my evil father and me?" He laughed. She didn't blame him, given her stabbing disapproval mere seconds ago. "You're enjoying it?"

"Of course," she said stiffly.

"And the plan?"

"A job in one of the top-five firms, of course."

"Speciality?"

"Corporate."

"You mean like banking? Counting beans? Helping companies raid others and earning yourself wads of cash in the process?"

"Nothing wrong with wanting to earn a decent wage in a job where you can sit down." She walked away to serve the customers she'd been ignoring too long. Her need to achieve wasn't something trust-fund-son over there could understand. She needed money—not for a giant flat-screen TV and a house with a lap-pool and overseas jaunts. She needed a new house, yes, but not for herself. For her parents.

She was conscious of his gaze still on her as he sat now nursing something non-alcoholic and taking in the scene. As she glanced over, she saw his eyes held a hint of bleak strain. Was it possible that behind the playboy façade, the guy was actually *tired*?

But he didn't leave. Even when the bar got quieter and they'd turned the music down a notch. In another ten minutes the lights would brighten to encourage the stragglers out of the dark corners. Mya felt him watching her, felt her fingers go butter-slippery. She kept thinking about the kiss; heat came in waves—when memory swept over control. She couldn't stay away when he signalled her over to his end of the bar.

"I've been thinking about the drinks for Lauren's party," he said easily. "It would be good to offer something different, right? Not just the usual."

So that was why he was still sitting there? He was party planning? Not surreptitiously watching her at all?

"There you go, see?" Mya said brightly, masking how deflated she suddenly felt. "You'll organise a brilliant party. You don't need me."

"I need your expertise," he countered blandly. "I don't think I can ignite alcohol."

No, but he could ignite other things with a mere look. Mya pulled her head together and focused on the task at hand. "You want me to come up with a couple of Lauren-inspired cocktails?"

"They're the house speciality, right? So, yeah, make up some new ones, give them a cute name, we'll put them up on the blackboard." He chuckled. "Something that'll be good fun to watch the bartender make. Definitely use a bit of fire."

"And ice," she answered, then turned away to scoop crushed ice into a glass and wished she could put herself in with it. How could she be this hot? Maybe it was a bug?

"What would you use to make her cocktail?" he asked idly. "What kind of spirit is Lauren?"

She took the question seriously. "Classic bones, quirky overtones. A combination that you wouldn't expect."

She turned her back to him and looked at the rows and rows of gleaming bottles. Reached up and grabbed a few and put them on the bar beside Brad. Then she poured. "Her cocktail would need to be layered." Carefully she bent and made sure each layer sat properly on the next. "Unexpected but delicious."

She smiled to herself as she added a few drops of another few things. Then she straightened and looked at him expectantly.

He just held her gaze.

Finally she broke the silence. "You don't want to try it?"

He studied the vivid blue, orange and green liquid in the glass in front of him. "Not unless you try it first. It looks like poison to me. Too many ingredients."

"I don't drink on the job." She smiled sweetly. "Are you too scared?"

"Don't think you can goad me into doing what you want," he said softly. But he picked up the glass and took a small sip. He inhaled deeply after swallowing the liquid fire. "That's surprisingly good."

"Yes," Mya said smugly. "Just like Lauren."

He grinned his appreciation. "All right, clever clogs, what cocktail would you put together for me?"

Oh, that was easy. She picked up a bottle and put it on the bar.

He stared at it, aghast. "You're calling me a boring old malt?"

"It needs nothing else. Overpowering enough on its own."

"Well, you're wrong. There's another like that that's more me than a single malt."

"What's that?"

"Tequila. Lethal, best with a little salt and a twist of something tart like one of your lemons."

She rolled her eyes.

"And what are you?" He laughed. "Brandy? Vodka? Maudlin gin?"

"None. I don't have time."

"You should make time. You shouldn't work so hard."

"Needs must." She shrugged it off lightly. "And you have to leave now so I can close up the bar."

"Have lunch with me tomorrow. We can brainstorm ideas."

She should have said yes to organising the party on her own. Why had she thought he ought to have active involvement? "I'm at class tomorrow. I'm doing summer school." She'd be in summer school for the next three years.

"Okay, breakfast, then."

She shook her head. "I'm working."

"This place is open all night?" His brows lifted.

"I work in a café in the mornings and some other shifts that fit around my classes and the bar work."

"And you work here every night?"

"Not on Sundays."

"Where do you work on a Sunday—the café?"

She nodded, looking up in time to see his quick frown. She rolled her eyes. Yes, she worked hard; that was what people did when they had to. Eating was essential after all.

"Why didn't you take a summer internship?"

She turned and put all the bottles back in their places on the shelves. The summer internships at prestigious law firms in the city were sought after. Often they led to permanent job offers once degrees were completed. But she wasn't going there again, not until her final year of study and she'd recovered her grade average. Not to mention her dignity. "I need to keep going with my studies and, believe it or not, I earn more in the bar."

"You get good tips?"

"Really good." She rinsed her hands again and wiped down the bench.

"You might get more if you let some more of that red lace stuff show." He glanced down the bar. "One thing we are going to do for the party is have better bartender outfits. You'd never guess what you wear beneath the undertaker's uniform you've got going on in here."

Heat scorched her cheeks again. Once again, why had she picked that wretched scarlet bikini? He was never going to let her forget it. "This is what we all wear in the bar. It's simple, efficient and looks smart."

"It's deadly dull and doesn't make the most of your assets. Not like that red underneath it."

"It's not underneath it."

"You took it off?" He looked appalled. "Why on earth did you take it off?"

"It was a *bikini*," she said, goaded. She closed her eyes and breathed deep to stop herself laughing. His wicked smile suggested he knew she was close to it anyway. She looked at him. Not at all sorry he had to shell out however many tens of thousands to hire the most popular bar in town outright for a night during the busiest time of the year.

"Why do men get so fixated on lacy underwear?" she asked aloud. "Don't you know sexy underwear is no indicator of how far a woman is prepared to go?"

"You're saying you'll go further than what your boring day-bra might indicate?" he said mildly.

"No!" she snapped.

"So you do wear boring day-bras?"

Oh, the guy was incorrigible. But, heaven help her, she couldn't help but laugh. So she'd see him some saucy talk, and raise him some flirt. She nodded with a secret smile. "No lace."

"Why's that?" The corner of his beautiful mouth lifted.

"No boyfriend to buy me some," she flipped tartly and stalked away, letting the clip of her high heels underline her reply.

"You wouldn't let some guy buy you frills," he called after her. "You're too independent for that."

Very true. Interesting he understood that. But she swung back to face him because she didn't want him thinking he knew it all. "Actually it's just that they're uncomfortable."

"They are?" His gaze lowered again.

"No woman can wear those things for more than five minutes."

"No woman in my presence would need to."

She ignored the comeback and cooed instead. "I'm very sensitive. Lace hurts." She watched his expression with amazement. Was he actually blushing? She smirked, pleased she'd finally managed to push him off his self-assured pedestal.

"How sensitive?" He walked down the side of the bar so he was close to her again. "Can they cope with touch?"

That was when she realised his flush wasn't from embarrassment but arousal. Her body clenched, drenched in fire. "No."

"No?" he asked, surprised. The flush on his skin deepened.

She was burning up with a blush to match.

"Hmm. That sensitive, huh?" He looked thoughtful. "What other bits are too sensitive?"

She couldn't look away from the teasing intimacy in his eyes. The intense drive of his words melted her. She hadn't meant this to get so personal. She'd been out to tease him. Only her too-sensitive bits were shrieking right now, liquefying in the heat he was conjuring—his words locking her in a lit crucible.

"Must make it difficult for you," he said softly. "I bet you pull away. You can't just go with it." He looked at her speculatively. "Just the way you pulled back from me before."

She was so hot, her soul singed by words alone. She couldn't even answer. Because in truth? He was right.

"Seems to me you need some practice coping."

She shook her head. "I'm not inexperienced." And she definitely didn't need to get any more experience by playing with him.

His mouth curved in disbelief. "Aren't you?"

Well, okay, she wasn't as experienced as *him*. She lifted her head proudly. "I've had boyfriends." Jerks, the pair of them.

"Yeah, but you've never been with me."

"And you're that amazing?" she asked, managing a tone of utter skepticism, which was quite something given her wayward hormones were shrieking that *yes, he was that amazing!*

His expression was pure intent. "You'll have to wait and see."

"You're so obnoxious." She recovered her sass, more determined than ever to shoot him down. "Why would I want to have sex with a guy who's been with every other girl in the city?"

"Not *every* other girl," he protested. "But I don't see anything wrong with sharing the love," he added. "If you have too much sex with one woman, she starts to get funny ideas. Better to have sex with too many women. Safer."

"Oh, real safe." She rolled her eyes. But he wasn't denying it. Brad Davenport wasn't a commitment kind of guy. He was a playboy.

He reached across the bar and ran a finger down her arm. Electricity sparked every millimetre of the way. She saw it. He saw it. There was no denying it. So she didn't.

"This isn't anything more than lust." She turned and literally burrowed out more ice from the freezer.

"So what?" he calmly said behind her. "It's still worth exploring."

"Even if I agree there's chemistry, I'm not sure I can bear to feed your over-bloated ego by saying yes." But the feeling the guy could inspire with just a look?

"You'll always regret it if you don't," he insisted.

"And probably regret it if I do."

"Damned either way, then," he said with a laugh. "You might as well have the good moment and enjoy it."

"Moment?" She suppressed the squeeze her muscles had in response to his laugh. "As in singular? What are you going for here, some orgasmic snuffle?"

"You don't need to worry. I'll take care of you."

"I don't need anybody to take care of me," she denied, affronted.

"Really?"

Narrow-eyed, she watched him draw closer. It seemed to her there might be an imbalance of attraction here. Was it all about her wanting him? Or was the chemistry as insane for him as it was for her?

"Maybe you don't. But you keep thinking about that kiss," he said. "I can tell."

She was shaking her head already but when she went to deny it he put his finger back on her mouth.

"You can't hide it. I see it in your eyes. It's the same for me," he said simply. "I want to kiss you again."

"Brad—"

He straightened. "I accept that you're saying no, for now, but don't deny that the desire is there."

"I haven't kissed anyone in a while." She shrugged. "What happened before was merely a reaction to that."

He shook his head. "You were every bit as into it as I was. You're as 'all or nothing' in your approach to life. It's just that you go for nothing and I go for all."

"Have you ever managed nothing?"

"I am right now."

"Really." Not a question, more an expression of disbelief. "Almost two hours with nothing?"

"Nothing," he said, as if it wasn't an experience he was enjoying. "Not so much as an eyelash flutter since you."

Mya chuckled and this time she reached across, clasping his wrist as if she feared he was about to have a heart attack. "How are *you* coping?"

"Moment by moment." He clapped his hand over hers. "But I'm quietly confident."

"Quietly?" she mocked. She leaned across the bar again and gave him some advice. "You shouldn't hype yourself up so much. It'll end up a disappointment."

"What orgasm was ever a disappointment?"

She tried so hard not to blush. "Is that all it is for you? The momentary thrill?"

"It's pretty much up there, yeah," he drawled. "I won't lie." He lifted her hand with his and pressed her palm to his heart. "I fancy you." He paused. "Now, can you speak with the same kind of honesty?"

For a moment she couldn't answer as she absorbed the strong, regular thud of his heartbeat. But while the moments of orgasm might feel good, it was the moments afterwards she was more worried about. She curled her fingers into a fist and pulled away from him. "I'm not on trial here."

"You're a coward," he accused. "Is having fun so wrong?"

Mya answered with absolute honesty. "Not wrong. Inconvenient."

"Never inconvenient. You need to sort your priorities."

She shook her head and laughed. "Oh, no, I have my priorities *exactly* right."

No burst of heat was going to blow her balloon off course.

Chapter 4

The next night Brad watched Mya stride into the all but empty bar like a bounty hunter on a hot trail. A satchel hung over her shoulder, she'd poured herself back into the black jeans, and her fiercely swept up hair all spelt *business* to him. The bar wasn't officially open yet, but she was here to work, and anyone watching would know it.

No Messing Around Mya.

He bit back the amusement, because he was going to mess with Mya. He knew he had to play it carefully or she'd block him the way she'd blocked all those other guys at the bar. But he knew the party was a brilliant idea, and having to work with her to plan it? Genius. Because he hadn't felt heat in nothing but a kiss in for ever. The chemistry between them had kept him awake and rock hard all hours. He'd never felt the thrill of the chase like this. Then again, he hadn't *had* to chase like this. He watched closely to see her reaction when she saw him but her face remained an expressionless mask—too expressionless. Now, that took effort.

Good. If she had to work hard to hide her reaction to him, that meant her reaction was extreme. As was his to her. But he wasn't going to hide it. No, he was all about having fun and being up front.

"Hi, darling," he called, hoping to raise a spark.

She didn't answer until she'd reached the bar and then it was with a mocking coo. "Have you forgotten my name? I'm Mya."

"I can't call you 'darling'?" He propped an elbow on the broad expanse of highly polished wood.

"I'm suspicious of men who rely on pet names." She moved to put the bar between them. "I wonder if it's because they can't remember the name of the woman they're with."

He smiled, enjoying the way she was so determined to put him in his place.

"You've been guilty of it, haven't you?" She raised her brows and said it as a statement of fact, not a question.

He always remembered a woman's name at the time, but a few months later? Yeah, he'd better plead the fifth. With growing disappointment he watched her wind the apron round her waist, hiding how well her thighs were shown off in the spray-on jeans.

"We're not open yet." She turned to face him. "So I can't serve you."

"It's all right." Brad nodded at his half-empty glass. "Your boss already has. I've been talking with him about the party. Saturday after next. That okay for you?"

Her teeth worried her lower lip as a frown creased her forehead. "I'll need to talk to Drew. I'm rostered to work that night."

"Not any more. It's already sorted. You're there as a guest, not a bartender."

That little frown didn't lighten. "Yes, but—"

"You work every night," he interrupted. "You're not going to take a night off for your best friend's surprise party?"

"Of course I am."

"Then there's no problem, is there?"

"No, but you didn't need to arrange that for me." Her vibrant green eyes rested on him, still frustratingly cool.

Was that what bothered her? Him interfering? Fair enough. "I thought it would help," he explained honestly. "I wanted your boss to understand that he couldn't call on you at all that night and that I was willing to pay for extra staff."

"And that's wonderful of you," she said through

a smile that couldn't be more fake. "But I can handle my own requests for a night off." She suddenly looked concerned more than cross. "But it's very soon and very close to Christmas. You'll have to work quick to make sure people are free that night."

"They'll be free." Where the food and drink were free, people turned up.

"You'll need to get invitations out." She pulled a rack of glasses from a dish-drawer beneath the counter and began stacking them onto another shelf.

He grinned, happy that she was being overly efficient. He hoped it meant he was under her skin. "Can't I just send a text?"

"You want the whole world and his dog to turn up and drink the place dry?" She turned and gave him a pointed look. "You'll need to have a list of bona fide invitees on the door at the very least. But you should do proper invitations."

"Right, okay." He nodded as if her every word were law. "And personalised, right?"

"Right."

Actually she was right. Lauren wasn't a store-bought-stationery kind of woman. Mya wasn't either. Brad had spent all last night wondering just what kind of woman Mya was.

"Maybe you should do the actual invitations?" he suggested. "You're good at taking photos and stuff. You have a real eye for composition."

She sent him a withering look before turning back

to stack the glasses. "I don't have time. I can come up with the guest list and get you some contact details, but you're going to have to put it all together."

"Okay, I can do that." He sighed. "What are you thinking of? Gilt-edged cardboard things?" Never in a million years.

She flattened him with another killer cool stare. "I think Lauren would prefer something a little more original than that."

"I'll get to thinking, then," he answered mock meekly.

She eyed him suspiciously this time before her gaze lifted to something behind him and brightened. "Nice of you to turn up, Jonny," she called. "Everything's ready."

"I knew I could count on you." The tall guy who'd just walked in winked at her. "But you need the music." He stepped behind the bar and the relentless, rhythmic thud began.

Brad watched Mya instinctively move in time to the beat. With her natural rhythm and grace and fiendish determination, not to mention her sharp tongue and challenging eyes? He was dying here. And he wasn't getting anywhere very far, very fast.

The bar opened and the stream began. Offices weren't shutting for at least an hour yet but these people were ready to party. He didn't want to leave. Instead he watched half the other punters eye her up just as he was doing.

She and the Jonny guy made a good combo. Jonny, tattoos on display beneath the sleeves of the regulation black tee, was tanned and tall where she was pale and petite. Brad watched them banter their way through the cocktail preps. Her competitive streak was right to the fore. It amused him seeing the clinical way she observed the guy. He saw her flicking her wrist in practice, mimicking the movement of the master.

"You're almost as good as he is," he said when she came to his end of the bar in a quiet moment.

She didn't pout at the honest assessment. Mya wouldn't want false flattery. She was too straight-up for that. "Give me another week or two and I'll be better."

Brad smiled. She wanted to be the best?

"The protégée wants to whip the master, but I'm not going to let that happen." Jonny slung his arm along Mya's shoulders.

Brad immediately felt an animal response, his skin prickling at the sight of another man touching Mya—since when did he have hackles?

"Oh, it's going to happen and you know it." Mya flicked Jonny's arm off as easily as she'd flicked off the flirty guys from the stag do the night before. "You're running scared."

Both Brad and Jonny chuckled and watched her swagger to a waiting customer.

"You've been teaching her?" Brad asked Jonny.

Jonny nodded. "She's a quick learner. Focused, driven, plus she's been practising. That's how she got the job here in the first place."

"And she wants to work here because?"

"It's the most popular bar in town." Jonny looked at him directly. "We get good clientele with a lot of money to spend. So we make good money. With her looks and the skill to match, she's popular."

"Why do you help her out? You're not threatened by her?" Brad texted some mates, determined not to turn into some sad stalker type who just sat there and stared at his fixation. He certainly didn't want to feel this needle as he watched the byplay of the two bartenders. It couldn't be jealousy, could it? Never.

Jonny laughed. "Wouldn't you rather work with her than some guy?" he pointed out with a sly smile. "We work well together—people like the competition. Some like to look at her, others like to look at me." He turned back to the bar and bluntly summed it up. "It's all for the show and to help them spend their money."

And Mya needed the money. She'd mentioned the tips last night. She could earn more here than on an internship? Even though the internship would progress her career. Brad frowned as he remembered what little he could about her. The girl his parents had been so disapproving of had actually become the Dux of the school—carrying off the elite academic prizes. It had only been because Mya was going to university that Lauren had decided to go too. So surely she was doing as well at university? By rights she should be bonded to some corporate firm already, with a scholarship in return for five years of her working life. Instead she was flinging bourbon around a bar and working back-to-back shifts between the club and a café while squeezing in summer school as well. Something had gone wrong somewhere; the question was, what?

Mya wished Brad would go do his thinking elsewhere. She'd spent all night trying not to think about him, and here he was the minute she'd walked into work. She tried to retain coordination as she checked round the tables making sure all were clean and had the necessary seating arrangements, but she felt his eyes on her.

She'd gone overboard in her reaction to learning he'd cancelled one of her shifts, but the truth was she couldn't afford to lose a night off work. As it was she worked the bar job and a café job in the daytime. But it wasn't just a silver spoon that Brad had been born with; it was a whole canteen of cutlery. He might work, but it wasn't because he needed the money. He had no idea what it was like for people on the wrong side of the poverty line. And he was so used to getting his own way she was now ridden with the urge to argue with every one of his suggestions.

She walked back to the bar. She'd gone uber-efficient when she'd seen him sitting there. It was a way of working off the insane amount of energy she seemed to be imbued with. It didn't help that he was so gorgeous wearing dark jeans, a belt that drew every eye to his lean waist and a red tee so faded it was almost pink—only Brad could put on pink and make it masculine sexy. Pure ladybait.

Eyes locked with his, she reached for the knife to slice more lemons. Her skin sizzled as he openly looked her up and down.

"You never used to dress so monochrome," he commented thoughtfully.

He remembered that? Mya had never worn normal in the past, but she didn't have the time to make her crazy outfits any more.

"Needs must," she said briefly. If she didn't have the time to do something properly, she preferred not to do it at all, so all the fun she'd once had in creating something from nothing had been put away. Lauren had never worn the latest in fashion either—another thing that had brought them together back at school. She too turned her back on the consumerism of the day, and together they'd done it with style. Mya knew how to sew. She could turn a rag into something unexpected—deliberately setting out to make a statement with her clothing.

He glanced up and grinned at her. "Still touchy?"

"I didn't sleep well." She sliced quickly.

"Nor did I. I kept looking at your picture on my phone."

She paused, eyes glued to the knife. No way could she dare look at his expression this second. "I don't want to know what you were doing with my picture."

"I never looked at you that way before."

Oh, like that was meant to make her feel better?

"I'm aware of that," she snapped. "It was not 'til you saw the bikini."

"No, I was otherwise occupied. I'm sorry about that in a way. But to be honest it was a good thing. You weren't ready for me then."

"I'm not now," she lied, snapping the knife down on the chopping board, ignoring the way the lemon juice stung her burn.

"Oh, you hold your own," he said. "And you know it."

Her phone vibrated against her leg. She frowned and pulled it out. But it wasn't a text; it was a reminder from her calendar.

Oh, no.

"Are you okay? You've changed colour." Brad raised his voice. "Mya?" He asked more sharply. "Bad news?"

She tried to smile but couldn't force the fear far enough off her face to manage it. How *could* she have made such a mistake? She had everything on file, had due dates highlighted *and* underlined, but she'd been too busy dreaming up exotic cocktails and daft names to christen them in the past twenty-four hours to check. In other words, she'd been having too much *fun*.

She'd been so distracted she'd said yes to the extra shift at the café when they'd called last minute, forgetting to check her diary just in case. She'd figured it was better to keep fully occupied and thus ward off dangerous, idle-moment thoughts. Brad-type thoughts and replays of an unexpected, crazy kiss. She'd been distracted by imaginary conversations with a guy. About a *party*?

As a result, the assignment due tomorrow for her summer course had slipped her mind. She'd not done it. She'd not even *half* done it. She hadn't done nearly the amount of research and reading she should have. She was playing everything close to the wire at the moment, every minute screwed down to either work or study, and last-minute deadlines had become the norm in recent weeks—so long as she had the info she needed. Mya was good enough to wing it. But just winging it wasn't good enough for her. She wanted to ace it. She wanted her perfect GPA back. She wanted her perfect control back. She didn't want to be sleepless and thinking saucy thoughts at inappropriate hours of the day. She was *such* a fool to let herself be distracted. Especially by Brad Davenport. She drew a deep breath into her crushed lungs. No more distraction.

"Nothing I can't manage," she lied and brought

the bottles back to the line-up of shot glasses to pour more cherry-cheesecake shots for the trio of babes at a nearby table who were wearing "so hot right now" dresses and drinking in the vision of killer-in-casual Brad.

"Really?" He watched her with absolute focus, as if he had no idea that he'd caught the undying attention of every woman in the building. But he knew it already—it was normal for him.

She nodded and looked down to concentrate on pouring the vodka in the glasses, not trusting herself to speak again without snapping at him. Suddenly she was too stressed to be company for anyone, and his utterly innate gorgeousness irked her more than was reasonable.

He put both palms on the bar and leaned closer. "Mya?"

That underlying note of concern in his deep voice didn't help her combat the melting effect his mere presence had on her bones. His observation of her made her butter-fingered—not good when she had to flip two glass bottles at once in performing-seal fashion. Smashing the spirits would see the dollars coming out of her pay packet. "I need to concentrate." She offered a vaguely apologetic smile. "We'll have to talk about the party later."

"Sure." He eased back and flashed her a smile that would easily have coaxed her own out had she looked long enough.

But she resolutely kept her eyes on the glasses as she fixed the cranberry layer in them, because she was not allowing him to distract her any more. She put the shots onto a tray, lifted it and slowly walked out from behind the bar, to carry them to the divas. They were all looking over her shoulder, checking out Brad.

"You know him?" one of them asked in an overly loud whisper as Mya put the tray on the table between them. "He's single?"

"Permanently," Mya answered honestly. She glanced around and saw he hadn't moved. Worse he had a smile on, not his usual full-strength-flirt one, but a small twist to the lips that somehow made him even *more* attractive. It was so unfair the way he could make hearts seize with a mere look. She turned back to the pretty women. "But he loves to play."

And no doubt he'd adore three women at once. Maybe if she were to see him go off with the trio for some debauched night, then she'd blast away the resurgence of this stupid teen crush and be able to concentrate wholly on the wretched assignment she had ahead of her.

One of the girls stood and went over to talk to him. Mya went straight back behind the bar and tried not to pay attention to the high-pitched laughter. But she knew it was exactly two and a half minutes until he joined the women at their table. Mya decided to let Jonny serve them from then on.

She ignored the way the women leaned forward and chatted so animatedly. She ignored the laughter and smiles that Brad gave each of them. Most of all she ignored the way he tried to catch her eye when she walked past a couple of times. Peripheral vision let her know he looked up and over to her; she refused to look back. She had far more important things to think on. And then she was simply far too busy. People began pouring in as the sun went down but the night warmed up.

"Jonny, if I don't take my break now, I'm going to miss it altogether." She leaned across to beg him.

"Go now." He nodded. "Pete and I can handle it."

She grabbed the oversized ancient laptop she always lugged round in her satchel all day and took it out to the small balcony Brad had led her to the other night. She didn't really know why she'd brought it with her—it wasn't as if she'd somehow type on her feet as she worked her shifts at the café and then the bar.

Her heart sank as she scrolled to the relevant document. The cases were all cited, but she'd have to try to get copies of them to read them in full. What library was going to be open at midnight? She didn't have the Internet in her small flat as she couldn't afford the connection. She didn't even have a landline. She'd have to go to a twenty-four-hour café with wireless access and try to do it from there. Downloading fifteen cases? Oh, she was screwed.

She'd hardly started the first paragraph when Drew came out and caught her hunched over at a corner table.

"You can't sit there studying. This is a bar, not a library," he grumbled. "It's not the right look."

It was the last thing she needed—her control-freak, this-place-must-maintain-its-cool-image boss coming down on her.

"It's my break—surely I can read?" She looked up at him. Didn't he get how desperate she was?

"Not there, you can't," Drew informed her coolly.

To her horror, tears were a mere blink away. She shut her laptop and stood. Swatting up screeds of legalese in the dark alley outside didn't inspire her but if that was what she had to do, she'd do it. It was going to be an all nighter anyway. Followed by the brunch shift at the café tomorrow. How could she have screwed everything up—*again*?

She walked out past the queue forming at the door and into the night, desperate despite the fact she'd only have a few minutes at most before Drew hunted her out. While the summer sun's heat still warmed the air, it was now dark. Hooray for the safety torch on her keychain; she'd be able to read the fine-print text on the step at the back entrance of the bar.

"Big essay?" Brad had followed her, gazing at the ancient computer in her hand.

She nodded glumly, her stomach knotting again.

"Due tomorrow and I've not done it and I don't have half the case law I need," she confessed.

"Tomorrow?"

She winced. Did he have to hammer home her incompetence? "I need to read up." In other words, she needed him to go back inside and keep chatting to those women.

"How long's your break?"

"Twenty minutes."

"You can't possibly concentrate here." He frowned at the giant recycling bin into which they threw all the empty bottles. Yeah, the sound of smashing glass was regular and went well with that thudding bass beat coming through the brick walls of the converted warehouse.

"I can concentrate anywhere." If she had the info she needed.

"And do an assignment in twenty minutes? You might be brilliant, Mya, but you're not a magician." He frowned. "How come you don't have the case law?"

"I did an extra shift at the café today," she said. "I forgot about the assignment."

"You have too much on."

"Yes, so I need to work now," she said pointedly. But he didn't take the hint. Instead he cocked his head and came over all thoughtful.

"I've got access to all the legal databases. Including the subscription ones at my place," he said.

The ones that cost money to print each article from? The ones that held the case law she hadn't been able to download because she'd done the extra shift at the café? The ones she couldn't get to because the libraries were closed at this time of night?

He pondered another moment. "Skip your break and ask Jonny to cover the last of your shift. You know he'll do it. He owes you for setting up alone tonight. Come home with me. You can print off all you need and work all night." He stepped closer, pressing the best point, decisive. "I'll help you."

She folded her arms, using her laptop as body armour, mainly to hide the way her thundering heart was threatening to beat its way right out of her chest. "This isn't a family law assignment." She tried to play it cool and not collapse in a heap of gratitude at his feet. Or a heap of lustful wishes.

"I covered commercial in my degree too, you know. You're not the only one with dibs on brilliance. I got straight As."

Of course he did; he was that perfect. And she wasn't. She no longer had the brilliant label at law school. She shook her head. "I can't cheat."

"You're not going to," he growled. Stepping close, he put his hands on her shoulders. "I'm not going to write the assignment for you," he said firmly, as if she were a kid who had to have the simplest thing explained to her twenty different ways. "Consider me your law librarian."

Mya just stared. Feeling the warmth from his firm hands, and seeing his fit frame up close, she felt as if he were like an ad for all-male capability and virility. He was also the least likely librarian she could ever imagine.

He laughed and stepped closer. "I used to work in the law library as a student. I'm very good at searches."

"You *never* worked as a librarian." That she just didn't believe.

"Okay, library assistant," he clarified, all humble integrity mixed with that killer charm. "Great job to have as a student." His wicked grin bounced back. "I got to meet all the cute girls, and their names and addresses were all on there on the system already."

"So you abused your position?" Mya drawled, trying to cover the way she wanted to abuse his closeness now and lean against him.

"You're accusing me of wrongdoing?" He shook her and she nearly stumbled that last step right into his arms. "How come you're so down on me? All I'm trying to do is offer you a little help."

She kept her balance. She didn't like having to accept help.

"Just some space and some computer access." He held out the offer as if it were as innocent as a plate of home-made cookies.

While access to those databases would be awesome, what she really couldn't resist this second was his charm. "Okay, I really appreciate it," she breathed out in a rush. "But I don't want to put you out."

"You're not putting me out." He let go of her shoulders and turned to walk back down the alley. "And I promise I won't bother you."

He didn't have to *do* anything to bother her. He only had to exist. And the nearer he was, the worse it was. But she was just going to have to control that silly part of her body because she had an essay to write.

"Relax and go finish your shift," he said, leading her past the queue and back into the crowded bar. "You'll get the info you need and you've got all night to nail it."

Yeah, but it wasn't the assignment she was thinking of nailing.

Chapter 5

As Mya went back to mixing concoctions behind the bar, she surreptitiously watched Brad head back to the three beautiful women. Okay, so he was just helping her out with her schoolwork. There was nothing more to his offer. That was fine, perfect in fact. Then a couple of his mates turned up and he introduced the babes to them. Then—Mya couldn't help but notice—Brad stepped back from the conversation. And every time she glanced over—purely to see if their glasses needed refilling, of course—he was watching her. Time and time again their gazes met. And the thing was, he wasn't even giving her the full maple-syrup look, but it had the same effect anyway.

Yeah, she still wasn't over the fact that he was the hottest man she'd ever laid eyes on. It seemed there was a part of her that would always want him, no matter what else she had going on or how much of a player he was.

And had he made the computer-access offer to win her over and into his bed? Possibly. Did that matter? Not really. Because she wouldn't be sleeping in his bed. She'd be getting her assignment written.

It was just before 1:00 a.m. before she could get away—early, as Brad had suggested. Brad's two mates and the three babes had already left the bar, so he was waiting alone, having swapped from drinking beer to soda water hours ago. He straightened from the wall he was leaning against as she neared, her heavy satchel over her shoulder.

"Your place is really only a few minutes away?" she asked, determined to stay matter-of-fact and not crawl up against him and beg him to take her to bed and have his wicked way with her so she'd mindlessly fall into sleep the way she ached to.

He nodded.

Sure enough, just down the road and around the corner from the row of eclectic shops and bars in the more "alternative" area of town was a street of small, old villas. Every single one of them had been stylishly renovated and looked gorgeous and no doubt cost a mint.

"Why do you live here?" It was nothing like the

exclusive suburb in which he'd grown up with the massive modern houses and immaculate lawns.

"I like the mix in the neighbourhood." He shrugged. "Lots of good restaurants nearby and it's central."

"You don't cook?"

"Not often," he admitted with a flash of a smile.

She waited by the potted rosebush on the wooden veranda while he unlocked the villa and put in the code for the security system. And she knew he was wrong. She couldn't possibly concentrate here, not with him around.

"Let me give you the tour," he said as he led her the length of the wooden-floored hallway.

"I don't need to see your private things." She regretted this now. She'd have been better off winging the assignment by cobbling together an average essay with reference to just the few textbooks she had in her flat.

"Yes, you do. Otherwise you'll be curious, and if you're curious you won't be able to concentrate."

She managed a smile. "Because all women are curious about seeing your room?"

"Of course," he said. "Kitchen and lounge are this way."

They faced out to the back of the house, the garden not visible this time of night. For a guy who didn't cook, he still had all the mod cons in the kitchen.

She stayed in the doorway, really not wanting to take in the atmosphere of being in his personal space.

"Guest bathroom this way." He brushed past her as he stepped back out to the hall and opened a door on the other side of it. "Then there are a couple of spare bedrooms. One is my office. The other is a library and workroom for my assistant." He opened the door opposite.

She didn't go into his office but into the one he'd said was the library. She wouldn't have guessed he'd have a library—certainly not such a varied one.

"You have a whole bookcase of children's books." She read the spines. She recognised so many she'd read in her hanging-out-at-the-library days when she'd avoided all the other students. Avoided the teasing. That was where she'd met Lauren—who'd been ripping a page out of a book she could have afforded a million times over.

"I work for children," he answered briefly. "I got a bulk lot from a second-hand store."

Internally she laughed at the way everything was shelved in the "right" place. Clearly he hadn't been kidding about his library-assistant job. She pulled one from the "teen-read" shelf and flicked it open. Inside the front cover a name had been written in boyish scrawl—Brad Davenport. Second-hand store, huh?

She smiled. "That was my favourite for years. I read it so many times."

"Uh-huh." He took the book off her.

"Did you cry at the end?" she asked.

He smiled but didn't confess.

"I did every time," she admitted with a whisper.

Still he didn't give it up.

"You don't want me to know that you're a marshmallow inside?"

"I'm no marshmallow," he answered. "I have them here for the look of it. Generally the kids only come here to meet and talk with me so they're not so nervous in court. I'm not their counsellor or anything. I'm merely their legal representative."

"But they're your books." And the kids he was supposedly not that close to drew pictures for him that he put on his walls?

His reluctant smile came with a small sigh. "I like to read."

"And you like kids?

"Sometimes." He drew the word out, his voice ringing with caveats. "But I have no interest in having any myself." He put the book back. "There are enough out there who've been done over by their dipstick parents."

"You think you'd be a dipstick parent?"

"Undoubtedly."

She smiled.

"I think parenting is one of those things you learn from the example you had," he said lightly. "I didn't have a great example."

"So you know what not to do."

He shook his head. "It's never that simple. I see the cycle of dysfunctional families in my office every day. Now—" he moved back out of the room "—the last room is my bedroom."

Mya hovered in the doorway, really not wanting to intrude as the sense of intimacy built between them.

He turned and saw her hesitating and rolled his eyes. "I promise not to pounce."

She stepped right into the room. He had the biggest bed she'd ever seen, smothered in white coverings. It would be like resting in a bowl of whipped cream. Definitely not a bed for pyjamas; there should be nothing but bare skin in that.

"Why is it so high?" she asked, then quickly cleared her throat of the embarrassing rasp that had roughened her voice.

"I'm tall."

"You wouldn't want to fall out of it, would you?" If she sat on the edge of it, her feet couldn't touch the floor. "It's like Mount Olympus or something."

There was no giant TV screen on a table at the foot of the bed. No chest of drawers for clothing. No bookshelf. No, it was just that massive bed with the billowing white covering demanding her attention.

"Nice to know I inspire you to think of Greek gods."

She sent him a baleful look. It was unfair of him to start with the teasing again when she had a whole night of work ahead of her. She was tense enough with unwanted yearning. But she couldn't resist pulling his string a touch—wishing she really could. "What do I inspire you to think of?"

His gaze shifted to the left of her—to that bed. "Better not say."

"Don't tell me you're shy?" She laughed.

"I don't want to embarrass you."

Oh, it was way too late for that. "I mistakenly sent you a picture of myself in a half-see-through bikini. I don't think I could be more embarrassed."

"That was just an image. I couldn't touch you."

Her breathing faltered, her pulse skipped quicker at the thought of where and how he was thinking of touching her. And when. Now? Mere words banished the chill she'd felt before as heat crept up her cheeks and across her entire body.

A half-smile curved his lips. "You like a little talk, don't you? For a woman who's planning to spend the rest of her life counting beans, you have to get your thrills somewhere, huh?"

"There's nothing wrong with chasing financial security." She chose to ignore the suggestion she might like a little sauce talk.

"Strikes me you chase all-over safety. Which isn't something I can give you," he warned, leaning close. "You're not entirely safe with me."

"Now you tell me, when you've got me alone in your house." Her insides were melting—that part of her had no desire to be safe right now. It was a dangerous game and one that was so irresistible.

"In the middle of the night."

She turned and looked at the pretty design on the lower part of the wallpaper. Not just normal wallpaper, but almost a mural. Good diversion. "The room came like this?"

"No, I chose it." He let her pull back from the brink.

"You did?" It made the room like a grotto—with that big bed in the middle and the soft-looking white pillows and duvet. "Okay, you chose it with women in mind."

"No, I liked my tree house when I was a kid. Remember that?"

She did remember the old hut up high in one of the ancient trees at his parents' house. She and Lauren had been banned from it. It had been padlocked and everything. His escape from the magazine-spread-perfect house. Lauren had got her escape by banning her mother from her room.

"This gives me the same feeling of peace." He walked towards her. "And women don't sleep in here."

Yeah, right. "Because you have a separate bedroom for your seduction routine? One with boxes of condoms and sex toys?"

"I don't need sex toys," he boasted with a self-mocking smile. "And you've already seen the spare rooms. One's my office, one's my library."

"So what, you're celibate?" She let her eyebrows seek the sky.

"I prefer to sleep-over at their houses. It makes the morning-after escape easier."

She shook her head but couldn't help the laugh. "You're bad."

"No, I'm good. It's easier for both of us. Women tend to be more relaxed in their own environment."

"Do you even make it to the morning, or do you sneak out while she's still asleep?"

"I never *sneak* out." He walked a step closer still. "There's nothing like starting the day with sex. I leave her recovering in bed after that."

"And dreaming of another encounter that will never happen." Mya desperately clung to some kind of mockery but all she could think about was kissing him, about starting the day with sex—with him.

"Why ruin a beautiful memory?" He smiled. "One perfect night is all that's required. More just gets messy."

She suspected just the one with him would get messy for her. Her one and only one night had been hideous the next day.

"Now," he said softly, so close in her personal space now her pulse was frantic. "You can either work in my office or the library. You've got your laptop." He glanced at the dinosaur beast in her bag.

It weighed a ton but still had a word-processing program that worked. That was all that mattered. "Let's go with my office." He made the decision for her. "I'll pull up the cases you need while you get reading. And my computer is faster in there than the one in the office. You can type up your assignment on that—be better for you ergonomically."

Mya dragged in a shaky breath, determinedly so *not* disappointed he hadn't kissed her, and followed him to the office.

There was really only one reason why Brad had offered to help Mya. One carnal, driving reason. But now she was in his house he fully regretted it. Her scent tormented him. The light sweetness overlaid with the tart lemon from the bar. Yeah, that was Mya. He switched on the computer with deliberately calm movements. In truth, he wanted to spin in his seat and grab her, have her over his desk in a second and kiss every inch of her skin. Here, in his bed, the kitchen, everywhere. He had the sinking feeling she'd haunt his house for ever if he didn't get her out of his system.

But there was no doubt she was waiting for him to make his move. His playboy reputation had all her barriers up, and though he knew he could eventually get her to say yes, he didn't want to be that predictable. He didn't want her thinking she knew all there was to know about him. Because she didn't. He wasn't *that* out of control. He didn't *want* to be that out of control. And he wasn't that shallow—at least he hoped not. So he bit back the raging lust and concentrated on the case searches instead.

He quickly read the list she pulled out. It wouldn't take him that long.

She had her textbook out and was making notes already. He smiled as he watched her discreetly while logging in to the online databases. She was so natural with her hair tied back and her pen in hand, ready to take notes as she read—fast. She'd eased right into it, looking more relaxed and at home than he'd ever seen her in the bar, for all the effort that she put in there. And that was the difference, he figured: there it was a big effort, whereas this—reading, studying, thinking—was effortless for her. And natural.

"You really like corporate law, or is it about the earning potential?" he couldn't resist asking when he was about halfway through the list.

She lifted her head and met his eyes for a too-short moment. "I really do like it." She looked at the pages. "Does that surprise you? I like the challenge. I like figuring out the rules. I like the power in negotiation."

He nodded but couldn't help thinking she was holding something back. Her drive was so strong.

"You think I'm shallow?" She looked up again and this time he saw the flicker of insecurity in her eyes. It mattered to her what he thought of her?

"No," he answered honestly. "Different people

enjoy different things. Different people have different things driving them."

She nodded, but to his disappointment didn't open up more.

"Why are you doing summer school?" He couldn't help asking. "Why do you work so many shifts? Aren't you on scholarship?"

"Not any more."

"Why not?"

Mya took in a deep breath. She never usually discussed this—but telling Brad might be a darn good idea. It might help keep her focused around him. "I failed."

His fingers stopped on the keyboard and he swivelled in the chair to face her. "You finally flunked an exam? Don't worry about it—everyone does sometime."

Somehow she didn't think he had. "I didn't flunk one. I flunked them all. Finals last year I completely crashed."

"What happened?" His eyes widened.

Yeah, it had been a shock to her too. She'd always been the super-bright one. The rebellious but diligent student who was there on sufferance because she dragged the school's academic rankings up single-handedly.

"What happened?" he asked again when she said nothing. "Your family? Is everyone okay?"

"It was nothing catastrophic." She turned away

and began underlining random sentences with pencil. "It was embarrassing."

"So what happened?"

She really didn't want to go into it but going into it would put the ice on any hot thoughts—hers and his—and she wanted to get through this night without being tempted. "I met a guy. I thought he was, you know, the *one*." Now she was blushing with embarrassment, because she'd been so naïve. "But he totally wasn't. He broke up with me two days out from exams and I…handled it badly." It was mortifying now to look back on, but she'd been hurt. She'd finally thought she'd found a place to fit in, and she couldn't have been more wrong.

"What a jerk breaking up at exam time."

She nodded. "He was. But I was an idiot. A big idiot." Because she'd gone out and made everything worse.

"How big?"

"I went out and got really drunk."

"Oh." He was silent a moment. "Did something bad happen?"

"Not bad. But not that great either." She glanced at him. "My own mistake and I've learned from it." The responsibility lay with her. She was the one who'd lain in bed crying her eyes out. She was the one who'd gone out and got drunk to try to forget about him and ease the pain. She was the one who'd brought home some random guy and slept with him just to feel wanted. She'd woken up the morning of her first exam with a dry mouth and a sick stomach and an inability to remember the name of the man in her bed. She'd been mortified and ashamed and sick. Hung-over and bleary-eyed, she'd not even made it past the first hour of the exam. The one that afternoon she'd turned up, signed her name and walked out again. The last exam she'd actually tried to do something on but had panicked halfway through and walked out. Her supervisor had called her in when the results came out. Had asked what had happened, had wanted her to get a doctor's note or something because her performance was so shockingly below her usual standard. Below anyone's standards. But she could never have done that. It was her fault, her responsibility.

She'd fed from the scholarship fund long enough. All her secondary schooling, now half her university degree. No more. She was making her own way in the world—and paying her own way. Nothing mattered more than gaining financial independence, by getting a good job. And if it meant it took longer for her to finish her degree working part-time, so she could live, then that was just the way it had to be.

"What have you learned?" Brad asked.

She turned and looked at him directly. "That I can't let anything or anyone get in the way of my studies again. Definitely no man, no relationship."

"That's why you don't want to get involved with anyone? That's why it's inconvenient?"

"That's right." She nodded, denying the other reason even to herself. "I'm busy. I'm working at the bar every night and at the café on the weekends. I've got lectures midweek and assignments and reading to do in and around that. I just don't have time for anyone or anything else."

"You can't let one bad experience put you off for ever."

"Not for ever. Just the next couple of years."

He frowned. "But you get time off over Christmas, right?"

"From lectures but I have assignments and I have shifts right the way through." The public holidays paid good money, and patrons were more generous tippers too. "I'm not interested in anything."

"Not a great quality of life for you, though, is it? All work and no play."

"It's not for ever," she said again.

"No? How many years are you off finishing your degree?"

"Part-time it's going to take me three. That's with taking summer papers as well."

"So no nookie for you for another three years?" He shook his head, looking appalled. "That's more than a little tragic."

"Sex isn't the be-all and end-all," she said with more confidence than she felt.

"It's up there. Without sex there can be no life."

"We're not talking biology here."

"You're going to be miserable," he warned.

"I'm not. I'm going to achieve what I want to achieve."

"With no help from anybody."

"You understand, right?"

"No, I don't."

Startled, she looked at him.

"I don't see why it has to be that miserable." He turned and met her eyes. "No such thing as balance with you, is there?"

"I have to do what I have to do. And I'm not into the casual-sex scene." She cleared her throat, trying to hold the blush at bay as she remembered that mortifying morning. "I learned that too. I don't want a fling. But nor do I want a relationship right now. I have too much else to do."

"All or nothing," he murmured.

"Right now it's nothing," she confirmed.

He looked at her, brown eyes serious. "Okay." He held her gaze. "Message received loud and clear."

She said nothing. He turned back to the computer and pulled the list of cases nearer. Mya watched his fingers fly over the keyboard. Serious, focused.

That was it? She'd told him as explicitly as she could that she didn't want an affair and he just accepted it?

Because here was the thing—she was still totally

hot for the guy. How could he be so focused when she was dying of desire? She'd gone for honesty and he'd taken it. He'd backed right off. But instead of feeling any kind of relief, she felt *more* wound up. She'd been so sure he'd make some kind of move. She'd been so sure she'd say no. Only there were no moves from him, and only *yeses* and *pleases* circling in her head.

She couldn't believe her madness. Her brain had been lost somewhere between here and the bar.

He stood and picked up the pages as they came out of the printer and put highlighters and sticky notes in front of her. She almost laughed. It seemed the guy was as much of a stationery addict as she was.

"It's all vital for doing an assignment." He winked. "I'm off to make you some coffee while you get started."

He'd left the documents open on screen so she could cut and paste quotes as necessary. Hell, he'd even opened up a documents file, named for her, and saved the other cases he'd downloaded. She stared at them, not taking in a word, just waiting.

Five minutes later he put the steaming mug in front of her and stayed on the other side of the desk.

"I'm turning in now. There's more coffee in the machine in the kitchen, fruit in the bowl, chocolate on hand too. Stay as late as you like. Don't go walking out there at some stupid hour of the morning."

"I can't stay the whole night." There was just no way.

"It'll probably take you all night to get the assignment done anyway. No point in taking unnecessary risks." He walked back to the doorway in jeans and tee—she noticed his feet were now bare.

"Thanks," she said rustily. "Really appreciate this." And was so disappointed when he disappeared down the hallway.

She stared at the screen. All this info was at her fingertips. All she had to do was read, assimilate, process, write. It wasn't that hard. She'd done enough essays to know what her lecturers wanted and what it was she needed to get that extra half grade.

But the house was silent.

Acutely aware of his presence under the roof, she sat stupidly still, listening for sounds of him. Imagining going to find him—imagining sliding into that mountainous cloud of a bed and...

She'd pushed him away and it had worked. For *him*. She still wanted what she couldn't have and with that she'd lost her ability to concentrate. That was a first. She glanced at the big printer on the table behind her. Half a tree's worth of paper and twenty minutes later she was ready to leave.

"What are you doing?" he asked just as she'd tiptoed to the front door.

She whirled around. What was she doing? What was *he* doing standing there almost completely bare?

Only a pair of boxer shorts preserved his modesty and even then they were that knit-cotton variety that clung rather than hung loose. And speaking of things being *hung*…

She burned. "I can't work here." It was a pathetic whisper.

"You're sneaking out." He crossed his arms. It only emphasised his biceps. It was so unfair of him to have such a fit body.

"I didn't want to wake you."

"How are you planning on getting home?"

"I can walk."

"It's after two in the morning."

"I walk home from the bar all the time. I have a safety alarm. I walk along well-lit streets. I'm not stupid."

His jaw clenched. "Take my car."

Could he make it worse for her? "No, that's okay. I'm fine walking."

"It's not fine for anyone to walk home alone this time of night. Take my car."

She sighed. "That's very kind of you, but I can't."

"You have a real issue accepting help, don't you?" he growled.

Possibly. Okay, yes, particularly from him. His whole "friendly" act was confusing her hormones more. "I can't drive," she admitted in a low voice. "I've never got my licence. I've never learned to drive."

For a second his mouth hung open. "Everyone learns to drive. It's a life skill. Didn't your dad teach you?"

Her dad didn't drive either. That was because the accident at the factory years ago had left him with a limp and unable to use his right arm. He'd been a sickness beneficiary ever since. Living in a house that was damp, in a hideous part of town that was getting rougher by the day. She was determined to get her parents out of there. She owed it to them. "You're assuming we had a car," she said bluntly. They couldn't afford many things most people would consider basic necessities, like a car and petrol or even their power bill most of the time.

"Okay." He turned and strode back to his bedroom. "I'll drive you."

"You don't have to do that," she called after him, beyond frustrated and embarrassed and frankly miserable.

"Yes, I do."

"I didn't want to disturb you."

"It's way too late for that." He returned, jeans on, tee in hand. "I'll drop you home."

She needed him to put the tee on, and she really needed him too. She'd had such sensual thoughts in the past hour she was almost insane with it.

But he read her fierce expression wrong. "Don't you dare argue with me any more."

He opened the front door and waited for her.

To her horror her eyes filled and she quickly walked out. She was too strung out to argue. She'd not admitted to anyone the struggle she'd been having. Not even to Lauren. But she was so tired. The relentless shifts, the constant pressure of squeezing in assignment after assignment, of fitting in lectures around work, of desperately trying to get the highest of grades every time, of never, ever getting enough sleep. But it was something she alone had to deal with. And she certainly couldn't lose more time or sleep fantasising about him.

Chapter 6

Brad's tension didn't ease as he unlocked the car and opened the passenger door in the middle of the night for her. For someone so independent, her inability to drive threw him. They lived in New Zealand. Everyone drove here. And she shouldn't be walking home alone night after night after work at the bar. She was so pale; the amount of work she had on bothered him. It didn't help that he'd lumbered her with this party as well. He was thoughtless. And, yes, selfish.

Because all it had been about was him stealing time with her. He'd wanted her—and any excuse would do to get that time. But now? Now he really was concerned.

"I'll teach you to drive," he said, putting his car in gear and pulling out into the quiet, dark street.

"Thanks all the same but it's not necessary. I live centrally. I walk to work. I use public transport—it's better for the environment."

"You're happy to learn bar tricks from Jonny," he pointed out, annoyance biting at her refusal.

"I wouldn't want to damage your car."

His body tautened to a ridiculous degree, urging him to pull over and kiss her into silence. Into saying yes—to this, to anything, to *every*thing. He wanted her more than he'd ever wanted a woman. Who'd have thought that a picture could have affected him like this?

No. It wasn't just the picture. It was every time she opened her mouth and shot him down while eating him up with her eyes. If they ever got it on, it would be mind-blowing. He knew it. But that wasn't happening. She wasn't into flings and he wasn't into anything else and he was man enough to back off. He'd drop her home now and go out tomorrow night and find a new friend to play with.

But the idea left him cold. Instead, he went back to thinking about her.

"About Lauren's party." He revved the engine while waiting at another infernal red light. The ten-minute drive seemed to be taking for ever. "If it's too much for you—"

"It's not too much." She interrupted him and he

heard the attempted smile in her voice. "I just got behind on this one assignment and I'll get that done tonight. At home. I want to help. I can do it. Just to the left here is fine." She pointed out her apartment.

"I haven't thought much more about it." He hadn't thought about the party at all. He'd spent all his spare moments imagining the delicious things he'd do to Mya the minute she let him.

She turned to face him as he cut the engine. "The cocktails will be fun. Just get in a good band and a DJ and good food. It'll be fine."

He flicked on the interior light so he could see her properly. "You wouldn't be lowering your standards for me, would you?"

The colour ran under her skin but she kept on her smile as she shook her head. "I'd never do that. I still expect the best."

Brad grinned despite his disappointment. She'd have got the best. Her automatic, instant refusals of anything he offered? They pricked his pride. He wished she'd come to him, wished she'd be as unable to resist their chemistry as much as he seemed unable to.

"I really don't know how to thank you." She clutched the door handle, her eyes wide and filled with something he really wished was desire.

"I can think of a couple of ways." He couldn't help one last little tease.

"You've a one-track mind, haven't you?" she

teased right back, but she looked away from him, drawing a veil over that spark.

The devil in him urged to press her for a date, but he already knew her answer. She was either working or studying, every waking minute. So he let her go and drove home in the darkness. But once there he remained wide-awake and restless and *hot*. Nothing was going to happen between them, but that hadn't diminished the ache and the hunger. Lust. He'd get over it. But as he sat in front of his computer, the sky lightened and he got to wondering whether she'd finished her assignment. Whether she was working her shift. Whether she was okay. And then he realised he wasn't going to be able to rest until he knew for sure that she was.

Mya knew that if she could survive tonight, she could survive anything. She showered to refresh her system but it was a bad idea. The warm water made muscles melt and her mind wander into dangerous territory. She flicked the jets to cold. Then she dragged herself to her desk and pulled out the piles of paper and opened her ancient laptop. She had four hours. She didn't have time to lust after anyone.

Finally she got in the zone. She read—fortunately she was fast at it—assimilated, analysed and wrote, fingers thumping the keyboard. Her phone alarm beeped at seven forty-five just as she was finalising the formatting. She packed up and sprinted to the café. There was Internet access there. She grabbed a coffee and hit Send on the email. Her assignment was safely en route to her lecturer's inbox. She straightened and stretched out the kinks in her back from hunching over her keyboard. Exhaustion hit her like a freight train. Only now she had to put on an apron and start making everyone else's coffees.

Two hours later she switched her phone to mute and put it in the cubby so she'd no longer be bothered by the zillion messages she was receiving. Brad had sent the invites to everyone about the same time she'd sent the assignment to her lecturer. She'd never expected he'd follow through so quickly or with such impact. She should have known better. Brad Davenport was all about impact.

She'd been impressed by the slick black-and-white mysterious message that had spread over the screen of her phone when she'd clicked on it. Yeah, she'd been fielding texts and calls all morning with people wanting the inside deal on what the plans were for the party—all excitement and conjecture. Because the Davenports were the ultimate in cool. Stylish, unique and rolling in it, and anyone who was anyone, or who wanted to be someone, wanted this invite. She'd answered honestly that she hadn't a clue what was planned but that they'd better be smart enough to keep it secret from Lauren. Mya had threatened them with a prolonged and agonising social-death sentence should anyone spoil the surprise.

Her shift crawled to its end. She was almost in tears with relief and at the same time ready to drag herself across town. She'd doze in the bus on the way. The last person she expected to see just outside the café door was Brad.

"What are you doing here?" Was she so tired she was hallucinating?

"I thought I'd give you a lift home. You must be exhausted."

Not a hallucination, he was real. Looking so strong and smiling, and she wished she didn't have any stupid scruples.

"I'm okay." She was so tired, it was harder to control her reaction to his proximity and the urges he inspired.

"You got it done?"

She nodded, glad he'd reminded her of her work. "Thanks for coming in but I'm not going home. I'm having lunch with my parents." She was due there this minute.

"I'll give you a ride."

"No, it's fine," she hurriedly refused. "I take the bus."

He looked at her. "I can give you a ride."

"Shouldn't you be working?" She really didn't want him taking her there.

"I'm due a lunch break too."

"But—"

"Can you stop saying no to me in everything?"

he asked. "I'm offering as a *friend*, Mya. Nothing more."

She opened her mouth and then shut it again as she registered the ragged thread of frustration in his voice. He must be tired too—that invitation would have taken some time on the computer. Had he not slept a wink either?

"You don't have to do this," she said softly ten minutes later as they headed towards the motorway that would take them right across town and to the outskirts.

"Don't worry, I won't embarrass you." He reached over and gave her knee a teasing squeeze. "I won't tell them you like sending people racy pictures of yourself."

She managed a light laugh but her discomfort mushroomed as she realised he was going to see the worst.

"Are *you* embarrassed?" he asked quietly. "You don't want me to see your home?"

"No," she argued instantly. "But you wouldn't be the first person to look down your nose at my neighbourhood. We come from totally different worlds, so don't act like you're all understanding and down with it. You can't ever relate."

"Your shoulders aren't broad enough for a chip this big."

"Oh, it's a chip, is it? It's just me being oversensitive?" She twisted in her seat to face him. "What would you know? Have you ever faced the judgments and expectations from each side of the economic divide? Girls from the wrong side of the tracks like me are only good for a fling." Never marriage material. That was how James had treated her. At first he hadn't known. He'd been attracted to her academic success, but when he'd found out about her background, he'd run a mile. "All *you've* ever wanted from women like me is sex."

"All I've ever wanted from *any* woman is sex," he pointed out lazily. "It has nothing to do with your family background."

About to launch into more of a rant, she stopped and mentally replayed what he'd said. And then she laughed.

"I mean really—" he winked "—you don't think you're taking this too seriously? We're in the twenty-first century, not feudal England."

She shook her head. "Twenty-first century or not, the class system operates. There's an underclass you know nothing about."

"Don't patronise me," he said. "I'm not ignorant. I'm aware of the unemployment figures and I've dealt with worse in my work. You've got no idea of the dysfunction I see. I can tell you it crosses all socioeconomic boundaries. Sometimes the worst are the ones who have the most."

"Yeah, but you don't know the stress financial problems can bring."

"That's true. I don't have personal experience of that. But I'm not totally without empathy."

"And salary doesn't necessarily equate with effort," she grumped. Her mother worked so hard and still earned a pittance. That was why she'd insisted Mya study so hard at school, so she'd end up with a job that actually paid well. And Mya wanted to work to help her parents.

"Mya." He silenced her. "I know this might amaze you, but I'm not that stupid or that insensitive."

She put her head in her hands. Of course he wasn't. "Sorry."

She heard his chuckle and let his hand rub her shoulder gently—too briefly.

"I'll let you away with it because I know how tired you are," he said.

But her discomfort grew as they neared. He'd been right—she didn't want him seeing it. She was embarrassed. Embarrassed she hadn't done something sooner to get her parents out of there. She should have done so much more already. "You can just drop me, okay?"

"Sure," he answered calmly. "They must be impressed with how hard you're working at the moment."

Mya chewed her lower lip. "They don't know."

"Don't know what?"

"Don't know anything."

"That you work at the bar, the café or that you're not at uni full-time?"

She shook her head. "They don't know I lost the scholarships. They don't know I'm at summer school. They can't know. Can't ever." She felt tears sting. Stupid tears—only because she was tired.

He took his eyes from the road for too long to stare at her. "And you're that stressed about them finding out?"

"Of course I am. Watch the traffic, will you?"

He turned back to stare at the road, a frown pulling his brows. "I think you should tell them."

Her breath failed. "I can't tell them. They're so proud of me. It's...everything."

"They'd understand."

They wouldn't. She'd be a failure. She didn't ever want to let them down. She didn't want disappointment to stamp out the light in their eyes when they looked at her. "You don't get it. I'm the only one to have even finished school. They're so proud of me, they tell everyone. I can't let them down now. This is what I am to them." It was all she was.

"Everyone stuffs up sometimes, Mya. I think they'd understand."

"They wouldn't. And I couldn't bear for them to know. It alienated me from the others. My cousins, the other neighbourhood kids... They gave me a hard time then. I don't want more of a hard time now.

I don't want my parents disappointed. Life's been tough enough on them."

She'd been bullied as she walked across the neighbourhood in her school uniform—the only kid in the block to go to a school with a uniform. Taunted—told she'd become a snob, torn down. *Freak. You think you're better than us?*

She hadn't thought that. She knew just how hard those in her 'hood worked—or worked to try to get a job. Sure, a couple hadn't. A couple had gone off the rails in the way Lauren had once threatened to. But she knew better than anyone that snobbery worked both ways. In the one hand she'd carried the hopes and dreams of her parents; in the other she'd been burdened with the spite and jealousy of others. She didn't fit in here any more, but she sure hadn't fitted in with her new school either.

And now she was held up as the neighbourhood example—her cousin's five-year-old daughter had said she wanted to go to uni and be just like her. She couldn't let them down.

She'd had opportunities others hadn't had and she'd squandered them on a man who was so removed from her own sphere—that elite, born-to-it world that she'd never once felt comfortable in. She couldn't let them know what an idiot she'd been. And she couldn't be that naïve girl again. This damsel was doing her own rescuing. No man, no fairy-tale fantasy, would come between her and her studies.

"How will you get home after lunch?" he asked as they neared her home.

"Same as always."

She knew he was looking at the gang symbols graffitied on the fences they passed. The lush greenery of the affluent central suburbs gave way to unkempt, sunburned brown grass and bare dirt. The old-looking swing-set in the park and the new activity set that had already been defaced, litter spilling from the bin. She knew what he was thinking; she thought it too. The neighbourhood wasn't just rough; it was unsafe and was worsening. Her resolve firmed. She was getting her parents out of here as soon as she could.

They were sitting on the porch when Brad turned into the driveway. The two-bedroom government-supplied house had been modified so her father could walk in easily. He didn't rise as Brad stopped the car, but her mother hurried over. Brad got out of the car and greeted her with his intensely annoying polite manners. Mya watched her mother blink a couple of times, watched his full impact on her—that overpowering charm. And she helplessly watched him accept her mother's invitation to join them at lunch. All done before she'd even said hello.

When Brad walked into the house, he was shocked—but not for the reasons Mya might have thought he might be. He'd seen way smaller, emptier properties. No, what shocked him was the wall in the lounge.

It was smothered in the evidence of Mya's achievements. There were certificates everywhere. Certificates going back more than a decade—from when she won spelling competitions at age six. Competitions far beyond her years at that. There were newspaper articles citing her academic successes. There were pictures of her in her uniform. Pictures of her accepting cups and prize-giving. But there were no pictures of her playing.

Proof of their pride in her was everywhere and he realised she hadn't been kidding about the pressure. No wonder her identity was so bound up in performance—*perfect* performance. But surely her parents weren't so success-obsessed for her that they'd disown her if they knew she'd failed? She was their only child.

"Brad's a lawyer. A tutor at university." Mya walked in with her father, who was leaning on her arm. "He's been helping me with my studies this year. He just gave me a ride because I was running late to get here." She bit her lip and looked at Brad as if worried she'd made a slip in mentioning law school given she was supposed to be on holiday.

"She doesn't need my help, you know." Brad went with her story with an easy smile. "She's just trying to make me feel useful."

The sad thing was he liked feeling useful to her. Even if in truth he wasn't.

"She's a genius." Even as he was saying it, he realised he was buying into the Mya-brain-box worshipping—doing it as badly as her parents. Talking her up until she was terrified of failing. Mya, who needed no help academically because she was such a star. Never-fail Mya. Never *dare* fail.

So he switched. "But she works really hard at it."

He encountered a beseeching green gaze just at the moment her mother's proud tones came from the other side of the table.

"Mya always works hard."

Brad worked hard himself then, keeping the conversation light—and away from work. Mya was abnormally quiet and giving him keen looks every so often. It bothered him she was so nervous—what did she think would happen? Did she trust him so little? He wouldn't let her down and give her away.

"I hope it wasn't too bad my staying." He finally apologised for butting in when they were back in his car and driving towards town. "But I really enjoyed it."

"It was hardly your usual restaurant standard," she answered brusquely.

"You couldn't get fresher than that salad," he pointed out.

That drew a small smile. "It's the one thing he

likes the most but tending the garden takes him a long time. He has chronic pain and he gets tired."

"It was an accident?"

"In the factory years ago." She nodded. "He's been on a sickness benefit since. Mum does the midnight shift at the local supermarket." She sighed. "So now you know why I want to get the big corporate job."

He nodded.

"I want to move them somewhere else. Somewhere much nicer."

"I can understand that." He paused. "You really care about what they think of you, huh?"

"Don't you care about what your folks think of you?"

He laughed beneath his breath. "It no longer matters to me what either of them think."

"No longer? So it used to?"

"When I was a kid I wanted to please Dad." He laughed—the small kind of laugh designed to cover up real feelings.

Mya didn't want him to cover up. "But you don't any more?"

"I'm really good at my job and I enjoy it. What he thinks is irrelevant."

"What did he do?"

"He didn't do anything."

"I'm not stupid either, Brad." She turned in her seat to study his profile directly.

"So you know what he does." Brad trod harder on

the accelerator and gave her the briefest of glances. His warm brown eyes now hard and matte. "Buys his way out of anything."

"What did he buy his way out of for you?" Mya asked quietly.

Attention. It was all about attention. For him. For Lauren. He'd once asked his father to come and see him in a debating contest of all things. Sure, not the most exciting of events, but he'd been fifteen years old and still young enough to want his father's approval. At that time he'd wanted to *be* his father. A brilliant lawyer, top-earning partner in his firm with the beautiful wife, the yacht, the two kids and the dog.

"I caught him." Brad surprised himself by answering honestly.

"Doing what?"

"Betraying us." He glanced at Mya. She'd revealed a part of her life that she preferred to keep private and that she wanted to fix. He wanted her to know that he understood that. So he told her. "I wanted him to come to see me in the debating final when I was a teen. But he said he had an important meeting he couldn't get out of. I won and went up to show him the medal." He'd gone up to his father's office, excited with the winning medal in hand, anticipating how he'd quietly hold it up and get the smile, the accolade. Instead he'd discovered that the very important meeting his father hadn't been able to wriggle out of had been with one of the junior lawyers. Fresh from law school, whether she was overly ambitious or being taken advantage of, Brad didn't know and no longer cared.

"The meeting was with a trainee," he said. "She was on her knees in front of him."

"Oh, Brad."

His father had winked. Winked and put his finger to his lips, as if Brad was old enough—"man" enough—to understand and keep his sordid secret. His scheduled screw more important than his own son. And the promises he'd made to his wife.

So many dreams had shattered that day.

The anger had burned like acid as he'd run home and hidden in the damn tree hut that he hadn't built with his father, but that his father had paid some builder to put in for the look of it.

Brad decided never to be a lawyer like his father. It would never be a father-and-son firm as his father had always envisaged. No insanely high billing rates for Brad. He'd turned to the far poorer-paying child advocacy in direct retaliation to his father. He had the trust fund from his grandfather. He was never going to be short of money. So there was something more worthwhile that he could do. Something that would irritate his accolade- and image-driven dad.

But eventually he realised his father really didn't give a damn what he did. Brad just wasn't that important to him. His gestures might be grand, but they were empty. Just purchases. There was a missing element—no true paternal love. All his father was, was hungry for success, money and women—and for maintaining that façade of the perfect family in society.

"I thought Mother didn't know," Brad scoffed lightly. "I thought I was protecting her." Brad had kept that bitter secret for months, feeling all kinds of betrayal—for himself, his sister and his mother.

"But she did," Mya said.

He nodded. "We have an annual barbecue at home for all Dad's staff. And that trainee turned up all confidence and Mother greeted her *so* politely. So knowingly. Coolly making it clear to her that while Dad might screw the secretaries, he'd never leave his wife."

His mother was as selfish as his father. She wanted what she wanted and was happy to put up with the inconvenience of having a faithless husband. Money and status mattered more than truth. She was so busy projecting the perfect image. That was the moment that Brad decided not to help her project that image any more. That was when he removed himself from home as much as possible. He'd gone off and found his own fun—with his own rules.

He looked at Mya. He'd never told anyone that. Not anyone. Had lack of sleep got to him too? And, yeah, he regretted mentioning any of it now he saw what looked like pity in her eyes. He didn't want pity, thanks very much; he had it all under control. He was more than happy with the way he managed his life.

"I'm never going to marry," he said firmly. "I'm not going to lie the way they both do."

"You don't think a long-term relationship can work?"

"Not for me."

"You're not willing to take the risk?"

"Why would I? I can get all I want." He smiled, acting up the playboy answer again. And he figured the women in his life got what they wanted too. Which wasn't really *him* but the things he could give them—good sex, fancy dinners, a flash lifestyle. And fun: "I care about my work. I like to have fun. I like my space. I like it uncomplicated."

"Easy."

"Is that so wrong?"

"No," she said softly. "Not if that's what both parties want. And understand."

He trod on the brake and turned to look at her. "I don't do relationships, Mya. I do fun and flings and nothing more."

"Message received loud and clear." She echoed his words of the night before, calmly meeting his stare.

He felt sorry, tired, resigned. "So this…chemistry between us," he said slowly.

"Goes nowhere," she answered. "It's just one of those things, you know—the friend's older brother…"

"The sister's best friend."

"We're such a cliché," Mya acknowledged with a lift of her shoulders. He'd have believed she was amused had her laugh not cracked at the end. "We've seen too many movies. And you know how it is—you always want what you can't have."

"We'll be friends." He did want to remain in contact with her.

She hesitated. Too long for his liking. "We'll do this party for Lauren."

And after that? Back to zero contact? It would be for the best. But it wasn't what he wanted at all. He still wanted her to the point of distraction. He'd just have to get over it. Another woman maybe?

He gripped the steering wheel with psycho-killer strength. Appalled with her schedule, he dropped her to university for an hour's lecture knowing she then had to go straight back to the bar for another night's shift. Despite the scratchy feeling beneath his eyelids, he found himself driving to his parents' house. He vaguely tried to remember when it was he'd last been there, and failed. But now was a good time. His father would still be at work and his mother would be at some meeting. He avoided both the house and them as much as possible.

"Hello?" he called out just in case as he opened up the door and disarmed the alarm.

No answer. He took the stairs. His and Lauren's rooms were still neat, still as they'd had them when they were growing up. On a separate floor to their parents, at opposite ends of the hallway from each other, with guest rooms and bathrooms in between. The physical distance was nothing on the emotional distance between the entire family. And though he and Lauren had grown a little closer as adults, the gap between parents and children had only widened.

His mother had read a home-organisation book at some point in one of her obsessive phases, and all their personal things were stored in crates, neatly stacked and labelled in the back of their wardrobes. Schoolwork from decades ago. When was he ever going to go through that? When would anyone? But it wasn't his room that he'd come to grab stuff from. It was Lauren's.

Because that photo of Mya at her parents' house had reminded Brad that, at one stage in her turbulent teen years, *Lauren* had taken hundreds of photos. For a long time she'd preferred the magic of the old-style camera before messing around with digital. The old playroom had been converted into a darkroom for her, their parents eager to do anything that might hold Lauren's interest in a topic that was actually palatable to them—not like boys and underage clubbing. It had long since been converted back into a study but the boxes of prints remained in Lauren's wardrobe.

He sat on her bedroom floor and flicked through them, his heart thudding harder and harder as he worked through the piles. Lauren's best friend, the natural model for Lauren's photographic phase. It had been the two of them against the world, right? The rebel and the reject—the kid who'd not been included by anyone at the hellish, snobby school they'd gone to. Except for Lauren.

Though it was subtle, Mya had changed. The planes of her face had sharpened, those high cheekbones, the big green eyes were able to hold secrets now. In her teen years the attitude was obvious. The resentment, the defensiveness. But so was the joy, effortlessly captured in every other photo—that pixie smile, the gleam in her eyes.

Often she had a battered library book in her hand. Every other photo it seemed Lauren had snapped while Mya was unaware—and she was so pretty. The ones where she *was* aware were funny. The madness of some of the pictures made him laugh—terrifying teen girls.

He'd gone to university as soon as he turned seventeen and missed much of this part of Lauren's life. It had been a relief to get out of the house. At the time he'd been too selfish to think of his sister. He'd thought she hadn't known but of course she had. He'd discovered that in their tennis sessions. It was the great unacknowledged truth, how unhappy and dysfunctional their perfect family unit really was. The affairs of his father, the obsessive illness of his mother. They all retreated behind the façades they'd chosen for themselves. His father the distant worka-holic, his mother the busy do-good wealthy woman, his sister the tearaway who acted out for any kind of attention. What was left for him but the playboy role?

He paused over one photo. Mya in that prom dress. He should have taken a better look at her in it back then. Then again it was probably better that he hadn't.

She was leaning against the wheel of a car, parked on a lawn that looked as if it hadn't seen a mower in a few months with ratty weeds. With broken head-lights and the weeds around the wheel, that car was going absolutely nowhere any time soon. Yeah, that'd be the car she hadn't learnt to drive in.

Brad put that picture to the side and shuffled through some more. He thought about taking the whole box home to look through at leisure but that was a step too far into stalker territory. He flicked through the pile more quickly—Mya wearing some mad hat, Mya draped in what looked like an old cur-tain. Mya in another dress apparently butchered and sewn together. He looked at the commonality in the pictures. Lauren's pictures of Mya in Mya's crazy—brilliant—creations. So many different things and so out there.

He flipped through them, faster and faster. She'd not always worn black. She'd always worn outra-geous. Uncaring of what society might think. She'd

made them herself, made that massive statement—
"here I am, look at me…"

Where had that fearless girl gone?

Why had she turned herself into a shadow? Now
in nothing but black, slinking round as if she hoped
she couldn't be seen. Why didn't she want to be seen?
Where had the crazy fun gone? She'd grown into a
pale, worried woman. A woman who worked too
damn hard. Brad held the picture and looked at the
smiling face, and slowly his own smile returned as
it dawned on him.

It wasn't Lauren who needed a party. It was Mya.

Chapter 7

Brad was lost in thought when his sister thumped his shoulder.

"What was that for?" He frowned, rubbing his biceps more from surprise than pain.

"What's wrong with you?" Lauren asked.

"What do you mean?"

"I mean those two women just swished past you with hips and bits wiggling and you didn't even look at them. Plus I almost beat you today, which has never happened in our whole lives."

Seated at the tennis-club lounge, Brad felt more confused than ever. "What women?"

Lauren's mouth fell open. "Are you sick?"

Okay, he had been somewhat distracted this

morning. "I've got a tough case on." He offered a genuine excuse. Gage Simmons was truanting again and still not speaking to his psychologist, and the idea of his parents coping with a mediation conference was a joke.

"Isn't that even more reason for you to scope out some action?" Lauren said sarcastically. "That's your usual stress release, isn't it?"

Once upon a time it had been, sure. But he hadn't looked at another woman in days—there was another consuming his brain space. "Have you seen much of Mya recently?"

"*My* Mya?" Lauren's pretty nose wrinkled. "Not much. Why?"

"I ran into her recently," Brad hedged. Seemed Mya hadn't told Lauren about the mis-sent photo. Good.

"Where?"

"At that bar she works at."

Lauren nodded and sighed. "She works all the time."

"Mmm." Brad knew if he left the space, Lauren would fill it.

"It was her birthday last month and she couldn't even come for a coffee with me, she was so crunched between work and study," Lauren said.

Bingo.

"Seems a shame for her." Brad hesitated, unsure of how to put his idea forward without his sister guessing what it was he'd really wanted. "Your birthday is coming up soon and you'll get your mitts on all your money." Her trust fund would be released. "We'll have to have a huge party."

Lauren shrugged. "I don't want it."

"The party or the money?"

"The money," said Lauren.

Brad paid proper attention to his sister for the first time all morning. "What do you mean you don't want it?"

"I'm going to give it away."

"What? Why?"

Lauren shrugged and looked self-conscious. "I want to make a difference. You make a difference."

Brad smothered his groan and at the same time felt affection bubble for his scamp of a kid sister. "It's easier for me to do that when I don't have to worry about how much I earn in my job. I can afford to take on the pro bono cases, Lauren. I couldn't do that as easily without the trust fund."

"That's what Mya said too." Lauren frowned. "But look at her, she's so independent."

"Yeah, but she's not having much fun with it. Life should include some fun, don't you think?"

"We all know what you mean by that." Lauren rolled her eyes and giggled.

"Not just that. Some simple fun too, you know—party fun." Brad stretched his legs out under the table. "What are we Davenports good at?"

"Not that much." Lauren sipped her lemonade through her straw.

Brad raised an eyebrow. "But we are. We're really good at putting on a show, right? Let's put on a show for Mya."

"Mya?" Lauren breathed in so quickly she choked on her drink. Coughing, she asked him the dreaded question. "You're not going to mess with her, are you, Brad?"

He shook his head. "No."

"Hmm." Lauren didn't look convinced. "She's not as strong as she seems, you know. She's actually quite vulnerable."

"Are you telling me to stay away?" Brad managed a smile.

"Would it make any difference if I did?" Lauren asked point-blank. "I just don't think it would end well. Things don't end all that well for your women, and Mya's had enough of that."

"Don't worry." Brad grinned, though his teeth were clenched. "She's like a sister to me." What did she mean things didn't end that well for his women? "And this is because I have a venue I need to do something with for a night."

"A venue?" Lauren leaned forward, and Brad smiled for real this time. Yeah, his sister had always liked a party. "So what were you thinking?"

"How's this for a plan?"

* * *

Mya got used to the random calls and quickly got in the habit of checking her phone for texts every five minutes. They were short queries about the tiniest details that most people would never think of. One thing to be said for Brad, he was thorough. Very thorough.

In the mornings now he came to the café and ordered a coffee. He never stayed more than ten minutes or so, always moved away when she got busy and had to serve someone. She spent the rest of the day looking forward to her shift at the bar.

Because now he turned up there early every night and urged her to do her worst in creating another cocktail or shot before the crowds came in. She loved the challenge and got the giggles over the often awful results. It didn't matter if she made something that tasted hideous. They laughed about it—with him naming them outrageously. His word play had her in hysterics. He made suggestions; she ran with them. Together they came up with some bizarre mixes that actually worked and many, many failures. But with Brad, failing was more fun than not. And while they worked on it in that calm twenty minutes or so before the crowds appeared, they talked.

She admitted more about her parents' troubles and told him about her cousins who lived around the corner. He listened and then, in turn, 'fessed up more about his parents, and occasionally referenced his work. She knew he was incredibly busy; sometimes he came in looking drained but he always switched "on" as soon as someone spoke to him. But she knew he went back home after their cocktail-mixing session to do more work. It was why he never drank more than a mouthful of whatever they'd mixed. But mostly they laughed—teasing about everything from taste in music and TV shows to sports teams, and swapped stories of wild, fun times with Lauren.

Mya laughed more in those few minutes each day than she had all year. But fun as it was, it was also slowly killing her because her teen dreams were nothing on the adult fantasies she had now about Brad Davenport. He was so attractive, so much fun and yet so serious about the silliest of things for the party. His concern over the finest of details was so attractive.

In days he became a constant in her life—the one person she saw most of aside from her workmates. It was only for a few minutes, but they were the highlight. And then there were all those texts and the never-ending playlist suggestions for the DJ.

Three days before the party, in between her shifts at the café and the bar, Mya was studying at the library. Her phone vibrated with a message from Brad.

Where are you?

She chuckled at over-educated Brad's inability to use any abbreviated text language. She was similarly afflicted. So she texted back her grammatically correct reply and went back to her books.

She didn't know how long it was before she glanced up and saw him standing at the end of the nearest row of books. "What are you doing here?"

"It's my natural home." He winked as he walked nearer.

"But you of all people should know you're not allowed food in the library." She gave the paper bags he was carrying a pointed look.

"No one will see us." He jerked his head and sneaked down the stacks away from the study tables and well out of range of the librarian's help desk.

"Brad," she whispered. But in the end there was no choice but to follow, and she'd come over all first-year giggly student in the library in a heartbeat.

In the narrow space, surrounded by thick, bound books, he opened the bag and pulled out a couple of pottles and put them on a gap in the shelves.

"What is this?" she asked, intrigued.

"Chocolate mousse."

Of course it was; why had she even asked? But she did, and she had to ask the even more obvious. "You want me to try them?"

"Yes, they come in these cute little cups, see?" he whispered. "Which do you think, mint or chilli?"

"You are taking this far too seriously." She shook her head, but licked her lips at the same time. Yum. She took a tiny bit on two teaspoons and tried them.

"They're both really good. I think Lauren would like—"

"Which do *you* like best?" he interrupted, his gaze boring into her.

Mya's skin goosebumped while her innards seared. She'd missed that look these past couple of days—that full-of-awareness-and-forbidden-desires look. She'd thought he'd gone all friendly and party efficient and had forgotten that kiss altogether—or didn't think it was worth anything. Now all she could think of was that kiss and how much it had moved her and that maybe, just maybe, he was thinking of it too.

"Why does it matter what I think?" She didn't have to try to whisper now. Her voice had gone completely husky. "This is for Lauren, not me."

"She'll like what you like," Brad insisted, stepping closer. "Come on, tell me."

She'd never had lust-in-the-library fantasies. Until now. And right now, all she wanted was for Brad to kiss her again in this quiet, still space.

"You've gone red," he said. "Was the chilli-chocolate too hot?"

"Must have been," she muttered.

He was looking at her mouth. Could he please stop looking at her mouth? Did she have a huge gob of mousse on her lip? Because he looked as if he wanted to *taste*, and she wanted him to, very much.

Mya had never felt so hot.

But Brad missed her scorching thoughts. "Mint it is, then."

She nodded. Just. "You've really got into this," she said, trying to pull herself together as he replaced the lids on the pottles and put them back in the bag.

"I've discovered my latent party-planning talent." The smallest smile quirked his mouth. He glanced at her and caught her staring. "So you're all set up to bring her?"

"It's all sorted." Mya nodded. She'd arranged it with Lauren a few days ago. But now that the party was so close, she felt irrationally ill at ease—even unhappy. She'd be glad when it was over, wouldn't she? She wasn't sure any more. But the worse feeling was the jealousy—she was envious of how much effort he'd gone to for his sister. Which was just mean of her.

She walked away from him, hiding from his intent gaze, back out to the table she'd been studying at. Hopefully he'd leave right away. But he didn't. He pulled out the seat next to hers, sat and flipped open his iPad, hooking into the university's wireless network.

How was she supposed to study now? He didn't get that when he was around, her brain shut down and all she could think of now was lewd behaviour in the library. She coped for less than five minutes and then she spoke without thinking.

"Did you ever get it on in the library in your librarian days?"

He shot her a startled look.

"I mean—" she felt her blush growing "—that'd be the kind of thing you'd have done back then, right?"

She trailed off as his intense look grew. He slowly shook his head.

He hadn't? *Really?* She'd have thought that Mr Slayer like him would have...but no. He hadn't. Nor had she, of course. And now here they were...

Oh, hell, why did that excite her all the more?

She looked at him and decided honesty was the best policy. "I can't concentrate on my study when you're around," she mumbled. "At the bar, the café, it's different. I don't need to think as hard as I do here. But I can't *think* with you..." She trailed off.

He didn't say anything, just looked at her with those penetrating eyes. He hadn't moved in the past ninety seconds. She wasn't sure if he was even still breathing. Mya felt even hotter than before but now there was a huge dose of embarrassment twisted into her inner furnace as well. She'd all but admitted she still fancied him. But the fact was now she fancied him more than ever. And he'd gone all *buddy* on her.

"Maybe it's best if we work out any last-minute plans over the phone or something," she said quickly, trying to recover. "It would be easier, don't you think?"

Slowly he blinked and then seemed to see straight through her. "That's what you want?"

"That would be for the best," she squeaked.

He remained still for a very long moment, still watching her. And then he whispered, "What are you going to wear?"

She froze; like his look, his question breached the boundaries from friendly to intimate—but she'd done that herself already. Now she felt she'd plunged off the edge of a cliff and was swimming in darkness. Who knew which direction the safe beach was? "I'm not sure."

"Not black," he said quietly.

"Probably."

"No," he muttered. "Give me that at least."

"Okay." Mya could hardly swallow and her skin was doing that hot-and-cold tingly thing again. "You've done such a great job," she said softly, aiming for that conversation-closing platitude—that she meant with all her being. "She's going to be so thrilled."

"You think?" His smile lanced her heart. "I hope so."

Suddenly he stood, not pausing to pack away his gear, just shoving it into his case as he left.

Instantly she felt bereft. But it was for the best. She looked down at the black-and-white text in front of her—the case names and details she had to understand and memorise. She didn't see any of them.

She sighed and blinked to refocus. The sooner the party was over, the better.

He didn't text the day of the party. He didn't need to, of course; he had everything planned to the nth degree. But he'd got her thinking. She wanted to get dressed up. Really get dressed up in a way she hadn't in years. *Her* kind of dressing where she'd been as loud and unconventional—deliberate, girly. Everything unexpected. She'd been in the black jeans so long she'd almost forgotten her old style. But she didn't have any money for anything new and had no time to make anything.

Yet there was one dress she could wear. She shied away from the thought—it would be so obvious, wouldn't it? But she could adapt it, she could wear a wrap or a cardigan or something to dress it down a little…she could get away with it. Maybe.

She went to her parents' house and picked it up, smiling to herself throughout the long bus-ride. She realised she was more excited about seeing him than she was about seeing Lauren's reaction to her surprise.

Once dressed, she went to Lauren's as she'd arranged for their "girly night out"—their first in ages.

"Look at you!" Lauren squealed when she greeted her at her door.

"Ditto." Mya laughed at how glamorous Lauren looked.

"Where should we go first?" Lauren asked, her eyes sparkling.

"I promised Drew I'd drop something in at the bar. Is it okay if we go there first?" Mya spun her line.

"'Course!"

Mya sent the "we're coming" text as they climbed into the taxi. All the way there she kept up an inane patter about one of her regular café customers—not Brad. Mya's heart thudded as they swept up the steps. Kirk was on the door and he winked as they walked up and he swung the door open for them.

There was a moment of silence. Then a collective scream.

"Surprise!"

The cacophony of almost a hundred people screaming momentarily deafened her, but Mya chuckled. The glitter confetti bucketing down on them might have been a touch OTT but that was all the more fun. She gazed at Lauren for her reaction.

Only then she noticed that Lauren was looking right back at her with a huge grin on. And then she heard the crowd chanting.

"Mya! Mya! Mya!"

"What?" Mya gazed round in confusion.

Then—who knew from where—a gong sounded and they all screamed again in unison.

"Happy Birthday, Mya!"

Mya clapped her hand over her mouth and shook her head.

"This is for you," Mya tried to tell Lauren.

"Uh-uh." Lauren shimmied closer with a wicked smile. "Fooled you. We all fooled you."

Shocked, Mya stood immobile. She didn't even breathe—only her eyes still functioned, sending images to her brain. And OMG they were all in on it. Jonny was laughing, her varsity mates. Even Drew was grinning. Her fellow baristas from the café were here. They'd all fooled her. They were all here for *her*.

It seemed Lauren had breathed in giggle-gas as she laughed delightedly, putting her arm along Mya's shoulders.

"But it's not my birthday." Mya's mouth felt as if she'd been at the dentist for a ten-hour procedure and she had all that cotton-gauze stuff still clogging it.

"You never had a birthday party because you were working." Lauren laughed more. "So we took matters into our own hands."

We.

Mya looked into the smiling crowd once more. Her mouth automatically curved into an answering smile even though she was still in shock, still couldn't believe any of this.

Then she saw him. Brad.

And heaven help her he was all in black—black suit, black tie, black shirt. It emphasised his height, his eyes, his aura of simmering sexuality. The tailored tuxedo a perfect foil for her recycled old prom outfit. If they were a couple, they couldn't have planned it better. Except they weren't and they hadn't.

But he'd planned it—this whole party. Had it been a set-up right from the beginning? What did he mean by all of this? Was this mere seduction? Or a gesture of kindness? Her heart thudded so fast she thought she might faint.

He strode forward from the throng of people and pulled her into a quick hug. "I changed my mind about the party once we got to talking," he whispered into her ear. "I thought it would be more fun to have a party for you."

Her fingers touched his smooth jacket briefly, the contact with his body *far* too brief. He pulled back and looked at her for a split second, a shot of truth in his gaze—serious, sweet sincerity.

So all the things he'd asked her about hadn't been for Lauren, but for her? No wonder he'd wanted to know which mousse *she'd* preferred. She blinked rapidly, emotion slamming into her. Pleasure, disbelief, gratitude, confusion.

She went cold again—and hot. She wanted this, she appreciated this, she did. But part of her wanted to escape as well. Part of her wanted to be alone.

Okay, not alone. She wanted to be with Brad.

Brad had lost all ability to move the moment he saw her. For a snatched moment of time his heart had stopped, his muscles froze solid, his brain shut down completely. When his system started again, it sped straight to a higher rate than usual. Adrenalin coursed through his veins and desire shot straight to his groin. Yeah, that was the part of him most affected. He drew a deep breath and forced his body to relax. Mya had made it more than clear it wasn't happening. And that was fine. He was man enough to handle rejection. Except she didn't look as if she was saying "no" now. Her green eyes were wide and as fixed on him as his were on her. He'd known all along she was attracted to him, but determined not to have a hot affair. He could respect that. He was a man, not an animal, and all this tonight really hadn't been about trying to make it happen. Only now he finally saw it—the surrender in her eyes, the seduction.

The *yes*.

She was in that dress. That damn beautiful pink prom dress, with her breasts cupped high and ribbons trailing down her bare back. His attempt to hold back his body's reaction began to falter. When she looked at him like that? His muscles bunched, rigid with the urge to push her three steps back to the wall and screw her 'til she screamed. Nothing sophisticated, nothing smooth. Just a wild-animal moment to assuage the white-hot lust consuming him.

But they were in a roomful of people and that wasn't the show he had planned for them. And it wasn't what she truly wanted either. She had her other priorities and he could respect them, right?

The only way he'd get through the night alive was to stay away from her and focus on his host duties. He'd been crazy taking this on, on top of his overfull caseload. He'd challenge Mya for her "world's most busy" title. But he'd done it. And that look on her face had been worth it. Now he could only hope she appreciated the other things he had planned for the evening. But jumping her wasn't on that list.

Mya was aware of Lauren watching her so she forced her gaze off Brad's tall frame as he disappeared back into the throng. "This is unbelievable." She smiled at her best friend.

"So good." Lauren grabbed her hand. "Come on, I heard a rumour about crazy cocktails."

They were there—listed on a chalk-board with Jonny standing behind the bar rolling his eyes over the contents. Mya grinned and ordered the only alcohol-free option—she needed to keep her wits about her.

A crowd formed around her—friends she hadn't seen or been able to have fun with in ages, workmates with whom she'd never been able to just hang out. Conversation was fast and snatched and fun, and she tried so hard not to keep watch for Brad. She was determined to enjoy this—the first party ever thrown for her.

But an hour or so into it, the lights suddenly dimmed dramatically.

"What's happening?" Mya leaned close to Lauren as the music switched so suddenly nothing but fierce drumming hit max volume.

"I have no idea."

Mya stared transfixed as about twenty black-clad figures swooped in, suddenly clearing a path through the crowds and pushing giant black boxes around the floor. The drums continued while the shadows put some kind of construction together.

Brad, looking sexier than a man had any right to be, was suddenly lit up from an overhead spotlight and appeared taller than ever. She realised those black-clad figures had created a small stage of sorts that extended down the middle of the room. Mya, like everyone else in the place, was stunned into immobility.

"If you don't mind, everyone, there's something we need to do tonight." Brad's voice boomed out. He had a microphone?

The black cloths that had been covering the windows behind him dropped, revealing two giant screens. The spotlight went off Brad while on screen an old-style countdown reel played. The guests joined in counting down. As they got to one the entire bar went pitch-black.

In the pregnant pause, Mya leaned in to Lauren. "When did he set this up?"

"You're asking me?" Lauren giggled. "He didn't let me in on this bit. I just had to get you here."

"You know we're here to celebrate Mya's birthday tonight. But the thing that you and I all know, but that Mya doesn't quite believe yet, is that not only is she an amazing academic and gifted cocktail creator, she's also an artist. And so for tonight, we're turning this place into an art gallery and seeing what other marvellous things Mya has done."

"He's *what*?" Mya asked, clapping her hand over her mouth to hold back the shriek.

Now she understood what the stage really was—a runway. And walking along the runway now were models. Slim, gorgeous girls in black bikinis and boots, modelling her hats, her accessories, her dresses that she'd created in her teen years and in the first couple of years at university. Where the hell had he got them all from?

She turned to Lauren, who held her hands up in the classic "don't shoot" pose and shook her head at the same time.

She glanced at Brad and couldn't contain the crow of delighted laughter. *Naturally* he'd found a way to get bikini-clad women on the scene. The crowd cheered and clapped, and she couldn't blame them as the leggy beauties strutted the length and Brad gave a running commentary on each item.

"There was a time in Mya's life when we all looked forward to seeing what it was she was wearing—the accessories, the clothes, sometimes the shoes."

Everybody laughed as a picture of silver-marker-decorated gumboots flashed up on the screens.

"She moved into this world of recycled clothing, making new from the old, turning someone else's rubbish into art for herself. Maximalist, statement clothing. More than clothing. It was wearable art."

Mya gazed at both stage and screen, her heart swelling. He'd created a multimedia display—a live modelling show interspersed with images from the past flashing up on those giant screens and a soundtrack made up of her fave teen beats. She pressed her freezing palm to her hot forehead. All those DJ picks he'd texted her. The really cheesy ones she'd sent back. He'd made a music mash-up and photo montage, and it was all so embarrassing and wonderful at the same time.

"Of course, she designed for men as well," Brad said as the tempo of music changed.

Oh, my. Mya's jaw dropped and she gripped Lauren's hand, giggling now. Because she'd *never* designed anything for a guy. But there was an extremely buff guy up there now in nothing but black boxers and some sort of butchered baseball cap. She hadn't designed it for a man, though one could wear it, of course, but it had just been for the fun of it. And the tie that was now being displayed by another guy with very little else on, that had been her school tie that she'd redecorated in a rebellious fit one day. But that mega-buff guy in nothing but black boxers really knew how to show it off.

"So come on, everyone, give it up for Multifaceted Mya."

Oh, no, someone had switched the lights on her. Literally shone the light on her, and some gorgeous thing came down to where she sat with Lauren. It was the buff guy with the cap. Nothing but the boxers and the cap. Mya looked over at Brad and saw his mouth twitching with amusement as he spoke.

"While Mya makes her way to the runway, here are a couple of stills from the collection where we can see her talent at her best."

Mya froze on her seat. He couldn't be serious—she had to walk up there? And OMG there were huge photos of her up on those screens?

The black-clad male model extended his hand to her. She had no choice but to take her turn down the damn runway with the hot stuff at her side.

"Let's face it," Brad concluded. "The lady has an abundance of talent."

Everyone in the place was on their feet and cheering.

Mya looked at Brad and saw his smile. Tender, a little mocking—self-mocking perhaps—but genuine. It pierced straight through the last thin layer of defence she had left and exposed her to the full glare of his attraction. In every cell, all the way to her toes it hit—how gorgeous he was.

He wasn't just sexy and funny and handsome. He was nice, thoughtful and caring. It was a side of him she'd never wanted to acknowledge. She'd preferred to keep him in the slutski spoilt-man stereotype. Mr Superficial Playboy. That was the easy way out. But the truth was he was utterly outrageous, utterly unashamed and yet utterly kind.

The lights came back on, and Lauren came up as the bar music resumed.

"It was all her idea." Brad curved his arm around Lauren's shoulders and drew her close.

"That's not true." Lauren shook her head firmly.

"Lauren found everything." Brad gave his sister a sharp look.

"He came up with it when we were playing tennis at the club the other week."

"It was supposed to be a party for you," Mya said, too shaky inside to look at Brad at this moment.

"I don't need a party." Lauren shrugged. "I go to parties all the time."

"I'm getting you back for your birthday," Mya promised.

Lauren just laughed as one of her boys claimed her for the dance floor.

"How did you do all this?" Mya asked Brad, her mouth dry and still not looking at him.

"I had help," he confessed. "With the catwalk and the lighting and the music and stuff."

Mya shook her head and looked across the room. "Where did you find all of it?"

"My mother's itemised storage system. Lauren had kept them all."

Well, it had mainly been Lauren's clothes Mya had messed with. The only thing Mya had kept was the dress she was now wearing.

"And you called on all your girlfriends to model for you." She felt overwhelmed. "Why did you do it?"

"I found some of the pictures of you," he said softly.

"You and your pictures." She stole a quick glance at him.

His mouth had twisted into a wry smile and that soft expression was in his eyes. "None as good as the one you sent me, but ones Lauren took when you guys were mucking around a few years ago. You were so bold and so creative. Why have you given all that up? You have real talent."

"No," she scoffed, totally downplaying it.

"Didn't you just see that standing ovation?"

"You set it up." She couldn't resist the urge to lean closer to tease him. "All those beautiful models and all their glorious skin?"

Her words drew a reluctant smile to his lips. "All that aside, you really do have talent," he insisted.

"I appreciate this, so much," she said softly, her

throat aching because it was such a kind thing he'd done for her. "But I don't have time to do that any more. It was a hobby. Life has moved on from that stuff."

She blinked as bleak frustration dimmed his eyes. "Mya, you don't *have* a life."

"I do," she argued, quiet but firm. "And I'm lucky enough to have friends." Ones who cared. She might even dare put him in that category after tonight. Except, grateful as she was for this night, she didn't want to lock him away in that neat and tidy box.

Something flashed in his eyes and was almost immediately blanked out. All that remained was resignation—she felt it too.

He smiled as another guest walked up to talk to them. It was that charismatic smile of his, yet strangely devoid of depth. Despite the excessive heat of a crowded club-floor on a hot summer's night, Mya's skin cooled as if the first spears of winter had bitten their way through the hot warehouse bricks. His walls were back up; that automatic charming gleam hid the honesty in his eyes. It felt as if she'd lost something precious.

Brad watched her mingle, the gnawing feeling inside worsening with each minute that she laughed and interacted and clearly had fun. She was having a great time, but it wasn't enough. He was used to getting what he wanted—easily. Giving up what he wanted wasn't nearly so easy. Especially when she looked at him with that expression in her eyes—the one that told him he could have what he'd wanted more than anything these past couple of weeks.

But successful though it may be to a point, this night was also a failure. She'd appreciated his effort, but she hadn't understood it. He wanted her to understand she had so much more to offer the world if she'd just give herself a chance, if she just let go of all the burden she took on and let herself be free. She should be doing the things she loved, not just doing things *for* those she loved.

The realisation hurt and with that came the worse hit—he cared too much about where she was at and what she was doing. When he looked at her now, there wasn't just that stirring in his groin—there was an ache in his chest.

He liked her—too much to mess around with her. *Things don't end all that well for your women.* While he wasn't sure he agreed with Lauren's statement, he wasn't taking the risk with Mya. He could get her to say yes, but she wasn't cut out for a fling, and he didn't want more than just that. Even if he did, she wasn't ready for that in her life. She had her other priorities and that was fine. The only thing to do, right now, was walk away.

So he did.

Chapter 8

It might have been one of the best nights of her life, but Mya wanted the fireworks to finish it off. She didn't want to be the wallflower walking home alone tonight as she had all those years ago at that miserable prom.

She glanced around. Lauren was flirting with yet another guy—she'd been collecting them throughout the night. Several other friends were propping up the bar getting outrageously hammered with her lethal cocktail mix. Others were up on the catwalk having a dance-off to the hits of their teen years. It was a crazy-fun night.

But Brad had quietly slipped off into the dark—

alone. He hadn't said goodbye to her or anyone. He'd flipped a wave at Lauren but he hadn't even looked at Mya.

That wasn't good enough.

Did he think he could do this for her—send her insides into such a spin—and then walk away?

Tonight had been her one night off in months. And didn't she deserve pleasure in it—pleasure for *all* the night? Didn't she deserve a treat? It wouldn't be like that mess-up last year when she'd thought she could handle a night of nothing but physical fun and had failed. This time she knew what she was doing—and she *knew* Brad. She even liked him. But not enough to cause confusion. She'd read the rulebook, was certain she could handle herself on the field. This time she already knew the score. And while there was that hint of insecurity about her performance, she figured Brad wouldn't be all that bothered. Ultimately all she'd be was another notch to him, right? But *she* would have the best sexual experience of her life. He'd teased that it would be, but she knew to her bones he'd follow through. She simply couldn't resist—not for one night.

So she blew Lauren a kiss and waved.

Her feet moved of their own accord, fast, determined, sure. She was stone-cold sober but in a blink she was there already—standing at his front door. Before she could take a breath and think better of it, she hammered the door so hard her knuckles hurt.

He opened it sooner than she expected. He'd lost the jacket but was still in the black shirt and trousers and, oddly, a cleaning cloth in his hand. He stared at her—saying it all with just that wild-eyed look—surprise to desire in a heartbeat. Only then he closed his eyes and bent his head. Sudden nerves paralysed her. Insecurity drowned her moment of boldness.

"Are you going to let me in?" she asked, her voice pathetically breathy even to her own ears. So much for chutzpah.

He looked up and she saw nothing but raw emotion in his eyes—not just desire, but torment. It was reflected in his stance too as he blocked her entry, his hand gripping the door. "You know what will happen if I do."

Relief shot into her belly, bursting into flame on impact. "Yes," she said. "That's why I'm here."

"But—"

"I don't want a relationship, and I don't want a fling. But I've changed my mind about the one-night thing."

He swallowed and then stepped to one side. She walked in, holding her head high while her blood fizzed round her body. She went straight to the place she'd fantasised about for weeks. The cover was stripped back, the light switched on—the brightness harsh on her eyes after the moonlit walk here.

"What happened to the vase?" The mess on the floor surprised her.

"Accident caused by frustration." He watched her as if he was afraid she'd disappear if he blinked.

"You're not usually clumsy."

"I'm not usually frustrated."

She paused. If he was "frustrated", why wasn't he happy to see her here now? "Why are you feeling bad?" she asked softly, stepping closer. "It was a great night. I loved every second of it. Everyone else did too."

"This isn't why I did it." He spoke low and rough. "I just wanted you to have some fun."

"I did," she answered. "And I'd like some more."

"Lauren said not to mess with you. That you're fragile."

Shock hit, embarrassment soon followed and both burned. What else had Lauren said? "Do I look fragile to you?"

"Not on the outside, but that vase didn't seem that fragile either and it still broke when I dropped it."

"You're not going to get the opportunity to drop me," she said. "I only want what's left of tonight. I don't want anything more. I'd never expect promises from you. I understand that." There were only a couple of hours of darkness left. A couple would have to be enough. "And you know I can't give more either. This isn't going to be anything more for either of us. This is just tonight."

He walked nearer. Intensity sliced into her as she saw the look on his face, the raw, unrestrained desire honed in on one focal point—*her*. Excitement swept over her and she backed up until the backs of her thighs hit his bed and she sat on the edge of it.

She gazed at him—unashamed in her admiration. He was so much taller, stronger. And looking at her like this? So lethal.

She realised that until now he'd kept a leash on his desires, letting her think she'd controlled this thing between them. But he could have pulled her to him any time he'd wanted. His potency was strong enough to render her will useless. She wanted to be his. But just as violent was the desire to have him ache for her in this same extreme way. Impossible, of course. Hence the one night.

"Are you sure?" he asked as he moved to within touching distance.

"Yes."

"I like you." He frowned as if that wasn't a good thing. "I want the best for you."

She just wanted to enjoy this attraction—and end up free of it. "Then give me the best."

He smiled, his eyes lighting up.

"Don't tease me any more," she begged. She needed him to come nearer, to stop talking, to make her feel as if she wasn't about to make a massive fool of herself.

"But it's all about the tease." A glimpse of humour.

"You know what I mean." She wanted it to be

fast. She wanted to get the release, to be freed from it. For it to be over.

He stepped close. The brilliant thing about the height of his bed was that she didn't have to crane her neck too far to look at him. With a single finger he traced the hem of her dress—now rucked up to just over her knees. She couldn't believe he wasn't moving faster already. But instead he put his hands on her pressed-together knees and exerted the smallest pressure.

"Let me in, Mya." His gaze didn't leave her face. "Let me in."

Mya trembled at the cool command. He seemed to be asking for more than access to her body. "I am." She swung her legs wide.

"No." He bent and his lips brushed her neck. "If we're doing this, then I want everything tonight." He ran two fingers down her cheek; the slight pressure made her turn her head. He whispered into her exposed ear. His words a caress, an intimacy. As if he'd somehow accessed her soul. "How much do you want this?" His lips brushed the whorls of her ear. "It better be as much as I do because otherwise you might not be able to keep up."

"You're that fabulous, huh?"

"I just want to be sure we're on the same page for this evening. Because it ain't over."

"I'm not fat and I'm not about to sing," she said with a hint of her old defiance.

"What about screaming?" He leaned closer until there was nothing but a whisper of air between them. She could feel the heat radiating from him, and her own emotions burned.

Tired of talk, tired of waiting, Mya wanted action. She lifted her chin and laid one on him.

For a moment Brad lost control of the situation. For someone who supposedly suffered extreme sensitivity, Mya could give a blisteringly hard kiss. Her fingers threaded into his hair, holding him there while beneath his mouth hers was lush and hungry. Startled, he gave it to her—the full brunt of the want that had burdened him these past weeks. He dived deep into her sweet mouth, tangling his tongue against her equally ravenous one. He pressed harder until he felt her trembling and moaning already.

He eased it back a bit, put his hands on her face, cupping those beautiful cheekbones with gentle fingers and pulling back just enough for their lips to barely be clinging. "I have no intention of bruising you," he said quietly.

That nagging feeling that she was holding back wouldn't leave him. What held her so reserved? While she smiled and joked with the bar patrons and Lauren's boys, there was that distance that he'd seen no one breach. He wanted to be the one who broke all the way in.

So while there was a time and a place for hot and

hard, quick and rough sex, this wasn't it. She wanted it that way. He knew she did. She was desperate to have him to have the release. And for it to be over. Because there was that part of her that was mad with herself for wanting him as badly as she did. She didn't want to be another of his conquests. She didn't understand yet that she *wasn't*.

Because there was his own confounding desire for her to come to terms with. He hadn't realised it was possible to want a woman this much. He'd craved sex before. Of course he had. But that had been sex. That had been about getting the pleasure and the release. This was about her. This was about seeing her shaking and out of control and filled with ecstasy. This was about seeing her weak with wanting him, with her unable to stand—only being able to lie on a bed and beg for him to come to her. Oh, yeah, the submissive fantasies were a first.

And now he had her—lying back on his bed with that dress even more rucked up, giving him a glimpse of lace-covered treasure. He tensed every muscle to fight the urge to dive straight in. Heat tightened his skin; he felt as if he were on the rack—stretched well beyond his usual limitations. And now she forced him closer than he'd like. Pushed him to intrude deeper than he normally would. Yes, he wanted it all from her.

He quickly stripped himself and then straddled her on the bed and let the ribbons slide through his fingers as he loosened them enough to pull the bodice of the dress down to bare her beautiful, bountiful breasts.

She shivered before he even touched them. He let his fingers trace near to their precious peaks, so slowly and gently—watching to see how she coped. She moved restlessly beneath him. He bent closer, traced his tongue around the tight, rosy nipples and blew warm air over the tips of them.

She shuddered.

"Too much?" he asked softly.

She shook her head, her chest rising and falling quickly. He carefully cupped her soft flesh, let the centre of his palm touch her nipple. She shuddered again and arched her back, pushing her breasts deeper into his hands. He pushed his hands together, pushing her breasts together, letting her nipples peep over the top of his cupped hands. Beautiful. Big and beautiful and so responsive. He blew on them again. And then so carefully bent to brush his lips over them.

"Oh, no," she whimpered.

"Okay?" he murmured, caressing them ever so softly.

She nodded and arched towards him again so he kept up the slow, wet caresses.

Her hips rocked now and he smiled at her giveaway reaction. Did she want the same treatment down there? He sure as hell hoped so. He stripped away her small briefs and then kissed his way down her flat stomach, his own excitement uncontrollable as he neared her most intimate curves. He'd dreamed of this for so long, he could hardly believe it was real now. But she was warm and writhing and tasted so hot. Her response deepened, her movements wild.

The pleasure of seeing her so wanting was more satisfying than anything in his life. He peeled her legs further apart, tasting her glistening femininity, holding her hips firmly so she couldn't escape him as she stiffened and then began to convulse. He sucked on her most sensitive nub and then buried his tongue inside her, quickly reaching up to cup her breasts and cover her nipples—diamond hard now, they pressed into his palms. He applied more pressure and tasted the reward as she came hard and loud, screaming for him.

He breathed hard, flicking his tongue to see her through the aftershocks and then he moved quickly. But his fingers were all thumbs as he tried to get the condom on.

"Damn," he muttered. Desperate, the need to drive deep within her the only thing circling in his head.

Now. Now. Now.

His lungs burned, his heart thumped—and he'd not even started. He was going to embarrass himself at this rate.

"Can I help?" she teased.

"No," he snapped hoarsely. Instantly feeling bad about biting her head off.

But she laughed. A throaty, sexy laugh as if she knew just how he was feeling.

It was all right for her—she'd had her first orgasm. Finally he was sheathed. He knelt and gazed at her. His gaze fixed on the cherry-red, too-sensitive nipples, lowered to her pink, glistening sex and then he looked up into her glowing eyes.

His heart seized.

Her laughter faded. "Brad?"

Her voice lifted a notch, the return of excitement even though she perceived the threat. Oh, yeah, he had plans. He leaned over her, relishing using his size to dominate her. But she wasn't intimidated. Not her, no—her smile returned. Those wide, uneven lips parted and revealed that sexy-as-hell gap. All petite, fragile, strong woman.

Take. Take. Take.

So he did. Peeling her legs further apart, he took position, his aching erection pressing against her slippery, sweet entrance. So hot for him. Meeting his gaze unflinchingly, her breasts rising and falling fast as she waited for him to finally take her.

And he did—surging forward to encase himself in one swift movement. But he was almost obliterated as he felt her clamp around him for the first time. He closed his eyes, clenched his teeth, locked still to stop the instant orgasm before he'd begun any kind of rhythm. That just *wasn't* happening.

He breathed hard, pushing back the blissful, delirious fog, refusing his release until he'd seen her too strung out to scream any more. And finally he moved, slow, back and forth, circular. Stopping to caress her breasts, her neck, her lips. Teasing, nipping, sucking—savouring every inch of skin he could access while locking himself inside her. And it was good. So damn good.

"Please let me come, please let me come," she begged him, writhing again, her face flushed and her skin damp.

Victory sang in his veins as he slowly claimed, withdrew and reclaimed his place right in the core of her. Her clenching, soft heat offered unutterable joy as much as it did wicked torment. And he was too ecstatic to care about the implications of the one thought hammering in his head.

Mine. Mine. Mine.

Breathless, pinned beneath his marvellous weight, Mya called to him. How could he bear it so slow? Wasn't he dying inside for the release? How could he hold back from coming inside her so long? Didn't he want to drive himself into her the way she ached for him to—furious and fast and hard?

Oh, hell—was it her? Was she not good enough at this for him? She certainly didn't know any tricks or anything much beyond the basics. And this was sex at its most basic, with him above her, no fancy positions or toys. She knew no tricks—was probably the most apathetic lover he'd ever had. All she'd been able to do the past half-hour was lie there and moan.

He slipped his palm beneath her bottom, pushing her closer so he could thrust even deeper into her, and all self-conscious thought was obliterated in the ecstasy of his onslaught. There was nothing she could do but absorb his decadent attention.

She tensed as that unbearably tense pleasure rebuilt in her. He pushed closer, closer. Her body tautened, her muscles, nerves, heart all strung out, locking onto every part of him she could. She was no longer begging, no longer coherent. Just gasping, grasping for that final step into oblivion. And then screaming. He tossed her into that river of delight. Sensations tumbled over and over—bliss shuddering through her in spasm after spasm. And she clung to him through it all as if he were her life raft as well as the source of the surge.

She gasped again as the last tremor shivered through her and she regained enough strength to sweep a hand down his sweat-slicked back. His skin burned, the muscles beneath flexing and rigid. She turned her face into his neck, wanting to hide how raw her emotions were. How close she felt to him in this moment.

With a feral grunt he pulled her head back so her mouth met his. A hungry, uncontrollable kiss. His tongue pummelling as fast and relentlessly as that other part of him was. Something broke free within her, that desire to *hold* onto him. To hold onto him so tight because he'd given her something so precious. She sucked on his tongue the way her sex was—tightly squeezing. Not letting him go. Stroking him back. A slick friction that set fire to her senses again.

He tore his mouth from hers, arching and shouting as his release ripped out of him. Her body quaked as she received it, intensifying her own pleasure to the point where she could bear no more.

It took a few moments for Brad to realise he'd blanked out and was slumped over her. Their bodies were stuck together—hot skin, locked limbs. Hell, could she breathe? He propped himself up on his elbows and looked at her.

"Wow." She nodded slowly. "Okay. I can see why."

It wasn't quite the comment he'd wanted. That hadn't been his usual wham and bam and "let's do it three times again, ma'am". Physical and fast and fun. He didn't know what had got into him with this so-slow-you-think-you're-going-to-die-from-bliss intensity.

"You sure proved your point." She swallowed.

He might have managed to laugh that off if he weren't so winded. Slowly, reluctantly, painfully, he withdrew from her warmth and rolled to lie beside her. He kept his eyes closed, holding back the exposed feeling. Because that had been so far from his usual behaviour that he couldn't comprehend it.

That hadn't just been sex. He didn't really know what it had been, but he knew it was not just sex. Part of him wanted to flee the scene immediately. Another part of him was stirring back to life, hungry for a repeat. How could the gnawing ache be worse now than it had been before?

"I'm sorry for being so useless," she murmured.

He flashed his eyes open and lifted his head. *"What?"*

To his amazement she'd gone bright red, more flushed than when she'd been in the throes of passion and about to come. "I just lay there."

He really did laugh then—and it was all genuine. "No, you didn't."

She'd sighed and moved in subtle, uncontrollable ways that had nearly driven him out of his mind. And she'd held him. He'd had the most incredible feeling when she'd held him.

He pulled her close. But sleep didn't claim him as quickly as it did her. Instead he lay still fully attuned to the signals of her body, his embrace tightening as her body relaxed into sleep. He'd never struggled to get to sleep after sex before. But he'd never had sex like that before either. He tried to process it, his body humming, his mind replaying fragments, sending flashes of memory to senses already overloaded and struggling with oversensitivity. Almost an hour later, still nowhere near sleep, he slipped away from her. In the moonlit kitchen he poured a glass of water.

He drank, trying to wash away the fever and regain his laid-back, carefree attitude. But the cool water didn't dispel the growing sense of discomfort and confusion.

The best moment of his life might also have been the biggest mistake.

Chapter 9

Mya woke early, panic clanging louder than an electronic alarm plugged into subwoofer speakers. Warm, sweat-dampened skin where they touched. Time to get out of here. She slipped out from his hot embrace, ultra-careful not to wake him because there was something she had to do first.

Quietly she found her phone and got it ready. Just as he stirred, she threw the sheet back and captured him in all his morning glory before he could blink.

"Now we're even." She laughed and teasingly waved the phone at him, determined to hide the ache pulling down her heart—from herself most of all.

He blinked and a slow, naughty smile spread over

his face—the return of the charmer. "Damn, you should have told me." He stretched. "I could have posed better for you."

He could *never* have been posed better. He looked like the Greek god he'd joked about.

"I'll delete this when you delete the picture of me," she offered. But it was a lie. Even if she trashed it from her phone, she couldn't ever wipe this image from her brain.

"I'm never deleting that." His laughter rumbled, rippling muscles over his taut, bronzed chest. "I've sent it to my computer. It looks brilliant on a big screen."

Oh, she should have known. "You're a perv."

"And you're an amateur. You think I mind you having a photo of me like this?"

"Well." Mya sniffed. "I guess half the city's women have seen you like this, so, really, it's nothing that personal, is it?" She had to remind herself who she was dealing with—and all that this had been.

"Miaow," he said and then reared up on the bed, moving towards her like a tiger on the prowl. "Why don't we make a movie instead? Come here and star in it with me."

The sight of him on all fours was almost enough to tip her over the edge, but she dug in her heels. "You really are a perv."

"Come on, back to bed." He knelt right up, the most X-rated fantasy Mya had ever seen. "It's early."

"And I have work to get to." She really *had* to get out of here.

"You're kidding."

She shook her head.

"Be late. Call in sick."

Oh, no, she wasn't letting him tempt her. It was finished. "You know it's over. The mystery is gone— the wondering of 'what'll we be like'—now we know. Now you can go back to your three-women-a-week lifestyle and I can get on with my studying."

There was a moment, the briefest of pauses when she wondered what he was going to say. He looked away, hiding his expressive eyes, and he flung back on the bed. "It's only three when I'm on holiday." He rested his head on his arm and looked even more like a Greek god reclining.

And all Mya could think was how he'd said there was nothing like starting the day with some good sex. She closed her eyes and forced away the whisper of temptation and the vision of one very aroused Brad. She had a shift to get to. She pulled her crumpled dress back on, hoping it was early enough for her not to get caught doing the walk of shame home.

"You can borrow some of my clothes if you want," he said unhelpfully.

No. That would mean she'd have to see him again to return them, and there was no way that was happening. There was no way she was indulging again.

It was going to take long enough to forget how incredible he was as a lover.

She didn't regret last night. But it had been so good she almost did.

"I don't think they'd fit but thanks all the same." She turned her back on him so he couldn't see her mega blush.

There was no reason for them to see each other again after this. He'd had what he'd wanted now and so had she. It was over. Outside work hours she'd be back to nothing but study, and he'd be back to saving kids during the day and romping his way around the city at night. It was one night and it was over.

Four days later her eyes hurt and she was exhausted but two coffees and a sugary doughnut saw her through the first two hours of her shift at the café. She'd already agreed to stay on and do a double shift before going straight to the bar. Desperate to fill every moment of her day. Study wasn't enough—it was in silence, and in silence her mind wandered. She needed noise and relentless activity.

Sex was sex, right? It was fun and physical, the release was great, and then it was over. Nothing more to it. So why was she so damn fixated on him?

Drew looked up when she finally got to the bar. She was running late from the café, but to her surprise he wasn't grumpy; in fact he smiled at her as if she were his employee of the week.

"We have another private function tonight," he said. "In the VIP room."

"We do?" Another person had hired out part of the place for some outrageous price this close to Christmas? "Who's the client?"

"Same guy as last time," Drew answered. "Brad. He specially requested Jonny. Double rates."

Mya's insides went solar-hot and her outsides ice-cold, while her heart soared and then dropped in the space of a second. He was supposed to be out of her life—in fact, he *was* out of her life. He hadn't contacted her; she hadn't contacted him… But now he was coming to her place of work but didn't want to see her? He'd asked for *Jonny*?

She didn't know whether to be mad, glad or amused.

"Trouble is," Drew said, "Jonny cut himself today. His fingers are all bandaged up and he'll be off the rest of the week. Are you up to serving the private party?"

"Do I still get double rates?" Mya asked.

"I'll have to check with the client."

Mya flicked her fringe out of her eyes and got down to prepping her cocktail trims. "Don't worry, I'll check with him." Her blood quickened as both anger and anticipation simmered. Why hadn't he wanted *her* to tend his bar, hmm?

Half an hour later, she walked into the small room that could be roped off for VIPs or small private functions. "Hi, Brad," she said coolly. "You've offended me."

"I have?"

"You don't like my cocktail skills any more?"

"I didn't think you'd want me to pay for your time." He turned on the smiling charm immediately—but then leaned a little closer to where she now stood setting up the small bar. "I thought you might prefer not to have to see me."

She shrugged. "It wouldn't matter to me." She carefully placed glasses. "Maybe I could do with the money."

"And that wouldn't bother you?" He watched her closely.

"You'd be paying me to pour drinks," she answered with some sass. "Not anything else. And you're offering to pay Jonny more than the going rate?"

"To secure the private space I had to. I didn't think you'd want me to treat you as a charity."

"But you wouldn't be, would you?" she asked coolly.

He studied her, a small smile playing around his way-too-luscious lips. Yeah, there was the problem—she now knew exactly how skilled that mouth was.

"I can be professional," she said—to herself more than to him.

"Can you?"

"Sure, can't you?"

His smile deepened. "I'm not at work. I'm here to have fun and flirt with the bar staff."

"You wanted to flirt with Jonny?" She laughed. "I'm sorry to disappoint you, but Jonny is off sick. You're stuck with me."

He looked at her.

"Am I worth double?" she asked him and tilted her head on the side.

"You do know what you're doing, don't you?"

"Stirring a cocktail, yes?"

"You're stirring, but not just the cocktail."

"We can still be friends, right? Isn't that what you said?" she said archly.

That was before they'd slept together.

"Of course." He inclined his head and walked to greet the first person coming through the door.

Mya watched the guests arrive and insecurity smote her—there were women here, seriously hot women. Smart ones too. Lawyers, the lot of them. And it was so dumb to feel threatened when she was ninety per cent on her way to being a lawyer too. And even if she weren't, she still didn't need to feel any less worthy than them.

Yet she did. The years of conditioning at that school had shaped her—that she should feel grateful for having that opportunity. That she shouldn't stuff it up. That her drop-kick family background meant she'd never be fully accepted by the social strata that most of these people came from—as James had pointed out.

She watched Brad laughing with one of the women. Oh, no, maybe that was why he hadn't wanted her to work the bar—had he been sparing her because he was here with another woman? Why hadn't she thought of that?

Brad knew all the guys were checking her out. It had been a dumb idea to come here, but he'd thought he could pull it off if Jonny had been doing the work. Then Brad could pop into the main bar and snatch a few words with Mya and see how the land lay. Only now she was right in front of him, smiling, joking and teasing with them all as she served them.

And all he could do was watch like some lovelorn pup hoping for any kind of bone to be thrown his way. Some small scrap that might show she wanted him again. It was more than his pride that was stung. Did she really not want another night with him? Had that truly been enough for her? He didn't believe it—was egotistical enough not to. All he needed was some proof. And to get that, he figured he just needed to get a little closer to her.

Mya fully regretted saying she'd do this. He was more handsome than she remembered, more fun with his wicked smiles and sharp words. And now she was assailed by images of sneaking him into the cupboard or some dark corner in the alley and having her wicked way with him. Quick and frantic and fabulous.

And to make it worse, he'd now taken up residence right beside her and was watching her every move with the full-on maple-syrup glow. Brad Davenport on full throttle. She fumbled with the bottle and was annoyed to glance up and see him suddenly smiling as if he'd won the lottery.

"Not on your game tonight?" he drawled. "Or is it because you can't concentrate when I'm near?"

She stopped what she was doing—but couldn't stop her blush. "Don't be mean."

His brows hit the ceiling. "I'm not the one who was mean—you're the one who said one night only," he whispered harshly as he leaned over.

"You only *do* one night," she whispered back.

"Not necessarily." He leaned against the bar. "Maybe I can do unpredictable."

Mya clutched the neck of the bottle with damp fingers and tried to joke. "Would you be saying this to Jonny?"

He didn't bother to reply, just kept those burning brown eyes on her.

"Why didn't you ask for me?" she added.

"Can you honestly say you wouldn't have got mad if I did? Can you honestly say you'd be happy for me to pay for your time no matter the context?"

She poured herself a tall glass of water. Damn, the guy actually understood her.

"I'll walk you home tonight," he said.

"You're hoping for a good-night kiss?" She squared her shoulders and asked straight out.

"I'm concerned for your safety," he replied, his eyes twinkling.

"Really?"

"Partly. Mainly I want more than a good-night kiss."

"Do you?" she asked softly. "What do you want?"

He didn't answer with words—just that look.

Mya turned away while she still could. "I'll get Pete to come in and finish serving you guys, and I'll meet you out the front at closing time."

To her pleasure, he was waiting as she'd asked, at the very end of the night.

"Where do you live?" he asked.

"Tonight?" she said. "I'm staying at your place." She walked up to him but he took a step to the side and back, out of reach.

"I'm not touching you now," he muttered. "If I touch you now we'll be all over each other in the nearest shadow and I don't want to do that."

"You don't?" Her confidence surged at his words.

He closed his eyes. "I don't want it to be sordid."

Delight and desire filled her, topped off with relief. All that pleasure was smashed away by the need that pierced her a second later. She walked faster. "It wouldn't be."

He stopped on the footpath behind her. "Mya." A warning, a plea, a demand.

She turned her head to look back at him and smiled. Then she walked faster still, her body slick and ready. "It would be fun."

As it had been the night of her party, she seemed to fly rather than walk. Her feet skimmed over the concrete. There was no alcohol in her system, yet she was in a haze as if she was under the influence.

She was under the influence of *him*.

She realised he was breathing faster than normal, and he was fit. The walk home hadn't exactly taxed him. Something else was bothering him—the same thing that was bothering her.

She walked up the narrow path to his villa. Under the veranda they were shrouded in darkness the streetlamps couldn't penetrate. The scent of the rose in the pot by the door was sweet and fresh. She stood in front of the door, like an impatient cat yowling to be let in, while he stood behind her.

"I can't get the key in the lock," he muttered, nuzzling her neck. "Don't go getting all Freudian on that." He chuckled with a groan.

At least they were almost inside his home. He hauled her closer, crushing her against him. She melted into his hot strength, almost delirious with ecstasy already. Yes, this was what she wanted—more of him. *All* of him. And she was too desperate now to wait a minute longer. On the darkened deck, no one could see them from the street. So Mya, bolder than she'd ever been in her life and on the brink of ecstasy because he wanted her as much as she did him, pulled her jeans down. She didn't get them very far, wiggling her hips side to side to tug them as far as she could, but she only made it to mid-thigh. She'd hooked her knickers with them, and despite the warmth of summer, the air on her bared butt was cool. She pressed back to feel the rough denim of his jeans against her.

He swore, pithy, crude, hot.

She looked over her shoulder as she put her hands to the cool paint and arched back, letting her butt grind against his pelvis.

He swore again, explicit and thrilling, and curled a strong arm around her waist, his other hand scraping the key in the lock. Finally he got it and turned the handle. He lifted her with that one arm and took the two paces inside. He turned them both and slammed the door, stepped forward immediately, his hands gripping hers and lifting them higher on the wood so they were above her head.

His feet moved between hers, pushing hers wider apart. But they couldn't go that far the way her jeans were only pulled to her mid-thigh. It excited her all the more—she wanted to be pinned by him again. It had been all she'd been able to think of for days. He leaned against her from behind, holding her still as he unzipped his jeans. She pressed her palms to the door herself, rubbing to feel the blunt head of him so near to entering her slick heat.

"Hell, Mya." He cursed again. "I want you…"

She heard the sharp rip, felt his movement behind her. A second later his hands circled her thighs. His fingers met in the middle, touching her intimately. She heard his roughly drawn breath as he felt how wet she already was. His fingers returned to her inner thighs, holding her tight now, and he thrust in hard. No preliminaries, just raw heat.

She gasped, shocked and delighted and desperate all at once. She put her hands on the door, bracing and giving leverage to push back on him and take him deeper. He moaned and immediately pressed his mouth to her shoulder to muffle the sounds of ecstatic agony.

Heat beaded all over her body. Her breath burned in too-short bursts. More moisture slicked where she needed it most, easing his sudden, forceful invasion.

He circled his hips and then thrust hard all the way home again, surging into a quick, hard, breathless rhythm. A coarse word of bliss rapidly transformed into a groan and he paused his rough thrusts into her. "Damn it…you can't possibly come this way."

"Oh, yeah?" But she could, she was almost there already. Desperately turned on. "Don't you dare stop."

He lifted her, flattening her against the door. Literally screwing her to it. A good thing given her legs were trembling so much they couldn't hold her up because she was so close to orgasm.

He forced his fingers between her and the wood, and for a second they stroked, as if to ensure she was as turned on as she declared. She pressed against his hand, trapping it, stopping the tease. Then arched her back as much as she could.

"Brad!"

He growled and withdrew his hand, slamming it against the wall by her head as he thrust hard again. "I want you so much."

She squeezed her eyes shut, breathing hard as his words struck like hot stones into her soul and his body rammed once more into hers. She felt his rough jaw against her cheek; the blunt demand inflamed her body.

She could hardly move her mouth to form the words. "More," she confessed. "I…want you. More… More."

It became a mantra and then a scream as the sensations skidded, becoming convulsions that twisted through her. Her hands curled into claws as she shook. She ground her hips round and round between him and the wall. Both immovable forces. With a harsh groan he resisted her attempts to milk him. His hands gripped her hips, holding her still as over and over he stroked as if trying to get deeper and deeper within her, as if he too couldn't bear for it to be over just yet. His need shocked her. The same need that had summoned her here, making her ignore both caution and reason.

"Oh. *Yes*." Her own primal reaction to his demand was an orgasm so strong she would have fallen to the floor had he not held her so tightly.

His fingers dug as the answering cry was ripped from him.

Breathing hard, he slumped against her, still pinning her to the wall, his head falling to her shoulder. She felt the harsh gusts of breath down her back as he held her close. She appreciated the contact—the comfort—as if he too needed the time and the proximity to process what they'd just shared.

And then he moved, lifting her into his arms and stomping a few feet into his spare room—the library. He sank into the big armchair, holding her in his lap.

Their eyes met in the dim light. He smiled at her and then kissed her. She kissed him back. The slow, tender kisses that they'd skipped in their haste for completion.

"We're doing this again," he said quietly.

How could she deny him anything when he was so skilfully stirring her body into blissful submission? "A couple more times," she muttered, barely able to think.

"More than a couple."

Okay, she could see the attraction in that for her, but what about him? "What's in it for you?"

He laughed silently, but she felt the vibrations all around her. "You have to ask, after *that*?"

She'd never thought of herself as a skilled lover or any kind of sexual goddess. "That other guy told me I was lousy in bed," she admitted. "And given James had just dumped me, I thought he was right."

"You're kidding," Brad groaned. "You're amazing. That was unbelievably amazing."

The glow he'd already lit inside her burned brighter. "Is this not normal for you?" she teased.

He stilled. She could sense him deliberating over his reply. She looked away, studying the shelf of books as if she could read the titles in the gloom.

He took her chin in firm fingers and turned her so she had to look him in the eye again. "No. It's not."

She felt her cheeks burn but he wouldn't let her turn her head away.

"That other night? And tonight?" he said softly. "Best sex of my life."

"No," she whispered. She didn't want him to flatter her with false praise.

"Do I have to print out a certificate before you'll believe me?"

She chuckled.

He was the one shaking his head now. "You don't have to get the awards, you know. You don't need accolades to be certified attractive. All you have to do is smile."

How could she not smile when he said things like

that? "Another confession?" she whispered. "It was the best sex of my life too."

He smiled.

"But this can't be anything," she added quickly.

"I don't think we need to label it, do we?"

"It's only for a little while." Only until she had her desire for him under control. If she didn't put her heart on the line, she'd be fine.

He shook his head. "Don't you get it? We can't put limitations on this because we'll both want more if we do that. You always want what you can't have. And we both have that fighter within who wants to defy the rules."

"So what do you suggest—no rules?"

"No rules." He leaned over her and whispered. His hand teasing the soft skin of her inner thigh. "And if you like, no boundaries."

Mya stared at him, incredibly tempted. He meant physical boundaries. She knew that. "None at all?"

He lifted his shoulders.

Her heart thudded so hard. "All or nothing?"

"Anything you want me to do, sure, I'll do."

"You're offering to be my love slave? You'll do whatever I want?" She couldn't help but smile at that idea.

He nodded. "You take pleasure from me and I'll take pleasure from you."

He was offering a licence to thrill. "What if I don't

want to do something you ask me to?" she asked curiously.

His expression deepened and he ran a gentle finger down her arm. "I think you'll want to."

She touched her tongue to her lip. Yes, she figured she would.

His fingers tickled as he suddenly grinned. "I wasn't actually thinking of anything that kinky," he teased. "But maybe you were."

Colour heated her cheeks. "What I think of as kinky you probably think of as tame," she muttered defensively.

"You can ask me for anything," he murmured.

She nodded. "It's not the right time for a relationship for me and you never want one...but for now—"

"There's just now." His arms tightened around her and he stood, carrying her down to his room.

Mya reached out and switched on the light as they passed it.

"I love this wallpaper." She gazed at the green vines climbing the white paper. "It still stuns me you're into floral."

"It's not floral," he said firmly, planting her on the bed and tugging off her jeans. "It's jungle."

"*That's* floral." She rolled onto her stomach and pointed to the small vase on the bedside table filled with sweet-smelling summer roses.

"Women like flowers," he said blandly, bending to kiss the small of her back.

Oh, he might talk all sophisticated loverman, but it wasn't quite as it seemed and she knew it. "No, you had flowers there that first time I visited, and you didn't know I was coming."

"I'm always prepared for an overnight female guest." He emphasised the tease with a nip of his teeth.

"No." She rolled to face him and grabbed a fistful of his shirt to pull him onto her. "You prefer to sleep at their houses so you can do the 'quickie and exit' in the morning. The only reason *I'm* here is because you know I'll leave early. You know I'm not going to linger and make for an awkward morning-after moment." She met his darkened gaze and determinedly ignored the way his fingers were stroking closer and closer to her nipple. "So the flowers are here because you like them. Furthermore—"

"There's more?"

"Oh, there is. I have all the evidence for this case. You grow the roses in your garden."

"Okay, so I grow the roses," he admitted. "Are you going to tease me about it?"

"Of course not." She rubbed her fingers against his stubble. "They're beautiful."

His amusement turned wicked. "I get pleasure from watching something bloom. I appreciate form, nature's 'curves'." His hand slid over her hips and between her thighs.

"You can try to hide behind some sexy talk, but

the fact is *you're* talented. You really care about your roses."

"I really like curves." He burrowed down the bed more. "I like pretty pink flowers too." He pulled her knees apart. "And you're right, I like to look after them." He bent and kissed her there, his tongue circling in ever-teasing strokes, before sliding inside.

Mya had given up on her analysis the moment he touched her. Her eyes closed as sensation rippled out from deep within her. He turned her on so quickly.

When she was wrung out and panting he rose, wearing the smile of a victor. She wound her arms around his waist and pulled him close.

"Mmm," he groaned appreciatively as she wriggled beneath him. "I've discovered a liking for clinging flowers."

"What about carnivorous ones?" She arched swiftly and ate him whole.

But later as she tumbled towards sleep in his arms she reminded herself exactly how long this fling was going to last. Brad might have said no limitations, but as far as she was concerned it was for one week and one week only. She only had two lecture-free weeks over the Christmas break. The first was his, the second was for her assignments and exam study. There'd be no room for him in her life from then on. Abstinence had failed; an overdose had to work. One week of indulgence.

Chapter 10

She came to him every night. And every night it was the same but different—variations on a theme. So many, many wonderful variations. He delighted in his deepening knowledge of her—he sought to learn what she liked, what made her shiver, the slow discovery of all her secrets. But finding enough time to see her was hard. Frantic sex followed by sleep followed by more frantic sex before she left for work. He sometimes had lunch with her—a snatched ten minutes before he was due in court or before she had a lecture. Ten minutes wasn't enough. He went back to the bar in the early evenings but then left to get more work done—and to let her work.

* * *

There wasn't enough time. Mya grasped the few moments they had but it felt like the glitter from the party—impossible to catch and hold. Just an ephemeral, beautiful shimmer. So she was determined to make the most of it. Brad seemed more intent than ever on "just having fun" too—as if he was also aware of how brief this would be.

She stretched in his big bed, slowly and so reluctantly coming awake after what felt like only five minutes' sleep. She could hear him talking—dozily she listened to one half of an incisive discussion on some point of law. She smiled as she snoozed. He sounded so authoritative—which he was on this, of course—quoting from case after case, and given that she could hear he was pacing down the far end of the hall, she knew he was recalling those cases from his own memory, not that of a computer. Geek. Question was why he was talking so early in the morning.

She sat up and looked at her watch. It wasn't just early in the morning—it was still the middle of the night. She'd really had only a little more than five minutes' sleep.

She slipped out of bed and wrapped a towel round herself and tiptoed down the hall. She could see the light in his office was on, and she paused in the doorway. He stood at his desk, his hair a crumpled mess, unshaven, circles under his eyes, still on that difficult call.

She took a step back and went back to the bedroom, not wanting to eavesdrop. But in the silent
house, his voice carried—his concern was obvious.
She waited a very long time for him to return to bed.
But even though he'd stopped talking quite some
time ago now, he still didn't come down the hall. So
she got up again—concerned.

From in his office doorway, she saw him sitting
at his desk, his face a portrait of worry. She'd noticed before how tired he sometimes looked when he
thought no one was watching. The animated, charming façade slipped on when people talked to him. She
didn't want him to feel as if he had to put that mask
on for her. She understood now that he covered up
with the charm factor. Why did he feel the need to
maintain the image? When he claimed to hate that
manufactured perfection in his parents' home? In a
way he was as guilty of it as they were.

But then he closed his eyes and put his head in
his hands.

"Brad?" She swiftly walked into the room, round
the side of his desk and put her arms around him. It
was an instinctive, caring gesture. Nothing sexual,
just the comfort of a hug. "What's wrong?"

For a long time he said nothing. But then there
was a sigh and a mumble. "Christmas is bad for most
of my kids."

My kids. The word meant much. She softened inside. He cared deeply, but he didn't like to display it for everyone. "Something's happened?"

"Gage has run away."

Mya bit her lip. Two days out from Christmas? Things must be bad. "Who's Gage?"

"A client. His parents split a while back. He's been shuttling between them for a few years, but it's never been easy. His father had a new partner on the scene but they've split up recently." He sighed. "What's worse, do you think? Being fought over, or not being noticed or wanted at all?" He glanced at her. "Or being expected to carry the expectations and dreams and ambitions of generations?"

She shook her head. "It depends."

"It does," he said tiredly. "I should have spotted there was something badly wrong," he added quietly. "I should have seen it. I knew he'd been truanting. I knew he hadn't been talking to the psych. But I—"

"You're not his parent."

"I'm his advocate. I should know what it is he wants."

"And do you?"

He stared sightlessly at the desk. "I'm not sure. He's on the run but if I were to guess I'd say he'll head to his dad's ex. She's been the one there. But she lives in another town now. She wasn't married to the guy. She's not a guardian. In theory she has no legal claim to Gage."

"But if he wants to stay with her, if she wants him—can you help them?"

"Maybe. That's if he is heading there, if he is okay." He looked worried. "Not all stepmothers are wicked."

And not all playboys were heartless.

"It's really sad," she said.

He nodded. "And if he doesn't turn up soon, he's only going to make it harder for himself to get what he wants."

"I'm sorry, Brad."

He rubbed his forehead, as if he could rub away the stress. "You should go get some sleep."

"Not without you." There was one thing she could give him—the one thing he'd wanted from her. It wasn't much, but it was all she had, and she wanted to give him comfort now. She didn't know how she was going to do it, but after Christmas she was walking away from him. She'd been such a fool to think she could handle this. "You do an incredible job," she whispered. He was an incredible person.

"Not good enough," he muttered. "Not this time. I should have spotted it, Mya. Hell, I hope he's okay."

"He will be." She hugged him tighter. "Don't feel bad," she urged. "You help so many people. You'll help him too."

Worry burdened Brad—burned inside him. Because he feared Mya was wrong—on several levels. "I do this job to make myself feel good. To pretend to myself that I have helped out in some way," he confessed. "But do I really?" He shrugged. "Who knows?"

"Of course you do," she said vehemently. "You're hugely talented and you give that talent to the most vulnerable. You're generous."

"Mya," he muttered, trying to claw back some cool. To joke his way out of this intensity the way he always did. "I thought I only did counsel for children to score chicks?"

"I don't think you're as selfish as you like to make out that you are."

Oh, but she was wrong. He knew he was selfish. He'd been told it many times by women. And they were right. "I'm not very good company tonight." He felt uncomfortable—felt vulnerable with her this moment. He wanted to pull it back in. His chest ached. Maybe he was coming down with summer flu. "I don't feel that great," he muttered, too tired to hold that last fact back.

"I know."

He turned and looked at her—beautiful, bright, *sweet* Mya, whom he wanted so much from and yet who couldn't give it.

Wasn't it ironic that the game-changing woman for him didn't want the game changed? He'd positioned himself as her bed-buddy—painted himself into a corner as her "good-time guy". And was that so bad? A few minutes of fun here and there in an otherwise hardworking life? He was the king of quick'n'fun, wasn't he? With the same woman for once, yet what difference did that really make?

It made all the difference. Tonight it hurt.

Because he cared for her a lot more than he'd like, and the reality was he didn't stand a chance. There was no room in her life for him. Her parents came first and that was fair enough. He'd played the playboy role too well for too long for her to see him any other way. He supposed it served him right. But this second he was so wrung out, he was at the point where he'd take all he could get. And so he tried to pull it back on again—his playful tease. "Is there something you wanted?" he drawled.

But she didn't respond with the same kind of light amusement. "Yes, there is."

She didn't tease him with her wishes or do a pretend strip to reveal her polka-dotted panties and mismatched cotton bra. Instead she looked serious. "Tell me what you want me to do."

He coughed; it felt as if something were crushing his chest. A crazy, over-the-top reaction. This was hardly the first time a woman had asked him to reveal a sexual fantasy. But he didn't want a fantasy tonight. He just wanted Mya. "I thought I made it clear you didn't have to do anything other than just be for me."

"No. You've done what I wanted you to do so

many times. Now it's your turn. I'm yours. What would you like me to do?"

He didn't answer. Frankly, he couldn't think with the way she was looking at him with all the promises of the world in her eyes and the sweetness in that unique smile.

"No ropes?" Finally, she teased. And her laughter tied his tongue—and his heart—the way no real binds ever could.

All he wanted was for her to welcome him the way she always did. All he needed was to see how much she enjoyed being with him; her response told him she was as enthralled as much as he in the passion between them. He ached for that total embrace, the softness in her body. Yeah, her embrace alone was enough. Her absolute acceptance. He took her hand and pulled her closer.

"Cover me," he whispered.

Deliverance finally came as she draped her warm limbs over his.

Chapter 11

She never got back from the bar until the early hours of the morning. Brad loathed the thought of her walking home alone, but she refused to let him pick her up after work, arguing it was too late for him. She wouldn't pay for taxi fares—certainly wouldn't let *him* pay for them. According to her, her scream-in-a-can and night-school self-defence moves were enough protection. Not for Brad they weren't. She didn't know it but he'd paid Kirk, the bouncer, to walk her home these past couple of weeks. He'd even concocted the lie for Kirk to tell her—that he'd moved into the city and walking her wasn't far out of his way. Mya hadn't argued much, which made Brad suspect she wasn't completely convinced about her self-defence skills either. It made his blood sizzle that he could only help her if he did it secretly.

His blood sizzled more because of the intensity with which he *wanted* to help her. It was crazy. And even crazier was that here he was, awake way beyond midnight, waiting to hear the sound of the key in the lock. Since when had he *ever* given a woman a key to his home?

He'd seen how tired she was today. She'd had two coffees for breakfast this morning. He knew she'd get something to eat at the café—and more coffee. Then she'd gone straight into her shift at the bar. She'd get more sustenance there too. But what the woman needed was some sleep. She needed to take better care of herself. He needed to take better care of her. He hated how hard she worked. And he hated how it had been his fault she'd had so little sleep last night—and not from energetic bedroom games but talking. Off-loading all his troubles about Gage. He didn't feel comfortable about that either. It was time to ease back a bit, get them back into the playful groove. Lighten it up the way he liked it. But his mood was bleak—worried about Gage, worried about Mya, and, frankly, worried about himself and his ability to handle it all.

Eventually he heard her arrive, her heels clipping along the hallway. He rolled onto his stomach and closed his eyes, feigning deep sleep—too late to switch the light off.

"Brad?"

A stage whisper that he ignored. He counted his breathing, trying to keep it deep and regular.

She touched his shoulder, and he braced to stop the flinch as her fingertips stroked. She had a soft touch, but not shy. He made the counting in his head louder so he wouldn't smile. The thing she needed most right now was sleep, not an hour getting physical with him.

"Brad?"

He was *asleep*; hadn't she got that already?

She sighed. The edge of disappointment nearly broke his resolve. He'd make it up to her tomorrow. He'd disable her alarm and let her sleep late. Then he'd wake her slow—morning sex was the way to start the day, and they'd never yet managed it in any kind of leisurely fashion. And Christmas morning meant the café would be closed.

She walked a couple of paces away. He carefully opened his eyes and saw her back was to him. He could see the weariness in her shoulders, in the way she rubbed her forehead as if there was a residual ache there before she began to undress. He wished she wouldn't work as hard as she did. He wished she'd damn well let him help her out. She could drop one of her jobs; he'd see to it that she didn't starve.

He was so busy thinking he didn't notice that she'd turned around. Or that he was supposed to be out like a light.

"You're awake."

He snapped his eyes shut but he knew it was too late.

"Brad!"

Busted. "I was asleep."

"You were pretending to be asleep!" She sounded outraged. "Why were you pretending to be asleep?" She supplied the answer before he could even open his mouth. "You didn't want to have to perform tonight? You're lying there feigning sleep like some unfulfilled spouse trying to avoid duty sex?"

"Mya—"

"Are you bored already?"

It was the hurt behind the indignance that got him moving. He shot out of bed. "Does it look like I'm bored?"

His erection was so hard it hurt, his skin pulled tighter than ever before. All he wanted to do was bury himself deep in her heat and find the release. He wanted those sensations that only she could give, to steal away all the thoughts that tormented him, to be as close as they'd been last night with nothing between them.

"If you didn't want me to come tonight, all you had to do is tell me." She ignored his evidential display.

"I want you to come." And yes, he meant that in the teenage double-entendre way.

"Then what are you doing pretending you're asleep?" Arms folded, foot tapping, she waited.

He sighed. He was a condemned man. His answer

would annoy her but she wouldn't let him get away with not explaining himself to her. "I thought you needed some sleep."

Her jaw dropped.

"Look at you," he said. "You're exhausted."

"The shadows beneath my eyes are a turn-off, is that it?" she queried—not hiding the hint of hurt. "You're not doing a lot for my ego here."

"Mya," he said coaxingly and reached for her.

She pulled back out of reach. Totally put out. "I work two jobs and study on top of that, so exhaustion is normal. I'm sorry if I can't live up to the high-gloss appearance of your usual lovers. Maybe you need to stick to ladies of leisure."

"Mya." He tried to laugh it off, gesturing at his erection. "It's perfectly clear your appearance is still lethal for me."

She wasn't buying it. "You can't tell me you didn't pull some all-nighters when you were studying. It's normal student behaviour."

"Not every assignment, I didn't."

"Well, bully for you for being more organised than me."

"No one can be more organised than you. Your problem is that not only are you studying, you're working two jobs. That's not a normal workload."

"In my world it happens all the time. You do what you have to do."

"Yeah, but *you* don't have to do that much."

"I do if I need to eat."

"Why not let me help you?"

She whirled away from him. "You don't need to help me. All I want from you is—"

"Yeah, okay. I got it." He didn't want to hear what *little* she wanted from him. He'd made the bed. But now the bed wasn't enough for him.

What was wrong with him? He'd never turned down sex. Ever. If a pretty woman was offering, he was on it. Easy come, easy go and a good time had by both.

She'd wanted to ravish him, and he'd lain there like a log. And ironically harder than a piece of petrified wood. He'd definitely come down with some kind of mind-altering fever. And now she was halfway down the hallway again.

"You're not leaving," he stated, striding after her.

"I'm not staying where I'm not wanted."

"You're wanted. You *know* you're wanted. All you have to do is look at me to know you're wanted."

"That's just a normal state of being for you."

White-hot fury ripped through him because this was *not* normal for him.

She turned in time to read his expression and suddenly shook her head. "Don't make this complicated." She kept backing up the hallway. "I think I'll spend tonight at my place. Catch up on my beauty sleep." A pointed look. "And I need to get to my parents' place early in the morning. We can get together next week."

He caught up to her in a couple of quick strides.

He pulled her against him and kissed her until she was panting. And so was he.

"You couldn't look more beautiful than you do right now," he said.

When her attention was riveted on him. When desire filled her eyes and blood pounded in her lips and she was seconds off breathing his name.

But that hurt look in her eyes grew—dimming that light. "You just don't like me walking out on you right now. But you started it."

"What I don't like is how hard you're working. Why not work smarter instead of harder?"

"What is that piece of management-mag speak supposed to mean?"

"Get just one job. A better job. Get an internship at a firm."

She shook her head.

"You could clerk for me over the summer." It was the worst thing to suggest; he knew it before he'd even opened his mouth but he couldn't stop the words.

"I'm not a charity case. I'm tired of charity. I want to do it myself. I want to deserve it myself."

"You do deserve it," he argued, his volume lifting along with his frustration. "You're super smart. You've got amazing grades. Any firm would want you."

"You only do because of this...connection," she said. "It's the sexual equivalent of the old boys' network. Only because you know me. I'd rather send my CV out and get a job on my own merit."

"Okay, fine. Will you send your CV to my firm?"

"Of course not."

"So you're doing the opposite. Because we do know each other, you won't work with me?"

"We couldn't. I couldn't."

"Why not? We'd make a great team."

She just stared at him.

"Everybody makes connections, Mya," he said, his body clenched with frustration. Wanting to shake sense into her some way or another and knowing already that he was doomed to failure. She was so *damn* obstinate. "That's why they have networking groups. Young lawyers, young farmers, young fashion designers. People have mentors. It's normal."

"You set up on your own," she argued. "You turned your back on any help your father could offer."

He drew a hard breath. "You know I had my reasons for that. And I still had help. I might have turned my back on my father's help, but I still had his name." He sighed. "And to be honest I know that helped. It helped that I had money."

"It helped more that you'd won all the prizes in your year at university. Your own merit, Brad. I want to do the same."

"I still had help," he ground out through his teeth, hating to have to admit it, but knowing it was the truth.

"Well, I'll get my lecturer to write a reference or something."

"So it's just me you won't accept help from?"

"I'm not using our personal relationship for professional gain."

"So we have a relationship." He pounced.

"No," she denied instantly, swallowing hard. "This is a fling. Stress relief." Mya stared at him in all his naked glory. What was the man thinking? Why was he changing the rules—why was he offering for her to work with him? As if that were possible? What did he think would happen when he decided he'd had enough of sleeping with her? No way could she take this from him.

"Look, I made the mistake of going for one job based on a relationship already. I'm not doing it again. James had suggested I apply for an internship at a particular firm last summer." She'd been thrilled when they'd both been accepted. "But then he found out some of my grades and I took him home to see my parents…and it was like he turned into a different person overnight." It wasn't until later that she learned how average James's grades really were. "But his grades didn't matter because he was getting a job at the most prestigious accountancy firm in town anyway because his dad was a partner there. Meanwhile I spent my first pay packet in advance buying clothes that might possibly be acceptable to work there, but after he broke up with me, and just before those exams, the company withdrew the offer, saying they had no need for so many interns. So no, I'm not trusting any job offer based on any kind of connection other than merit. I'm not having any kind of relationship interfere with my future."

"So you have to earn everything yourself? You can't accept a gift? I only have money thanks to *chance* at birth. You can't take anything from me?" he asked, completely frustrated.

"That's right." She wouldn't take anything from him. Because what he was offering wouldn't ever be enough. "I need to earn it myself."

"You have to be so independent, don't you? You have to be the best," he said bitterly. "So insanely competitive you're on the brink of a breakdown from the sleepless nights and caffeine overdoses. Well, why don't you go ahead and study yourself to death? Then work yourself to death and become a corporate lawyer."

"Is that such a crime?"

"It is when you have huge talent in another area."

She rolled her eyes. "Don't go there."

"You should make time for your wearable art. It's important to you. You should be happy as well as successful."

That wasn't what was going to make her happy.

"It's something you're so good at," he continued. "You should take the opportunity. You should put your work out there."

"I can't."

"You'd rather not compete at all rather than come

second?" He shook his head. "Is being the best *so* important to you?"

"Success requires sacrifice," she said firmly. "What would you have me do, Brad? Give up all I've worked so hard for, to try and scrape a living selling some recycled tat? That's not realistic. It's not going to happen. Yes, I love doing that but I also love the law."

"So strike a *balance*."

"I can't yet."

"You won't ever," he said, going quiet. "There'll always be something else you feel you have to achieve. Your parents wouldn't want you to live like this. Your parents want you to be happy."

"Don't talk to me about what my parents want. I know what they *need*." And she was the only one who could help them.

"You don't. You can't face up to what *you* need, let alone anyone else," he argued. "You lie to your parents. What's worse is you lie to yourself. You're so scared of failing you can't take any kind of real risk."

"And you can?" So hurt, she poured it all back on him. "*You're* the one who constantly has to be the epitome of charm. You're as bad as your parents. You project this perfect façade—all funny and capable and unable to admit to anything being wrong or *needing* anything. *You're* the one who's scared. You're the one who can't take any kind of support." She paused and saw he'd gone pale.

He drew in a deep breath but she didn't give him

the chance to try to argue—because there was no argument. "We want different things, Brad," she said sadly.

He didn't answer. And she turned and left.

Chapter 12

As dawn broke on Christmas Day, Gage Simmons pushed his blistered feet and aching back onward. He knocked on the door. She opened it in less than a minute—the woman he wish, wish, *wished* were his mother. The one he'd walked miles and miles to get to. The one he wanted to stay with. The one who'd shown him more love and compassion and simple fun than any of his blood relatives.

"Will it be okay?" His voice wobbled as she pulled him into a super-tight hug.

"I don't know," she murmured into his hair. "But we're going to try." For a moment they watched the sunrise together. "We have to call them, you know.

It's not fair on your parents not knowing where you are."

Gage closed his eyes and thought none of it was fair. But he nodded.

"Look at the day, Gage." She kept her arm around him. "It's going to be a beauty."

He didn't want the sun to move. It had taken so long to find her and he didn't want to leave. Not yet. He didn't want another second to pass.

"We'll work it out, Gage. I promise."

There was a single-sentence mention in the morning news bulletin—that the boy who'd gone missing had been located and was well. Mya desperately wanted to call Brad and ask if everything truly was okay. But it wasn't okay enough between them for her to be able to do that. And there was something else she had to do—urgently.

Utterly sleep-deprived, Mya walked up the overgrown path towards her parents' house. She'd fantasised for so long about turning up there with a property deed in hand tied by a ribbon. Her gift to them—a Christmas gift. Wouldn't that be wonderful? To be able to move them somewhere so much better. And she would do it; one day she would. It just wouldn't be as soon as she'd hoped it might. And she was so sorry she hadn't been able to be everything they'd wanted her to be.

Brad was right, she had lied—to her parents and

to herself about what she really wanted. Because she was so scared of letting them down and of being let down herself.

She sat on the sofa and told them—about losing the scholarship, about working two jobs on top of summer school, about what she wanted to do for them more than anything.

Her parents were appalled, but not for the reason she'd feared.

"We wouldn't expect you to do that for us!" her mother cried. "We're okay here."

"You're not." Mya wiped her own tears away. "I wanted to do this for you so much. I wanted you to be so proud of me and I've let you down."

"You've never let us down," her father argued gruffly. "We let you down. I gave up. I got injured and gave up and put all our hopes on you. That wasn't fair."

"No wonder you're so thin and tired," her mother exclaimed, rubbing Mya's shoulder. "All we want for you is to be happy." She put her arms around her. "What would make you happy?"

So many things—her parents' comfort now certainly helped. There was that other thing too—but she didn't think he was hers to have.

"Can we get rid of all those photos of me winning prizes?" Mya half laughed and pushed her fringe from her eyes, determined to focus on the future and fixing things with her family.

"They bother you?"

Mya nodded. They took down most of them to-gether, leaving a few, finding a few others with the three of them together. The cousins turned up, and the Christmas eat-a-thon began. As the day faded, Mya picked up the discarded lid from a soda bottle and started playing with it, twisting it—tempted for the first time in ages to create something silly-but-stylish just for the sake of it.

Brad was almost two hours late getting to his par-ents' place for the obligatory big Christmas lunch. The calls between Gage and his stepmother and his parents and their lawyers had gone on and on until they'd wrangled a solution for today at least. Gage would stay with his "stepmother" until this after-noon, when he'd have time with each parent.

Poor kid. But at least now Brad knew what his client wanted, where he wanted to be and who he wanted to be with. He'd demonstrated it in an ex-treme way, but Brad was determined they'd work it out. He'd not stop working on it until they did.

He walked into the ridiculously decorated home and spied Lauren looking sulky at the overloaded table. He wasn't in the least hungry and stared at the twenty perfect platters of food for the four of them. Hell, it was the last thing he felt like—some fake happy-family thing. Surely there was a better use for them today?

"Why don't we take all this food down to the local homeless shelter?" he asked his mother.

She looked appalled.

"We can't eat it all." Brad shrugged. "Honestly, Mother, what's the point? Let's do something decent with it."

He looked at his mother, who looked at his father, who said nothing.

"Great idea," said Lauren, standing up.

"Okay," said his mother slowly.

"I'm not that hungry anyway," his father commented.

"Good," Brad said. "Why don't you two go down together to deliver it?" He stared at his parents, who both stared, rather aghast, back at him.

"That's more your mother's scene," his father eventually said.

"It's Christmas Day," Brad answered firmly. "You should be together." He moved forward. It'd be a relief to escape the picture-perfect scene with the empty undercurrents. "We'll *all* go."

Open-mouthed, Lauren watched him gather up a couple of platters.

"Come on," Brad said insistently. "Let's do it."

He was surprised that they actually did. They loaded all the food into his father's car, and Brad and Lauren followed in Brad's car.

For two hours they stood and served food to the people who'd come to the shelter. Their platters had gone into the mix, and his parents were now fully engaged in dishwashing duty.

"This was so much better than a strained dinner with them," Lauren muttered under her breath.

"I know," Brad agreed. "Genius. But are you hungry now?"

"Yeah, but not for any kind of roast." She looked slightly guilty. "How bad is that?"

"Why don't we go get Chinese?" he suggested with a half-laugh. "The restaurant round the corner from me does really good yum char."

"Shouldn't we have dinner with Mum and Dad?"

"Nah, let's leave them to it. We've done enough family bonding for the day."

"I actually think they're happy the way they are," Lauren said as she pulled a chicken dish towards her, half an hour later.

"You think?" Brad asked.

"Yes." Lauren chewed thoughtfully. "Surely if they weren't, they'd have done something about it by now?"

"I think they're just used to it." He sat back and toyed with the food on his plate. "They're apathetic and simply don't care enough to do anything to change things."

"It's a waste," Lauren said.

"It is," Brad agreed. "Maybe they'll learn something at the shelter." He grinned. "It might be a Christmas miracle."

Lauren suddenly looked serious. "Have you seen Mya recently?"

Brad's moment of lightness fled. He shook his head and stuffed rice into his mouth to keep from having to answer.

"She's not really a sister to you, is she?" Lauren said slyly.

The observation caught him by surprise—he half laughed, half choked and shook his head again.

"Is it going to work out?"

He shook his head again—slower that time.

"Have you stuffed things up so badly I'm going to lose my best friend?"

He shook his head more vehemently. "Be there for her."

Lauren studied him closely. "Why can't you be?"

"She doesn't want me to."

"Really?" Lauren frowned. "Mya had a thing for you for years. Even when you never saw her."

Yeah, but the trouble was Mya had got to know him properly now. And though he'd offered her all he could, she'd turned him down. It hurt.

"Don't tell me you're too apathetic to do anything about it, Brad," Lauren said softly. "Don't make the same mistake as Mum and Dad."

Lauren's words haunted him over the next week. The memory of Mya positively tortured him. Night after night he replayed their last conversation in his head and he dreamed of the too few nights they'd been together.

She'd been furious with him for not opening up. She claimed he maintained as much of a false façade as his parents did. He'd not realised he did that. But she was right. He had opened up to her, though—a couple of times he had, and she'd been there for him in a way that had made his heart melt. So why was it that when he'd wanted to support her, she'd pushed him away? Until now he'd been too hurt to try to figure it out, but now he had to *know*.

Lauren was right too: he couldn't be apathetic. He needed courage—Gage's kind of courage. To run towards what you needed most—the one person you needed most. The one whose love and laughter meant everything.

He went to the bar and pushed forward to the front of the bar section she was serving. Her eyes widened when she saw him and she asked his order ahead of the people he was standing beside. He refused to get a kick out of that—it was probably because she wanted to serve him so he'd leave asap.

He inhaled the sight of her like a man gulping fresh air after a long, deep dive in the abyss. And as she mixed his deliberately complicated cocktail, he tried for conversation. "I like your hairclip." So lame. But true.

She put her hand to her head where her homemade clip resided and smiled self-consciously. "You do?"

"Absolutely."

She nodded, looking down to stir some awful collection of liqueurs before speaking quickly. "I don't have the time right now for entire outfits," she said. "But hair accessories I can do. Pretty clips, small statements. Just a little fun and it keeps my fringe out of my eyes."

"That's great."

"It's enough," she said. "But you were right. I needed it."

"Good for you." He wished she needed him too.

For a moment their eyes met, and Brad was too tired to hide anything any more. He was too tired to try to make chit-chat and break the bulletproof wall of ice between them. He just wanted to hold her close—to have her in his arms and by his side and have it all. For ever.

But she moved to serve another person, and it was like having scabs from third-degree body burns ripped off. Coming here was the dumbest thing he'd done. For a guy who was supposed to be smart, he'd picked the world's worst time to try to talk to her. New Year's Eve was the busiest night of the year. Jonny was back—there were five bartenders there and all of them run off their feet. And she couldn't even look him in the eye.

He didn't even touch the cocktail she'd made for him. He just turned round and walked away.

* * *

Mya glanced up from making the next customer's cocktail—desperate to make sure he was still there. But he wasn't. She stretched up on tiptoe and just got a glimpse of his back heading towards the exit.

Oh, no. No, no and no. He wasn't turning up for the first time in a week looking all rough-edged and dangerous and for one heart-stopping moment *vulnerable*—and then leaving again. She had things to say to him. Things she'd been rehearsing in her head for days and days and no matter the outcome she was still determined to say.

She pushed her way out from behind the bar and barged through the throngs. "Brad!" She didn't care who heard her.

But if he did hear her, he didn't stop. She ran out onto the footpath and charged after him. "Brad!"

This time he stopped.

She looked at him, oblivious to the revellers on the street and the heat in the summer night. And now all those words that she'd been mentally practising just flew out of her head—when he looked at her like *that*?

"Oh, hell, don't cry," he groaned.

"I'm not *crying*!" she denied. And then sniffed. So what was the point in denial? "Okay, I'm…crying."

"Mya." He sounded strangled. "Please go back."

"Mya! Drew is having a fit." Kirk came puffing up beside them. "We need you back at the bar."

"I don't give a damn about the bar," Mya snapped.

Kirk scuttled away like a dirt bug escaping daylight.

"Mya, you should go back. You don't want to lose your job."

"I don't, but—"

"And you need to focus on your upcoming exam."

"I don't give a damn about that exam either!" she shouted.

Brad stared at her, waiting.

"Okay, I do, but…" She broke off to draw a ragged breath. "I don't care about the bar. But I do. I don't care about the exam. But I do. I don't care about anything that much but *you*," she admitted softly. "And I don't want you to walk away from me." Another fat tear spilt down her cheek.

He sighed and took a step towards her. "Mya, I've always believed that no one can ever truly put another person first. That ultimately we're all selfish and do what's best for ourselves. But I was wrong about that." He stopped and breathed out. "Because I will do whatever *you* need me to do in order for you to be happy. If that means walking out of your life, then that's what I'll do. It's the last thing I want to do. But I want what's best for you."

She shook her head angrily. "You might be brilliant but you're not a mind-reader. What makes you think walking out of my life would be best for me?"

"It's what you asked me to do," he pointed out.

"Well, I was an idiot."

He stared at her. "What do you want me to do?"

"I don't know that you can offer me what I really want from you."

"I know you want to hold onto your independence. I respect that. If you want the big corporate law job, then fantastic. I'll suck up my stupid fears and be right there behind you. If you decide you'd rather make your creations and try selling them, I can afford to support you. You can ask me for anything," he said.

She shook her head. She didn't want any *thing*. "I can't be dependent on you. I just can't." She couldn't give herself so completely to a guy who didn't feel the same for her as she did for him.

"You want me to give it all away?" he suddenly exploded. "Okay, I'll give all my money away. I'll give a guy the shirt on my back and stand here naked and with nothing. I just want to support you," he roared at her. "And you won't take it from me!"

"It's not your money I want!" she shouted back. "It's everything else. You have *everything* to give me. Love and *emotional* support, rather than financial. Strength. Humour. Play. Everything that's so wonderful about you. I love you and all I want is for you to love me back."

He stared at her. Stunned. "Why didn't you tell me?" He gestured wide. "You never showed me. You never wanted anyone to know about us. You were embarrassed to want me."

"I was never embarrassed about wanting you. What was I supposed to do? You're the ultimate playboy. Never with any woman more than a week. I had to protect myself somehow. I had to think of it as just a fantasy. If no one else knew then it wasn't really real."

He gazed at her, now motionless. "What do you think I feel for you?"

"Lust."

"Absolutely. Lust is right up there. Right now so is annoyance." He walked towards her. "Also admiration. Frustration. But above all, love."

She bent her head.

He put his fingers under her chin and lifted her face back up to his. "Mya, why do you think I want to give you everything I have?" He gazed into her eyes. "I love you more than I've ever loved anyone. Even myself," he joked just that little bit.

"Brad," she choked out.

"Has it not occurred to you that I'm the best person to help you with your studies?"

She laughed, but it was in despair. "I failed so badly at concentrating that night you found those cases for me. I had the wickedest thoughts going on that night. I can't concentrate with you around."

"We weren't sleeping together then. We were both frustrated. Wouldn't it be different knowing you can have your way with me when your study goal is met? Won't it be different now you know I love you and that you love me? And that we can be together as much as we want?"

Yeah, she still couldn't quite believe that.

He muttered something unintelligible and then just swept her close, his lips crashing onto hers as if there were no other way to convince her. And she *ached* to be convinced, desperate to feel the security that should only be a breath away. She burrowed closer, opening for him, wanting to give him everything and get it all in return.

"Do I really have to give away my money?" he asked gently. "If I was a starving student, you'd share everything with me, right?"

"Of course. But you're not a starving student. It feels so unbalanced." She sighed.

"Only in that one aspect and that's only temporary. In another couple of years you'll be qualified and raking it in, and I'll take early retirement and you can keep me in the manner to which I am accustomed."

She couldn't help it, laughter bubbled out of her. "And in what manner is that?"

"Restaurant meals every night," he said promptly.

"I can do salads from the café down the street."

"Sex every night of the week." He waggled his brows.

"And every morning."

"That too." He kissed her again. "You were right, by the way. I do my job because it makes me feel better about myself as a person. I tell myself I'm okay because I help kids. I make a difference, right? So I can't be all bad." He sighed. "But I'm not all that great. I chose not to get too close to anyone and never let anyone see behind the façade. That was because, like you, I don't like failure. Growing up in that house with my parents, I saw the falseness of their relationship. Swore I'd never have such a marriage. And that I'd never fail kids like that. That I'd never have them."

"You don't want to commit. I know that." She'd never try to fence him in. She'd have him for as long as he was hers to have. No way she could walk away from him now.

He laughed. "I don't have the choice, darling," he teased. "I'm not interested in anyone else. I don't want to be. I want this to work with you. You inspire me to be more."

"I'm not some perfect creature." She shook her head.

"No one is. But you kill yourself *trying* to be perfect and you don't have to. You don't have to get the top grade. You don't have to be the best bartender in town. You don't have to excel at everything. You can fail at everything and I'll love you anyway. Do you understand that? I'll love you no matter what."

Her eyes filled as she felt the intensity of his

words, the full emotion behind them. And finally she did understand that.

"You're wonderful and human, and you make mistakes like I do, but you pick yourself up and you fight on," he said. "You face your failures and you get it together."

"I don't fight on," she cried. "I gave up on you, on us, before we'd hardly started. I was so scared. I didn't want to change my priorities only to find out what we had wasn't anything more than a bit of fun."

"It's a whole lot of fun." He smiled. "And you don't have to change your priorities. We can have so much more fun together if you'll take a chance on me."

He stood before her, his expression open, no protective façade in place, just pure honesty and an offer she could never, ever refuse.

Now she saw behind his mask to the genuine, loving man he was. While he could act all cocky, come up with the most outrageous statements as if he fully believed he was God's gift to the female of the species, beneath that bravado was a guy as insecure as any other normal person. Despite that silver spoon, that money, all that success…there was still someone who doubted that another person could love him for just being him. But that was the part of him she loved the most.

"I need nothing but you," she answered simply.

And he needed someone who didn't give a damn

about anything he had, or his image. A person who cared only about him. The *essence* of him. The good-humoured, gorgeous, arrogant guy.

Happily that someone was her.

She wrapped her arms around him and lifted her face for another kiss. Offering her heart. It was a long time before he drew back and sighed. She felt the elation in every inch of him, but also the tension.

"You need to go back and finish your shift," he groaned. "New Year's Eve is the biggest night of the year."

"It is." She nodded. "Will you wait for me?"

"Always."

"We'll go on a two-hour rotation," he said firmly the next morning after they'd had breakfast. "Two hours' solid study, two hours' solid sex."

"That's finding balance?" she asked incredulously.

"I think so." He nodded in all seriousness. "Round the clock."

She giggled. "Yeah, that's really achieving balance."

"No point in trying to fight our natures, now, is there? Might as well roll with it." He winked. "Right now I'm on case names and caffeine duty. And then massage services."

"Massage services?"

"Inside and out." He lifted his brows lasciviously.

Deep inside her, muscles shifted, ready.

He laughed, reading her thoughts. "Later, babe. You've got facts to memorise."

How was she supposed to concentrate when she knew what was coming? She was insanely excited already. "I think you should feel me up first."

"No. Work now, reward later." He put himself on the far side of the desk and refused to look at her.

She sighed and sat up in her seat, pulling her pages of notes closer. "Better be a good reward," she grumbled beneath her breath.

"Mya, darling," he drawled from his desk. "You know it's going to be out of this world."

And it was.

TWO YEARS LATER

You know you want this.

Mya smothered a giggle at the photo she'd just been sent on her phone. Brad, buck naked and bold with a party hat magically positioned in a very strategic place. She quickly closed the message and acted as if she were paying complete attention to the orientation speech for new recruits at the multinational law firm she'd signed with. But her phone vibrated again.

Tonight. Our place. Come as soon as you can.

As soon as the spiels and slideshows were over— as interesting as they were—she escaped. She walked through the city, the warm summer air delightful on her back. Her first week had gone well, long hours, of course, and that competitive component. She relished it. She loved coming home too. Especially to Brad in playboy mode.

"Brad?" She closed the front door and called down the cool empty hallway.

"In the garden," came his distant shout.

She walked through the house, her footsteps ringing loud. The rest of the house unnaturally silent—until she stepped out onto the back deck.

"SURPRISE!"

There were five hundred people in the backyard.

Mya put out a hand and it was immediately gripped. Lauren laughed as she squeezed her hand to bring her back from the light-headed faint feeling.

"Oh, wow!" Mya couldn't move. Certainly couldn't think of anything to say.

"Breathe, woman, you need some colour back."

It was already back. Mya felt the blush burning over every bit of her body. OMG, there was a huge surprise party. Here. For her.

Dazed, she glanced around.

Her family were there—her mother beaming, her father standing by the barbecue helping Stella turn the steaks. They were in a new home only about ten minutes away. Brad had insisted he help them as soon as they'd got together that New Year's Eve two years ago. It had made such a difference to her parents.

Jonny and Drew were there from the bar. Some of

her cousins were there, also beaming. Many of Lauren's men. Brad's buddies. Some of her law school mates, a whole mishmash of people from her life. And they were all smiling, all celebrating, and they'd managed to keep this whole thing secret from her?

But there was only the one person she really wanted to see this second. And that was the tall hunk coming towards her through the crowd with a glass of champagne.

"You did all this?" she asked as he stepped unnecessarily close to hand the drink to her.

"You know what a good party planner I am." He bent to whisper in her ear and steal a kiss at the same time. "But don't be disappointed—we'll have our own private party a little later."

She giggled. As if she could ever be disappointed! And she knew that they'd have their own time tonight. Everyone else would leave, but Brad would always be there for her.

She sipped her champagne and stepped forward with a smile, Brad alongside her.

She'd dropped the café work and many of the shifts at the bar, working only during the weekends so she saved the weeknights for the two of them. The nights she did work, Brad came down to the bar and kept her company. His gang of mates had been more than happy for it to become their regular. And she'd gone back full-time at university to finish her degree—with a promise to pay Brad back sometime for all the free rent. He didn't bother arguing or answering that one, just rolled his eyes.

She'd had four job offers before her final exams. She didn't win the gold medal for top law graduate of the year, but she did take out the prize for top family law student. She'd thrown that in with all the contract and company law courses so she could understand what Brad was going on about in the evenings. He'd been right, he was a brilliant coach—firm, but he had a super-fun reward system going.

Yeah, she had the best prize already. She didn't think she could be happier.

She loved the party. There was no catwalk this time, no "wall of fame" either. It was all friends and family and laughter.

His parents were there too. Mya chatted with them. They all worked the façade to a degree but Brad had become a lot more open about talking with them—quite blunt in some of his views. Mya backed him up. They were his parents, and if he could make that effort, so could she.

"I'm so proud of you." She leaned back against him several hours later as they stood at the door and watched the last guests leave.

His laugh rumbled in his chest. "That's my line."

"I mean it." She turned to face him, pressing her breasts against his strength. "You're the most generous man I know."

He laughed even harder. "You have rose-tinted glasses."

Her smile blossomed too. "You grow the roses for me."

He brushed his lips against hers and took a step backwards into the hall to close the door.

"I have a graduation present for you." His breathing quickened.

"I haven't graduated yet."

"Mere technicality." He gifted her a teasingly light kiss. "I was going to give it to you when they were all here because I figured you couldn't refuse it in front of everyone. But then I thought that wasn't fair." He put his hand in his jeans pocket and pulled out a box.

Her heart stopped. "Brad—"

"Two years we've been together," he interrupted mock crossly. "Don't you think it's time you made an honest man of me?" He opened the box.

She went hot and cold and hot again in a nanosecond.

His hands gripped her shoulders as if he knew she'd gone light-headed. "You can't take advantage of me so long. Taking what you want, when you want it. Demanding all those pictures of me and treating me like some kind of sex object."

"And you're not?"

He shook his head, his eyes dancing. "No, I need solid commitment from you. I want a public declaration. I want this rock flashing on your finger to show those pups at that law firm that you're taken. And I want a family."

"Oh, you do?" Her sass answer was totally undermined by her breathless gasp.

"Yes."

She took a moment to inhale a few times. "Got anything else to add to this list of demands?"

"Speed," he snapped. "I want the big wedding as soon as possible. And one hell of a honeymoon. In fact—" he drew breath "—I've already started planning it."

"The family?" Her voice rose. She was still getting to grips with that idea. She'd thought he never wanted kids.

"No, that part can wait 'til after you're crowned biggest fee earner at the firm and you've taken me on a round-the-world trip." His reply was tinged with laughter.

She didn't care about being the biggest fee earner. She cared about her parents and him and everybody staying well and happy. So happy. "So it's the honeymoon you're planning?"

"No, the wedding. I've decided on the flowers already." He winked.

She giggled. "Well, we know party planning is your niche. You should jack in the law practice and just do parties."

"Now, that wouldn't be fair on my clients."

"No." She sobered and placed her palm on the side of his face in the gentlest caress. "They need you." He'd worked so hard mediating with Gage's parents and the stepmother—finally hammering out a solution that had made that sombre-eyed boy so happy. She leaned closer. "I need you too. More than I can ever tell you."

"Same here." He wrapped his arms around her and pulled her right into his heat. "So that's a yes to my proposal, then?"

She rested her head on his chest. Her big, strong playboy loved her no matter what, supported her no matter what, and together they could build it all. "Yes."

"It's going to be one hell of a party, Mya," he whispered.

Yes. One that would last the rest of their lives.

* * * * *

We hope you enjoyed reading

THE HEAT IS ON

by *New York Times* bestselling author
JILL SHALVIS and

BLAME IT ON THE BIKINI

by reader-favorite author NATALIE ANDERSO

Discover more fun, flirty and sensual contempora
romances from the new Harlequin® KISS™ line
books. KISS is all about the delirium of a potent
new romance.

Try one today, with a FREE ebook
WAKING UP MARRIED from
USA TODAY bestselling author Mira Lyn Kel
Visit www.TryHarlequinKISS.com.

⬦HARLEQUIN® KISS™

Fun, Flirty and Sensual Romances

Look for four new romances every month fro
Harlequin KISS!

Available wherever books are sold.

www.Harlequin.com

NYTH

you're not here for—" He broke off and almost looked omfortable. "Me."

No, your brother did not pay me to come and be a al plaything for you." Caitlin smiled sweetly. "And don't think—" she cocked her head "—that if I were such a essional,' I'd have chosen to be in your bed wearing some- g a little more sexy than one of your thousands of identical irts?"

hough the shirt was damn sexy on him—the gray bringing the depth in his eyes and the fit stretching across his chest seriously pulse-pounding fashion.

is lips thinned as he turned back to glare at her. She was to full-on media "glare," but his dark-eyed look was just t the fiercest, most cutting scrutiny she'd had to withstand. m—"

orry," she snapped. "The word you're looking for is *sorry.*"

ired," he said firmly. "I'm tired and I made a mistake. I'm *sorry,* but you can't stay here."

kay, maybe she was a little in the wrong here, too— n the guy actually owned a third of this apartment. But couldn't afford anywhere else. And with her only clothes ging wet in the bathroom? *Damn.*

ecause worst of all she needed this space for more than ing money reasons. She needed to hide. "Well, it's just that your brother said I could stay for the next month."

"Month?" His jaw fell open. "No. No. No."

Yeah, she already got that her month wasn't going to hap
But she needed to buy time to find a new plan. "Well, I'm
going anywhere else tonight."

"You have to."

She needed this bed. George had said she could use it.
Grumpy James here was going to ruin it for her.

"Look." She abandoned all dignity and pride. "We can fi
out something. I'll take the floor."

He was rigid, and his glare pierced deeper. It was a wo
her bones didn't snap from the force emanating from him

"You are *not* sleeping on the floor."

Caitlin sighed. "Don't pretend to be all chivalrous now.
seen the real you unmasked, remember? You know, the
unsurprised to find what he thinks is a hooker in his hon

"You are not sleeping on the floor."

Implacable? Yeah—he had the whole stubborn attitude

"Fine." She switched tack. "We'll *share*."

**Find out what happens next for James and Caitl
in WHOSE BED IS IT ANYWAY?
available in October 2013, only from Harlequin® KI**

REQUEST YOUR FREE BOOKS!

2 FREE NOVELS
FROM THE ROMANCE COLLECTION
PLUS 2 FREE GIFTS!

YES! Please send me 2 FREE novels from the Romance Collection and my 2 FREE gifts (gifts are worth about $10). After receiving them, if I don't wish to receive any more books, I can return the shipping statement marked "cancel." If I don't cancel, I will receive 4 brand-new novels every month and be billed just $6.24 per book in the U.S. or $6.74 per book in Canada. That's a savings of at least 22% off the cover price. It's quite a bargain! Shipping and handling is just 50¢ per book in the U.S. and 75¢ per book in Canada.* I understand that accepting the 2 free books and gifts places me under no obligation to buy anything. I can always return a shipment and cancel at any time. Even if I never buy another book, the 2 free books and gifts are mine to keep forever.

194/394 MDN

Name	(PLEASE PRINT)	
Address		Apt. #
City	State/Prov.	Zip/Postal Code

Signature (if under 18, a parent or guardian must sign)

Mail to the **Harlequin®** Reader Service:
IN U.S.A.: P.O. Box 1867, Buffalo, NY 14240-1867
IN CANADA: P.O. Box 609, Fort Erie, Ontario L2A 5X3

Want to try two free books from another line?
Call 1-800-873-8635 or visit www.ReaderService.com.

* Terms and prices subject to change without notice. Prices do not include applicable taxes. Sales tax applicable in N.Y. Canadian residents will be charged applicable taxes. Offer not valid in Quebec. This offer is limited to one order per household. Not valid for current subscribers to the Romance Collection or the Romance/Suspense Collection. All orders subject to credit approval. Credit or debit balances in a customer's account(s) may be offset by any other outstanding balance owed by or to the customer. Please allow 4 to 6 weeks for delivery. Offer available while quantities last.

Your Privacy—The Harlequin® Reader Service is committed to protecting your privacy. Our Privacy Policy is available online at www.ReaderService.com or upon request from the Harlequin Reader Service.

We make a portion of our mailing list available to reputable third parties that offer products we believe may interest you. If you prefer that we not exchange your name with third parties, or if you wish to clarify or modify your communication preferences, please visit us at www.ReaderService.com/consumerschoice or write to us at Harlequin Reader Service Preference Service, P.O. Box 9062, Buffalo, NY 14269. Include your complete name and address.